D0409682

# THE CHANGING VALLEY

*Also by Grace Thompson*

A Welcome in the Valley
Valley Affairs

# THE CHANGING VALLEY

Grace Thompson

**HEADLINE**

Copyright © 1990 Grace Thompson

The right of Grace Thompson to be identified as the Author of the
Work has been asserted by her in accordance with the Copyright,
Designs and Patents Act 1988.

First published in 1990
by HEADLINE BOOK PUBLISHING PLC

Reprinted in this edition in 1990
by HEADLINE BOOK PUBLISHING PLC

10 9 8 7 6 5 4 3 2 1

British Library Cataloguing in Publication Data

Thompson, Grace
The changing valley.
I. Title
823'.914 [F]

ISBN 0-7472-0246-X

Printed and bound in Great Britain by
Richard Clay Ltd, Bungay, Suffolk

HEADLINE BOOK PUBLISHING PLC
Headline House
79 Great Titchfield Street
London W1P 7FN

To my dear friends Pam and Fred
who make it all such fun

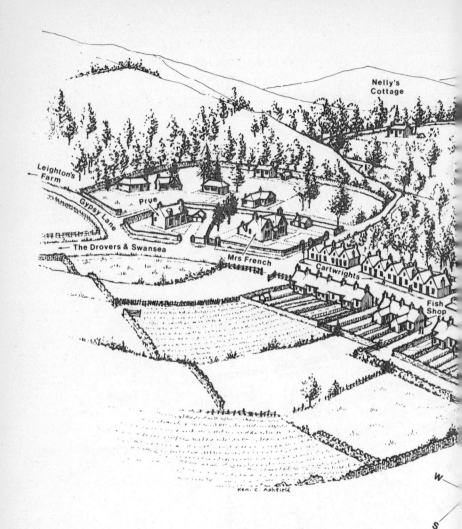

Nelly's Cottage

Leighton's Farm

Gypsy Lane

Prue

The Drovers & Swansea

Mrs French

Cartwrights

Fish Shop

Ken. C. Ashfield

W

S

# Hen Carw Parc

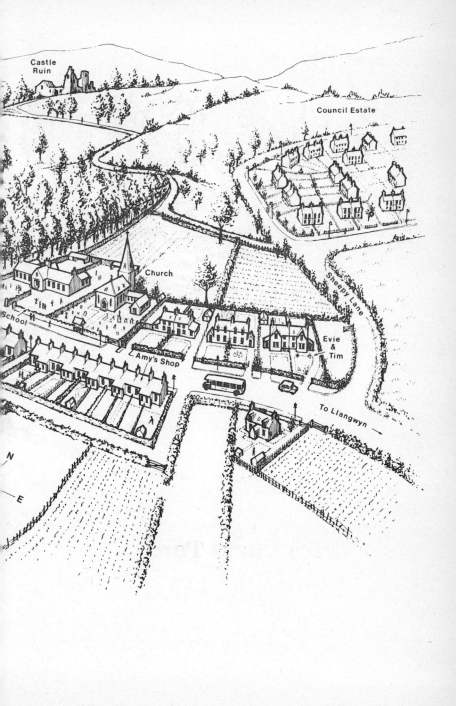

Castle
Ruin

Council Estate

Church

Sheep's Lane

School

Amy's Shop

Evie
&
Tim

To Llangwyn →

N

E

# *Chapter One*

It was a Sunday morning in late May and after three days of rain the hedges and fields sparkled with fresh colours. Nelly, making her way down the lane to the main road, stopped frequently to admire the star-like daisies, golden sun-filled cups of the buttercups and the flat white heads of yarrow. Pale primroses were visible to her sharp eyes, deep in the tangled hedge, and scarlet pimpernel threaded its determined way through the rest, its cheerful flowers open to the brightness of the day after remaining stubbornly closed during the rain and cloud of the past week.

Along the main road through the village of Hen Carw Parc, a steady stream of people made their way eastwards to the stone church. Their dress was as smart as the flowers as if, like the scarlet pimpernel, they had remained closed up and dowdy during the overcast days and only now had woken up and put on their best and newest display.

'Hats,' Nelly muttered, watching two elderly women pass across the end of the lane without seeing her. She pulled on the leads of the two large dogs to make them pay attention.' 'Ats an' 'igh 'eels is as important of a Sunday as prayer books an' the Bible, seems to me.' She stared into the brown eyes of Spotty and Bobby who gazed adoringly up at her, their tails wagging happily, then went on, 'I wonder if Gawd thinks better of 'em fer puttin' on 'ats an' 'igh 'eels? A sort of penance? Damned

1

uncomfortable they looks to me but p'raps it makes 'em sing better. After all, they all sings very 'igh don't they, as if they're in pain too, some of 'em!'

She held the dogs back and waited until the worshippers had ceased to pass the end of the lane before stepping out from the concealment of the hedge on to the main road. She was not a person to worry unduly over the opinion of others but somehow, seeing even Farmer Leighton dressed in his best tweed suit which he wore only for Sundays and market days, she was conscious of her appearance. The short skirt unpressed, the over-large coat flapping about her, the ancient felt hat with a brim large enough, George often remarked, to protect her shoulders from sunburn, and, on her size-five feet, George's size-nine wellington boots.

Her own wellingtons had been left out in the garden and, when found, had been full of water. They were now stuffed with newspaper and drying by the fire. As the lane was too muddy for shoes, George's boots seemed to Nelly utterly sensible.

Because the wellingtons were too large by several sizes they pulled on her stockings and on one fat knee and the elastic band intended to keep her stockings up was visible below an expanse of white flesh. Careless now of being seen, as most people were ahead of her making for the church, she hoisted up the stocking with a groan of effort, fixed the elastic high up on her thigh and tucked the leg of her knickers under it to help in the difficult task of keeping herself covered.

'Come on boys.' She yanked the amiable dogs to their feet and after waiting for Gerry Williams and Pete Evans to roar past on their motor bikes, crossed the road to the general stores and post office. It was closed of course but she had arranged with Amy to go and help with some weekend cleaning.

The shop door was open and as she climbed the step

2

and threw off the first boot she heard a gale of laughter behind her. Amy Prichard, her long glittering earrings dangling and shaking, her blue eyes almost closed with mirth, pointed to Nelly's foot dangling in the air and about to discard its ungainly wellington.

'Nelly love, what are you wearing?'

'George's wellies, what d'you think? Me own is full of rainwater. Yer wouldn't want me to get pneumonia would yer?' She threw off the second boot and stumped through the shop to the cupboard where she kept her slippers. Returning with furry slippers on her feet and a sacking apron around her middle she stood, arms akimbo in front of Amy who was still laughing.

'Where d'you want me to start, Amy? Shelves again?'

'Please, Nelly. These, where I keep the knitting wools need a clean-up.' She dabbed her eyes to wipe away the tears of laughter and shook her head. Nelly would never change.

Humming cheerfully, Nelly began to take out the skeins of wool, sorting them carefully into colours and thicknesses, and soon emptied the shelves. The wooden compartments were washed and refilled, drawers which held needles and pins and dozens of small items on which Amy made little profit but which saved the villagers many a tedious trek into the town of Llangwyn were tidied up and cleaned.

'Cup of tea, Nelly love?' Amy asked as she finished cleaning behind the row of biscuit tins in front of the counter.

'I thought you'd never ask!' Nelly kicked off her slippers and sat on the chair intended for customers to rest on while they gave their orders. Amy returned with the tea and sat down on an empty box. She dropped her shoulders and her pretty face looked sad.

'I'm getting fed up with all this, Nelly,' she sighed. 'My life seems so full of work there's never a moment to

3

relax.' As if on cue, a baby began to stir and a thin wail filled the shop. 'See what I mean? I swear baby Sian knows the moment I sit down!'

Nelly put down her cup and saucer and went to where the carry cot was resting on two chairs in the small kitchen behind the shop. She picked up the little girl and carried her through the shop to Amy. 'Bit of wind I expect, Amy. She's good really, ain't she? You'd 'ardly know she's there.'

'But what happens when she starts to crawl and walk and need more attention than her feeds and an occasional cuddle? What will I do with her then?'

'Won't Prue be well enough to take 'er back by then?' Nelly asked, watching Amy patting the baby's back and soothing her back to sleep. Baby Sian was the daughter of Amy's sister, Prue Beynon, and since the birth, the baby had lived with Amy, as Prue had been too ill to care for her.

Amy shook her blonde head.

'She doesn't seem to improve at all, in fact she seems to be institutionalised already. She sits there staring into space for most of the time when I visit her, as if she's waiting for me to go so she can return to her room and wait for the next meal.'

'Don't she take no notice of 'er little girl?'

'Hardly any. I suppose, when you think of how she lost her husband, after she learnt that he was being unfaithful – and with me, her sister – *then* found she was pregnant so late in life, it's small wonder she couldn't cope with it all.'

'Amy, it ain't my business I know that, but wouldn't it be better if you come back to live 'ere above the shop? That 'ouse 'Arry Beynon left yer it too far away, tight at the end of the village and, nice as it is, it's a lot of extra work for yer, goin' backwards and forwards.'

'I was so thrilled to be left that house, Nelly. Not for

4

the value as much as the gesture. Harry showing he cared for me in spite of refusing to leave Prue and marry me. I thought it would be a proper home for Freddie and Margaret, a place where they could bring their friends, room to breathe after years of being stuck in those cramped rooms above the shop. But I suppose it's all gone wrong. Freddie's joined the army and, as for Margaret, I don't have time to have her friends round nearly as much as I dreamed. I don't have time for anything! Except the things that keep us ticking over.'

'Then tell them Powells upstairs to hoppit! They can go back to livin' with 'er mother, can't they, up on the council 'ouses?'

'I couldn't do that. They've only just settled in and Mavis helps me in the shop, and—'

'Sod to all that. You got to look after yerself, Amy. Tell 'em to go. Be sorry an' polite but tell 'em you need the flat, why don't yer?'

'In some ways it would be easier. But there's Margaret, she loves her new bedroom.'

'Tell 'er it's only fer a while. Kids can put up with anything if it's only fer a while.'

Both women stood up and continued with their work. They were silent as they washed and scrubbed and dusted and stacked, Nelly thinking of how, if Amy left the house and returned to the flat she would lose some hours of work, Amy wondering if she should do as Nelly suggested and return to the cramped flat and leave the house she and Harry had dreamed of making their home.

'Perhaps the Powells would rent the house and let me come back here,' Amy said half an hour later.

'You'll miss the garden.'

'Yes, but honestly, Nelly, when do I have time to enjoy it?'

'An' what will yer boyfriends do to impress you if they can't see to yer lawn and weed yer flower beds? Blimey,

5

talk about rivalry! Gawd 'elp us, as soon as a poor little daisy dares to open its eye, Billie Brown or Victor Honeyman swoops down and slaughters it before it can admire the view! Them two'll be desperate, lookin' fer jobs to do to impress you with their devotion!'

'Everyone was marvellous when I moved, Nelly, including you. People never stopped turning up with gifts and offers of help. Honestly, I was overwhelmed.'

'People *like* you, Amy.'

'Tolerate me, you mean. Two children and no husband, affairs with two married men. That doesn't do much to endear me to the locals!'

'People like you and don't think no different.' Nelly went to the door which stood half open and looked down the quiet street. Being Sunday, there was little traffic apart from the few cars taking people home from church and chapel. Small groups of pedestrians were scattered along the pavements and from one group a figure separated and waved enthusiastically.

'Oh gawd, it's Milly Toogood,' Nelly groaned. 'What's she run out of this time?'

'I swear that if I open that door at midnight she'll come running in asking for something or the other. *That's* why I'm tolerated, Nelly, because I'm useful.' She turned and gave a dazzling smile to Milly, who was panting with the effort of getting to the shop before the door closed, 'Morning Milly, we're closed,' she said firmly.

'Out of sugar, I am. Spilt the lot, I did.'

'There's a shame.'

'Oh, come on, Amy, just a little half pound.' Then, as she saw Amy weakening, she added, '—and you couldn't let me have a bit of bacon off next week's rations could you?'

'No I couldn't!'

'All right then, just the sugar.' Milly made a face to

Nelly but received no sympathetic response.

Amy put some sugar in a bag which she disguised with a wrapping of newspaper before handing it to Milly Toogood. 'I don't want half the village knowing I'm a soft touch on a Sunday morning!'

'Thanks, Amy, you're a good sort. Pay tomorrow, all right?' Milly's eyes swept around the shop, noting the wet floor and some of the shelves empty of their contents. 'Having a bit of a clean-up, are you? And on a Sunday too.' She tutted disapproval.

'Cheerio Milly.' Amy closed the door with some haste behind her customer and turned to Nelly. 'Nosy old devil!'

'You'd better open that door again. Here's a visitor you will want to see,' Nelly smiled.

Coming across the road, waving goodbye to Mrs French the music teacher, was nine-year-old Margaret. Her long hair was a rich red, her eyes a warm brown. She wore a dark-green coat with a velvet collar and pocket flaps and in her hands she carried a few sheets of music as well as a Bible and a hymn book.

'Hello, darling,' Amy said, opening her arms to hug her daughter.

'Mam, I've got news for you.' Margaret smiled to include Nelly. 'There's going to be a concert and lots of other things as well, to raise money to build a new church hall.'

'And you're in the concert!' Amy guessed.

'Playing piano, singing in the choir, and I want to enter the painting competition *and* write a poem!' Margaret danced on her toes in excitement.

'What about us?' Nelly asked. 'Ain't there somethin' we can do? I can sing yer know.'

'Yes,' Margaret said hesitantly, 'I've heard you. Um – there'll be lots of other things too.' Her brown eyes darted from Nelly to her mother, anxious not to offend.

'The Reverend Barclay Bevan says he wants to involve everyone in the village.'

'Don't worry,' Nelly chuckled, 'I don't want to ruin the 'ole thing by singin'. I don't sing till I'm drunk an' then there's no tellin' *what* songs I'll choose! What about my grandson? Ollie's a bit shy but 'e can do somethin' quiet, like the paintin'.'

'Come on, Margaret love or we'll never get any dinner tonight.' Amy suddenly looked tight-faced and sad.

'What's up? Ain't yer pleased that your Margaret is singin' and that fer the church?' Nelly whispered.

'It's just reminded me,' Amy whispered back as they put on their coats, 'if we do move back to the flat, where will we put Margaret's piano?'

'Small room be'ind the shop o' course,' Nelly hissed back. 'You won't want this kitchen if you've got the one upstairs, will yer?'

'Oh dear, I never seem to settle into a trouble-free existence, do I?'

'Aw, poor you! Get the violins out, shall I?' Nelly teased and was relieved to see Amy's pretty face relax into a smile.

Amy gave Nelly an affectionate push. 'Go on, you, I want Margaret to see you crossing the road in those daft wellingtons!'

'You could always marry that Billie Brown,' was Nelly's parting shot. 'Life of luxury you'd 'ave then, bein' married to a wealthy farmer.' She was surprised at the thoughtful expression on Amy's face as she left her.

As Nelly crossed the road, lumbering slowly and with exaggerated difficulty to make Margaret laugh, the two motor bikes returned.

'Hi-ya Nelly? Want a lift?' Pete Evans shouted. The dogs barked at the deafening noise and Nelly was almost pulled out of George's wellingtons before she reached the safety of the lane.

8

There were sounds of activity in the garden of her cottage as she and the dogs approached it. The front of the house looked away from the village towards the wooded hills, and the the back garden, rarely thought of, was overgrown and neglected. It was from here that the sounds came. She peered through the hedge and could see branches swaying as the sound of something being dragged along the ground came closer. Nelly waited curiously to see the cause of the disturbance.

'That you George?' she called, then smiled as a tall, white-haired and bearded man appeared, his blue eyes crinkled with pleasure.

'Yes, Nelly, I'm making a start on the worst of the garden. Look at it. It's like cutting a way through an Amazonian jungle. Come round and give me a hand. Dinner won't be ready for an hour.'

' 'Ang on, I'll push through.'

'No! Don't spoil the—' George fell silent as Nelly turned herself backwards and, leaning on the neglected privet, forced a way through with her ample hips. '—spoil the hedge,' George finished sadly.

The back of the cottage was wrapped in a shawl of leaves. A creeper had spread across the walls and the windows, with only a small opening cut at an upstairs window to let light into George's bedroom. It had reached the roof, where it swayed occasionally in the breeze like fronds of seaweed in a gentle tide. It had also travelled across the ground and curled itself lovingly among the trees and bushes. It was on this convoluted confusion that George was working.

'Blimey, George, that ain't 'alf grown!'

'Think of all the candles we'll save when we let the daylight in,' George laughed.

They worked together for an hour, pulling the creeper free from the stones of the building, and piling the resulting leaves and stems into an ever-growing bonfire. When the area immediately near the house walls had been cleared, Nelly stood back and admired the result.

'Smashin' that is, George, you deserve a cup of tea.' Leaving George still cutting through some thick stems, she walked inside through the front door. She made tea from the sooty kettle simmering on the black-leaded oven range, refilled the kettle from the tap in the lane before carrying the tray around to where George was working. A pile of cut branches impeded her path so she went back into the house and into the small room over-looking the back garden.

'George,' she called, looking through the newly revealed window. When there was no reply she placed the tray on a cobwebby chest of drawers that had not been used for years, and stretched out through the window to look for him. Hearing the sound of chopping some distance from the house, she stretched further and further out and called again. Suddenly her call ended in a terrified shout as she felt the window frame, weakened by neglect, groan and give way. The corners distorted, trapping her in a tenacious grip.

With an anxiety that could be clearly discerned in her complaining voice, she struggled forward to escape the painful hug of the splintered wood and distorted nails. Forcing herself forwards, she fell through the window on to the ground as George finally appeared. Momentarily his concern was banished by laughter at the sight of Nelly's plump hips encased by the broken window, the hinged frame tilting around her like battered wings.

'Nelly, my dear, are you trying to fly?'

The talk in the shop during the following days was mainly about the forthcoming fund-raising events. It had been decided in the various committees that events would continue for the whole of the summer, ending with the school half-term holiday in October. People were already busy with plans for squeezing money out of reluctant pockets. Sewing and knitting circles were piling up small articles for the stalls which would be a part of the end-of-summer fair. Timothy Chartridge, the headmaster of the village school and Nelly's son-in-law, was beginning to select those pupils who would take part in the grand concert which he hoped would raise two hundred pounds. Prue Beynon, although she was so often confused by her illness, had understood what was planned and had agreed that the building firm left to her by her husband, Harry, would build the hall at low cost.

'Tell yer what,' Nelly offered one evening, when other plans were being discussed, 'if my 'orse wins the Derby, I'll give me winnin's to the fund.'

'What horse are you betting on?' George asked.

'I ain't bettin' on the 'orse so much as the jockey,' Nelly explained. 'I likes the look of that young Lester Piggot. Only eighteen 'e is, so I've backed Never Say Die.'

The Reverend Barclay Bevan, who was chairing the meeting in Mrs French's comfortable lounge, frowned as if wondering whether he should thank Nelly or show his disapproval. He decided to pretend he had not heard. He was a short, plump man, with a balding head that emphasised his roundness. He would lean slightly towards the person he was addressing in an attitude of rapt attention but the blue eyes gradually became vague. It was easy to see that his attention had gone, leaving his mind free to wander over more interesting things. A cough from Bert brought him back to the meeting with a jerk and a slight blush of embarrassment.

'We must look further afield than the boundaries of the village,' he said hurriedly. 'The amount we need cannot possibly come from us, no matter how generous we are as a community.'

11

'I hope my concert will attract people from Llangwyn and even further away,' Timothy Chartridge said. 'I am aiming high.'

'Where will we hold it?' Bert Roberts demanded acerbically. 'We haven't got a Hall big enough! That's why we're here, remember?' He went on muttering about educated idiots through the laughter of his quiet wife Brenda and others of the group, but Timothy, with his calm voice, quietened the disorder and went on, 'I suggest that, as the present accommodation is so inadequate and holds only sixty people with any degree of comfort, we have three performances, to be held in the School, and also arrange to visit other locations. I feel sure that with our local talent we can find audiences for more than one concert.'

'Can we ask you to investigate the possibilities and report back to us, Mr Chartridge?' the vicar asked. As Timothy nodded agreement, he looked to the others for further suggestions. Bert Roberts bobbed up again.

'I think I might persuade the Drovers to hold a darts tournament in aid of the fund, Vicar.'

'That's a splendid idea! I do think we ought to aim at giving full entertainment value with everything we plan. Yes.' The round, rosy face beamed and the little man nodded enthusiastically. Yes.' he said again. 'Will you make enquiries, Bert, and report back?'

With a slightly inflated chest and a smile of satisfied importance, Bert sat down, to be congratulated by Brenda.

Nelly, sat at the back of the meeting, leaned towards her friend, Netta Cartwright, and muttered audibly, 'That'll be a disaster for a start off! Bert Roberts couldn't organise kittens on a cat farm!'

'He does try,' Netta whispered, trying to hush Nelly's loud comments.

'Tries everyone's patience!' Ignoring the glare aimed

at her by Bert and his wife, Brenda, Nelly smiled across at her son-in-law. 'Well done, Timothy, you can put me an' George down fer two tickets.'

'Thank you Mother-in-law, most kind.'

Nelly mimicked his words and added, 'Pompous old stick, ain't 'e? Tedious Timothy I calls 'im.'

As Nelly and George walked home with Netta, they stopped at the end of Nelly's lane and looked along the main road towards the church and its hall.

'It seems a shame to pull it down,' George said. 'I know it's too small, but it's as much a part of Hen Carw Parc as the church.'

'I don't think that's the intention,' Netta said in her gentle Welsh voice. 'A committee room it will be, and for smaller meetings when the new hall will be too big.'

'I wonder what I can do,' Nelly mused, 'beside me gambling?' The following day, Phil-the-Post brought her an idea.

Nelly was weeding around the new carrots, wearing George's wellingtons again as hers were still unfit to use, when Phil Davies propped his bicycle against her gate and walked down the cinder path. Nelly threw down the hoe and kicked off the loose boots.

' 'Ello, Phil, stoppin' fer a cuppa?'

'Got any cake left?'

' 'Course I 'ave.'

'All right then.' He threw his sack down beside the back door and bent to scratch the heads of the two big dogs. 'What have they roped you in for with this fund-raising, Nelly?' he asked as he settled into the wooden chair near the door. He took the steaming cup and added with a grin, 'Selling teas, is it?'

'I couldn't sell teas, Phil. I likes people to come an' 'ave one free. No, I don't know what George an' I will do, but we'll think of something.'

13

As Nelly refilled the plate with her small cakes and replenished his cup, Phil delved into his bag and handed her a letter. She opened it as he sipped noisily at the hot drink.

'Damned if I ain't got an idea fer raisin' some money!' she gasped, a leery grin on her face. 'This'll make a bit of fun, Phil.'

Phil stretched up to see what the letter said, his dark eyes bright with the prospect of curiosity being satisfied.

'What is it, Nelly? From the council, isn't it?'

'It's about me new drains, and the bathroom an' posh lavatory. Seems George an' I got to dig the trench fer the drainage ourselves.' She stared skywards, her uneven teeth showing in a crooked smile. 'I'm goin' ter do what that Tom Sawyer did in one of Mark Twain's stories, Phil. I'll get the drain trench dug an' charge people to do it for me!'

'You want people to dig your trench and pay you for the privilege. I always thought you were daft, woman. Now I know for sure!'

Nelly threw back her head and laughed loudly, her harsh roar disturbing a flock of sparrows in the apple tree.

'If I succeed, then I ain't so daft, am I? You remember the story, Phil. Tom Sawyer 'ad to whitewash a fence an' 'e persuaded 'is friends that it was a rare privilege to be allowed to do it. They paid 'im with tadpoles and a dead rat on a string an' stuff like that. I'll ask fer money fer the fund.'

'Damn me, Nelly, if anyone can persuade people to do your work for you and pay for doing it, you can!' He was still laughing as he finished his third cup of tea and set off to deliver the rest of his mail and spread the news.

Nelly watched him go, a smile on her face as she thought of the day of fun to come. She had the local councillor, Mrs Norwood Bennet-Hughes, to thank for

14

it. That large fur-coated lady had called on her, driving her Rover up the narrow lane and parking near her gate. They'd shared a pot of tea and had soon been chatting like old friends. Before she left, she had promised to see that the cottage would have a bathroom as soon as it was possible. Nelly's smile widened, her crooked teeth showing as she thought of how jealous her social-climbing daughter had been to learn that Nelly had made a friend of such an important local dignitary.

Nelly went up the curving staircase and into the back bedroom, which, although an attempt had been made to clear it when George came to live, still had a clutter of half-explored boxes against two walls, leaving only a narrow space for George to walk to his bed. Kneeling on the beige counterpane, she looked down at the village of Hen Carw Parc in the distance, the spire of the church gleaming in the sun. The church and its hall had once been the centre of the village and an inn had stood beside it, but the sprawl of new council houses to the east and the loss of cottages in the fields behind the main road, had distorted the shape. The inn had long disappeared and a school built in its place.

She had lived in the village since 1940 – fourteen years – and despite beliefs to the contrary that newcomers were never accepted, felt she truly belonged. Her London accent had not faded but even that failed to dissuade the locals from believing her to be as much a part of the place as the church spire.

Her reputation as an easygoing, untidy and careless housekeeper bothered very few among the house-proud locals, but when her daughter Evie had returned to live in the village with her headmaster husband, Timothy, things had been difficult for Nelly. Evie had tried, unsuccessfully, to prise Nelly out of her primitive cottage where she lived so contentedly, and Nelly's marriage to George, who had wandered the fields and farms as a

15

tramp, caused further shock. Finally Evie had reluctantly seemed to accept that her mother was in the cottage to stay.

The dogs ignored the rule about climbing the stairs and jumped up beside her to look out of the window, wanting to share with her whatever strange occupation she indulged in. She hugged them both with her fat arms, smiling in contentment as she looked down at the mess of the half-tamed garden. Her uneven teeth distorted the smile, three having being knocked out some years previously. Her dark eyes were intelligent and they glowed as she studied the garden and imagined the teams of men she would soon see out there, digging the trench for the drainage.

She left the window and, collecting the dogs' leads, walked down to the village shop.

'Amy, will you put a notice in the shop winder for me?' she asked, dragging Spotty from an imminent clout from Amy as he tried to wet against a sack of potatoes.

'Take that dog out, Nelly, for heaven's sake,' Amy sighed. 'I've just disinfected the floor after Billie Brown's sheep dog!'

'I just want you to put up a notice for me. I won't stay.'

'All right, what is it?'

'Finish servin'. We ain't in no 'urry.' She slapped the dogs' rumps to make them sit and, when the shop was empty, told Amy of her idea.

'Daft!' was Amy's comment, 'but it's likely to work.'

'Put the kettle on, Amy. I'll carry these crates of vegetables outside while I'm 'ere. Constable 'Arris won't be around fer a while. Wheezing and puffing, Nelly moved the vegetable into a neat row on the pavement.

When Amy carried in the cups of tea, she stared at the wooden baker's tray on the counter near the door.

'Have you sold one of those iced cakes, Nelly?'

16

'No, just some 'taters to Brenda Roberts. The money's
on the till.'

'That's funny, there were three of them and one is
missing. Nelly – if one of your dogs—'

'No, they ain't bin near.'

'Could someone have nipped in and taken one?'

'P'raps, but I never saw no one.'

The cake that had disappeared was a snow cake,
covered in marshmallow and with a cherry on the centre.
As Nelly walked back up the lane, the dogs began to pull
and, when they were released, they pushed their way
through the hedge of Mr Leighton's field with great
urgency. Curious, Nelly peered over the hedge by standing on the sloping grassy bank and saw them tucking in
to what looked suspiciously like the missing cake.

'What d'you think of that?' she said to George later as
they sat eating baked potatoes outside their back door.
'Someone pinched it then threw it over the 'edge. Why
would someone do that, eh?'

George smiled, his clear blue eyes laughing, the pink
lips within the neat white beard parted. 'A mischievous
child?'

'No one I know would take a cake an' not eat it.'

'What about the little girl we saw the other morning,
running out of the garden with a hen's egg? We found
that smashed on the lane, didn't we?'

'You think it might be the same girl? But why,
George?'

'Mischief, like I said, or a game of Dare.'

'Why are you smilin' George?'

'I know who she is.'

' 'Oo then? Is she starvin'? We could coax 'er in an'
give 'er a good meal, couldn't we?' Nelly's face wrinkled
with compassion as she thought of a child in need of food.
Her mind raced with ideas for meals to tempt the child.

'She's called Dawn and her mother is dead. She lives in

the council houses with her father, and no, he doesn't neglect her from what I hear, but she is what you might call difficult.'

'We'll look out for 'er an' see if she'll talk to us. Sometimes it ain't yer nearest an' dearest what's best able to 'elp.' She looked at George and smiled. He was her nearest and dearest now, even though their marriage had only been an arrangement to frustrate Evie's efforts to get her out of her cottage. They had settled to a life many would envy. No sex to cause aggravation and turbulence, just serene untroubled friendship. Nellie didn't pray often but when she did it was to thank God for sending George to her.

When Phil-the-Post arrived the following morning, Nelly was just leaving for work. It was Wednesday, the day she 'did' for Mrs French. She took the letters he offered and nodded towards the fire where the blackened kettle simmered gently.

'Kettle's on the boil, make yerself a cuppa, why don't yer? I got to go or Mrs French'll be worryin'.'

'No time, Nelly. Late I am, thanks to some kind person who stole my bike!'

'Stole yer—' Nelly laughed. 'What did I just see you ride up on then, a Rolls Royce?'

'Borrowed one from Mam. Been in the shed for years it has. Proper fool I feel, riding a sit-up-and-beg woman's bike. What with the high handlebars and the cords across the wheels to stop me skirts from catching in the spokes! Damn, the kids have been running after me, laughing their heads off! Never live it down I won't, if one of my mates sees me.'

'Pinched? Are you sure you never rode it to the Drovers an' forgot to ride it 'ome?'

'Someone took it from outside the front window. There's typical, isn't it. I wanted to finish early today.

18

Mam's birthday it is and we were planning a surprise. All of us pretending we've forgotten, then tuning up this evening with presents and mine not bought yet! When I find out who took it I'll give it to him proper! Sorry he'll be that he tangled with Phil Davies!'

'He – or she,' Nelly said thoughtfully.

When she had finished her morning's work, Nelly did not go straight home. She walked past the cottage and up through the woods to the ruins of the castle. She sat on a low wall and watched as the dogs wandered through the ruins, sniffing out trails and following tracks, their long tails wagging in excitement. After a while, Nelly followed them, looking into the only surviving room that had been used as a kitchen when the village had celebrated the Coronation the previous summer. It was a few moments before her eyes became accustomed to the poor light but when she could see clearly, her eyes picked out a bundle of clothes in the far corner. She gasped with shock. At the time of the Coronation someone had slept here for a while: Mrs French's son, Alan, who had come back from the war, despite having been presumed killed. His return had ended with his tragic suicide and the silence of the place and the sight of the heap of clothes just where he had slept shocked Nelly's memory. For a moment she thought Alan had returned once again from the dead. She shuddered and stepped towards the clothes, then bent to look closer. Moving some of them, Nelly recognised the outline of a bicycle, Phil's bicycle. She tugged it upright and with the dogs following, pushed it through the broken walls and overgrown stones to the path.

She stood for a moment, wondering whether to go to Phil's mother's house or take the bicycle home, when a small figure ran past, almost knocking her and the bicycle to the ground. The dogs began to bark angrily,

19

their front paws leaving the ground as emphasis to their disapproval.

' 'Ere,' Nelly shouted angrily, 'Come back 'ere, cheeky little perisher! Oi, you, is that Dawn?' she shouted the last words as the idea of the child's identity came to her.

'No business of yours, Dirty Nelly!' the girl shouted back.

'Enough of yer "Dirty Nelly", cheeky little devil!'

The dogs began to run off in pursuit of the fleeing girl but Nelly called them back.

'Come on, boys, time we was gettin' back. 'S funny,' she frowned. 'I thought people was beginnin' to ferget me nickname.' She walked towards the lane, pushing the bicycle and stumbling occasionally in her angry haste. 'Cheeky little sod, I'll give 'er Dirty Nelly!'

# Chapter Two

Griff Evans lived in one of the cottages in the row which included the fish-and-chip shop. His wife, Hilda worked at the shop or rather outside it, cleaning fish and chipping the potatoes and making the batter so everything was ready for when Bethan, Milly Toogood's daughter, opened for business. Griff was a regular caller at the shop, but he did not go there to work but to spend a pleasant hour with Bethan.

He was not a very attractive man, caring little for his appearance, even when calling on his lady love. He was short, dark and rather overweight with a stomach that was already beginning to bulge over his leather belt. He worked at the forestry and rarely changed out of his work clothes. He put on an old mackintosh when he went to the woods to poach on the estate far to the north of the village, and added a peaked cap when the weather was wet. He also earned money carrying bets for the local bookie and it was to him that Nelly had taken her two-shilling gamble on the Derby.

He came down to the fish-and-chip shop each lunchtime to collect the urn of tea Bethan made for the forestry workers and he always found time to call in to the Drovers to collect any bets. He occasionally held back the bets, when he thought the horse was unlikely to win and in the case of Lester Piggot's horse, he had done just that. Now he was faced with finding almost two pounds to pay Nelly. Two pounds he did not have.

She was waiting for him outside the Drovers, those big dogs of hers lolling against her legs and she smiled a greeting, obviously excited at the prospect of receiving her winnings.

'Got me money 'ave yer?' she asked. 'It's fer the church 'all fund. Pity really, it's a long time since I 'ad a thirty-three-to-one winner. Still, it's in a good cause, ain't it?'

'Sorry Nelly, but I didn't get it to the bookie in time.'

'You what?' She stared at the two shillings he had placed in her palm, then glared at him, her head held forward in an aggressive stance. 'I give it to you *days* before the race.'

'I found it in my pocket this morning. Forgot it, I did. Terribly sorry, love, but I just missed it when I went to deliver them.'

'Funny 'ow you fergets only the big wins, ain't it Griff Evans!'

'Now now Nelly, Everyone makes mistakes and there's no cause for you to accuse me of dishonesty.'

'Ain't there? Just you get me that money! I'm entitled and you know it. Spend less on yer lady friend and you'd be able to pay up!'

Griff walked past her and into the pub where a group of men would be standing waiting for him. The remark about his lady love had startled him: he had believed that no one knew about him and Bethan. He had better be careful, he didn't want Hilda to find out. Life was comfortable at home and he had no desire to change things. Hilda was no beauty and their marriage no love-match, but she looked after him well. Damn. If he had not held back that one bet he might never have known his secret was out. Ignorance is bliss, he thought ruefully.

Nelly looked at the two shillings in her hand, tempted to throw it after him and call out again about his dishonesty and carrying on, but she changed her mind and

22

went into the pub to buy herself a glass of stout. She stood at the bar, glaring at Griff and taking small satisfaction from knowing he was uneasy, afraid she was going to blurt out her accusations again. She pushed her way past him, knocking roughly against him as she left and said only, 'So, you'll be givin'. me me money tomorrer, will yer?' Griff did not answer.

Griff would have been surprised at how many people knew about his affair with Bethan. Spending so many night-hours poaching in the woods, he thought no one would be surprised to see him out, whatever the hour. But Nelly had known for a long time and Phil-the-Post missed nothing that went on. It was only because of his irregular life that Hilda suspected nothing.

Nelly decided to say nothing and hope that her silence would persuade him to pay her the money he had cheated her of in the next few days. She told George and laughingly threatened to warn Constable Harris of the regular exchange of betting slips that went on at the Drovers each lunchtime and evening.

'You should have seen the goings-on the last time the police raided,' she laughed. 'Everyone trying to burn their slips on the fire and kicking the logs to make them burn faster and Bert Roberts setting fire to his trousers. Little Archie Pearce who couldn't get to the fire was chewing 'is list of 'orses like mad and 'im with not a single tooth in 'is 'ead! But it ain't funny bein' cheated, George.' she added sadly. 'I'd 'ave bin pleased to 'and that money to the vicar.'

'Never mind, Nelly, it seems that there has been quite a lot of interest in your trench-digging idea so we'll make up for it with that. And have a lot of fun as well.'

It was raining as Amy left the shop on Saturday evening and set off on the twenty-minute walk to her house. Margaret skipped beside her, unbothered by the drizzle

23

which soon made a silver-fur covering on their clothes and sent dampness in a chilling barrier between their skin and the warmth of their clothes. Amy bent her head forward in a vain attempt to keep the insidious moisture from her face and pushed Sian's pram like a battering ram before her.

She was so intent on hurrying home and getting the evening tasks under way that she almost bumped into Billie Brown.

'Hey, you three, what are you trying to do, flatten me?' He moved Amy's hands from the pram handle and began pushing the baby. 'Put your hands in your pockets, Amy, it will keep them warm.'

'I'm not cold,' she grumbled, 'just wet. And what are you doing walking about in this weather?'

'I'm a farmer. Weather isn't often a bother, and a bit of a wetting certainly wouldn't keep me in, would it? Out in it all, I am.'

Margaret smiled up at him. 'Oliver and I aren't put off by the weather either, Uncle Billie, we want to be farmers when we grow up.'

'And good you'll be, too. Damn me, there's a lovely job you two made of washing out the milking parlour last week. Soaked yourselves more than this bit of rain though, if I remember?'

'Can we come again soon?'

'Welcome you are. My sister will be there to make us all a nice tea.'

'You must say if Margaret and Oliver are being a nuisance,' Amy said as she walked, still crouched against the insistent rain, beside his tall figure. There was a comfortable feeling about walking with Billie, she decided. He seemed like a bastion against anything that threatened. She looked up at him and he smiled, turning his head to encompass Margaret in his affection and protection.

'I walked along the stream for a bit of a blow, and when it came on to rain I thought I'd come and walk home with you as it was near time for the shop to close.'

Amy smiled but a bubble of irritation rose in her. On a day like this, all she wanted to do was get inside and close the door. Now she would have to invite him to stay a while and the ironing wouldn't get done. Her mind wandered ahead to what they would eat. She had bought chops for Sunday but there wasn't an extra one.

'I hope you don't mind,' Billie began, when they reached the drive which led to the half-hidden house.

'Mind you walking us home?' Amy asked curiously. 'Of course I don't, although I have the ironing to do and—'

'Not walking you home, girl. Mind me going into your house uninvited? I used the key you hide under a stone and went in and lit your fire. I thought on a day like this you'd like a bit of a welcome.'

'Billie, that is kind of you. Thank you!' She opened the front door and at once smelt the warmth. 'That's lovely!' She thought of the chops and wondered if she could make do with a couple of eggs for herself. 'Stay for something to eat, won't you?'

'No, no. I expect Mary is cooking for me. Another time eh?'

She saw that he had filled the coal scuttle and had left some chopped sticks drying near the fire. She watched him go, disappearing into the misty rain, a tall, burly figure in his oilskins and heavy wellingtons, guilty at the irritation she had felt. He really was very kind. She was tired after a busy day at the shop and it was tempting at moments like these to push down the last barrier and allow herself to fall in love with him.

Her pulse quickened at the thought of his love-making but admitted that her attraction for him was no great passion. Not like it had been with Harry Beynon whom she had loved from the first moment she had seen his wicked blue eyes behind his rimless glasses, and the smile that promised every delight except honesty. Harry had been the one real love in her life but he was dead, although he still filled her dreams with remembered joy.

Now there was Billie Brown, a farmer who loved her and was unattached, and Victor Honeyman who loved her but was not. It would be very easy to slip into an affair with Victor whose blue eyes reminded her of Harry's. But Victor's were paler and had a gentleness and calmness Harry's had rarely had. Victor made her laugh, his company was restful and as easy and comfortable as a long time friend. She was always excited at seeing him and her body responded to his touch in a most disconcerting way but he was married and even if he and his wife were unhappy, she determined never to involve herself with a married man again.

She picked up the post which Billie had placed on the small table and glanced through the assorted letters to decide if any were interesting enough to open while the meal cooked. One, in sprawling, boyish writing, she tore open at once, calling to her daughter as she did so.

'Margaret love, there's a letter from Freddie.' As soon as she heard Margaret tumble down the stairs to hear the latest news of her brother, Amy chuckled. 'Where's my dainty little girl gone? These days you're so long-legged you sound like a cart-horse with seven legs!' She handed the letter to Margaret and hugged her. 'Go on, you read it first, tell me what he says.'

'He's coming home, Mam! He's got a whole week's leave! He's not quite sure when – he'll let us know later. He asks about Sheila Powell of course. He never forgets to ask about her! And, er, he says he will spend a part of his leave planting some extra roses around the front borders for you.' She put the letter down. 'Freddie loves gardening doesn't he, Mam? Why did he go away to the army instead of finding work with flowers d'you think?'

'Sheila Powell was the reason he went away, love.' Amy tried never to lie to her children and although the subject of Freddie's love for Sheila was one which made her angry, she forced herself to explain. 'Freddie was fond of her and I think for a while thought she was fond of him. But she married Maurice Davies after announcing she was – how can I explain this to you—'

'Sheila was going to have a baby and it was Maurice who was the father, right?'

'Well, yes.' Amy was startled by Margaret's outspokenness and apparent understanding.

'So Freddie couldn't stay, he had to go into the army? Seems silly to me.'

'We all do silly things, love. Me more than most, so I can't blame him, although it seems a pity he didn't stay with Auntie Prue's building firm where he had a good future.'

'Would Sheila have been my sister if Freddie had married her then?'

'Sister-in-law. Yes, love.'

'And your daughter-in-law?'

'Yes.' Amy's pretty face curled into a scowl.

'Wouldn't you have liked that, Mam?'

'Whoever you or Freddie marries will be welcome here and made to feel a part of our family.'

'But you don't really *like* her?' Margaret insisted.

Amy smiled and tugged at Margaret's long red hair. 'You, young lady are far too sharp for a nine-year-old! Now go and wake Sian. There's time to feed her while our meal is cooking.'

'I'll feed her, Mam, then I'll do my practice. There's an exam Mrs French wants me to enter soon. Can I tell her I will?'

'Would you really like to?'

'Oh yes, I love playing the piano.'

27

'Then of course you can.'

With the baby fed, bathed and in her cot, and Margaret in her pyjamas snuggled in an armchair listening to the wireless later that evening, Amy felt loneliness creep over her again. She had a busy and interesting life, with the shop and family life with Margaret, baby Sian and on occasions, Freddie, but it wasn't enough. She thought of Billie only a few miles away in the large farmhouse he shared with his sister, Mary, and wondered if she could cope with a life so different from all she had ever known, just for the sense of belonging, of coming first with someone. She became aware of her daughter's brown eyes watching her. Jerking herself from her daydreams she said, 'Shall I make us a nice cup of cocoa? I brought us some biscuits from the shop for a treat.'

'Is something wrong, Mam?'

'Wrong? What could be wrong? I've got a beautiful daughter, enough money to make life pleasant, Freddie's leave to look forward to. No, nothing is wrong. I was indulging in a bit of a daydream, that's all.'

On the following morning, Amy busied herself with the routine tasks while Margaret was in church. Then after lunch they went to see Ethel Davies. Although she was only going to see a neighbour, Amy spent time dressing and applying makeup with care. She looked at the weather, which seemed likely to give rain, so she wore a bobbleweave navy skirt and a paler blue blouse over which she put on a lightweight mac. She had bought new makeup, changing the colour slightly for the beginning of summer. The Cremepuff shades varied with skin colour and from Truly Fair she had moved darker to Candle Glow preferring to appear slightly tanned, although she rarely had time to sit in the sun. She put on a sparkling rhinestone necklace and matching dangling earrings and fluffed out her hair until she was satisfied with the result. She stared at herself in the mirror of the compact for a while, wondering if her face showed her thirty-eight years to others as kindly as it appeared to her. Perhaps she mused, we remain young inside and are deceived into believing it's how we look. She snapped the compact on the thoughts of lonely middle age and ran down to where Margaret was waiting.

Instead of walking along the main road and going up Sheepy Lane to Ethel's, they turned up towards Nelly's cottage. The lane would take them past the ruined castle and along the edge of the wood before reaching the entrance to the council houses and turning down again to return to the main road as Sheepy Lane.

Nelly was in the garden. With a long-handled hoe she was working between the newly sprouting vegetables, singing to herself, accompanied by the wireless on the chair beside the open door.

'Where are you off to?' she called as Amy and Margaret waved.

'I'm going to ask about Sheila,' Amy explained. 'We had a letter from Freddie and he always asks for the latest news.'

'Phil says she ain't too well,' Nelly reported. 'It's getting near 'er time, ain't it?'

Amy saw a paper carrier near Nelly's gate. 'Did you know there's a parcel here, Nelly?' she asked.

'Yes, that Griff owes me some money an' instead of payin' 'e brings me rabbits. D'you think they'll be all right? There's all this talk about some disease in Kent.'

'We're a long way from Kent, Nelly,' Amy laughed. 'Do you mean myxomatosis?'

'Yes, terrible thing to do to rabbits ain't it? D'you think them are safe to eat?'

'I haven't heard anything in this area. Besides, wouldn't you be able to see if they were affected?'

'I'll wait till George 'as 'ad a look. 'E'll know.'

Amy felt a brief stab of envy at Nelly having George to discuss things with, and her departure was hurried. Why did she never meet someone who was free to love her? If even Nelly could find a man to share her life what was it that *she* lacked?

Amy and Margaret walked on, stopping to enjoy the quiet of the woods that was disturbed only by birdsong and the chuckle of the nearby stream. When they reached Sheepy Lane they saw an ambulance hurry past from the direction of Hywel Rise. Amy wondered anxiously if Sheila was being taken into hospital already.

At Ethel's house her fears were confirmed. Ethel was stepping into the back of the ambulance and, as the door closed, Amy saw she was upset. Phil, Ethel's postman son was standing beside the door of the house and he beckoned to Amy.

'Something wrong, I'm afraid. They're rushing Sheila into hospital. There's some doubt about the baby – gone well over her time she has.'

'Oh, I'm very sorry,' Amy said. 'Poor little thing.' Her thoughts, rather unkindly, were not for Sheila but the distress Sheila had caused to Maurice, who had been forced to leave Delina Honeyman whom he loved, and marry the pregnant Sheila. What if Sheila were then to lose the baby, the innocent cause of it all?

'Come in and wait for Mam to come back,' Phil said. 'Catrin has made a pot of tea and, you know Mam, she's left plenty of food.'

'All right, Phil, for a little while.' Amy turned to Margaret. 'Why don't you go and see if Oliver's home? I'll call for you when I leave.' Margaret ran down Sheepy Lane to the main road where Nelly's grandson lived.

Amy went inside the cheerful room with the roaring fire and the neatly laid table. She looked at the plateful of bread and butter and the homemade meatloaf and salad ready to serve. It was a constant source of wonder

30

and admiration that even through the years when rationing restricted supplies of food severely, Ethel managed to fill her table generously.

It was with a start of surprise that she realised that the room was not empty. In a corner near the back kitchen door, away from the fierce heat of the fire, waiting for her to see him, sat Victor Honeyman.

'Victor! I didn't see you there. What's the news about Sheila then. Very bad is it?'

'It's such a mess, isn't it? There's my Delina grieving over the cancellation of her wedding to Maurice, Maurice is in Australia where he went to escape from the girl he was forced to marry and the little baby who upset everything is likely to die.'

'I'm so sorry, Victor. Delina didn't deserve such unhappiness, and neither, really, did young Maurice. I'm afraid I don't think very highly of Sheila Powell. She asked for trouble.'

'Be fair, Amy, the girl is suffering too. It was far more humiliating for her to marry and have her husband go thousands of miles away rather than live with her, and now this.'

'I know. I shouldn't be so unkind, but she used my Freddie, using him to cover up for her meetings with Maurice, and for a while people thought he was the father. But you're right, it's our sympathy Sheila needs now.'

'I thought I might go down to the main road and telephone the hospital in an hour or so – see if there's any news.'

'Yes, I'll ring when I get home. Freddie will want to know what's happened. Still fond of her, he is.' She frowned and asked, 'I suppose her parents are at the hospital too?'

'No, that's why Ethel went. No one knows where they are.'

31

Victor rose from his chair and stood beside her, 'Amy, can't we meet. Just for a chat,' he added hurriedly as her head began to move in refusal. 'I don't have anyone to talk to. Delina is so subdued since her wedding was cancelled and as you know, my wife ignores me almost totally.'

'There are your sons?'

'Polite, that's all.'

'Victor, love, I have my daughter to consider. I've attracted a lot of talk in the past but now she's growing up and, well, I don't want anything to spoil her life.'

'There wouldn't be any talk, I promise. I just need to feel I can call on you and perhaps take you for an occasional drink. I've joined the darts team at the Drovers. Couldn't you at least come and cheer me on?' He smiled encouragingly. 'My aim would be straighter if you shouted for me, honest.'

The Drovers was where she used to meet Harry, and her voice was sharp as she said, 'Not the Drovers.' Then more kindly she added, 'Come at the weekends, when Margaret is there, not in the week. All right?'

His smile was so warm that she felt a moment of guilt. She was becoming a selfish woman, what with her lack of sympathy for Sheila and now here she was treating Victor as if he were a peasant begging for a crust. How could it possibly harm Margaret if her friends called to see her? That one of the friends was male should make no difference. But she knew she was kidding herself if she pretended it would not result in gossip. 'Sometimes,' she said, surprising Victor with her vehemence, 'I wish I lived in the middle of a big anonymous town!' Not being privy to her thoughts he asked, 'Why? Aren't you happy in Hen Carw Parc?'

'Everyone knows what everyone else is doing. I swear I only need to think of changing my dress and everyone knows!'

'You can't really mind. It shows people care about you. Nosy people are often generous hearts who find out when there's help needed and offer it.'

'You're right, Victor.' She touched her lips lightly against his cheek. 'I'm a misery lately.'

'Is Sian more than you can cope with?' He leaned over and looked at the baby who was staring up at the flickering firelight on the ceiling with apparent interest. 'She's a good baby isn't she?'

'Very good, but it's still a lot of work, what with the shop, the house and trying to find time to spare for Margaret. It was easier when Freddie was home but I suppose I was unfair to him, leaning on him. It wasn't right.'

'Lean on me, Amy,' he said softly, 'lean on me.'

She sighed, touching his arm affectionately. 'If only I could.' He leaned towards her and kissed her lightly on the cheek.

'You can, Amy. I know I'm not free, but one day I will be and then I'll look after you proper. Unless that Billie Brown steals you before then. He's got more to offer you, I know that, and he's free to offer it all now, but he can't love you any more than I do.' His lips touched her cheek, travelled across to her lips and as she was about to surrender to his kiss a shadow crossed the open door and a voice asked, 'What you doing?'

Amy turned at once but the shadow had gone. She hurried to the open door and Victor followed but there was no sign of anyone.

'Did you see someone come in then, Phil?' Amy called to where Phil stood outside the gate with a knot of others, discussing the fate of Sheila and her baby.

'No, why?'

'It doesn't matter,' Amy frowned. 'Was it Margaret' she asked Victor. 'Or Oliver?'

'No, but it was a child.'

33

A noise from the back kitchen made them stare into the room and Victor went on tip-toe to investigate. He was just in time to see a young girl disappearing around the door post. On a small table near the sink was a cake, left to cool and hurriedly broken in half.

'That girl who's been a nuisance, it was her! Stolen some of Ethel's cake she has. I'm going to see Constable Harris about her. She mitches from school and hangs about all day and no one seems to care about her.'

'Perhaps her parents don't know,' Amy defended.

'Then it's time they did! There's all sorts of trouble a child like that can get into wandering about on her own all day. Some parents just don't care!'

The group who had stood to watch the ambulance drive away moved towards the house. Milly Toogood was there with Sybil Tremain, her constant shadow, Bert Roberts was loudly offering his opinion on the stupidity of the doctors, and Amy suddenly became aware that they were all talking sympathetically about Sheila; even Milly, who rarely spoke well of anyone.

'It was only Ethel who showed any concern,' Milly was saying, trying to out-shout Bert. 'She's been up to see her regular, and her with her bad legs too.'

Amy silently agreed with her. No one had bothered with Sheila except her mother-in-law, who she sensed felt love for the girl as well as responsibility.

Victor looked through the door and saw that Phil had been called by Constable Harris. He pushed past the people waiting for Amy to make tea and called to the constable. 'I've just been saying to Amy, I think you should do something about this girl who's making a nuisance of herself. D'you know what she's just done?' He stopped as he saw from the men's faces that something was wrong. 'What's happened?' he asked.

'Constable Harris has just told me I'm not going to be

34

an uncle again after all. Mam'll be so sad. Looking forward to the new baby, she was.'

'You mean, Sheila's lost the baby?' Amy's face drooped with sadness when she heard the news. She felt partly to blame for the way she had criticised Sheila. 'I'm really sorry. Ethel would have so enjoyed having a new grandchild.'

'Ethel phoned me from the hospital, and asked me to find Sheila's parents. Seems Sheila isn't too good either.'

'Mam.' Margaret squeezed into the now crowded room and pushed towards her mother. 'Oliver isn't in but I think I know where he is. There's a meeting at the vicarage to make arrangements for tomorrow's Whitsun outing.'

'Of course, and that's where the Powells will be. Be a love and run after Constable Harris and tell him, will you?'

Margaret pushed her way out of the room, where Milly was passing round cups of tea, and ran down the lane. In Ethel's house the talk was subdued. There was concern for the girl few could honestly say they liked but for whom they all felt sympathy.

Johnny Cartwright arrived as Milly was refilling the cups. Not knowing the news, having just finished his shift on the buses, he said cheerfully, 'What d'you think I saw yesterday? Evie and Timothy and young Oliver in a car, but the surprising thing was, Evie was driving! Yes, learning to drive she is, fancy that now, and she hasn't said a word to anyone. At least, Phil didn't know and that's almost the same thing!' He stopped his cheerful chatter and looked around him. 'Where's Ethel, then? And what are you all looking like a funeral for?'

'It's the baby, Johnny,' Phil explained. 'Sheila's lost the baby and she isn't too good herself, like. Mam's at the hospital and PC Harris is looking for Sheila's parents.'

'Damn, I didn't know. And there's me going on like that— Sorry, Phil.' He took the cup of tea that Victor passed him and sipped hurriedly. 'Is there anything I can do? Will your Mam want a lift home from the hospital?'

While everyone was discussing the arrangements, Amy prepared to leave.

'I'll walk back with you,' Victor said. 'Come on, here's Margaret back.'

They walked silently up the lane which curved past Nelly's cottage. At her gate, Nelly was trying to control the excited dogs.

'Any news? she shouted above their enthusiastic barking. 'About that Sheila, I mean?'

When she heard the sad report about the baby, her face crumpled exaggeratedly into dismay. 'Shame it is, a real shame. What with all the trouble the girl caused, and Ethel looking forward to having a new grandchild. It's hard that it's all ended with nothing at all, ain't it?'

'I feel guilty,' Amy admitted. 'I've never said a good word, and now—'

'I told her it's nothing to feel guilty about,' Victor said. 'As if her not liking Sheila could have changed anything.'

'Only Ethel showed any love for 'er,' Nelly said. 'P'raps we're all a bit to blame.'

Amy realised that Nelly was wearing her navy coat, fastened across the front with a safety pin.

'Are you off to see Ethel?' she asked. 'She's still at the hospital. I don't know when she'll be back.'

'No, I ain't callin'. It's someone else I want to see, name of Dawn Simmons. That girl what's been tormentin' us and 'elpin' 'erself to cakes an' eggs. Remember 'er takin' a cake from your shop, Amy? Well, she's opened up me chicken coop an' that could mean the fox gettin' me chickens again. So I'm off to see 'er father.'

'I think we should have a word with the police.' Victor showed a ruffle of anger.

36

'No, let me an' George talk to 'er dad first. She ain't got no mother. Best if we 'ave a word with the dad before the police.'

'Oh, I didn't know about the mother,' Victor said. 'We seem too willing to jump to accuse, don't we?'

Because they were still feeling ashamed at the lack of care they had shown to Sheila, forgetting the part Maurice obviously played in his own downfall, they agreed not to involve Constable Harris with regard to Dawn Simmons until her father had been told.

'Me an' George are going up now to find 'er. She's only ten and I expect 'e'll be glad we saw 'im first.' Nelly looked back at the cottage, mellow in the early evening sun, a few early roses drooping heavy heads, the last of the blossom on the apple tree patterning the ground below it. There was a peaceful stillness and beauty about the place, which Nelly's loud ear-piercing voice suddenly shattered, calling for George to hurry. This started the dogs off again and Amy, Margaret and Victor thankfully left her.


'Will you stay for tea, Uncle Victor?' Margaret asked as they walked out of the village, past the house where her Auntie Prue used to live. 'I never have a game of Monopoly now Freddie's gone to the army. It's boring with only Mam.'

'What d'you mean?'

'Only it's better with three,' Margaret smiled. 'Will you stay?'

'I'd love to, Margaret, but it's up to your mam.' Victor lit a cigarette as an excuse to give Amy time to reply. When he looked up again, Margaret was smiling.

'Mam agrees, so, will you?'

'I bet I beat the pair of you!'

'One game only,' Amy said firmly, 'and put that cigarette out before you come in!'

37

The one game went on a lot longer that they expected and Victor was amazed to realise that Margaret was cheating. Not to win, but to prolong the game. Every time he was getting low in money she would conveniently forget to demand rent when he stood on one of her properties. When Amy went to see to the baby, he leaned towards the grinning girl and said, 'You, Margaret Prichard, are a cheat!'

'I know I am,' she whispered back, 'but it's making Mam forget it's bedtime.'

The baby was settled into her cot and Amy had put Margaret's nightdress to warm. Victor sensed he was outstaying his welcome. He stood up and gestured to the clock.

'Sorry Margaret, but I really have to go. I think when we count up, you will have won. And there was me boasting I'd knock you both out of the game in an hour!'

He picked up the cups and plates left from tea-time and took them into the kitchen, collecting his coat from the hook on the back of the door.

'Don't go for a moment,' Amy said. 'I'll just see Margaret into bed and we'll have another cup of tea.'

'If you're sure—' His eyes held a question.

'I'm sure people will gossip whether you stay an extra hour or not.'

While Amy read a story to Margaret and tucked her in, he counted up the score and put the game away. When Amy returned he was sitting near the fire, staring into the coals, looking thoughtful and a little sad.

'What's the matter' she asked.

He turned and smiled, opening his arms to her and as she stepped closer he held her tightly against him.

'I enjoy being here with you and Margaret and it makes me sad too.'

'Why?'

'Because it's such a small, precious part of my life.

The rest is so empty. Amy, I only come alive when I'm with you.'

'Victor, I won't—'

'You know I love you.'

'I won't get involved. I won't!'

'I just want you to know, I will leave Imogine one day.'

'Will you? Will you leave Delina? Or Daniel, or David? David is only twelve.'

'I know I can't leave until David is old enough to cope. It's a long time to ask you to wait, but when he's eighteen and able to manage without the little I give to the family, then I'll leave.'

'Five or six years? And how many years after that before you are free?'

'I know it's asking too much. You're still young and there's that Billie Brown with so much more to offer than I'll ever have. But I want you to know how I feel and that my constant dream is that miraculously we'll find a way to be together.'

He sat holding her hand and staring into the fire. Amy stood beside him breathing shallowly, silent, and moved by his words. The slightest move on his part then and she would have been in his arms and kisses would have opened the locked doors and allowed love to flow free. She almost made that first small move herself; the temptation was so strong it was choking her to stand mute and unyielding.

It was as he rose to reach once more for his coat that the magnetic force drawing them together became irresistible. He reached past her for the garment which he had thrown across a chair and Amy moved at the same time so they touched. Their arms circled each other and the kiss that followed was so sweet that tears escaped from Amy's closed eyes.

'I want you so much,' he murmured and she pulled free.

'No, it would make things impossible. It's wrong for us.'

'Ill-timed, yes, but not wrong.'

'Wrong for us now with so many obstacles in our way. Please, Victor, you're making it very difficult. Margaret is upstairs and not even asleep. I can't risk hurting her.'

His arms slowly released her and he stepped away from her. 'Neither can I, love. You're right.' He picked up his coat, walked to the door and left without another word.

A few moments later there was a knock at the door and she gave a cry. If Victor walked back in she would not be able to turn him away. She held her breath as she opened the door and her heart fell into a chasm of disappointment. It was Morgan Morgan, who was running the building firm while her sister was ill. He called each weekend to collect the books which she was supposed to inspect. She handed them to him with a forced smile, unable to decide whether she was relieved to have escaped the ultimate decision with Victor or sorry she had lost the chance to change her mind.

# *Chapter Three*

Nelly had failed to see Dawn Simmons and her father on the previous day, so after her morning's work for Dorothy Williams, who lived near the Drovers, she went home for a sandwich and a sleep, then set out again hoping to find either Dawn or her father at home. As she reached her gate she saw the sheep dog belonging to Farmer Leighton and looked up and down the lane, smiling at the prospect of a chat, although chatting was difficult with Leighton, who rarely said more than two or three words at a time.

She saw him walking up the lane from the direction of his field beside the lane. He was carrying two buckets which he proceeded to fill at the tap beside her gate.

' 'Ello, what you doing with my tap?' she joked.

'Hello, Nelly. You've got a couple of new neighbours.'

'Sheep?' she asked. 'I won't let Bobby an' Spotty bother 'em, you know that.'

'No, my horses will be permanent residents now. I've retired them and bought a tractor,' he explained.

'You ain't?' Nelly said in disbelief. 'You workin' without your 'orses? I never thought I'd see the day.'

He filled the buckets and walked beside her towards the main road, stopping at the gate on the corner to enter the field. There, beside the hedge was an old bath which he was filling with water.

'Your George and I will be busy over the next few days

41

building a shelter for them,' Leighton smiled. 'Good with the tools, he is.'

'An' so is my Ollie,' Nelly said. 'Can 'e come an' watch yer? 'E'll 'elp too if you'll let 'im.'

Leighton nodded, his burst of conversation ended. Nelly watched him walk over to the bath and empty his buckets and return to the tap for more water. She'd never known him to smile so widely. Was it excitement at the prospect of the new tractor or pleasure at the thought of his beloved horses enjoying a well earned retirement, she wondered.

She looked back up the field and noticed that a pile of wood had been left in the corner near the gate, presumably for the new shelter. She felt a brief sadness. Nothing stayed the same, not even the village. No horses on either Billie Brown's farm or Leighton's – it didn't seem possible. Life was just about perfect, why did everything have to change?

She looked across the road at the row of cottages which included the fish-and-chip shop and Amy's shop. That row seemed to stay the same. The people who lived there seemed never to quite belong to the rest of the village. It was as if the main road were an impenetrable barrier and those behind it hid themselves away. Many of the houses had belonged to the same families for several generations, the tenancies passing from mother to child and, oddly enough, most of the people in that row went out to work. Even after retirement from the shops and offices which had encapsulated their careers, they prefered to shop in Llangwyn, and only used Amy's shop for emergencies.

For no other reason than a desire to pass a little time before calling on Dawn's father, she crossed the road and went along the back lane behind the cottages. She glanced into the yard behind the fish-and-chip shop and called a greeting to Griff Evan's wife, Hilda, who was washing freshly cut chips in a bath of cold water. Although it was June and not particularly cold, the woman looked chilled.

She wore a wrapover apron and an old black cardigan, and on her feet were short boots as she stood in the running water, dealing with the potatoes. Her hair was in Dinkie curlers and to Nelly's eyes seemed rusty, having been inexpertly dyed black to hide the greying. Nelly wondered how Griff and Hilda had ever come to be married. She was so dull and he treated her no better than a drudge, never even taking her to the pictures.

'Tell your Griff I want ter see 'im!' Nelly shouted and the woman looked up from her task and waved.

'You're as likely to see him as me, Nelly. Never in, always busy at something or other,' Hilda complained. 'If it isn't work it's darts and if not darts then he's out in the woods setting his traps, or with our Pete, doing something to the motor-bikes!'

' 'E owes me some money,' Nelly growled.

Hilda shrugged her thin shoulders. 'Join the queue!'

The back yard of the shop had been built on so there was little more than a path leading to the open-sided area where Hilda did most of her work. In the newer part of the building were two small rooms in which Milly Toogood and her husband, Tommy, lived. Milly's daughter, Bethan, lived above the shop with her son Arthur who was the same age as Nelly's grandson. Although Bethan had lived in the village all her life, few called her Bethan; to everyone she was "Milly Toogood's daughter". This was mainly due to the mystery of her husband who had been an American soldier and who had failed to materialise in time to welcome his son into the world. Doubt as to how to address her had led to her odd, nameless state.

As Nelly passed the back of Amy's shop she heard the sound of children shouting as they were released from

43

the confinement of school. She quickened her pace, now she was certain to find Dawn at home. There was one certainty regarding children of nine and ten; as they left school their first thought would be food! She was greeted by several children as she crossed back over the road and began to walk up Sheepy Lane to Hywel Rise where Dawn and her father were living.

This time there was an answer to her knock. The door opened almost at once and she guessed that the man was about to go out. Tad Simmons was small, slim and anxious-looking, his fair hair untidy, as if he had forgotten to comb it, even though he was wearing a lightweight overcoat and had a trilby in his hand. His face wore a mask of stubble which gave him a slightly wild look. The blue eyes were large and bellicose, the jaw tight, with an aggressive tilt that made Nelly step back.

'What is it now?' the man demanded irritably.

'That ain't much of a greetin' is it?' she said, and guessed, in a flash of sympathy that she was one of many who called to complain about his wayward daughter. 'Best form of defence is attack, eh? Bin a lot of people to complain?'

'Some. Is that what you've come to do, Nelly Luke?'

'Oh, knows me name, do yer?'

'I haven't lived here long, but everybody knows Nelly Luke.'

'Well yer wrong for a start off, me name's Nelly Masters. I married again.'

'What is it. I'm just off to work.'

'I only wanted to ask if your Dawn would like to come an' 'ave some tea with me grandson, Oliver, on Saturday.'

The man was surprised and he stared at her with a brief pleasure which quickly turned to suspicion.

'Why?'

'Well, she's new 'ere an' my Ollie's got lots of friends.

I'll ask young Margaret Prichard too an' 'ave a bit of a party. 'She turned to go, dragging the dogs from their attempt to go inside. 'I expect you know where I live? Bring 'er about three, why don't yer?' She waved and walked off down the hill, leaving the man still staring in disbelief at her retreating figure.

He slammed the front door and sat for a moment in a kitchen chair. He wondered at Nelly's motive. Not kindness, that was for sure. No one had shown him any kindness since the sympathy surrounding the death of his young wife had faded away. He was on his own and he was happy to accept that. He would look after Dawn and make sure she suffered as little as possible for the loss of her mother. He looked around the sparsely furnished room. If only he could work at a proper job and earn enough for them to be comfortable. He had long since given up his dream of returning to college to complete an engineering course interrupted by the war, but he longed to be able to work more than the few hours he managed by leaving Dawn in the charge of unwilling neighbours, to clean floors in a factory in Llangwyn.

Nelly still didn't go home, her dinner was cooking in the oven heated by the fire and needed no immediate attention. She walked down Sheepy Lane and, holding the dogs as close to her as possible, called to see her daughter. Evie showed no pleasure at seeing her.

'Tie those animals up, please, Mother,' she said in her careful, slow voice. 'If you intend coming to visit me, why don't you leave them at home?'

'My Mrs French don't mind me takin' 'em there, an' she's a *real* lady,' Nelly retorted. She shortened the leads even more and stood outside the back door. 'Beside, I ain't visitin'. I just called to invite young Ollie to tea on Saturday.'

'Oliver. Your grandson's name is Oliver. And no, I

45

don't think he can come. Timothy and I have to go to town to buy him some summer clothes.'

'Aw, you'll be back by three, won't yer? Send 'im up to me while you unpack yer shoppin' an' 'ave a bit of a sit-down, why don't yer?'

'Well, all right, if we're back in time.'

'Right. Tell 'im there'll be baked potatoes done under the fire, just as 'e likes 'em.'

'For tea?' Evie looked horrified.

'O' course fer tea! An' some jellies and cake.'

Nelly chuckled as she set off again, this time to the shop. Evie was such a snob. It was nothing but cucumber sandwiches and tiny cakes that would hardly fit into an egg cup, for her. Potatoes burnt with the ashes of a wood fire and, before rationing, running with butter, were most uncouth! 'What she's missing!' Nelly sighed. 'Poor Evie and 'er fancy ideas of what's right.'

She wondered, as she reached Amy's shop, whether there was any chance of some butter scraped from the paper and too stale to sell as someone's ration, which Amy sometimes spared her. She would ask. When the fifty-six-pound block of butter was packed into two-ounce allowances the remnants were often scraped off and passed to her by a generous Amy.

When she walked the dogs she usually held her head down and it was only as she reached the shop steps that she looked up and noticed Mr Leighton's new tractor parked outside the shop. Further down the lane was a van, marked with the name of Billie and Mary Brown's dairy farm. Behind the tractor was another van. This one, she knew, was one driven by Victor Honeyman when he delivered from the wholesaler in Llangwyn. The shop was full and she thought she might be better served not to bother Amy at the moment.

Two people came out of the shop before she could move away. One was Billie Brown, the tall, strongly built farmer in his cowboy shirt and brown overalls, the other was Farmer Leighton. The two men stood discussing market prices and gave her a casual nod. With those two out of the way the shop did not seem so full and as Victor was there, it might be an idea to interrupt. Nelly thought it her duty as Amy's friend to protect her from the advances of Victor Honeyman.

'Amy, got a minute, 'ave yer? I wondered if your Margaret would like to come to tea on Saturday with my Ollie? 'I've asked that Dawn Simmons as well but don't tell my Evie or she won't let Ollie come.' All this was shouted from the doorway, trying to prevent the dogs from entering.

She stretched further in to hear Amy's reply and trod on Bobby's paw. He yelped and the dogs belonging to the two farmers, and which she had not noticed, came running towards the shop, heads down in an aggressive manner. They growled and in seconds the air was filled with barking and snarling as the four dogs tried to assert their positions. Nelly let the leads go as snapping jaws threatened to bite her hands. It seemed an age before Billie separated the angry animals by walking in and using his knees to force them apart. He held his hands high before grabbing the necks of his own dog and Leighton's bitch and dragging them in opposite directions. Leighton stood on the leads of Nelly's dogs to prevent them following as Billie shut the offender in the van.

'Didn't know there was a farmers' convention this afternoon,' Nelly grumbled into the sudden silence. She looked up to where Amy was standing, arms akimbo, glaring at them all. Behind her was Victor.

'Sorry, Amy,' Nelly said. She stood expecting a telling-off but all Amy said was, 'Go and put the kettle on, Nelly.'

With Bobby and Spotty tied in the yard and the two

farmers departed, Nelly left her dogs licking real and imagined wounds and made tea.

'Shall I sweep up the mud while I'm 'ere?' she offered. She gestured to where the hard-pressed patterns of mud had dropped from the boots of the farmers. While this was accomplished, Victor backed his van into the lane and took Amy's order into the storeroom behind the shop.

'I couldn't get in before,' he explained. 'That Billie Brown's van was in the way.'

'Blimey, Amy, them two are like Milly Toogood and the Pup – you never see one without the other turning up! They must be telepathic where you're concerned. Each seems to know when the other comes visitin'!'

Milly Toogood was rarely seen without her friend, Sybil Tremain, who always walked a few paces behind her as if in a constant effort to catch up. Nelly's nickname for Sybil, "the Pup", was now commonly used.

'Victor always delivers on the same day,' Amy smiled.

'Yes, an' I bet Billie manages to find a reason to call at the same time, to shop any chance of you two 'avin' a moment together!' Nelly sighed in exaggerated despair. 'Why don't yer marry one of 'em an' put them both out of their misery?'

'Victor is married!' Amy's voice was sharp.

'Oh, an' 'e's the one, is 'e?'

'Neither of them is "the one" as you put it. They are both good friends.'

There was a sadness in Amy's eyes that made Nelly hurriedly change the subject. 'Well, can she?'

'What are you talking about now? Got a mind like a butterfly you have, Nelly Luke!'

'Can Margaret come to tea on Saturday?'

'Of course she can and thank you for asking her.'

'An' you won't tell Evie that Dawn's comin'?' Chuckling, Amy mimicked Nelly and mimed cutting her throat. 'Hope ter die!'

*　　*　　*

On Saturday afternoon, George and Nelly set up a table in
the garden and laid it with cakes and jellies and a variety of
salads. the cakes were made without fat, the custard with
fresh eggs and the potatoes were taken from their jackets
and mashed with a few slivers of corned beef saved from
their lunch, and sprinkled with cheese before being placed
on plates in front of the hungry children.

'Thank Gawd cheese is off ration at last,' Nelly said as
she stood to watch the children eat.

'They were quite excited to see such a grand spread, and
it does look lovely with the coloured jellies and the iced
cake,' George smiled. 'I hope they leave some for us!'

'I thought it best to let them eat on their own. Give 'em a
chance to talk, then I can find out from Ollie what sort of a
girl Dawn is.'

'From the way she's tucking in, she's pretty normal!'

After the children had eaten and filled up on some of
Nelly's homemade lemonade, Nelly expected them to
play games in the garden, but as soon as she had eaten,
Dawn disappeared.

'She filled her pockets with what was left of the cakes,
told us we were horrible and ran home,' Oliver reported.

'Never mind, we'll ask 'er again,' Nelly said. 'I ain't
goin' to be beaten by a ten-year-old!'

'She's a rebel and perhaps always will be,' George
warned. 'Don't expect too much.'

Phil-the-Post came later that evening and brought a list of
names.

'There you are. These idiots have volunteered to dig
your trench for you, Nelly, me included, *and* we've all
paid out for the privilege.' He turned to the tall white-
haired George and scowled. 'Your name's goin' down
too, isn't it boy?'

'I thought I'd be foreman and whip you all into action,'

49

George said innocently. 'I haven't got to dig as well, have I? And pay you for digging my own trench.'

'I ain't diggin',' Nelly said quickly. 'I'm doin' teas!'

'And selling them,' George added.

'There's something even you didn't think of,' Phil said with a laugh. 'I'm selling tickets to them coming to watch!'

A few days before the day arranged to begin digging the trench for new drainage, Nelly went once more to Hywel Rise to see Dawn.

'We're doin' a bit of fund-raisin',' she explained as Dawn's father opened the door. 'Comin' are yer, you an' Dawn?'

'I'll see.' Tad Simmons began to close the door.

'Don't yer want to know where an' when?'

The door opened a little and she hurriedly explained the plan. 'It'll cost yer,' she said, but the door had closed again. 'Miserable old devil,' she muttered, then her frown cleared as the door reopened and Tad asked for more details.

'Sixpence to come an' look, a shillin' to 'elp with the diggin'.' Then she added, 'Dawn can come fer free an' 'elp me with the teas.'

'Right, er, yes, we'll come.' Looking confused but unwilling to ask for further clarification, he again closed the door.

'I don't think 'e'll come,' Nelly told George later, 'but you know. I think young Dawn was hidin' behind the door expectin' I'd come to complain about 'er behavior. She probably enjoys people getting on at 'er so I disappointed 'er there.'

The digging of the trench achieved several things, some not long-lasting. Firstly the trench was swiftly and neatly dug, ready for the council to connect Nelly's cottage to the water supply, a prospect she half dreaded, being so used to using the woods for her toilet and the tap in the lane for water. The second result of the afternoon's work was a pile of oddments found as the spades overturned the ground. Thirty-seven broken clay pipes were evidence that someone had once sat on a garden seat and dreamed away the hours, old kettles and a brass fender, an old bicycle wheel and even an almost complete pram were unearthed as the tangled shrubs were cut back and the earth opened up. All these were piled up at the furthest corner of the garden, near an even larger pile of branches and old wood.

Half the village appeared to watch the fun. They pushed their way through the gate and after dropping a coin into Phil's eager hand, hurried to the back of the house, where, as usual, Bert Roberts had appointed himself as organiser. Nelly busied herself in the kitchen, watching as the stream of people passed, in the hope of seeing Dawn Simmons. The visitors slowed to an occasional trickle and she had almost given up hope when she recognised Tad Simmons in a rather untidy raincoat pushing his reluctant daughter in front of him.

She's feigning reluctance, Nelly thought, watching the girl's face. Just as she enjoys all the complaints her father gets about her. She put down the plate of sandwiches she had prepared for the time when the digging was finished and, hands on fat hips, stood at her door watching the man and young girl walk down the cinder path.

'Come on, you're late, ain't yer?' she said as if the arrangement to help had been a firm one. 'You go 'ome, Mr Simmons, Dawn an' I got things ter do.' As she guessed, with such an emphatic greeting, Tad and Dawn were too surprised to argue. Nelly rolled up her sleeves and stuck the girl's hands into a bowl of warm, soapy water, swished them about then handed her a towel.

'That'll do. There's too much fuss about washin' if you asks me. Now, get them sardines out of the tins and mash 'em for me, why don't yer?' She hummed softly, secretly watching the girl as the sardines were spread on to slices of fresh bread. Dawn hardly spoke and when she spilt a dish of grated cheese and pickle, she just stared belligerently at Nelly, waiting for the complaint to come.

'Bobby? Spotty?' Nelly called and grinned at the girl as the spoilt food was quickly cleared. For the first time, Dawn smiled back.

'Come on, let's go an' see 'ow they're gettin' on.'

She guided the girl up the curved staircase and into the cluttered back bedroom used by George. From the window, they looked at the village *cwtched* between the fields and hills. Only a few roofs and the tall church spire were visible, but columns of smoke rose into the still air and the hills shone a brilliant green in the sun.

'Look down there, it's Brenda 'avin' a go,' Nelly pointed and Dawn opened the window and leaned out. They were both kneeling on George's bed and the girl jigged up and down in excitement.

'What a big garden. And it's full of trees!'

'It was a real muddle before my George started to clear it,' Nelly said, delighted that Dawn was enjoying herself. 'Down there, where young Arthur Toogood is banging on the oak tree with a stick, there used to be a nest of owls. Bleedin' 'eadache they'll 'ave if they're still there!'

Dawn giggled. Then she shouted down to Arthur, 'Oi you! Stop that banging, you'll frighten the birds!'

'Yeh,' Nelly joined in, 'bang yer own 'ead if yer want to bang somethin'!'

Laughing, they closed the window.

'We'd better go an' see if they're ready for some grub, before we get Milly Toogood on to us.' At the doorway she stopped and saw that Dawn was looking at something in one of the boxes of abandoned treasures, things Nelly no longer used but was loath to throw away.

'What's this?' she asked Nelly, holding up an old camera.

'Ain't used it fer years. It took some good snaps of my Evie once. Ain't you seen a camera before?'

'Not one like this. My dad's got one but I'm not allowed to touch it.'

'Not allowed? I bet that doesn't stop yer!' Nelly laughed. 'Bring it down if you like, we can look at it together. Pity we ain't got a film. There'd be some good pictures in my garden today!' She picked up the kettle and made a large pot of tea. 'Come on, carry them sandwiches and I'll carry the teapot.'

They went into the garden, Nelly's face beaming with delight at the hordes of people standing and sitting watching the antics of the men and women digging out the trench. It was Johnny Cartwright's turn and Netta, his mother, was teasing him, pretending to help him lift the spadeful of soil.

'Come on you lot, come an' 'ave a cuppa while it's 'ot.'

Johnny threw down his spade and others followed suit and everyone crowded around reaching for the cups as soon as Nelly had filled them. The table which had been used for the children's tea party was in service again and Dawn carried out tray after tray of food. Although she was kept very busy, Nelly noticed that Dawn seemed ill at ease.

'Probably seein' so many of the people she's teased and pestered,' she whispered to George. 'I'll keep 'er busy.'

It was as they were all eating that Delina arrived. Since the trouble with Sheila had caused Delina's wedding to be cancelled she had rarely been seen in the village apart from her journey to and from the school in Llangwyn where she taught. Nelly offered her a cup of tea and invited her to help herself to food.

'Come to 'elp with the diggin', 'ave yer?' Nelly asked. But Delina shook her head.

'I'm looking for Dad. Mam isn't too well. I'd like him to decide whether or not we call the doctor out.'

'What is it?'

'Her arm. She fell a while ago and broke a bone. It's still painful and she has to go to the hospital occasionally to get treatment to ease it.'

'Ain't that yer dad over there with Phil, talking to young Dawn?' As Delina made to go over to her father, Nelly called her back. ' 'Ere, you're a teacher, what d'you make of Dawn? She be'aves badly and leads 'er dad a right dance, but I don't think she's that bad, just un'appy.'

'Would that be Dawn Simmons? I've heard about her escapades. I'll have a chat to her if I get the chance. You're probably right, Nelly, she needs friends. A new area and only her father for company, it must be difficult for her to enjoy being a little girl.'

Victor's face lit up when he saw his daughter approaching.

'Come to join the fun, love?' he said. But his face changed equally fast when she explained her presence.

'Mummy didn't want me to come,' she told him, 'but I don't know whether she needs a doctor or if we'd be wasting his time. It isn't as if she were ill, but she is in pain. Perhaps I should get some aspirin?'

'I think the shop will still be open. I'll slip across and get something and go home to see how she is. Unless it's serious, I'd like to stay and do my part of the trench. Daft, I know, but it's money in good cause. Stay here and talk to Dawn.' He turned to introduce her but Dawn had disappeared. 'Oh, she's here somewhere, helping Nelly with the food. Look out for her, will you? She's supposed to be a bit of a nuisance but she's got no mam. Makes a difference, that does.'

He was anxious that Delina should stay, now she had faced the village again. The news about Sheila was good, Maurice was far away in Australia and there was no longer any need for Delina to hide herself away. He had no real interest in Dawn who he thought needed a good smack rather than sympathy, but he used the girl as persuasion for her to wait for him.

He went past the kitchen door and up the path to the gate, intending to go to Amy's shop for some tablets. He was smiling at the legitimate excuse to see her. A man was standing at Nelly's gate, looking hesitantly into the garden.

'Come to help with the digging?' Victor asked. 'Better hurry, man, there's not much left, although I wouldn't put it past Nelly to fill it in and start again!'

'I've come back to fetch my daughter, a little girl aged ten. Seen her have you?'

'Would that be young Dawn?' As the man nodded, Victor added, 'Helping Nelly with the food and working very hard too. Go on in, Phil will charge you entrance mind,' he warned, before hurrying off down the lane to the main road.

Tad Simmons walked down Nelly's path to where Phil stood waiting.

'Sixpence if you're coming to watch,' Phil said.

'I've only come to fetch my little girl. Don't have to pay for that, do I?' The man's belligerent reply startled the good-natured Phil and his face opened up with shock, eyebrows raised, his mouth an "O". 'You going to stop me going in?' Tad demanded.

'Go you,' Phil said. 'And if it's Dawn you're wanting, she's probably with Nelly.' Phil pointed over his shoulder towards Nelly's kitchen. 'In by there.' He stared after the scowling man, who looked briefly into Nelly's living room then pushed his way past Phil to stand looking at the increasingly boisterous crowd churning the soil around the trench.

Victor Honeyman returned from buying the aspirin for his wife and, passing Phil, offered another sixpence entrance fee.

'Is Delina still here?' he asked in a whisper.

'I haven't seen her pass,' Phil told him. 'Hey, did you see that misery that came in now just? No wonder that kid's a nuisance if that's her father!' He put a finger to his nose as a warning for Victor not to reply as Tad walked towards them.

'Found her, have you?' Phil asked.

'Yes, she'll be staying a while longer.'

'There's a cup of tea in the kitchen,' Victor offered, curious about the surly man who looked downwards, his thin shoulders hunched as if trying to avoid acknowledging anyone.

'No thanks.'

'I'll treat you,' Victor said, 'it's only a couple of coppers and it's for the church-hall fund.'

'Oh, I didn't understand. I thought it was some sort of party.'

'It is really. It's Nelly Luke's daft idea. She's charging people to dig her trench for her. The funny thing is that it's working. There's a few pounds been made this afternoon. The trench is looking a bit sick, mind.'

Delina approached them, holding Dawn's hand.

'Dad, I have to go. I want to make sure Mummy's all right.'

'I went up and she was asleep,' Victor told her. 'Stay five more minutes, love.'

'This is Dawn's father. Get him a cup of tea, will you?' Phil asked. 'I've got to go and see George and Nelly.' He pushed Delina gently in the direction of Tad Simmons, winked at Dawn and hurried around the side of the house to see how the trench was progressing. Victor had been right, the once-neat trench was sagging sadly on each side as too many people crowded around to watch the fun.

Victor followed Phil, with a glance back to see his daughter, still holding Dawn's hand, talking to the still-scowling Tad. She was already looking more relaxed than she had for weeks. If she could be persuaded to take her place in the village again the afternoon would achieve more than money for the fund. As Tad, Dawn and Delina disappeared in the direction of the back door, he crossed his fingers and offered up a brief unholy prayer. 'Please God, don't let that miserable old bugger upset her.'

Delina was someone who loved stray dogs, and Dawn plus her scowling father were certainly in need of a friend. He thought that a difficult and unhappy child might be just what his daughter needed, as long as Tad would allow her to help. There's nothing like a "cause" to help you forget your own troubles, he mused as he strode off.

Johnny Cartwright arrived late. He drove the local bus and finished in the early evening. He brought his wife, Fay, who had dressed sensibly but smartly in a blue tweed suit and thick leather brogues. She wore a scarf around her shoulders and a small hat with a band to match the scarf. As her job was selling hats, she was rarely seen without one, considering herself as much a display as a shop window. Even on an occasion like this, in the churned-up mud of Nelly's garden she was dressed as neatly as when she went into town to meet a client. Johnny was very proud of her. He had loved Fay all his life and couldn't believe his luck when she consented to be his wife. But their wedding had, for a time, been cancelled when Alan French, Fay's previous fiancé, turned up having been believed killed in the war. A few weeks later, with only a few friends to witness Fay and Johnny's wedding, they had finally married. Johnny never felt sure of her though and even now there was anxiety in his dark eyes, knowing that for her village fun like this was just a duty.

'Sorry about the mud, lovely,' Johnny said as they reached the chewed-up part of the garden. The constant tread of feet had changed the almost untouched area into a sea of crumbly soil, and they saw that Nelly had changed her black shoes, worn on special occasions only, for her wellington boots.

'Damn me, she's a character,' Johnny laughed, pointing to where Nelly was struggling through the loose earth to carry a tray of tea to the men supposedly working hard on the gradually curving trench.

There were three men trying to complete their stretch but they had been stopped by Bert who held out a rule and was trying to explain to anyone who would listen that they were heading in the wrong direction. Bert was red in the face as he gesticulated towards the wavering line of string marking where he thought the trench should go.

'What's going on, Bert? You holding up the works again? Never saw a bloke so set on following the rules.'

'They won't take a blind bit of notice!' Bert shouted. 'I'm trying to get the trench straight. Off at a tangent they are and they won't listen!'

'Never!' Johnny gasped in mock horror, 'You don't say! Never mind, Bert, you can come back tomorrow and put it right, all by yourself.'

'Someone will have to, for sure!'

Johnny took the string with which Bert was desperately trying to mark the direction of the trench, that now wavered right, then left and seemed to be heading for the lane.

'Damn me, Bert, you've really put the mockers on this,' Johnny teased.

'Me!' The irate man threw the stick marking the end of the trench into the air and strode off. 'I'm going for a cup of tea!'

'Quick, George, while he's out of the way,' Johnny said and with Victor, Phil and young Oliver, they set to work. When Bert emerged from Nelly's kitchen, where Delina and Tad sat talking, he nodded his approval importantly.

'Yes,' he said, as if the improvement were all his doing. 'That's what I wanted.'

'Well done, Bert.' Johnny grinned at Phil and winked at Oliver. 'Damn good job you've done by here today.'

Bert smiled contentedly.

When Delina reappeared, she was not content. Her blue eyes blazed with anger. As she came round the house into the garden, Victor approached her and asked at once what was wrong.

'That insufferably ill-mannered man in there!' she said. 'I tried to talk to him about Dawn. It's obvious the child is unhappy, but he accused me of interfering and of accusing a ten-year-old child of crimes, over what was simply childish fun.'

'It's not like you to upset people, Delina,' Victor said anxiously. 'Are you sure you didn't say too much too soon? What *did* you say, love?'

'Very little. All I did was gently agree with him, then he turned on me and told me not to talk about things I couldn't possibly understand and—'

'All right, love, don't get upset. He's lost his wife apparently and the little girl is quite a handful for him, no doubt about that. Afraid of having her taken off him I suppose. That would be enough to make him over-sensitive.'

'He isn't the only one to have lost someone. Why should he think he's so special?'

'People do, don't they, when trouble hits? It's easy to forget that others are in the same situation, or one that's worse. I know that,' he added gently.

'I feel as if I've been isolated from everyone for months and the very first time I try and step outside my circle of misery I have to meet someone like Tad Simmons!'

'Come on, love, we'll go home. I'm glad you came though, aren't you?' He turned around to see the laughing and jeering that accompanied Nelly's latest attempts to dig out a section of the trench. 'It's good to laugh even if you're sad inside.'

Bert Roberts was being helped on to an upturned, broken barrel that had once been used to collect rainwater. He stood rather nervously upright and demanded silence. There were murmurs of "what now?" and various criticisms but they all stopped to listen.

'I think we could all stay a bit longer and help Nelly and George with the clearing up,' he said, and this was greeted with groans. 'I mean,' Bert added slowly, 'we could have a bonfire and burn some of this rotting wood that's no good for anything else.'

'Smashin' ' Nelly agreed and went at once to find paper and kindling.

'Gran,' Oliver followed her, 'Gran, can we cook some potatoes?'

Delina took her father's arm. 'Perhaps we could stay a while longer, if you're sure Mummy's all right?'

Parents came to find children, children came to find parents, and several, including Amy, arrived as soon as their day's work had finished. Some of the men brought flagons of beer and the garden was full of laughing, chattering people enjoying the unexpected party.

So it was almost eleven o'clock when the digging party finally departed. The trench, the reason for it all, was a sorry sight. Children had had a lovely time jumping across it, slithering down it and the walls in several places had collapsed and, even where it was not weakened, the dampness and the threatened overnight rain would help it to slither into a snake of disturbed earth with nothing to suggest it would allow a line of drainpipes to be buried.

George put an arm around Nelly's shoulders as she carried in the last of the china, and chuckled.

'Tomorrow's my day off, and I'll have to spend it re-digging the trench! But,' he added, hugging her plump shoulders tightly, 'it was a good day and we've raised six pound seventeen shillings and threepence halfpenny!'

'Gawd only knows where the half-penny came from!'

When Nelly went inside, she noticed that the camera she had been showing to Dawn had disappeared. 'I 'ope she didn't pinch it, George, I wanted to give it to 'er. Shame if she's spoilt my little surprise, ain't it?'

# Chapter Four

Oliver was a quiet boy and, at nine, was small and thinner than most of his school friends. Margaret and he spent a lot of their time together and it was with her that he wandered the fields and visited the farm where Billie Brown lived with his sister Mary. They walked there one Sunday in June and watched as Mary finished the last of the evening milking, then helped her to wash the milking parlour with the snake-like hose and the thickly bristled brushes.

As the children hoped, Mary invited them to stay for tea in the big farmhouse where a fire burned, whatever the strength of the sun. Today, the weather was cool enough for the fire to be a welcome sight, and while Margaret went into the stone-flagged kitchen to help prepare the food, Oliver sat in an old wooden settle with sides and a roof that made it similar to a half-completed sedan chair and where he sat to dream about being transported to imaginary lands, and wonderful scenes of colour and exciting smells and sensations.

Today, his daydreaming was halted by an item in the local paper which Billie had left, half-folded on a stool. Oliver did not read well. It was a constant worry to his ambitious parents that with a headmaster for a father he failed to achieve even an average result in his academic endeavours. But with Nelly's gentle coaxing, he had improved to the point where he could read enough to understand at least the general outline of a newspaper article.

The headline that had attracted him referred to a celebration planned to mark the one hundreth-and-fiftieth anniversary of the opening of the famous Mumbles Railway, the first passenger train in the world. He could not grasp all the details but learnt that there was to be a replica of the various trains that had been used on the track. It would begin with a horse-drawn carriage and end with the present tram engine which ran from the centre of Swansea along the edge of the beautiful Swansea Bay to the pier at Mumbles in view of the lighthouse.

When Billie came downstairs, having changed from his working clothes into a cowboy shirt and dungarees identical to those he had taken off, apart from their cleanness and neatness, he found Oliver on the floor, bending over the newspaper, his finger laboriously following the words as he concentrated on reading them.

'What's that, Oliver? Something has attracted your interest. You usually sit and daydream in that old chair.'

Oliver blushed. He had not realised anyone had guessed. Billie saw his discomfort and added, 'I don't think many sit in that old chair and not dream. There's something about it. The sides hide you from everyone else and you can feel safe to enjoy letting your mind wander. Magic in that chair, Oliver, at least, when I was a boy I used to think so.'

Oliver smiled at him, his small face still showing the red cheeks of his embarrassment, the need for it already fading. Billie understood. He was a bit like Gran, he decided. She never made fun of anything he said or did. Billie was becoming one of his favourite people, along with Gran and Margaret. He held out the newspaper and pointed to the relevant item.

'It would be fun to go and see, wouldn't it?' The light-blue eyes were bright, his straight fair hair falling over them pushed hurriedly back as he thought of the day out.

Billie noticed that the boy's hands were grimy from his work in the yard and he patted the boy affectionately and suggested, 'Why don't I read this while you go into the kitchen and wash your hands for tea?'

'Will you tell me all about it then?'

'Discuss it we will, all four of us.'

After an enormous meal, eaten around the big table which had been covered in dishes of food that all but obliterated the snowy-white table cloth it was time to leave and Oliver suggested calling on his gran.

'I'd like to tell her about the Mumbles Train celebration,' he explained to Margaret. 'Perhaps we can go and see the fun? Gran loves a bit of fun.'

They walked through the green fields, stopping to count Billie's sheep to see if that would really make them fall asleep, following the erratic course of the stream for part of the way and, as they climbed up to the woods and approached Nelly's cottage, Oliver asked, 'Margaret, do you sit in Billie's settle chair and dream?'

'When you give me a chance! Yes, I love to daydream and play pretend, don't you?'

'I dream about being top of the class.'

'I imagine playing the piano with a big huge orchestra and Mam and Freddie, and you of course, clapping in the front row and Mam crying as she sometimes does when she's happy.'

'Your dream will come true, Margaret, but I can't see me ever understanding sums and writing.'

'Of course you will! Besides, Billie says there's more than one way to be clever. He thinks you're clever with machines, knowing how they work before he's explained to you. That's really smart.'

'I do understand machines a bit. That's why it would be so great to go and see the Mumbles trains. There'll be a horse pulling dozens of people in a carriage on rails and everyone will be dressed up. I bet Gran'll love it.'

*    *    *

Nelly and George went to see Tad Simmons to deal with the loss of the camera. They knocked on his door somewhat nervously, wondering how to broach the subject without Tad becoming angry.

'It's about the camera I was showin' Dawn,' Nelly began.

'The camera you gave her you mean. Don't suggest she took something that didn't belong to her,' Tad said at once. 'I've met people like you before, Nelly Luke – er Masters. Giving something then changing your mind.'

'We haven't changed our mind,' George said calmly, 'we just want to show her how it works and buy a film to put in it.'

'Oh.'

'No sense givin' only 'alf a present, is there?' Nelly added. 'Tell 'er to bring it down after school on Monday and we'll fix it up for 'er.'

'We covered up for her with her father,' George said as they walked back down the hill, 'but I think we should let her know we don't approve of what she did.'

'She'll be told, George. It's best for 'er to be told.'

When they reached their gate, they heard voices. Margaret and Oliver were using the swing Billie Brown had made for Oliver and which had been set up in Nelly's garden. Oliver jumped down when he saw Nelly and greeted her with his suggestion of a day out.

' 'Course we'll go, Ollie, an' if Amy can't shut the shop Margaret'll come with us. Dawn too, an' anyone else you can think of. Make it a real outin' we will, picnic, ice-cream, chips, the lot!'

Nelly walked to the main road with the children and watched as Margaret turned right and Oliver turned left, both stopping several times to wave to her and each other before passing out of sight. She had the dogs with her

66

and decided to walk along the main road and up Sheepy Lane to call on Ethel and enquire about Sheila.

It was as she turned into Sheepy Lane and was bending down to release the dogs from their leads that a taxi passed her. To her surprise, Sheila was inside, obviously on her way home from hospital. With her, in soldier's uniform, was Freddie Prichard, Amy's son.

'What's 'e doin' with that Sheila Powell?' she muttered with mild anger. 'I'd 'ave thought 'e'd 'ad enough of that one!' She was distracted from thoughts of Sheila and Freddie by Oliver calling from the bottom of the lane.

'Gran, can I come back with you? Mam and Dad are out'

Although curious about Sheila and knowing that a visit to Ethel would satisfy her curiosity, she put the dogs back on their leads and turned back. A car pulled up in front of Evie's house and she and Oliver waited. Evie stepped out from the driving seat and called irritably to her son. 'Oliver, come on in and get cleaned up, it's time for your tea.'

'I've had tea with Uncle Billie and Auntie Mary,' he explained.

'Then come and get your homework done. I don't suppose you found time for that, did you?' With a brief nod to her mother, Evie opened the door and went inside, leaving Timothy to drive the car into the garage.

' 'Ello, Timmy, bin 'avin' fun, 'ave yer?' she asked with a wry grin.

The burglaries began on a Wednesday evening in the middle of June and the first victim was Archie Pearce who lived near Netta Cartwright. Archie worked at the forestry and each Wednesday evening he went to play darts at the Drovers. It was his only regular evening out. His other visits to the public house were last minute decisions based on the attractions, or lack of them, the wireless had to offer.

He always drank too much on Wednesdays and came home on the late bus, often assisted to his door by the good-natured bus conductor who worked with Johnny. He would fall into bed, pausing only to throw off his clothes and wind his alarm clock. The clock went unheard on Thursdays and this time the driver of the bus which took the workmen up to the forest was the one who helped him.

On this Thursday morning the driver issued a few threats, thumped on his horn and eventually left his cab to knock on Archie's door, shouting loudly as he did so. But instead of the little man bursting out of his door, hurriedly pushing his shirt into his trousers, tightening his belt and apologising for the delay, a very sober Archie opened the door and said, 'Oh, I thought you must be the police.'

'Police? Why, what you bin up to, boy?'

'I've been robbed, that's what. Money I'd put away for rent and insurance. Someone broke in and stole it. Left me without a penny to my name. Lucky I wasn't murdered – like poor Harry Beynon when he was robbed.'

'Look, I've got to go. Sorry I am, but these men'll be late. Called the police then, have you?'

'I put a note through PC Harris's door last night. Damn, it sobered me up proper it did, coming home to find all this mess.'

The row of faces in the bus windows all stared at Archie as he stood waving them off, his face shrunken and old at the shock of his home being invaded by strangers. He knew he should go and find PC Harris in case his note had not been found, but he was afraid to leave his house for fear of another break-in.

He had lived alone since his mother had died and had

never worried about the house being empty every day. He rarely locked his door, except when he went out in the evening and he frowned with concentration as he tried to remember if he had done so the previous evening. He shook his grey head, the frown deepening, and closed the door. He must have, the lock on the back door had been broken. How ironic that the house had been open all day and robbed when it was locked. He sighed with relief. At least he wouldn't be thought a fool when the police questioned him. He made himself a cup of tea, washing the cup before using it as if everything in the house was tainted with the touch of a stranger.

The contents of drawers had been strewn across the linoleum, his clothes pulled out of the wardrobe and even handkerchiefs were no longer in the carefully ironed piles, but crumpled as the thief had searched for money. He felt sickened and would not use anything before it had been washed, cleansed of the filthy grubbing hands that had trespassed on his privacy.

Constable Harris called at nine and noted all the information Archie could give him. Archie told him of the fear he held that the burglar was the same on who had broken in and murdered Harry Beynon. PC Harris reassured him.

'Different altogether this one, Archie. Amateurs who went into the Beynon home. Killed in panic. No, not the same at all. I don't hold out much hope of you getting the money back, mind, there's a look of an expert here. He broke in round the back and at a time when he knew you'd be out. And these terraced cottages with their fences between the yards are very private. I doubt if anyone saw anything unless they happened to be upstairs and looking out. I'll ask, mind, but in the evenings most people are listening to the wireless, or television for the lucky ones. I'll ask along the row and if there's the slightest clue we'll get him, but as for the money' – he shook his head – 'I bet that's already spent.'

69

'The only clue is a couple of leaves on the bedroom floor,' Archie muttered. 'Not much help, is it?'

Archie spent the day sitting staring into the fire and wondering if he would ever be able to go outside his door again. Or, if he did, whether he would have the nerve to cross his threshold and walk back in. He went to look at the mess the intruder had left but which he, as yet, felt unable to clear away. He stood on the front door for a while at intervals but could not explain why. He had an unconscious need to feel less shut off from others, but did not speak to anyone who passed: his need to see people was stronger than his ability to discuss what had happened.

The village was full of talk, most people believing that the murderer of Harry Beynon had returned. This opinion was scorned by Nelly, although she couldn't tell them why. She alone knew the truth about Harry's death. She had witnessed his wife Prue strike the blow that knocked him against the hearth and had sworn to remain silent, believing the death to have been simply a tragic accident.

Netta Cartwright called and brought some cake for his tea, and later in the evening Griff Evans came, having heard the reason for his absence from the forest.

'Come on, Archie, it isn't that bad. Look, the boys have made a collection to pay your rent, so at least you aren't going to be put out on the road. Now, isn't that something to smile about? Come on, boy, cheer up. It'll never happen again. Who ever it is will know there's nothing to steal now, won't he?' He tried to cheer Archie but the old man hardly acknowledged the envelope filled with an assortment of coins amounting to almost three pounds. Griff finally gave up and, accepting the mumbled thanks and promising to convey it to the rest of the gang, he left.

Nelly discovered the second of the burglaries and George was the first person suspected of committing them. Since Prue Beynon had given birth to Sian, early in April, she had been in a mental hospital. The shock of her husband Harry's death, followed by the realisation that at forty she was pregnant for the first time, had unhinged her and she had surrendered into a silent and uncaring life within the walls of the large hospital from which she emerged only rarely. Her uncaring attitude included the welfare of her daughter, and she showed little interest in her when Amy visited. Her house, not far from that belonging to Mrs French, stood empty, cleaned every few weeks by Nelly.

It was as Nelly opened the front door to begin dusting one afternoon soon after Archie had been burgled, that she realised that something was wrong. The hall looked the same except the door to the small room that had been Harry's office was wide open and the door to the kitchen was ajar.

Her heart raced with fear as she stepped cautiously inside and stretched out to push the doors further to see into the rooms. They were all empty and she stared anxiously up the stairs. Should she go up or get some help? So far she had seen no evidence of anyone entering, yet she knew that someone had been in the house since her last visit. Prudence won and she left the front door open and walked across to Mrs French to explain the situation.

'What with poor old Archie bein' robbed, I thought I'd better not go in until someone knew where I was, just in case.'

'I don't think you should go in at all! I'll telephone for the police and we'll wait until Constable Harris gets here,' Mrs French said firmly.

With Nelly's help, the policeman made a careful note of all that was missing.

'There ain't much that I can see, only the little vase she used fer flowers occasionally, like violets or a rosebud.

Glass it was.' Nelly looked around. 'P'r'aps 'e 'oped fer money and didn't find none.'

Nelly tidied the contents of the drawers and cupboards upstairs and cleaned the rooms, looking nervously behind her as she did so, half afraid that the man was still there, even though the constable had searched, even up into the loft. She was glad to finish and go home to start cooking George's dinner.

The first thing she saw when she walked through the door was the vase she had missed from Prue Beynon's house. George was sitting near the fire, taking off his thick socks and feeling under the big armchair with a toe for his slippers.

'What's that?' she demanded.

'A present for you,' George smiled.

'From – not from you, George?' she asked fearfully.

'No, from young Dawn.'

'Hells' bells! Get rid of it quick!'

'Why, don't you like it?'

'I love it but it ain't 'ers to give. It's the one that went missing from Prue's kitchen!' She hurriedly told him about the burglary and about the small glass vase being one item she had realised was missing.

'I see. I think we should go and see Dawn at once. No, perhaps I'd better take the vase back first, the sooner it's back where it belongs the better.'

'Hello in there?' a voice said, and a shadow filled the doorway as PC Harris stood peering in.

'Constable Harris! You gave us a fright! Stay an' 'ave a cuppa, why don't yer?'

George deftly removed the vase and slipped it into the table drawer as he took out spoons and knives. He helped Nelly make the tea and cut a slice of bread pudding for the policeman and, if their chatter was less relaxed than usual, PC Harris did not appear to notice. He had called to ask if George had seen anyone in the area who did not belong.

'A stranger is usually quickly observed in a place like this,' he explained, 'and I think, or hope, that this thief is not one of the locals. Who would take from Archie, poor dab?'

'And a local would know that Prue's 'ouse 'as bin empty fer weeks and wouldn't 'ave anything valuable in it, wouldn't they?' Nelly agreed. 'Yes, this ain't the work of no local.'

When it began to get dark, Nelly and George set out down the lane, the dogs left protestingly at home. Before they reached the main road, George slipped through the hedge and ran across the field where the two friendly horses trotted over to greet their surprise visitor. He soon reached the house belonging to Prue. He walked quickly but with no attempt at concealment, believing that to walk boldly would attract less attention or curiosity than if he were furtive. He went into the empty house using Nelly's key and placed the vase in the back of a kitchen drawer where it might reasonably have been overlooked. He was outside, turning the key in the lock when he felt the heavy grasp of a hand on his shoulder.

'Now George, what are we doing in Mrs Beynon's house at this time of night, eh?' Constable Harris asked in a loud voice.

'Nelly left her purse here,' George said, using the story they had prepared.

'Oh? And what did you put in the kitchen drawer, then? Go and have a look, shall we?'

Nelly, who was waiting anxiously in the lane was horrified when George returned accompanied by the policeman. They went back to her cottage and after taking out his notebook and sharpening his pencil, the uniformed man began to ask questions.

They hesitated at first, not wanting to involve the girl in further trouble, but eventually George looked at his wife and shrugged. 'Seems we have no choice but to tell, Nelly.'

73

Nelly agreed and they told the constable about the girl's wanderings and the mischievous stealing.

'She brought me the vase as a present an' bein' as 'ow I cleans fer Prue Beynon while she's in 'ospital, I recognised it. We thought that if George put it back and hid it, you might think it 'ad bin overlooked an' not missin' at all.'

Harris considered it his duty to lecture the pair on the foolishness of concealing crimes, even those carried out by juveniles, and of tampering with evidence.

'But I do understand your motives,' he added. 'It's so easy to set young people on the wrong path by too heavy a punishment for youthful devilment. But I'll have to see the girl, and I can't really avoid telling how I got on to her, can I? Besides, if she has broken into a property then it's well past what we could call youthful devilment, and on to real crime.'

'Can we go up there with you? That Tad Simmons is a bit of a bad-tempered bloke and if we were there to explain how it happened—?' George said.

The policeman smiled. 'Coming along to protect me, George?'

'No need of that. He isn't half your size and I think my fighting days are long past. But we've tried to help the girl and we don't want her to lose confidence in us without a fight – of the verbal sort!'

'No. Best not.' Harris shook his head and pursed his lips as he finally made the decision. 'Best you don't. I'll go now and catch the man before he goes to bed, with any luck.'

'Then come back an' tell us 'ow you got on, will yer.'

'A bit of toast and a cup of tea?' George coaxed.

'All right then. I'll come back and let you know what happens.' He hesitated at the door. 'No butter for the toast, I suppose?'

'No, but a bit of 'omemade blackcurrant jam.'

They sat in the doorway after the policeman had left, waiting for news. They spoke little, content to watch the night settling in around them, the darkness slowly creeping into the garden, hiding the corners and making the bushes grow larger as deeper shadows filled out the spaces beneath and beside them. A robin sang a sudden song as if disturbed by a dream, a blackbird clucked as he settled for the night and a mouse crept out quite close to them, so Nelly bent and held the dogs' collars to allow it to search for food undisturbed.

At the gate a fox peered through the wooden slats and, seeing the dogs, trotted on up the lane. The silence was like a blanket; warm, comforting and utterly peaceful. Only worry about Dawn spoilt their contentment. Then, they saw her.

Like a wraith she slipped past the gate, hesitated before running on, her small feet making only the faintest pattern of sound on the firm surface.

'Did you see— ?' George stood up.

'Poor little kid, what's she doin' wanderin' about at this time of night all on 'er own?'

'Just as long as she isn't breaking windows and going into houses to steal,' George said anxiously. 'It will be hard to help her then, Nelly.'

Constable Harris returned after an hour and he looked serious. 'There was no one in when I got to the house,' he said, 'and when Mr Simmons arrived he was not pleased to see me. I explained what had happened and he lost his temper and accused you two of making it all up. Said Dawn was asleep and refused to wake her.'

'Then the little girl came home, no coat, just a thin dress and only daps on her feet. With her father interrupting constantly, I asked her what she knew about the vase and warned her that you were suspected of entering with intent to steal and she told me the whole story, although I'm not sure that her father is as innocent as he makes out, between you and me.'

He stopped and took the cup of tea Nelly offered and nodded agreement when she held a small bottle of whisky over the cup. 'I shouldn't be telling you this, mind, but I know you have the girl's interests at heart. Anyway, she said the door was unlocked and slightly ajar and she went in, saw the vase and picked it up. She went no further than the kitchen and that's all she knew.'

'So who's the burglar?' George asked. 'If what Dawn says is true you're no further ahead.'

'Tad's house is poorly furnished. There's food on the kitchen shelves and the coal bucket was full, with a good fire burning, but it's a sad place with little comfort. I wonder if perhaps Tad Simmons is short of cash. He's very bitter about something too, isn't he?' he mused.

'Ain't 'e got no job then?' Nelly asked. 'I've bin told 'e leaves the girl with neighbours while 'e goes to work.'

'I'll find out more tomorrow. The constable put down the cup and saucer and stood to leave, his head almost touching the ceiling of the room. 'You won't discuss anything I've told you, will you? Thinking out loud, that's all I've done.'

'No fear of that, we wouldn't do nothin' to cause more trouble fer the kid, would we, George?'

They sat for a long time discussing the evening's events before taking a candle each and climbing the stairs to their beds. There was a moon and, with sleep evading her, Nelly sat looking out towards the lane, wondering what would become of Dawn if her father were to be taken to prison for burglary.

In the other bedroom, George also lay awake. An owl hooted, its mournful cry saddening him. He was so lucky here with Nelly and all the comforts of a home. If he and Nelly could help that tormented man and his unhappy child, he would feel satisfied that he was giving

76

something back as payment for his own good fortune.

There was a good excuse to go and see Dawn and her father. They hadn't sorted out what had happened to the camera Dawn had – borrowed. The word 'stolen' came into his mind but he blocked it. She had borrowed it and not told them. They would make the camera a gift and relieve her of the guilt she must be feeling.

He rose from the bed and went quietly into Nelly's room to see if she were sleeping. When he called softly, she answered at once and he went on and sat on the edge of her bed.

'About that camera,' he began.

'Yes, I've bin thinkin' about that too. We must go up and let her know it's a gift, 'cos she never came down with it like we asked. We'll thank 'er too for bein' honest about the vase, George. That saved us a lot of embarrassment.'

'Exactly my thoughts.'

'My Evie stole once, you know. I bet she wouldn't want to be reminded of that now! It was only a doll. A baby doll with eyes that opened and closed and a mouth where a dummy fitted. It belonged to a friend of 'ers and I took it back when I found it 'idden in Evie's bedroom. I never said nothin' much, just that it was cruel to take something someone loved and deprive them of it. I remember the word "deprived" was a favourite word with Evie fer a while an' so far as I know she ain't never touched a thing that wasn't 'er own since. I wonder, George, would she be as understandin' as that with young Oliver, if 'e did something stupid?'

'I know children are often tempted when they want something badly but I don't think Oliver is like that. He accepts what he has and seems to yearn for very little, except perhaps for a bicycle.'

They sat while the moon rode the skies, until Nelly dropped off to sleep with George still sitting beside her. He kissed her soft cheek and tiptoed back to his own bed.

Constable Harris went steadily around the houses asking questions, making a note of everything unusual and in this way received reports of a motor-bike being heard at night. He went to the house near the fish-and-chip shop where Griff and Hilda Evans lived with their son, Pete. Pete and his friend Gerry Williams from the council houses were keen motor-cyclists and always roaring around the roads on their machines. Both Griff and Hilda were out. Pete welcomed the constable in, excited at being invited to help with the enquiries.

'Gerry and I have heard that bike. Powerful it is, like mine, but we don't know who it belongs to. Dad had one too but his is in pieces, has been for months.'

'I've like to have a look, if you don't mind,' Harris asked politely. 'Unless you'd rather your dad be there?'

'No. He won't mind.' Pete led him to the corrugated iron garage which led out into the lane behind the houses and showed him the shining bike he used, and also the one which lay in pieces on a wooden work bench near the grimy window. 'See? Dad's lazy about getting his fixed. Now me and Gerry, we keep ours up to scratch, like. Always working on it we are, just ask our mam.'

When his father came home, having been up in the woods to inspect his traps, Pete greeted him with the news of the policeman's visit.

'Gave me a bit of a fright, seeing him standing there, like. I thought he'd come to ask about the betting slips, you being a bookie's runner! Relieved I was when he only wanted to ask about our bikes!'

When George finished work the following day it was later than usual. Hay-making was almost finished and he had spent the day taking out the machines used for the harvesting, making sure everything was in good order, while Leighton finished the final field. After they had eaten, he and Nelly walked up to the council houses to see Dawn and Tad. Tad opened the door and stared without speaking for a moment, unnerving Nelly and making George pull her back.

'It's Dawn we've come to see,' George said, but the man began to close the door.

'Can we see Dawn? We want to talk to 'er,' Nelly shouted. At this the door opened slightly and Tad growled, 'I don't know how you've got the neck to come here after what you did to her! Coming to apologise are you, for hiding behind a child of ten? You ought to be ashamed!'

Dawn appeared round the corner of the house and Nelly smiled at her, the missing teeth on the left of her mouth turning it into a grimace. 'Dawn, about the camera.' Then, as shock registered on the child's face, she added quickly, 'The camera you borrowed, well, we've bought you a film for it and you can keep the camera as a present from George an' me. Just promise to let us see any photos you take.' She handed the girl the film and George stepped forward to show her how to load the camera.

'Leave her alone. Take back your presents, we don't want them. If Dawn wants a camera, *I'll* buy her one. Right? Hiding behind a child. Shamed you should be, the pair of you.'

With a hint of firmness in his voice, George said, 'Mr Simmons, don't you think you should stop all this aggression? No one thinks ill of Dawn; her behaviour is understandable in the circumstances and—'

The door swung suddenly back against the inside wall and Tad leapt out and struck George a stabbing blow in the face.

'What d'you know about our circumstances, eh? Should be minding your own business, not ours!'

He did not say any more as Nelly began kicking him in the shins, her skirt pulled up – not to impede the

79

strength of the blows for she used one foot after the other in a well-aimed attack, careless of showing her fat knees.

She had kicked him at least three times before the pain of it reached him and he began to dance about with a wailing cry. The brief fracas ended abruptly as Dawn covered her face with her hands and began to laugh. She twirled on one foot then the other, pointing at her father, then at Nelly and George, who was holding his nose and looking tentatively for signs of blood.

Tad, bent almost double, holding his shins, disappeared inside, leaving the three of them standing looking at the closed door.

'Always like this, is 'e?' Nelly asked as she examined George's face for damage. 'An' don't stand there laughin', get a cold wet cloth to stop this bleedin'.'

The laughter stopped as Dawn saw the trickle of blood from George's nose.

'I'm sorry. He usually misses by miles.' She ran around the house to emerge with a dripping towel. 'Will this do?'

'George,' Nelly said solemnly, 'I think you're goin' to 'ave a black eye and everyone'll think I did it.'

They walked home with Dawn following at a distance. When they reached their gate, she followed them through, the camera and film in her hand.

'There's a competition at school for the best photograph,' she said. 'Can I enter?'

'Why not?' Nelly said. 'Just so long as you don't want a picture of George's black eye!'

Bert Roberts called soon after they got home. Archie Pierce was unable to play in the darts tournament since the burglary had made him afraid to leave his home in the evenings.

'I thought you might like to take over his place, George?' Bert explained. 'He's through to the second round and there's a prize at the end.'

'It seems a shame Archie can't stay in the contest. He's a regular in the Drovers' team.'

'Oh, I agree with you,' Bert said stiffly, 'but I can't spend any more time arguing with him. There's a lot to see to, you know – the tournament, and selling tickets for the concert and solo competitions. And now some bright spark has the idea of organising an outing from the Drovers and, of course, guess who they've asked to arrange it? Me, of course. Muggins gets landed with it again!'

'Perhaps if Nelly and I had a word with Archie?'

'Go on, you. Try if you like. I wash my hands of him. Let me know what's happening though, will you.' He added sarcastically, 'I am the one supposed to be running it all.'

'That's not what I hear,' George chuckled as the man bustled his way up the cinder path and back down to the village. 'Seems they've tried to persuade him to let someone else do the job but it's no good. He wants to do it and nothing short of murder will prise it out of his grip.'

Phil confirmed this the following day when he brought a letter for Nelly. He sat in the chair near the door and touched the side of his nose in a familiar gesture which Nelly knew as a sign that some gossip was about to be told.

'Seems there was a bit of a ruckus at the darts match last week,' he began. 'Three of them tried to persuade Bert he should let someone else run things as he's mixed up the date of the next round and forgot to let the teams from the council houses know about an alteration. Turned up they did and were landed with no one to play.'

' 'E came to ask George to play instead of Archie but never said nothing about no ruckus, but we 'ad one of our own. 'ave you 'eard about Tad and—'

'Yes, I heard about your George 'avin' a black eye,' Phil interrupted. 'Shamed you should be, Nelly, hitting a bloke twice your size!'

'I knew it! I knew I'd get the fault!' Nelly laughed as she picked up the dogs' leads. 'I'm goin' ter call in to Amy's on the way 'ome from work to tell 'er what 'appened so she can spread the news before I gets meself arrested fer assault!'

# Chapter Five

George persuaded Archie to go to the darts match on the following Wednesday, and he and Nelly went with him.

'We'll go back with you and make sure everything is all right. We'll have the dogs with us too – they'd soon tell us if anything was wrong, so you will be able to sleep easily,' he assured the nervous little man.

The Drovers was full that evening. The tournament was an attraction, with families following the games and supporting the players. Nelly and George pushed their way in with the two dogs and found a place in a corner with a table under which the dogs could settle to sleep.

Nelly was short of money and she glared at Griff when he smiled and said he was sorry not to have any winnings for her.

'No chance you didn't get it to the bookies in time then, not like when I 'ad a thirty-three-to one winner!' she accused loudly.

'Bad luck that was, Nelly, don't try to make more of it. Bad luck it was. Accuse me of cheating on you and I won't take no more bets. Right?'

He glared at her, hissing the words and she curled her lip and retorted, 'Watch it, or I'll be takin' bets on 'ow soon your Hilda finds out about you an' Milly Toogood's daughter!'

Through the smoke of the fire that burned brightly in the grate and the cigarettes, Nelly peered about her and recognised several friends. Phil was there with his quiet wife, Catrin, in support. Two of Freddie's friends, Griff's son Pete and young Gerry Williams, who were determined to show the older ones how to play, were teasing Bert and refering to him as 'Sergeant' much to his irritation. They were streaked with grease, having come straight from the garage where they both worked, repairing motor-bikes.

Bert Roberts managed to keep a space in the over-filled room to allow him to walk up and down, peering at the board accusingly to confirm or deny a disputed score and march back to his position, from which he followed the play and yet managed to add a cursory remark to one or other of the various conversations going on around him.

The two local farmers were present. Leighton silent as usual, merely nodding in reply to any remark, and Billie Brown, who constantly glanced at the door as if expecting someone.

'Amy,' Nelly whispered, nudging George. 'Billie's waiting fer Amy, I bet yer.'

'So is *he*.' George gestured to the opposite corner where Victor sat in a cloud of smoke as he puffed nervously on a cigarette.

When Amy did arrive, both men half moved towards her but it was to the young boys she went first. 'Pete, Gerry,' she greeted them, 'heard from my Freddie have you? I thought he was coming home but he didn't turn up. He hasn't told you why, has he?'

'Home? But he was home, Mrs Prichard.' Gerry said. Too late his friend dug him viciously in the ribs to hush him.

'No, he hasn't been, not for a while.' Amy laughed. 'I'd know for sure, wouldn't I?' The light caught her earrings as she shook her blonde head. 'No, you must have been dreaming!'

'He's been back in camp for a few days,' Gerry admitted. 'But not weeks.'

84

'Shut up, you fool,' Pete muttered. But the look on Amy's face made Gerry realise it was too late.

'Sorry not to have told you, Mrs Prichard, but he asked us not to say, like.'

'But I don't understand. If he came home, where did he go?'

The boys looked at each other, their heads lowered guiltily.

'He said not to say,' Pete murmured.

'Where did he go? I insist you tell me. I'm his mother and I demand to know!' Neither boy spoke and she leaned closer to them and whispered through clenched teeth, 'I'll just go and have a word with the landlord, shall I? About boys of sixteen drinking in his bar?'

'He stayed with Sheila Powell – er Davies.'

'What? You're telling me Freddie came home on leave and didn't come to see me or his sister? I don't believe you!'

'It's true, Mrs Prichard, honest.'

Nelly had overheard most of the conversation and she waved to attract Amy's attention.

'Budge up, George. Hey, Amy, come an' sit with us, why don't yer?' Nelly moved the dogs along with her feet to avoid Amy stepping on them. 'Something upset you?' she asked.

'You might say so!' Amy snapped angrily. 'Did you know my Freddie came home on leave and stayed up on the council houses with that Sheila?'

'No, er, yes. Er, sort of.'

'What do you mean, Nelly?' Amy's voice was still sharp.

'I saw Sheila in a taxi, comin' 'ome from 'ospital, an' I thought I saw Freddie in the taxi with 'er. Only thought I did, so I said nothin'.'

'Gerry Williams let it out just now. He and Pete promised not to tell me. Great, isn't it? My son home on leave and I'm not supposed to know!'

She picked up the drink that Victor had brought and

85

sipped it before banging it down on the table. 'Thanks, Victor. I'd better go home after this or I might decide it's a night for getting drunk!'

'Don't do that, Amy,' George said, offering a couple of crisps to the dogs, under the table, 'Freddie will explain when he feels able to. Until then try not to question him. He's very sensitive about his feelings for Sheila, knowing you don't approve, and it's easy to make things worse.'

'Worse? How can things be worse than my son not telling me when he's home? Staying in the village, and I bet everyone knows. That Milly Toogood will know for sure and she couldn't keep her tongue still if it was tied to a hand grenade!' The two boys nodded sheepishly at her and left, their turn in the darts match completed. Amy glared at the door as it closed behind them, her blue eyes like ice.

'I never dreamt Freddie would do such a thing. What will people think?'

'Sorry Amy, but I knew as well but decided not to say anything.' Victor appeared at her elbow and squeezed her sympathetically. 'Sorry you had to find out at all.'

'But why didn't he tell me? Am I such a villain of a mother?'

'Come off it, Amy,' Nelly laughed, her crooked teeth making her look more a villain than Amy. 'It was because 'e didn't want to upset you, not 'cause 'e was afraid to tell yer.'

Billie was standing at the end of the long rubber mat marking the position for throwing darts, but he turned several times before throwing. Seeing that Amy was upset and hearing a part of what was being said, he wanted to go to her. He threw the darts carelessly, his score jeered at by the good-natured watchers. As soon as the score had been written up he walked through the crowd to Amy as George took his place in front of the dartboard.

'Amy, what's wrong?'

'Nothing really,' Victor answered for her. 'It's just that Freddie came home on leave and spent it up in the council houses with Sheila.'

'Very considerate boy,' Billie surprised them all by saying. 'Sheila rang from the hospital and told him she was very depressed and felt utterly alone. He couldn't refuse to help, even if she didn't belong to him. For a youngster he's very mature. You made a good job of bringing him up, Amy, for him to care like that.' He pushed his way back to the bar and returned with a tray of drinks, including a brandy for Amy. He was glad he had overheard the conversations – it had given him time to think of a suitable comment, even if it had meant him losing his match.

'You really think that was why he did it? Because he took pity on her, having no one who understood?'

'I know for definite. Thoughtful and kind, that's your Freddie, and what's more, he knew you'd understand when he explained.'

'Budge up again for George,' Nelly said, 'an' make room fer Billie.' They all managed to squeeze into the bench seat as George returned from his match. It was Johnny's turn to play against the players from a nearby village and the noise as supporters encouraged their favourites made it impossible to hold a reasonable conversation.

Billie happily put his head close to Amy's as she asked, 'How did you know? Did you see him?'

'No, Sheila's gran told my sister Mary when she ordered extra milk. There's a lot of clues in the ordering of milk, Amy,' he laughed. 'He stayed close to her, his large frame threatening to press Nelly into the wall.

Victor shouted to Nelly, 'I think Archie wants to go home.' He pointed to where Archie stood, his cap in his hand, waiting near the door. He came closer as Victor beckoned.

'Leave, shall we, when you've finished your drinks?' he suggested hopefully.

Nelly had two drinks lined up with the half-empty one she was drinking. ' 'Ere, Archie, 'ave one of these,' she called.

To Billie's delight, they were all pressed closer on the bench to make room for Archie and he ended up with Amy seated comfortably on his lap. Victor watched silently. In the hubbub of the noisy bar it surprised Amy how many people were able to follow what was going on at their table in the corner. Johnny came over when he had won his match and whispered, 'Sorry, Amy. I knew about Freddie too. Saw him and Sheila arriving. Thought it best to say nothing.'

'Everybody knows!' Amy said.

'—what a kind boy your Freddie is,' Nelly finished with a wink for Billie.

'What a fool he is,' Amy whispered sadly.

The door opened, making the smoke in the room swirl and eddy like liquid, and Tad Simmons came in. He looked around the room but did not acknowledge anyone. Nelly watched as he ordered a drink and went to stand where he could watch the game in progress.

'I wonder where 'is little girl is while 'e's boozin' away 'is money?' Nelly said, with little attempt to whisper.

'Hush, Nelly love, he'll hear you,' George warned. He touched his eye tenderly. 'I don't want another black eye.'

Nelly stood up, pushing Billie and Amy close to the edge of the seat in her haste. She banged her glass on the table and said, again to George, but loud enough for Tad not to mistake the words, 'I wonder where poor little Dawn is, while 'er Dad is boozin'?'

Tad turned his head sharply and stared at her red-faced challenge, but she might have been a painting on the wall for all the notice he took after his instant reaction.

Slowly, he turned his head back to the darts players and raised his glass to his lips.

'Looked right through me, 'e did, the cheeky—'

George smiled and patted his wife's arm with a sigh. 'Time we went home, I think.' To his relief, Nelly gave in, if not gracefully then with a subdued protest, and he guided her out of the crush to the door, the dogs following in his wake.

Archie, who had been standing anxiously waiting for them to leave, his flat cap twisting in his fidgeting hands, promptly opened the door for them and stepped outside.

Nelly could not resist a parting shot and, as the door began to close behind her, she burst back in and said, 'Some people don't deserve kids! Blimey, you're worse than my Evie!' Her voice began to get more and more maudlin as she went on, 'Poor little Dawn, poor little kid, love 'er cotton socks—' George good-naturedly dragged her away from the door, her fingers grasping the edge like a child hanging protestingly on to a sweet-shop counter.

Delina Honeyman was angry every time she thought of Tad Simmons. She cycled to the school in Llangwyn where she worked each day and had to pass the house in Hywel Rise where he lived. After her attempt to discuss his daughter, she had been tempted to avoid passing his house by using Heol Caradoc instead, but she contented herself with glaring at the door as she freewheeled down the steep hill instead.

She thought repeatedly of the way she had forced herself to go and try to help with Dawn, only to be told rudely to mind her own business, which had startled and then humiliated her. Her emotions were tender since the sudden cancellation of her wedding to Maurice Davies and she was easily hurt.

Going down to see the trench-digging in Nelly's garden

was the first time she had mixed with the villagers since that awful occasion when Sheila had announced that Maurice was the father of her child. She had been aware of the hastily turned faces every time she walked from the bus, or had ridden along Sheepy Lane past the house where Ethel, Maurice's mother, lived. She guessed that as she passed groups of people, the conversation would immediately become a sympathetic revival of the day Ethel forced her son to marry Sheila Powell. It would be a long time before Delina could convince herself she was not the centre of almost every conversation in Hen Carw Parc.

That Tad Simmons had spoilt her first effort made it worse. She could see his face every time she remembered the incident, the blue eyes starting out of his head as anger exploded from him. The familiar curl of embarrassment twisted her stomach as she tried to force the memory from her. The words she had used had implied interest and understanding and surely had not warranted such an outburst?

She had not seen him since, but as she rode on her bicycle to the point when she would have to dismount and push it, she felt herself becoming more and more tense. If the sensation of panic did not cease soon she *would* use the other hill and avoid passing his house. But for the moment, there was enough defiance in her to make her refuse to take the easier option and change her routine.

She rode further up the hill that usual, puffing with the effort of the steep gradient, and the bicycle began to make complaining noises. She wished she had taken the other hill. How embarrassing it would be if she should break down outside his house. Her imagination flew and she imagined him seeing her and believing she had arranged the whole thing. Anger against him grew until she was having imaginary arguments with him. Her face had lost its usual calmness and a faint blush of colour had become a moist redness which increased the blueness of her eyes. She put on as much speed as much as possible, bent on passing his house before admitting defeat and getting off to walk.

To her alarm the pedals slipped occasionally and the noise became worse. The locking, followed by the slipping of the pedal, caused her to jerk forward and she looked down at the source of the creaking and groaning, wondering if she could make it past Tad's house. She couldn't get off now, not until she had passed it. She pushed more determinedly against the pedals in agitation. The creaking and groaning changed, there was a moment's blessed silence apart from the hissing of the tyres on the road surface, then there was a crack and the chain came off.

The road, which had been empty, soon filled with people either curious or wanting to help, as she stepped away from the machine and looked anxiously at the chain. She had no idea how to get the chain back on and was grateful when a man came from a house near that of Tad Simmons and offered help.

She bent to watch as he expertly replaced the chain, but her words of thanks were cut off as he said, 'Sorry, love, you'll have to get it mended properly. The link's gone, see?' With hands already covered with the grease which coated the chain, he pointed out the distorted link and shook his head sorrowfully.

'Thank you anyway,' Delina smiled. 'If you could put the chain in a wrapping of some sort, I'll walk home and get it fixed.'

'I have a spare joining link,' a voice said and she stood up from her perusal of the offending chain into the eyes of Tad Simmons. She felt the shock of arriving at a situation she had foreseen and had dreaded. Yet there was warmth too in seeing him looking at her with such interest. She disliked him yet was attracted at the same time. His blue eyes held a promise of something special and now, even the mouth had lost its accustomed tightness and the hint of suppressed anger. She was flustered and her reply to his polite offer of assistance was curt.

'No need, thank you. My father will be able to see to it for me.' She took the chain, which the first man had had wrapped in a piece of brown paper, and pushed her bicycle up the hill and around the corner into St Illtyd's Drive without looking back.

Her heart was racing. The encounter had unnerved her and put her out of sorts with herself. Why had she allowed the man to affect her so? He was rude and ill-mannered and therefore not worth a second's thought. His offer of help would not change that. But why had she been so angry at what might have been a peace-making gesture? It had seemed genuine – he had offered an open palm on which was a small metal object that she presumed was the link she needed. But no, she had to act like a spoilt child and storm off.

'What's happened, love?' Victor asked when he saw her throw her bicycle with unaccustomed anger on to the front lawn.

'The chain has broken on my bicycle.'

'That's nothing. I'll get a new link tomorrow and fix it in no time.' He studied her flushed face, wondering at her ruffled expression. 'Something else wrong?'

'No, just that Tad Simmons, offering to help. As if I'd let *him* help me. I wouldn't take his hand if I were drowning!'

'Upset you proper, didn't he?'

'I simply don't like him.'

'Funny that,' Victor mused, 'how we have to like someone to accept their help.'

'It's usually a two-way thing, offering and accepting, but there's no friendship in either direction between Tad

Simmons and me. I feel sorry for the little girl, though,' she said more calmly as she slipped off her coat and began to wash her hands. 'If I could find a way of helping her without having to meet her dreadful father, I'd gladly do so.'

'Call and see Nelly. She seems to have taken a liking to the girl. She'll have a few ideas, I bet you a shilling.' he covered his face in mock dismay. 'Whoops! Mustn't say "I bet" in case your mother's listening!'

'You aren't, are you, Dad? Betting again, I mean?'

'Now and then, like,' he admitted quietly. 'Life is pretty dull and a little flutter adds a bit of spice.'

'You and Nelly are a fine pair!'

'Now Nelly, there's a woman who loves the horses. I called there the other day while she was listening to the racing results and she was so close to that wireless of hers I could only see the soles of her feet!' He watched as Delina's smile slowly wiped away the frown, hoping he had succeeded in cheering her up as well as taking her mind off his attraction to gambling.

Victor did not find gambling a problem and it was only occasionally he risked a few shillings on a race, but Imogen, his wife, was a very religious woman who frowned even on the purchase of a raffle ticket, except when it was in aid of some charitable cause when, she insisted, it was to be considered a gift and not as an attempt to win something without paying for it.

It was his Imogine's strong determination to live a rigidly straight and honest life that had caused the serious rift in their marriage. Although never a loving couple, they were reasonably content until Victor found himself in court accused of theft. He had stolen from his employer, Harry Beynon, and his wife's fierce religious beliefs had made her cut him out of her life, except for the basic necessities of food and laundry. From that day, his wife had never addressed a word to him, communicating where necessary through Delina or one of her brothers. She had cut herself off from the village too, bitterly ashamed of what had happened.

He was honest enough to admit to himself that even if his homelife were not barren and loveless, he would still have been attracted to Amy. But coming from the emptiness of his marriage she was like a dream to him, a hope that kept him sane. Amy, so cheerful and loving, who he could imagine sitting opposite him while they chattered through relaxed mealtimes, and who would share his lonely bed.

On the following morning, Delina opened the front door and looked towards the lawn where she had thrown the bicycle, but it was not there. It was standing against the hedge and when she stepped closer she saw that the chain had been mended and the bicycle cleaned and polished like new. She went back and called to her father.

'Dad, thank you! What a lovely surprise. You must have been up since the crack of dawn to fix it for me.'

'Fix what, love?' Victor asked, shaking on his overalls ready to leave for work.

'That bicycle. The chain is on and you've cleaned it so the chrome gleams. Thank you!'

Victor looked confused.

'But I didn't, haven't, I mean. I intended to buy the link today and see to it this evening.' Still puzzled, he went out to look at the shining machine, then turned to his daughter with a frown. 'Someone's fixed it, love, but it wasn't me, unless I've been working in my sleep!'

Delina looked at the secure chain and her face wore a frown to match her father's.

'I wonder if the man who came to help me did it? But why should he?' Then her face changed, tightened in anger. 'Oh, no! *he* couldn't have—'

'Who are you thinking of?' Victor asked. He smiled teasingly as he guessed, 'Not that awful Tad Simmons!'

'Why would he? If he thinks this will make me forget his rudeness he's mistaken.' She felt a childish impulse to kick the bicycle but satisfied herself with only glaring at it before walking out of the gate, head held high. 'I'd rather walk!'

Victor thought he'd have another word with the man who had upset his daughter so badly and, on the way home from work that day, he stopped at Tad's door. There was no reply to his knock and he walked around to the back of the house and peered through the window to see if anyone was home.

He could see that the house was very bare and lacked comfort. There were only hard chairs, no big soft armchairs drawn up near the fireplace, which, it being summer, lacked even the normal cheer of a glowing fire. A table stood against a wall and two wooden chairs were near it, askew, as if the occupants had risen suddenly and had left in haste. Victor felt a sudden rush of pity for the man who was trying to make a home for his daughter and himself.

He felt the stirrings of a need to help and wondered how he could offer assistance without offending the man who, he knew, had a short temper. His gentle thoughts were interrupted suddenly by a slap on the shoulder and when he turned around, a smile half prepared to greet Tad, he was punched once and fiercely in the face.

'Get out! I won't have snoopers nosing about!' A low, almost growling voice muttered the words, which Victor heard through a humming mist of pain. His nose felt distorted and huge, the blow had made his eyes water profusely and he could see nothing. It was moments before he could make out his attacker standing before him, arms on hips, raised on the balls of his feet as if preparing for retaliation on Victor's part. Nothing was further from Victor's mind. All he wanted to do was get past the man and hurry out of the gate.

In a voice Victor hardly recognised as his own, he said, 'I came to thank you for mending my daughter's bike. If it was you.'

'Came to see what was to be seen, more like,' the man snapped.

Victor fumbled in his pocket for a handkerchief to quell the blood now beginning to flow. His lips felt like rubber tyres as he explained, 'Looked in to see if you were there, that's all, man.'

Tad handed him a handkerchief. He didn't apologise but, as Victor later decided, he came as close to it as he was able, when he muttered, 'That's what everybody round here does, poke their noses in. It's what I expect.'

'Damn me, there won't be any noses left to poke, the way you're going on!' Victor gasped, bending his head back and trying to hold his nose firmly as he spoke.

'You'd better come inside and clean up.' Taking a key from under an old flower pot, Tad opened the door and gestured for Victor to enter. Victor hesitated.

'Will I get another swipe if I don't keep me eyes to the floor? Shut them, shall I, and let you you guide me?' he said sarcastically.

While he washed his face and cooled the sting of the damaged nose and mouth with cold compresses Tad spoke in short bursts and again the words were close to saying he was sorry.

'I've got nothing to hide here – Dawn and I manage all right, if people will stop interfering. It's hard, only being able to work part time. Afraid they'll take Dawn away.'

'No chance of that, is there? Everyone can see how hard you're trying. She's a handful though, your Dawn.'

Victor stepped away as he said it, expecting another violent reaction but the man hung his head and once again Victor felt a surge of sympathy.

'She will wander,' Tad told him. 'I rarely go out after I finish work but occasionally I have to get away and have a drink and hear other voices around me. Then I leave her with a neighbour, but she always runs off.' He washed out the basin where Victor had been cleaning his wounds. 'Punishing me I suppose. Sometimes in the night I wake up and go to look in her room to see if she wants covering up and her bed's empty. I look out of the window and she's sitting in the garden. Other times I've found her wandering through the streets, looking through other people's windows.'

'Stays near though, does she?' Victor was half afraid to speak in case the man stopped talking to him; he felt in the other a need to share his problem, at least briefly.

'Several times she's gone further afield and I've had to go looking for her. Frightening, that is.'

Now he had begun to talk he went on, explaining all the difficulties of a man caring for a small child, hardly looking at Victor who sat holding a cold cloth to his stinging face.

'And there's school, dozens of things to remember there and half of them I can't get for her. Costumes for the end of term play. Now how can I make things like that? I know she refuses to take a part when she's offered it, because she knows I won't be able to get the things she needs. Then there's help with homework. My mind is an adult one, used to dealing with adult problems. I can't bring myself to her level somehow, although I badly want to.'

Victor wondered if his meal would still be waiting for him, cold and congealing on the kitchen table, or whether it would have been thrown in the ash-bin as on previous occasions. His nose had stopped bleeding and, apart from the sensation that his mouth and nose were of exceptional size, he felt sufficiently recovered to leave.

'Where's Dawn now?' he asked.

'Down with Nelly Luke or whatever her name is. Teaching her to use an old camera they gave her.'

'Kind old soul, she'll help you with Dawn, if you try to give up your hobby of clouting people,' Victor dared to joke.

'When her mother died I promised her I'd never let Dawn be taken into care,' Tad went on, not heeding Victor's remark. 'You can imagine how easy that seems when you say it. But in reality the responsibility is enormous. Trying to work and, in the few hours available to you, to earn enough to feed us both and make a home, it's damned near impossible.'

'Trying to be independent doesn't help, mind,' Victor felt brave enough to say. He glanced at the man warily to see if he was taking offence. 'People round here, they're great, and they'll help if you stop quarrelling with everyone, and give up punching noses.' Seeing Tad calmly listening to him, he went on more confidently. 'In fact, we've got a couple of armchairs we don't use, out in our shed, they are, and we could bring them down if you like. Only as a thank you for fixing Delina's bike, mind, not charity. Perish the thought!' he joked. He risked a smile and was relieved to see Tad smile back. 'It was you, wasn't it? You who fixed Delina's bike?'

'Delina, is that her name? I never caught it the first time we met. At Nelly Luke's party, it was.'

'That's her. How did you know where to find her?'

'I do know one or two things about the village, you know,' Tad answered brusquely. There seemed to be nothing further coming, so Victor left, with Tad's handkerchief still held over his nose. He would have to explain how, between stepping off the bus and reaching home, late, he had managed to get involved in a fistfight. Lucky for once that Imogine did not speak to him, he thought wryly. He would enjoy keeping her guessing.

Why not? And in any case, he did not intend to let Delina know who was responsible.

Constable Harris was on his way up the hill, gaitered legs wobbling a little as the hill grew steeper and the bicycle harder to push. Victor hoped he was not on his way to complain about Dawn, as he had once wanted to himself. He turned his head away. A third bloody nose would bring Tad Simmons a lot more trouble than a ruined handkerchief.

Johnny Cartwright swung himself off the bus as it slowed near the bottom of Sheepy Lane, shouting thanks to the driver and the conductor. He had just finished his shift and had taken the bus back home. He began to walk up Sheepy Lane towards the council house he and Fay rented but changed his mind and went instead to see his mother. Fay would still be out. It was rare that she was home before six o'clock and could be even later when she travelled down to Pembroke or up to Brecon to visit her newer areas.

He wished Fay didn't work. With shift work, he had spare time during the day and it would have been wonderful to be able to go home and spend the time with his wife instead of pottering around the house and garden, constantly watching the time, hoping to hear her car stop outside the gate. One day, when she decided it was time for them to have a baby, then he would really feel they were married. At present he felt that their relationship, although loving and warm, was still precarious.

Netta opened the door as he reached the gate, having seen him approaching. Her once-dark hair was a halo of white around her gentle rosy face and her well rounded figure was neatly dressed in a cotton frock and an embroidered apron.

'Mam, any chance of a cuppa and a *cwlff*,' he gasped. The slice of bread, thickly cut and covered with jam was his favourite and something his fastidious wife did not approve of. He stopped at the door and sniffed appreciatively. 'No, changed my mind, I can smell your cooking from here. Bake-stones, is it?'

'Yes, some bake-stones and a few pancakes. Will that do you?'

'Like you, Mam, lovely!'

He heard Phil's voice call him and said loudly, 'Oh, *he's* here is he? Not still delivering them letters, are you Phil Davies?'

'Catrin is out and he has to shift for himself today,' his mother explained with a chuckle.

'Never! Phil-the-Post make his own tea?'

He went into the living room where a low fire burned and settled to enjoy an hour of chatter. Before he could drink his tea, there was a knock at the door and Nelly arrived with her two dogs.

'Nelly Luke!' Johnny teased, 'Might have guessed you'd smell the teapot!'

'Johnny, I think people ought to call me Nelly Masters now I'm married to George.'

'I agree, Nelly,' Netta said in her quiet voice. 'It's almost an insult to George that no one uses his name, the name he gave you.'

'Nelly Masters you shall be,' Johnny promised. He sat again as Netta busied herself with extra food.

'Did you find out any more details?' Netta asked her newest visitor and Johnny asked, 'What's this then, something I should know about?'

'There's a celebration on the twenty-ninth to mark the hundred-and-fiftieth anniversary of the Mumbles Train,' Nelly explained. 'I'm going with Oliver and Margaret.'

'And you, Mam, are you going?'

'Of course, Johnny. Why don't you and Fay come too? It should be fun. There'll be all sorts of entertainment and some of the passengers are going to dress up in the clothes of years ago.'

'Yes, come why don't yer?' Nelly coaxed. 'We can all go on the bus an' we'll take a huge picnic an' 'ave a lovely time.'

'I might be working,' Johnny said. 'I'll have to check. Someone has to do the driving!'

'Then we'll invite Fay,' Netta said. 'Will you ask her, Johnny? You'll see her before I do.'

'There was talk of hiring a bus,' Nelly grumbled, 'but Bert forgot to book, thinking Phil was doing it.'

'Best keep it simple and make your own way,' Phil advised. ' 'Specially after last night!'

'Last night?' Johnny asked.

Phil settled into the armchair to tell the story, his finger rubbing the side of his nose in a familiar gesture.

'Someone suggested an outing for the darts teams,' he began. 'Good idea that, but then they were persuaded to let Bert organise it. So far, they've had four meetings and Bert has been in the chair. He's tied them up so tightly in rules and formal democratic procedures, they haven't even been able to decide on a date! Damn, it's funny, even if it is frustrating for them that's hoping to go. ''Must speak through the chair'' is one of his favourite sayings. According to little Archie, Billie Brown stood up and lifted a chair and shouted through the rungs, telling Bert to get on with it.

'Bert banned him! He did!' he said as the others laughed. 'Banned him, until the landlord threatened to ban Bert till Christmas if he didn't behave.'

Before Johnny left, he decided that even if he didn't go on the outing, it might be fun to sit it on the meeting called to arrange it.

# Chapter Six

Amy always rose early. During the weekdays she needed to prepare for opening the shop and on Sundays she liked to get her weekend work finished early so she had some time to spend with Margaret. On this Sunday morning she was surprised to hear the sound of activity in her garden long before six. Curious and a little alarmed, she leaned out of the window and realised that someone was digging.

'Victor? Is that you?' she called softly. She waited while the man below her window stepped in to view.

'No, it's me,' Billie said. 'I'm sorry if I woke you, Amy.'

'What are you doing at this time of the morning. Couldn't you sleep?'

'I've been up since five and, as Mary didn't need any help, I thought I'd come and give these borders a bit of a dig. I've brought you some annuals too. Clarkia, verbena, zinnias and some lobelia and alyssum for the edges.'

'You'd better come in.' Amy closed the window and, putting on her satin dressing gown which was trimmed with fluffy swansdown, went quietly down the stairs.

Billie removed his heavy boots and washed his hands, then stood as Amy filled the kettle and put it to boil on the electric cooker.

'You look lovely, Amy.'

'Without a spot of makeup and with my hair uncombed?' she laughed.

'You don't need anything, in fact. I've never seen you like this before and I think you're more lovely than when you're dressed for the day.' He spoke quietly and she was surprised at the earnestness of his remarks. Perhaps she should have made him wait while she dressed. Foolishly she imagined how his sister looked in the mornings. It was difficult to imagine Mary in anything other than her work clothes. She found, glancing at Billie, it was not so difficult to think of him wearing less than the dungarees and cowboy shirt, which was all she ever saw him wearing.

She busied herself with cups and saucers and, as she reached across to get a couple of spoons, Billie moved towards her. He kissed her clumsily, touching her ear with his lips as she turned away from him in alarm. Then he put his arms around her and pulled her towards him and kissed her again.

This time there was no awkwardness about his embrace and she felt herself submit to the lips moving gently over her own. His hands slid lower on her back and he pressed her against him.

'Billie, I'm not ready for this,' she protested weakly. 'Margaret's upstairs too and—'

'Amy, you know how I feel about you. Think about it, don't say anything now, just think about it.' He released her slowly and went to see to the impatient kettle, his back to her, his presence filling the room as he went about the mundane task.

'As for Margaret,' he added, 'you know I would never do anything to distress her.'

'It was unexpected, that's all,' Amy said.

'I'll finish planting these flowers for you then I'll go.'

'No need,' Amy said, 'I'll go up and dress then you can stay for breakfast if you like. I'll call Margaret. She'd love to see you.'

He reached for her again and this time she responded

with a feeling of wonderment at the idea of Billie –
plodding, quiet Billie – revealing a passionate side. The
thought excited her. His hands, warm through the
thinness of her dressing gown felt possessive and strong.
She eased herself away with some regret and pushed him
out through the door with a forced laugh and a threat. 'Go
you, before I call for help,' she laughed and the laugh
sounded harsh with the tenseness of her feelings. When
the borders were cleaned and filled with the plants he
had brought, he came back inside and joined Amy and
Margaret for breakfast. Margaret was pleased to see him
and her being there eased the tension and made the meal a
relaxed occasion. 'Uncle Billie, what have you been
planting in the garden?' she asked, and he took her out
and described the flowers that would be in bloom in a few
weeks' time.

'I've brought some carrots for Mr Leighton's horses.
Ask your mam if we can go now and feed them. I've got
the Landrover. Like a ride in that, would you?

'Yes please! Oliver will be jealous!'

Leaving Amy to continue her work and think about the
sudden declaration of his feelings, Billie took Margaret to
the field beside Nelly's lane. Leaving the car on the main
road they walked up to where the horses were leaning over
the gate. Nelly was there, offering the large and gentle
animals some bread. She had just refilled the bath with
clean water, a task she and George had taken on willingly.

'Just too late to 'elp carry the buckets,' she complained
light-heartedly.' Lovely, ain't they? My George is
buildin' 'em a shelter.' She pointed to the top of the field
where, protected by a small stand of trees, a wooden shed
was receiving the finishing touches from George, assisted
by Oliver.

'Goodness, is everyone awake early today?' Billie
laughed. 'I thought it was only farmers who rose with the
sun.'

'Some days is too good to waste,' Nelly said.

Margaret climbed over the gate and called to see Oliver who was sawing a piece of wood to finish the doorway of the new shelter. Nelly stroked the velvet noses of the horses and laughed with pleasure as they took the carrots from the children's open palms.

'Gentle giants, ain't they?' Nelly smiled. 'Peaceful things to 'ave about.'

'Come on, young Margaret. Time I took you back home. I don't want your mam shouting at me,' Billie said with a smile. The smile widened as he remembered Amy's kisses. 'I'll come and fetch you later and you can have tea with Mary and me. How's that? You and Oliver?'

'I'll go and ask Mother straight away. Can I ride down to the main road in the Landrover, Uncle Billie?'

'An' me,' Nelly shouted, 'I ain't never ridden in one of them.'

Billie loaded up his passengers and, after going up the lane a short distance to turn, drove back down to the main road. He was in a mood of elation. Amy had not refused to consider him as more than a friend and the morning was full of beauty and calm contentment. Then, as he turned the vehicle left to take Oliver home, everything changed.

There were two policemen outside Netta Cartwright's house, and this being such a rare occurrence in Hen Carw Parc, Billie knew something unpleasant had happened.

Netta Cartwright was short and dark-eyed like her son Johnny, but she was round and rosy-faced, while he was slim and boyish. She always spoke quietly and people found her presence relaxing and restful as her brown eyes showed a calm and gentle expression. But today her face was bright with shock, the dark eyes anxious and afraid. One of the policemen was Constable Harris and when he saw Billie he signalled him to stop.

106

'Another burglary, I'm afraid, Mr Brown.'

'No! Not Netta?'

'Makes you angry, doesn't it? That someone could break into the home of someone like her and take the little she has.'

'Go and fetch Johnny shall I?' Billie offered.

'Will you? That will save time.'

So Oliver, Margaret, Nelly and the dogs had an extra long ride as Billie went up to the council houses to tell Johnny about the robbery.

'It must have been last evening when I was out visiting Prue Beynon,' Netta explained when they got back, bringing an anxious Johnny with them. 'I came in and went straight to bed. No need to check the doors, as I'd locked them before going out. It was this morning when I went to go outside that I noticed the lock was broken.'

Nelly put an arm around her and, together with Johnny, guided her back inside. 'Makes yer want to kill 'em, don't it, Johnny?' she grumbled. 'Fancy all this upset fer seven pounds. 'Oo could do it, eh?'

'Someone wants money badly enough not to care what it does to their victims, Nelly. Someone in Hen Carw Parc.'

Nelly shivered. 'I 'opes they get caught soon, Johnny. We're all gettin' a bit jumpy.' She wandered back home after Billie dropped her again at the bottom of her lane, and tried to think of who would be in need of money urgently enough to steal for it. Dawn was the first name that came to mind but she discarded that idea. This was not the work of a child. Victor was always broke and Griff seemed desperate enough to cheat on the betting slips he carried to the bookies. And what about those boys with the expensive motor-bikes? And that miserable Tad Simmons? He needed money, no doubt about that. But by the time she had reached home she had discarded all the names. Surely none of them would cause such distress to people like old Archie and gentle Netta?

Billie drove Margaret back to get ready for Sunday School and stopped to tell Amy about the robbery. He did not stay this time. Amy's polite, but firm 'I have to see to Margaret now' was enough to warn him not to risk spoiling what was an encouraging start to this new stage in their relationship. With Margaret's promise to bring her mother for tea, he drove back home well contented.

Amy watched him go with mixed feelings. Lonely for a man's affections, she had responded too eagerly to Billie's sudden advances and now she felt ashamed. Leading him on was what people would call it, and her with no intention of marrying the man. Because, now the moment had passed and she had recovered from the surprising tenderness of his kisses, she knew that she did not feel enough love for him to make him the one man in her life. He was big and strong and utterly dependable but he was not what she wanted. Unbidden, images of Victor Honeyman filled her mind and she knew that if he were free, he would be the one. Billie was available and he obviously loved her. Why was life so perverse?

Johnny ran home from his mother's house one afternoon, smiling at the conversation they had had about Bert Roberts and his attempts to organise the darts team outing. They had decided to sit in on the next meeting to see the fun. He hoped he could persuade Fay to go with them, although Fay never seemed to see the fun in the ordinary happenings of the village. The meetings were held at the Drovers and, as there was no spare room, they were held in the bar, so anyone could attend, much to Bert's annoyance.

Johnny half ran up Hywel Rise to St David's Close

where he and Fay now lived, looking eagerly to the end of the close to see if Fay's car was outside their house. It was not and his footsteps slowed in disappointment. He glanced at his watch. It was almost five: she wouldn't be long, but he always preferred it when she was there waiting for him.

He went inside and began to prepare the vegetables Fay had left on the draining board. He turned on the wireless to hum along with, to take away the emptiness of the house which he always felt when she was not there. His mother's house had been so different from the simply furnished home Fay had made. Mam's chairs were big and there were too many of them for her small room which seemed to overflow with comfort. He adored his wife but missed the bustle and friendliness of his old home when Fay was not with him.

He heard the approach of a car and ran to the front of the house, his dripping hands held against him to avoid spotting the shining floors. It was Fay, so he ran back and put the kettle on and opened the door to greet her.

The sight of her gave him a shiver of pride: she was so beautiful. He still marvelled at his luck in winning her. Her slender figure, always immaculately dressed, her long blonde hair almost touching her shoulders and shining in the sunlight of the June day. As always she wore a hat and today she had on a pale-green suit with shoes and handbag of soft cream leather. The hat was a green straw with a feather in the band to match the suit exactly. A gold brooch on her lapel and small gold earrings were her only jewellery.

She came down the steps to the front door, carrying a small shopping bag which he took from her.

'Fay, my lovely, there's glad I am to see you. Thought you'd never get home.'

'Not late, am I?' She glanced at the gold watch on her wrist and then, safe inside the front door, she kissed him.

'I know I can never be too early for you.' She smiled at him, her blue eyes closing slightly as she added, 'Now, Johnny, what have you been up to that I should know about?'

'I've driven my bus out and back again a couple of times, been to see Mam, and all the time, I've been thinking of you.'

'Best for you too. Don't stop thinking of me and telling me you love me, will you Johnny?'

He looked at her closely. 'Nothing wrong is there, lovely?'

Looking away from him towards the steaming kettle she shook her head lightly, 'Wrong? Nothing at all. Come on, let's see to that kettle before it blows up!'

They sat in the garden after their meal, the summer air silky on their skin. Johnny had made a small flower bed and improved the lawn and they spent some time each evening in the quiet peace and talked. Mostly they discussed their day, entertaining each other with stories of people and events that had amused or saddened or simply interested them. Johnny heard about difficult customers and Fay heard about the abortive meetings chaired by Bert Roberts. But that evening, Johnny felt Fay was holding something back.

As the light began to fade Delina came to borrow a book and Fay jumped up to greet her friend with more than usual delight. Fay, calm, serene Fay, began to chatter as if grateful for the interruption. Johnny frowned. He would never feel secure in this marriage, he thought sadly, always looking for a sign that Fay was less than content with him. Fay was probably a little out of sorts and here he was trying to make a mystery out of it. He stood up and closed the deckchairs and, after putting them away, followed the chattering women into the house.

'Got your bike mended then?' he said to Delina.

'Isn't it marvellous!' Delina laughed. 'I fall off my bike and everyone knows about it!'

'How many know it was Tad Simmons who mended it for you though?' Johnny said conspiratorially. 'Saw him I did. On the way to my early shift and he was polishing it as enthusiastically as a terrier shaking a rat. *Duw*, he worked hard on that bike.'

'Bad-tempered, ill-mannered man. I hope I never see him again,' Delina said with a scowl.

Johnny looked at Fay and gave her a broad wink. Fay gave him a weak smile but she was definitely distant. He wondered if she were starting a summer cold.

Delina did not stay long and soon they went to bed, where Fay slept at once but Johnny lay wide-awake, worrying about her. The night was still, quiet and long as he lay, trying not to disturb her with his tossing and turning. Something was wrong but how was he to find out if Fay did not talk to him about things that worried her? Dawn crept around the curtains before he finally dropped into a restless, dream-disturbed sleep.

Delina also found it impossible to sleep that night. She was trying not to think about Tad Simmons. It couldn't be that she was attracted to him. How could she be interested in such an unpleasant man? She wondered if it was something to do with love on the rebound, finding someone else, pretending to feel something for them in an effort to ease the pain of losing the one you loved? She had certainly loved Maurice Davies and, if Sheila had not ruined things, she would be his wife now, watching him go off to work each morning at Beynon's building firm, and saving to buy their own home. But even thoughts of Maurice, now far away in Australia, could not take the image out of her mind of the small, irritable, blue-eyed man who was so ridiculously over-protective of his daughter.

\* \* \*

The day before the Mumbles Train celebrations, Nelly went into town. She went with a suitcase containing several dresses and skirts and two winter coats given to her by people who, seeing her in her usual over-sized coat, believed she was in need of them. In fact, she sold them to Greener's second-hand clothes shop and enjoyed spending the money more than she would have enjoyed wearing the good quality clothes.

The shop was over-full with racks upon racks of suits, coats, dresses and jackets. There were drawers and cupboards filled with blouses and scarves as well as hats and jewellery and even underwear. As usual, Nelly was shown into the storeroom behind the shop where Mrs Greener, the proprietress, kept her waiting and then bustled her in as if she had but a moment to spare before being swallowed up once more by her busy shop.

Mrs Greener was at least seventy but she wore carefully applied makeup and on her head was a bright wig of red curls which bounced as she walked. She smiled at Nelly and gushingly asked how she was, all the time moving to prevent Nelly getting the impression she had time to chatter.

'How lovely to see you, Nelly dear. So sorry you've caught me at a bad moment, my dear. I'd have loved to stop and hear all your news. Perhaps next time, is it?' She frowned as she opened the case, her varnished nails covering her dazzlingly white false teeth in dismay. 'Winter things. What a pity. This means I can't be as generous as I might have otherwise have been, dear.' She named a price and Nelly, who was speechless under the fast flow of words simply nodded agreement. Mrs Greener knew she would not want to carry the heavy case all the way back to Hen Carw Parc.

When Nelly waved goodbye to the still apologising Mrs Greener, she was tempted to step inside the nearby pub.

'I needs a drink after five minutes with 'er,' she told the dogs. There were a few things she needed to buy so she ignored the enticing doorway with the sounds of chatter and chinking glasses issuing from it, and made her calls at the stores near by.

Her purchases were mainly food for the planned picnic on the following day but she also bought a few surprises for Oliver. She caught the bus but did not alight at her usual stop but instead at the end of Sheepy Lane.

At the top of the lane she turned into Hywel Rise and as she walked, she extracted from her pocket a note she had written in readiness. As she pushed it through the letter box, the door opened and Dawn stood there. The girl wore martyred expression and stood silently waiting for some criticism, or so it seemed to Nelly's sharp eye.

'Dawn! I thought you'd be in school.'

Dawn continued to stare, a defiant look on her young face making Nelly want to smile.

'Read the note why don't yer?' Nelly waited as the girl picked up the piece of paper and studied it.

'You want me to come with you on some picnic?'

'If yer dad says you can. My Ollie's comin' an' Margaret.'

'I'll ask Dad.' The girl's eyes showed excitement but the mouth remained unsmiling.

'Taken any snaps yet with that camera?' Nelly asked, when she realised that was all the answer she would get.

'Yes.'

The girl went back inside and closed the door. Nelly bent to shout through the letter box. 'Come early in the mornin' if you're comin'. Bring yer camera. Tomorrow could give you a chance of some real good pictures an' maybe you could enter the competition at school, eh?' Nelly waited a moment, frowning as she listened for further communication, then shrugged as none came.

\* \* \*

113

Nelly woke early on the day of the trip to Mumbles and her first move as always was to open the door and let the dogs run out. They ran eagerly up the path and waited while she opened it for them. Barking their delight at being free and having her for company, they danced inelegantly on their back legs, a parody of a ballet, before disappearing temporarily through the trees that bordered the edge of the lane.

Nelly stood breathing in the quiet after their departure. There was a calmness, a solitary sensation as if all life around her was oblivious of her presence. Birds sang and a hedgehog strolled past her feet, unperturbed by her intrusion into his world.

Lost 'is watch an' is late gettin' 'ome, she thought with a smile.

A lizard lay on the bank where a stream once ran, soaking up the gradually strengthening sun. In a tree close by a blackbird was already busily flying to and from its nest with billsful of worms for its young. The sounds were all hushed as if she were listening to the world slowly wakening as the sun drew the curtain on a new day.

In the distance other sounds began to intrude; a tractor driving across a field, the sawing of wood as someone mended a fence and far away, beyond the ruins of the old castle, the bleating of lambs and ewes, temporarily separated as the ewes were shorn of their untidy fleeces. They sound more like children, Nelly thought, not for the first time. Every year the plaintive sound disturbed her momentarily until she remembered the innocent cause.

Giving a sigh of contentment, she turned towards the cottage. The dogs were waiting for her; their routine told them that breakfast came next and their eyes stared unwaveringly at her, urging her silently to hurry. Nelly's sigh and the reappearance of the big dogs caused the blackbird to call his alarm and he clacked and flew deeper into the wood, his wings touching the branches in his haste.

Leaving the dogs inside, Nelly returned to the woods to perform her own morning functions and, after a wash in the enamel bowl set on the table, she began to prepare food for the picnic. She sang as she worked, accompanied by the wireless, and the dogs settled down by the fire, raising their heads occasionally to watch her, looking for clues as to what the day was likely to hold.

The plan was for the children to meet at Nelly's cottage and, as she guessed, they all arrived early. They played on the swing in the garden while Nelly finished packing the wickerwork basket that had been among her possessions when she had said goodbye to her small, top-storey room in 1940, leaving behind the bombing and the terrors of a London at war to join her evacuee daughter, Evie, in Hen Carw Parc. The basketwork case had been fitted with rope to replace the worn leather straps and, to Nelly's eyes, it looked elegant. She filled it with the few pieces of china and cutlery she thought they might need, together with some of the food. When she had arrived in the village, it had been filled untidily with the pitifully few clothes she possessed. She smiled as she remembered.

The cottage had been in a neglected state and she and Evie had camped out in one room, sleeping on the floor with some blankets of dubious cleanliness over them. Evie had cried and complained, resentful of the mother who had followed her and taken her from the comfort of the home where she had been placed. For her mother to reappear when she had begun to hope never to see her again was a depressing blow to Evie, Nelly knew that. Everything about her mother embarrassed her then and the feeling had intensified through the years.

'Poor Evie,' Nelly whispered as she pressed the lid down on the basket.

Evie arrived on the morning of the picnic, neatly dressed and with her face wearing a look of disapproval as she entered the room and greeted her mother. She was half dragging a protesting Oliver, who fought back against coming in as he pleaded with her to let him wear something different.

She had dressed him in a short-trousered suit and knee-length socks with turned-down tops. His shoes were heavy and polished like mirrors, the shirt was fastened at the neck with a bow tie and his hair was so flattened with water that the ends rose away from his head in timid protest. His face was wild with despair and embarrassment, and his eyes, enlarged by tears, were enormous.

Nelly wiped her fingers on one of the dogs as she fought back anger. 'Oliver, come on, love, you're just in time to 'elp me with this 'amper.' She moved closer to him and winked.

'Mind his clothes, Mother, your hands are probably covered with fish paste. It's only his second best, but I don't want it ruined,' Evie warned as Nelly went to hug the boy.

'Just you go 'ome, Evie, an' leave Ollie to me. 'E won't get a spot in these clothes, not a spot, I promise yer.'

Evie kissed the boy, warned him to behave, remember what he had been told about eating too much, not to eat any rubbish and managing to succeed in wringing every hope of an enjoyable day out of him.

Nelly watched her daughter leave and winked at Oliver again. 'Go an' look in the bag on the stairs,' she said.

Oliver opened the carrier bag and, with his eyes shining, unwrapped the shorts and summer shirt. A pair of rubber soled daps for his feet and a pair of short socks completed the outfit and he went joyfully upstairs to change. They set off soon after with Oliver proudly admiring his new clothes and each of them carrying something towards their day out.

Oliver carried a bag containing two bottles of Nelly's homemade lemonade whilst Margaret, who'd arrived shortly after Ollie, carried a blanket on which they planned to eat their picnic. They sang as they marched in front of Nelly and the dogs, around the bend in the lane towards the main road. Nelly looked behind them several times, hoping to see Dawn, but it was not until the cottage was out of sight that she appeared. She hung back, allowing Nelly only a darting glimpse before moving back out of her sight. Nelly spoke without turning around. 'Come on then, young Dawn, give us a 'and with some of this stuff.'

Dawn came forward and took the coat from Nelly's arm and, as Oliver and Margaret, seeing the interloper, slowed their pace to walk one each side of 'their' Nelly, she pushed Oliver aside and walked between him and his grandmother. Margaret then pushed between Oliver and Dawn, glaring at Dawn to remind her she was the newcomer and should remember her place. Nelly laughed, her mouth wide open to reveal her uneven teeth. 'Blimey, it's like a game of draughts walkin' with you lot!'

Amy was waiting for them at the end of the lane, with the baby in her arms. 'It seemed less work than struggling with the push-chair,' she explained, 'but I'm glad she isn't an ounce heavier!'

They caught the bus and, with the three older children upstairs in the front seat, Amy and Nelly settled themselves with all their luggage near the platform. Nelly thought Amy looked strained and worried and wondered if she should ask what was wrong, or wait to be told. Amy was a good friend but inclined to be sharp at times so she decided to wait.

'Prue is coming for the day on Sunday,' Amy said and Nelly wondered if this was the reason for the tension.

'Want any 'elp, do yer? I could 'ave Margaret fer the day then you an' Prue could concentrate on the baby.

117

Giver 'er a chance to get to know 'er, won't it? Let me an' George take Margaret off yer 'ands, why don't yer?'

'That is tempting, Nelly. I'll think about it, shall I? I hope Prue will be well enough to have Sian back one day. I keep pretending I only have her for one more week.'

'Is it too much for yer?' Nelly's brown eyes saddened in sympathy for her friend.

'It's partly that and partly because I don't want to become too attached to her.' She stared out of the window for while, an unhappy and strained expression in her blue eyes that made Nelly worry. She waited for Amy to continue.

'And there's Freddie, still after that Sheila, in spite of the way she's carried on,' Amy added after a pause.

'Don't worry. 'E's young an' there's bound to be plenty of girlfriends before 'e settles down. She ain't fer 'im, an' all 'e feels is sympathy, like what Billie said. After all, she was 'is first love, even if it was a one-sided carry-on. Freddie's a good sympathetic boy ain't 'e?' Nelly said, repeating Billie's words.

To Nelly's relief, Amy turned and smiled at her. 'You're right Nelly, as always.'

When they reached their destination they were at once caught up in the excitement of the occasion. Bunting hung from every available space: from lamp-posts, trees and cavities in the rocks along the shoreline. Music came from groups of musicians and Nelly could see that choirs from schools were gathering to add to the air of carnival. Everyone seemed to be shouting as they tried to make themselves heard above the din of the ever-thickening crowd.

There was colour everywhere. Among the normally dressed onlookers was a large number of people dressed in the clothes of earlier times. Assorted Victorians as well as Edwardians with leg-of-mutton sleeves stood side by side with a modern miss wearing a sleeveless dress and

118

stilletto heels. Nelly wandered through the crowds, with Amy shepherding their charges to follow behind, marvelling at it all.

Along the track, small grottos built of sea shells and attractive pebbles gathered from the beach shone with lighted candles and even, in some cases, torches. The architects of these waited hopefully for passengers and onlookers to throw coins into them as appreciation of their artistic endeavours.

'Can we have an icecream?' Margaret pleaded.

'Look at the queues!' Nelly protested. 'You'll be there all afternoon,' but she and Amy shrugged and handed the three children a coin each and prepared to sit and wait for them to be served.

'Be sure an' come straight back 'ere!' Nelly warned them at the top of her voice and, although the noise of the crowd was deafening, they heard and acknowledged with a wave. When they returned, licking around the cornets which threatened to lose their contents in the warmth of the day, Nelly and Amy set off to find a place to sit and wait for the celebrations to begin.

'Not too far from the station, or we won't see a thing,' Nelly warned.

'We can sit on the sand, can't we?' Oliver asked.

'As long as we stay together we'll do anything you want to do. It's your day out,' Amy said.

As they pushed their way through to find a place where they could spread out their belongings and make themselves comfortable Nelly still looked around her, memorising everything so she could tell George when they got home.

There were groups of flappers in cloche hats, strap shoes and long strings of beads, with skirts just below their knees and even, in some cases, the short Eton Crop hair style that had been popular in the twenties. Bloused tops overhung waists, straight skirts, pleated skirts, and

119

double-breasted jackets, intended to hide any shapely curves and give a mannish slimness, were all represented. As they walked past, Nelly smelt several gusts of mildew from dresses and hats obviously recovered from an attic or a half-forgotten trunk.

' 'Ere, Amy, I bet I could 've found somethin' to wear if I'd looked in the back bedroom!'

'Thank goodness you didn't think of it, then,' Amy laughed. 'We'd 've been thrown off the bus!'

The shouting from the crowd told them the first train was in sight and, leaving their belongings on the beach, Amy picked up the baby and they all pushed their way forward. From the sea wall, Oliver and Margaret saw the horse-drawn coach approaching. Nelly found a place for Dawn and the camera began to click as the girl took several photographs, not of the train, but of the faces of the crowds watching and cheering its arrival. The coach had open stairs and on these people sat, filling every possible space so that, as the commentary explained, the poor conductor had to swing from passengers and any available hand-hold to move around and collect his fares.

'He had to use the passengers as a ladder,' Nelly shouted to Oliver in case he missed the words. 'Blimey, that must 'ave bin dangerous!'

Dawn climbed down from the wall and, while keeping near to Nelly, managed to take a full film of snaps, sometimes asking people to pose for her, and at others sneaking in to snap the unwary. She went as close as she was allowed and took a picture of the horse, whose name, Oliver discovered, was Kay.

'Why don't you take pictures of the coach?' Oliver asked.

'You can borrow the camera and take one if you like,' Dawn offered, so Oliver went through the crowd, watched by an anxious Nelly, to take a photograph of the coach and the horse who was enjoying all the attention.

When the next train arrived they were in a better position and watched the approach of the steam engine with its bustled and long-skirted passengers in the carriages behind. Cinders blew back from the engine and the passengers were all dishevelled and dusty. Dawn ran forward and, ignoring Nelly's shout, managed to reach the train in time to snap a woman who ran out in a red flannel petticoat and a cap. She was carrying a bucket which she filled with hot water from the engine and began to wash the train free of the grime that resulted from the short journey in a replica of a once-regular routine.

Nelly laughed as young boys cartwheeled beside the train and girls skipped and danced to music, filling the area with colour and happy sounds. Nelly absorbed it all, although rarely taking her eyes off Dawn, Margaret and Oliver. It was so easy to become separated with so many crowded into the small seaside village and once she became worried when Dawn was lost to her sight. She was only missing for a moment and, when Nelly learnt that the little girl had asked a man to refill her camera with fresh film – which he paid for – she doubted her wisdom in bringing her. She was not sorry when, after the electric train had deposited its passengers, Oliver announced that he was hungry and was it ever going to be time to eat?

They returned to their spot on the sands and began to unpack their picnic. Nelly and Amy exchanged glances as Dawn ate with great enthusiasm. The girl did not say much but tried occasionally to squeeze between Oliver and Margaret. This manoeuvre Margaret swiftly thwarted, much to Nelly's amusement.

'There's me thinkin' your Freddie's too young fer girls an' look at my Ollie,' she whispered proudly, 'got girls chasin' 'im already, 'e 'as!'

Flirting seemed a major part of the afternoon and

121

when Gerry Williams and Pete Evans turned up, it was clear they were intent on finding a girl with whom to spend the evening. Amy and Nelly watched them teasing and laughing as they approached some of the prettiest girls, and wished Freddie were with them.

'That's what Freddie should be doing, having fun with lots of girls, not bogged down worrying about someone like Sheila, whatever you say about him being sensitive,' she said as she waved to the two friends.

People pushed past and Nelly was constantly brushing the dirt from the cloth set out on the table of sand made by the children. When one of the passers-by stopped, she did not look up for a moment. Then a voice said, 'Cafe open, is it?' and Phil sat beside them and helped himself to a sandwich.

'Phil, there's a cheek you've got,' his wife scolded gently.

'Sit down, both of you. There's plenty,' Amy invited. 'We thought Fay and Johnny might come and one or two others, so tuck in, you.'

'Bert and Brenda Roberts are here and Milly and her daughter with that son of hers. I haven't seen Johnny and Fay though.'

When Johnny did come he was on his own.

'Fay must be working,' he explained. 'I went home to fetch her but there's no sign. No note either so she must have decided to work. Can't stop her and that's a fact. Never idle, that girl.'

Nelly thought he really meant Fay was never at home.

The food was rewrapped and the children once again queueing for icecream when Victor and Delina found them.

'Missed all the fun, have we?' Victor groaned.

'By the look of things it will go on for hours yet.' Amy pointed to where there were couples dancing and he gestured to her to join them.

'Go on, Amy, Catrin and I'll look after Sian,' Nelly coaxed, but her smile of encouragement was forced. She was afraid that Amy was heading for another disaster if she became seriously involved with Victor Honeyman. 'Enjoy yourself,' she went on, hiding her fears. 'You don't get many days off.' She watched as Victor led her through the crowds, a protective arm around her shoulders. Why can't she settle for that Billie Brown? she thought sadly. Delina felt uneasy as she watched her father escort Amy towards the dancers. They looked like a couple; relaxed and comfortable with each other. Should she show her disapproval instead of encouraging them? Then she thought of the barren life her father led because of just one mistake, and she knew she could not. Loyalty to her mother fought against love to her father, and lost.

'Give me the baby,' Delina offered. 'You go and look around for a while.' Nelly shook her head.' Me legs 'ave done enough lookin',' she said, laughing at her confusing remark. 'Glad to sit down,' she admitted, 'although Gawd knows 'ow I'll get up again!'

The baby was restless, aware of the strangeness of her surroundings and Delina picked her up and cuddled her.

'Will her mother be well enough to take her back soon?' she asked.

'We hope so, but she's still poorly. I think Amy's got Sian fer a long time. Pity really, it doesn't 'elp 'er chances, does it?'

'Chances?' Delina queried. 'Chances of what?'

'Finding a 'usband,' Nelly replied.

'Damn me, Nelly, you don't think that would stop any-one falling for Amy, do you?' Phil laughed.

'Yes, a good catch she is, with the shop an' everything,' Johnny agreed.

'I can see that having a child would be an extra strain on a new marriage but if the love was strong enough it would work,' Delina said.

'I don't know, 'ow would you feel if you fancied a bloke an' found 'e 'ad a baby to look after. Put you off, wouldn't it?'

Nelly was surprised to see Delina blush. Blimey, she thought, there is someone. That didn't take 'er long!

Dawn came back and, with an icecream held awkwardly, took some photographs of the group around the sand-table. She glared at Delina, who tried to talk to her, ignoring Delina's attempts at conversation.

'Have you had a good day, Dawn?' she asked, 'What have you enjoyed best? Tell me about the trains, I missed seeing them. Will you let me see the photographs you took when they're developed?' To all these, Dawn made no reply. She just hung her head and looked sulky.

'What you got against 'er then?' Nelly asked when Dawn helped her to pack the wicker basket.

'She's a teacher, isn't she? Fishing for something to complain about, that's all she's doing.'

'Don't be daft,' Nelly said.

'Well, why else would she want to talk to me? And she isn't seeing my photos either.'

'Tell *me* then. 'Ad a good day, 'ave yer?'

'Best I can ever remember.'

When it was time to leave, Victor offered Amy and Margaret a lift in the van he had borrowed but Amy declined. 'I came with Nelly and I'll go home with her. Although,' she added, 'if you could take the luggage it would be great.'

But eventually, Amy, Margaret and Oliver did go with Victor, delighted at the prospect of a ride home in the back of the van. Johnny, Phil and the rest travelled home with Nelly and Dawn on the bus. Nelly could see the sense in Amy having a more comfortable journey with the baby but she was not happy about the increasing ease with which Victor was slipping into her life. He had a wife and Amy had had enough trouble with her love affairs. Why hadn't Billie Brown come to take her home? She had hinted to him and explained where he would find them.

'Life ain't never perfect, is it, Dawn?' she sighed. Dawn was mystified but didn't ask Nelly to explain. She was over-full with food and lemonade and icecream and very tired. She wished she could have gone home with Oliver but she didn't mention that to Nelly, contenting herself with pouting all the way home to show that her day had been far from perfect too, in spite of her earlier remark to the contrary.

They all left the bus at the bottom of Sheepy Lane and Nelly began to walk up the narrow road to the council houses. A car approached, the engine screaming protestingly as the driver accelerated in a low gear and Nelly turned to see that her daughter, Evie, was driving. She waved, but Evie seemed to be looking down at her feet and she did not acknowledge her.

'See that, Johnny?' Nelly shouted as he strode ahead, anxious to see if Fay was home. 'My Evie's drivin' Tedious Timothy's car! What d'you think of that, then?'

'I think she should stick to using buses!' Johnny laughed.

'Don't you think she'll pass 'er test?'

'Snowball in hell's chance! Too conscious of herself to think about driving, and she's cruel to cars!'

'But if she's determined?' Nelly insisted, shouting at the top of her voice as Johnny had all but disappeared.

'I wish her luck, but she'll never be as good as my Fay.'

'My Dad says women shouldn't be allowed to drive,' Dawn said.

'Another endearing trait! 'E's determined to be popular, ain't 'e?'

# Chapter Seven

Earlier, on the day of the Mumbles celebration, Sheila Davies had a visitor. She had not encouraged the visitor to stay and had stood watching Ethel Davies walking painfully and slowly down the hill. She felt no sympathy for the effort Ethel had made to walk up Sheepy Lane and the steep St Illtyd's to see her. Sheila still thought of Ethel as Mrs Davies and was unable to refer to her as 'Mother-in-law'. How could she have a mother-in-law when she didn't have a marriage, or a wedding ring? When she had no husband?

Ethel had called on numerous occasions following the travesty of the marriage between her son and Sheila Powell after which Maurice had hurriedly left for Australia. She had brought gifts of knitting and crochet for the expected baby, the grandchild she was longing to welcome and love. Unfortunately, the baby had died but she still came, bringing not clothes for the infant but cakes and an occasional pie. This time she had brought a sponge cake, flat and rubbery being fatless, but generously filled with homemade jam, and cream illegally made from surplus milk on one of the local farms.

Turning away from the sight of the limping figure, Sheila closed the door and went to put the cake in the kitchen. She had not invited Ethel inside to rest after the walk up the hill. She was still bitter over the fact that although Ethel now often suggested she called in to the

127

house on the lane, neither Ethel nor Maurice had invited her before the proposed wedding made it necessary to convince the neighbours that Sheila was welcomed into the family.

When Ethel had produced the cake from her shopping basket, Sheila had waited to see if she would have anything else for her: a letter, or at least news of Maurice. A change of heart perhaps and a promise to send for her, or to return home to look after her. She had not asked if there was news from Australia but when Ethel offered none, she took the cake rudely and bid her a good morning.

She put the cake on the wooden draining board and looked around her. The kitchen was a mess. Another reason for not inviting Ethel inside. Washing was piled up on the tiled floor in sorted heaps ready for washing in the oval galvanised bath set up on a bench near the sink and half filled with soapy water. The sink was filled with clear water for rinsing the clothes once they had been washed and a bowl of blue water stood ready to receive the whites. With a sigh, Sheila threw the table cloths, tea towels and white pillow cases into the suds and began to rub them against the ribbed wash-board.

The whites should have been boiled but she could not face that steamy, tedious and dangerous task. Ladling them out of the boiler with the short wooden stick and lifting them into the sink for rinsing was a job she dreaded and, with her grandmother out, was one she determined to avoid.

As garments were rubbed against the wash-board, wrung by hand and thrown into the rinsing water, Sheila grew tired and bored. She spent less and less time rubbing them clean until the last garments had no rubbing at all, just a moistening and a half-hearted squeeze before being thrown into the sink. Her face was flushed and her hair hung around her face, damp and lacking in any curl, when she heard the knock at the door. She hesitated and almost did not answer it, but curiosity overcame her reluctance to show herself in such an untidy state and, giving a desultory push to the strands of hair across her forehead, she opened the door.

'Freddie!' she gasped. 'Where did you come from?'

'Don't look so surprised, I haven't come from the moon!'

'Come in.' She wished she had at least combed her hair. 'You'll have to excuse how I look. I've been doing the week's washing.'

Freddie was shocked by her appearance. When he had collected her from the hospital she had been expecting him and had made up her face with care. Her hair had been neatly brushed and she had appeared surprisingly fit. Now, there was no colour in her cheeks and her fair hair, of which she was so vain, looked like that of an old woman. He had never ever seen his mother looking so unkempt, and it frightened him. Sheila must be ill.

'Help me put the washing on the lines will you?' Sheila asked. 'Gran won't be back for an age and I want to get it dry and ironed if I can.'

'Sit down, you, I'll see to it.' Freddie put down the rucksack he was carrying and guided her to a chair. 'Sit by there and watch me through the window, then I'll come back and make us both a sandwich and a pot of tea.'

'If you say so, Freddie,' she whispered, widening her blue eyes as she looked up at him. They spent the afternoon sitting in the comfortable, if shabby front room, and when Sheila's grandmother returned from a visit to a friend, Freddie stood up to leave.

'Hello Freddie,' the elderly woman smiled. 'Sheila, why did you do all that washing? I told you to leave it till your mam came to help. Still weak, you are. You should have more sense.' She tutted as Freddie helped her off with her coat and then headed off into the kitchen, leaving Sheila and Freddie alone.

'Sheila, I want you to come with me to Mam's,' Freddie said firmly.

'No, Freddie. She doesn't like me.'

'She doesn't know you. You lived above Mam's shop for only a few weeks before leaving home and coming here to your gran's. That's the only time she's seen you. Come back with me now. I want you and her to be friends.'

'I certainly need a friend,' she sighed. 'But no, I can't go with you. She wouldn't want to share you with me. Never forgive me for keeping you here on your last leave, she won't.'

'Today is all I've got, Sheila, and before I go back to camp I want you and Mam to talk to each other, right? I need to know that when I'm not here there's someone to keep an eye on you, make sure you're all right.'

'No, Freddie. Perhaps next time you're home.' She flickered her eyes wearily, and seeing his concern, lowered her high voice a pitch and went on, 'Not today. Anyway,' she remembered, 'your mam isn't there. My mam is in the shop and yours has gone to Mumbles for the celebrations.'

'Good. You can come home with me and settle in before she comes. When she sees you there with me, she won't be anything but kind. You don't know my mam.'

'I know she won't like me!'

'She will. Come on, get your coat. We'll take it steady and if you get tired I'll carry you,' he smiled.

Accepting his determination, Sheila obeyed and, taking a black, bobbly-wool coat that was far too thick for a day in late June, but which she knew would make her look paler and thinner, she followed him through the village to his mother's house on the road to the Drovers.

\*     \*     \*

130

Amy knew there was someone there before she stepped inside. She could not explain how, but there was something about the doors being in a different position and the kettle on the cooker set askew.

'Anyone there?' she called nervously, thoughts of the recent burglaries making her heart race. She pushed Margaret behind her and clung tightly to Sian. Into the lengthening silence she called again.

'It's me, Mam,' came a familiar voice.

'Freddie!' She hurried into the living room but stopped when she saw Sheila sitting near the fireplace, where a bar of the electric fire burned.

'Sheila isn't well so I brought her down for a walk. I thought we'd have some fish and chips and a chat, then I'll take her back before I go for my train.'

'Go for your train? Now you've just come! Don't say you're off already, or have you been home a while and staying up with Sheila like last time?'

'I was given a twenty-four-hour pass and I'll have to leave at nine to be back. Special leave, it was. I told them I was worried about Sheila, her being just out of hospital, like.'

'I see.'

'Go and fetch the fish and chips, shall I, while you and Sheila talk? I'll go on the bike, won't take me long.' Not waiting for a reply, he left, taking the bicycle out of the shed, giving the tyres a pump and riding back to the village.

When he returned with the parcel of hot food, Sheila still sat near the electric fire, Margaret was practising her piano pieces and Amy was in the kitchen.

'Had a nice chat?' he asked, pretending not to notice the strained silence between the two women.

'Your mother's been busy,' Sheila said. 'She's been out all day and has to catch up on the work. I offered to help but she prefers doing things herself, her own way. I quite understand.'

131

Freddie gave the hot, steaming, newspaper-wrapped package to his mother and she began sharing it out between four plates.

'Mam, I want to talk to you,' Freddie said.

'About her?' she whispered.

'Yes, Mam, about Sheila.'

They sat at the table and, while Sheila silently ate and Margaret sneaked occasional glances at a book she had hidden on her lap, Freddie explained to his mother that he needed her to look after Sheila while he was away.

'Still weak, are you, after the baby?' Amy asked and her voice became less harsh. A sudden memory of the baby she had lost all those years ago came to her and reminded her that the position she had been in then was not dissimilar to Sheila's now.

'I'm all right, Mrs Prichard,' Sheila smiled, 'but I'm mixed up. I can't decide whether I'm most sorry about the baby or that Maurice left me. It's all the upset that's making me feel so bad. Mam and Dad hardly talk to me or each other. Shamed they are, and blaming me for embarrassing them. Your Freddie's been a real friend. He's making me face things and I don't know what I'd have done without him. I wouldn't have coped at all.'

'Well,' Amy said stiffly, 'you can come here and talk to me and Margaret if you're ever lonely. I know there are times when a mother isn't the one to confide your thoughts to. Good as your mother is, I'm sure,' she added hastily. 'If you need to talk things over, you know where to find me.'

'Thank you Mrs Prichard.'

Amy stood up and pushed the plate away from her. 'Now, if you two'll excuse me, I'd better get Margaret pointed towards bedtime!'

'Let her stay up a bit longer. I've hardly seen her,' Freddie complained.

'Bit better than last time though. At least you *have*

132

seen her!' Amy said, the sharpness back in her voice.

'Last time I spent my days off with Sheila because she was unhappy and ill and I thought I could help. I should have told you, but – well, I didn't. If Sheila hadn't wanted to have me there I'd have come home, but she did and I stayed until my leave was up. I didn't intend to, Mam, it just happened.'

Sheila smiled at Amy. 'He's so thoughtful and kind, isn't he Mrs Prichard?'

Amy thought how mature he seemed for a boy hardly sixteen years old. She felt proud of him yet sad that the days when she could plan and arrange his life for him were so soon over.

But later that evening as she closed the door behind them Amy found herself muttering crossly, 'Thoughtful my foot. The boy's a fool to get caught up with someone like that! A fool to himself.' She still found it impossible not to blame Sheila for attempting to blame Freddie for her pregnancy. She simply couldn't help it.

On that same day, Fay had intended, albeit unwillingly, to go with Johnny to the Mumbles Celebrations. She constantly refused to join in any local activities and tried to explain to Johnny that village life was a trial rather than a pleasure for her. She had finished her work before lunchtime and had stopped in Llan Gwyn for a cup of coffee before the drive home. She went to a local hotel where she sat in the comfortable lounge to relax and prepare for the doubtful pleasures of an afternoon near the sea. She was neatly dressed as always, her clothes immaculate and smart. She considered her appearance a part of her stock in trade, something as important to the prospective customer as the goods she sold. Everyone she met wanted to look as beautifully turned out as she did. She never stepped over her doorstep, or even showed herself to anyone, apart from Johnny, without

133

knowing her appearance was faultless. For most that would have been hard but Fay enjoyed it and did not begrudge the time involved for a moment.

Now, after several hours driving and persuading buyers to order some of her expensive hats and accessories, she was as neat as when she began her day's work. Still, she went first into the Ladies Room to touch up her makeup and comb her fair hair which she wore in a pageboy style, touching the collar of her beige linen suit.

She chose a table near the window where she could look down on to the main street of the small town and, when the waiter appeared, she ordered coffee and a tea-cake. She rarely ate at lunchtime and only ordered with the subconscious hope that it would delay her sufficiently to make the visit to Mumbles not worth while. If she could say with honestly to Johnny that she had arrived home too late to go, then she, and he, would be satisfied. She knew that Johnny would be disappointed, for he loved showing her off to his friends, but sitting on a beach or in a small cafe talking boring talk to such people as Nelly was more than she could bear. She failed to understand the attraction of such times.

The man was already seated at the next table when she sat down and, although he appeared to be reading *John Bull* magazine as he ate his lunch, she knew he was watching her. It was as if she had extra peripheral vision, seeing at the very edge of her view that his head had turned towards her. Moving her head a fraction she saw with amusement that his eyes were lowered, yet there was the clear knowledge that his gaze had been upon her and with, she was also sure, interest and admiration.

There had been many encounters with men as she travelled throughout the towns of South Wales and many opportunities to flirt, but she had never been tempted. Today, wanting an excuse to stop her having to join Johnny and his friends at Mumbles, she allowed a moment's pause before she turned back.

Her tea-cake arrived and she spread the butter, watching it melt into the hot toast, apparently needing all her concentration for the simple task. She became aware once again of the man's attention. Then, before she could raise the first small portion to her lips, he leaned over and asked, 'Wouldn't you like a proper meal? I would be glad of some company.'

Fay frowned and shook her head. 'Thank you, but if I had wanted a meal I would have ordered one.' She was disappointed. Surely he could have thought of a more original approach?

'I hate eating alone,' he went on. 'My wife is still shopping and I am sure she would welcome the company of an attractive stranger too.'

'You mean your wife wouldn't object if she returned from her shopping to find you entertaining a stranger? Another woman?'

'Of course not.' He moved his chair slightly closer to her. 'We have been divorced for three years and we're only meeting to discuss something regarding a house she wishes to buy.'

He gestured politely to the chair beside him and, curious, Fay moved to join him, waiting while he carried her simple meal to his table. She observed him as he busied himself with the rearrangement. His hair was reddish and his eyes could only be described as tawny. Like those of a lion, she thought foolishly. He was tall, slim and dressed in an expensive suit, a spotlessly white shirt and a tie that was clearly pure silk. His hands were well manicured and there was about him an air of confidence that pleased her. She guessed he was between thirty-five and forty. Wealthy, assured and sufficiently good company, she suspected, for her to enjoy making her return home too late for the trip to Mumbles.

In less than ten minutes she had told him about her job

and where she lived, and about Johnny and the visit to Mumbles which she wanted to avoid. He in his turn described the house where he lived with his mother and a housekeeper and the business which he ran with his brother.

'Will you meet me again one day when you have an idle hour?' he asked as she stood to leave. 'My wife will be so sorry to have missed you when I tell her about what you do. She's a great one for hats,' he said with a low chuckle.

It was the sound of his laugh and the remembrance of his eyes, half-hooded, glinting with specks of gold, that filled her mind as she drove home. Remembering, she was conscious of a warmth spreading throughout her body, disconcerting but undeniably pleasurable.

Approaching the outskirts of Hen Carw Parc she slowed the car. It was still early, time enough for her to go in and change into something more suitable and join Johnny at Mumbles. Stopping the car, she looked both ways and, seeing the road was empty of traffic, turned and went back the way she had come. Better call on a few more customers. That way she could tell Johnny that work had prevented her going to the celebrations. Her faced was slightly flushed, her blue eyes glowing with excitement and a guilty pleasure as the car went once more towards Llangwyn.

When the shops had closed and there was no further excuse for delay, still she did not want to drive home. It was almost six o'clock and she knew that Johnny would have given up waiting for her and would be on his way home. There was a film showing, 'The House of Wax', a 3-D production which necessitated each member of the audience wearing the red and green spectacles which could be bought for sixpence at the cinema box-office. She drove to Swansea with a feeling akin to that of a disobedient schoolgirl.

Johnny was frantic. He had expected Fay to be at home when he returned, and probably wearing a look of defiance as she faced him with reasons for not meeting him as planned. Finding the house empty and with no sign of a note to tell him she would be late, he began to prepare the meal, watching the clock, first with disappointment, then anger and finally consternation. Proping up a piece of paper listing the places he intended to visit in search of her, he left the house.

He went first to Ethel Davies, but she had seen nothing of Fay. Then to his mother's, and there he also drew a blank.

'She probably got to Mumbles late and is still on her way home for there,' Netta suggested.

Refusing the offer of something to eat, he ran back up Sheepy Lane to St David's Close to see if the car had returned.

At the corner he hesitated. Would it be foolish to go and tell PC Harris that his wife was missing? It sounded melodramatic on on a quiet summer's evening to worry about a grown woman, yet where could she be? Reluctantly he admitted that it was not an unusual occurrence for Fay impulsively to go and visit someone or even just drive around for an hour or two without first telling him. He saw Freddie walk up the road with Sheila and waved, tempted to ask if they had seen Fay but held back feeling that the urgency and alarm were foolish. He walked to the end of St David's Close and let himself into the empty house to wait.

He had the wireless on but heard the car as soon as it entered the Close. His emotions were tangled as he rose to greet her. Anger, hurt and relief exchanged places in his thoughts and on his boyish face. But it was relief that showed the moment he saw her stepping out of the car. He ran to help her.

'Fay, my lovely, where have you been? Worried I was *Duw annwyl!* I thought you were lost. Not knowing where you were and expecting you hours since. Not trouble with the car, was it? I'll take it out after we've eaten and check that everything's all right, shall I?' He was talking too fast, he knew that, and from her face she was already irritated by it. Forcing himself to be silent, he waited for her to tell him what had happened. Busying himself at the cooker with bedraggled vegetables, unable to watch her, afraid of what she might tell him.

He would never feel anything but vulnerable in his relationship with Fay. She was so clever and beautiful and he had loved her since he was a boy, never dreaming that one day she would consent to marry him, a bus driver. He would wake after a terrifying dream, in which she had left him, or else believing momentarily that the marriage had been the dream and the reality was waking and finding himself back in the bed in his mother's house, alone. He would put his arms around her, breathing in the sweet scent of her, wondering at the fate that he granted his wish and made her his own.

He returned from his thoughts to see her walking down the stairs wearing a silky dressing gown and fur-edged mules. She had cleansed her face and her hair had been brushed and pushed back from her face with a towelling band which she used for her makeup.

'Sorry, Johnny, but I didn't finish in time to come.'

'Come off it, Fay. Working until this time? That's a bit strong even for me to swallow, isn't it?' He didn't raise his voice but the criticism was was there and it added to her irritation and not her guilt.

'I don't know why but I didn't want to come home and hear all about the excitements of a picnic with Nelly and a gang of children!'

'Boring! Is that it? You find everything about our life together *boring*, right? What harm would there be in sparing an hour or two to enjoy a bit of innocent fun? Am I such a boring husband and companion that you have to drive around till this time of night rather than face coming home?'

'I went to the pictures.'

'Who with?' For the first time he raised his voice above a whisper.

'With no one. I went on my own to see "The House of Wax" in Swansea.' She took out the spectacles to show him.

'The one we were going to see together? Not so *boring* with me safely out of the way?'

'Don't keep saying "boring". I love you Johnny, but I hate the way you try to involve me in the lives of people I have nothing in common with. People like Nelly Luke. Even Evie has nothing to say that I find remotely interesting, although she would be horrified to hear me say so.'

'Nelly's a good sort and she's never done you any harm. I don't expect you to arrange dinner parties and invite her, but a bit of socialising wouldn't hurt, now would it? Better than going to the pictures on your own, I'd have thought.'

'Tell the truth, Johnny. You miss being a part of your mam's life with half the village traipsing in and out of her house day and night.'

'Yes, I do. There's always someone to enjoy a few minute's chat with, swop news with people who care if you have a problem, big or small. Yes, I do miss it. I find this place'—he waved his arms around the neat and sparsely furnished room—'this shell of a place as cold as my bus on a winter's morning, unless you're here. When I come here and you are working, it's got no welcome for me. Mam's place was never empty.'

'You like being a part of the community.'

'Yes, I do.'

'But Johnny, don't you understand, *I* don't.'

Johnny was startled at the vehemence in her voice and stared at her in alarm.

'Today I suppose I was rebelling at your attempt to make me mix with people I don't have anything to say to. It isn't how I want us to spend our time. I work hard and when I'm free I want us to be quiet and on our own, just you and me, Johnny. I married *you* and that didn't mean treating half the village as our family.'

'You do get tired, don't you? Is that why you don't have time for friends?'

Fay looked away from him. He was intelligent, but he seemed incapable of understanding one simple fact. She did not enjoy the free and easy camaraderie of the village. Even Phil, the postman, would stand for irritating minutes, holding back the letters in his hands until he had asked a dozen questions and passed on items of so-called news. Everyone was crowding her, expecting her to be someone different from how she had always been, simply because she had married Johnny Cartwright. As if she should become the same sort of person as those filling Ethel Davies's house day after day, or just 'popping in' to Netta for endless cups of tea and an exchange of gossip. She reminded herself that meeting the man at lunchtime was in no way responsible for her present strange mood.

'Yes, I do get tired,' she said, giving up trying to explain. 'I want my spare time to be spent with you, Johnny.'

He pulled her to him and she bent her head to rest on his shoulders. Unhappy she might be, but with a little pretence she could at least keep it to herself.

'Hungry?' Johnny asked and as she shook her head, he said, 'Me neither. Let's go to bed.'

He pressed her close to him and kissed her. She returned the kiss with hunger and warmed to his love, his arms protecting her from her doubts.

'Yes, Johnny, let's go to bed.' She moved away from him and walked up the stairs.

Johnny stayed down a while, inexplicably nervous. He threw away the mess of the abandoned meal, locked the door and went up to the cream-and-coffee-coloured bedroom and watched as she prepared for bed. He didn't know how to handle her present mood. That she was unhappy he knew but hoped that it was her lifestyle and not him that made her discontented. She smiled at him as he closed the bedroom door and slipped in between the sheets. She was so lovely he felt his breath rasp as he had held it too long.

'Fay, my lovely, I love you and I'll do anything to make you happy. You know that, don't you?'

She opened her arms for him and he got in beside her, taking her in his arms and pressing her slim body against his own. If only he could make her content, make her as happy as she made him every time he looked at her and told himself she was his.

The next morning they were both getting ready to go to their respective jobs. Johnny was on a split shift, giving him the afternoon free.

'Will you be in Llangwyn for a few hours today?' he asked.

'I can be. Shall we meet for a cup of tea?'

'Great. You say where. Remember I'll be in my uniform, mind. I won't have time to come back and change.'

She frowned and then said with a suspicion of a smile, 'Oh dear, I'll have to find a dirty little back street where I can hide you in case we're see by some of my posh customers.'

She had meant to joke, but Johnny's face stiffened. 'Is it my job that makes you unhappy, Fay? Tell me if it is. I don't know what else I can do, but together we'll think of something if that's what you want.'

141

'I don't want you to change your job. I think you'd be unhappy if you did. You love driving and enjoy meeting people. And the shifts mean you have spare time in the day, so you've got a sense of freedom. No, please don't ever think I'm ashamed of you or what you do.'

When he met her at three o'clock he surprised her by being dressed, not in uniform but a pair of grey trousers and a black and grey herringbone-tweed jacket. His shoes were brightly polished and his white shirt gleamed. She greeted him with delight.

'Johnny! You've been to all this trouble for me.'

'Worth any amount you are, my lovely.' He felt the same warm glow of pleasure as always as she took his arm and led him toward the cafe outside which they had met. 'Thank you, Johnny.'

'No, we aren't going in there.' He stopped at the doorway of the small, friendly cafe where they often ate. 'Not wasting all the effort of racing home and back. Come on, we're having tea at the hotel.'

Fay pulled back, afraid of going to the place where she had met the man and shared a few moments of innocent companionship. Superstition, she knew that was what it was. As if Johnny could pick up from the air, or the face of the waiter what had happened the previous day.

'No, let's go to the usual place.'

'Not today, my lovely. It's a proper tea with fancy cakes and everything. Come on.' Refusing to change his mind, he led her into the carpeted entrance of the hotel and to the restaurant. He ordered tea and only briefly wondered if it was expense or something else that had made her hesitate. He did not notice the way she looked around the room as if searching for a familiar face. And only showed mild curiosity when the waiter recognised her.

'Been here recently?' he asked. 'He seems to know you.'

'Yesterday, in fact. I came in for a tea-cake and a coffee at lunchtime.'

'Should eat better than that,' was his only comment.

The man did not appear and Fay gradually relaxed and enjoyed the hour they spent there. Johnny whispered remarks about other customers and made her laugh, and in a happy mood they left about four o'clock to go their separate ways. Johnny went to change back into his working clothes and Fay to call on three more customers. Both were smiling and each felt that their rocky marriage was on a lee shore again, if only for a while, and for that they were thankful.

# Chapter Eight

Victor arranged his delivery rounds to fit in with a lunchtime visit to the Drovers. He had bet on three horses the previous day, an accumulator bet with the winnings from the first horse going entirely on to the second and the winnings of the second going on to the third. It was rare to be fortunate enough for the three horses to win and, having seen the results in the previous evening's paper, Victor was impatient to hold the twenty-four pounds plus in his hand.

He was at the pub early and stood for a while wondering how he would spend his unexpected windfall. Taking out the morning paper from his overall pocket he studied the runners, contemplating spending at least some of the money on another bet. His luck was obviously in and it seemed a good idea to try again. Not another accumulator. That would be asking too much of Lady Luck.

He heard the sound of the van as Griff and Archie arrived to collect the betting slips, and he waved enthusiastically to the dark-haired Griff. Griff did not seem very pleased to see him.

'Bit of luck yesterday, Griff,' Victor called as the man slid from behind the steering wheel. 'Who'd have thought it?'

'Can I pay you later, Victor? I've come out without the cash. Got up late we did and—'

'None of those tricks with me,' Victor interrupted. 'You might manage to con Nelly out of a few pounds but you owe me nearly twenty-five pounds and I want it, now.'

'I'll see how much I get in from the bets. I might be able to let you have some of it today.'

'All of it, Griff. I want all of it, now.'

Victor was not a large man, and his pale-blue eyes were usually mild but Griff could see that he would not be able to fob him off, not with the large amount of money he had won. Damn it all, who would have guessed that such a stupid bet would have come off? He had not placed the bet, thinking the stake money would be his for the cost of a few words of comfort. Now he had to find all that money. It would wipe out all he had gained by holding bets in the last three months. He glanced across to where Victor stood, puffing nervously at a cigarette, obviously determined that the van would not leave until he had been paid. He had money in his pocket but it was not his. It was the money Hilda had set aside for various bills and would have to be replaced very quickly.

'Coming in for a quick half?' he asked Archie, and the old man, who spent his days clearing up and burning rubbish up at the forestry, eagerly stepped out of the van and followed Griff into the pub.

Griff ordered a drink for himself and Archie and surreptitiously pocketed the betting slips and money he'd taken from the group of men waiting for him. He stood in a corner shadowed by a partly closed curtain and handed out the few small payments, but as he turned to go back to the bar, found Victor blocking his way.

'Come on, Griff, man, don't let's have any bother.'

'You couldn't see your way to waiting till tomorrow, can you, Vic? I'll have it for you then, no trouble.'

'I'll have it now, no trouble,' Victor said warningly. He knew how wily a customer Griff Evans could be and was determined not to let him get away with even a day's delay. One day easily led to several, until Griff confused

146

his victim into accepting less than his entitlement.

'All right, I only wanted a favour, a day to get the money from where I left it. No one's trying to diddle you, Vic.'

'You diddle anyone? Never!' Victor held out his hand for the notes and silver that Griff handed to him and smiled his thanks. He took out the slip on which he had written his new bet but hesitated as he went to hand it over. He stared at Griff, now drinking his beer and chatting to the men crowded around him, discussing present and past racing, all fawning, begging him to take their money. Luck like winning on an accumulator bet happened very rarely, why should he give it all back? Victor knew the likelihood of still having any of the twenty-four pounds after a few more days of betting was low. He would lose it all for the sake of a few days of artificial excitement. He tore up the list of horses and threw them into the fire.

Griff drained the second glass of beer that Archie had bought for him and prepared to leave. At the doorway he stopped and said to Victor, 'Congratulations on the win. Got a cigarette, have you? I'm right out.'

On an impulse he never understood, Victor gave him the packet. 'Here, take the lot. I'm giving up smoking, it's bad for you. Them doctors in America say it causes cancer.' He threw the packet across to Griff and ordered another half pint of beer. He felt ridiculously pleased with himself, as if he had already succeeded in banishing the long-standing habit. Amy would be pleased. She was always complaining about the smell. He smiled as he raised the glass to his lips. Yes, Amy would be pleased, but he wouldn't tell her just yet. Already the brief feeling of success was fading and doubts over his ability to manage without the comfort of tobacco were rising.

He patted the money in his pocket and smiled again. With a sum like this to start with, he might be able to save

147

and get a bit of money behind him. He smile faded a little as he wondered how the money could bring the day when he had Amy were together any closer. He could not see how having a few pounds tucked away could possibly help, but it would give him the sensation, however false, that he was doing something, not just drifting along and day-dreaming about Imogine leaving him, and the divorce magically happening and Amy becoming his own. He put down the glass, waved to the barman and went out to continue his deliveries.

Griff drove back to the fish-and-chip shop where Bethan had the small churn of tea ready for him to take up to the forest for the men's lunch break. Several had ordered chips and these were wrapped in newspaper packages and tucked in beside the churn. He didn't speak to Bethan other than to thank her for the supplies and hand over the money for them. As he and Archie walked down the path carrying the churn, Bethan whispered, 'Mam and Dad are going to watch television with the Owens tonight.' Griff nodded briefly, a dark eye watching Archie for a sign that the old man had overheard the brief remark and, seeing his vague expression, decided he had not. As he closed the gate, he risked a wink at the smiling Bethan.

When he went home that evening he asked Hilda if she had some money to spare.

'Only a loan, like. I overdid the holding on to bets and I'm a bit short. Can't lend me a few pounds, can you?' He held her back as she went to look in the box where she kept the money for the electricity and rent. 'No, don't bother to look now. You must know if you've got some extra?'

'Not more than five pounds and that only for a week. I've borrowed from the box myself.'

'You've borrowed? Not in debt, are you?' He was

startled at the idea of Hilda not managing the living expenses on the little he gave her each Friday. It rarely crossed his mind how she bought food for the three of them, and managed to replace clothing and household items, month by month. 'There's your wages from the chip shop. Isn't there any spare?'

'I gave Pete money this week and last. He needed a part for his motor-bike.'

'Soft, you are. The boy is working and should manage on his own.'

'Loves that bike, he does. I can't bear to see him without it.'

'Without it? Damn, it's never on the road, always in bits in our garage. Him and Gerry are a right pair for stripping the thing down. You shouldn't have let him cheat you for the sake of a part he probably didn't need.'

Griff felt unreasonably angry with his wife. She should have had bit of money apart from the box money. He wished he had not asked. Now she was sure to go and check how much was there and find that there was more than twenty pounds missing. Damn Victor Honeyman and his accumulator bets!

Towards nine o'clock he put on the dark-green jacket he used when he went up into the woods and put a shapeless trilby on his head. Announcing that he was going to set his traps, he left the house, walked down the lane and slipped in through the back gate of the fish-and-chip shop. He glanced in through the window of the rooms used by Milly Toogood and her husband, Tommy, and seeing them empty went through the back door of the shop.

Bethan was serving as he looked carefully through the half-open door between the shop and the passage behind it, but she saw him and gave a brief nod. A young girl was behind the counter with her and he saw Bethan whisper some instructions before she joined Griff in the

149

passageway. Silently they went upstairs to the living room where the curtains were drawn. Bethan closed the door and ran into Griff's arms.

'How long have we got?' he whispered.

'Till ten, no longer. Mam and Dad will be bringing Arthur back then. I tried to persuade them to let him sleep in their rooms but he didn't want to.'

They kissed urgently and Bethan regretfully warned him that the minutes were slipping past.

'Don't want them to find you here, not tonight. It's too soon after last time.'

'I'm always in and out, they won't suspect anything. Hilda works for you, I do the occasional odd job – why shouldn't they find me here? Best there's no secret.' He kissed her again, his hands reaching under the white overall and finding the plump warm flesh. Bethan wore very little under the prim, white starched overall. Incongruously she always had on her feet a pair of thickly lined boots as the shop was draughty and on the rare occasions when there was time to undress Griff took great pleasure in leaving the boots until the last, seeing in the plump woman the childlike shyness that he loved.

'Fancy wanting to see me in these old boots, Griff Evans. There's daft you are!' she would complain laughingly.

There was no time for any fun and games that evening and he had to ask her a favour so he explained about the bet he had held and which had cost him a lot of money.

'I've taken it out of Hilda's box but I'll have to get it back in there before rent day,' he said. 'She'll spot the missing notes for sure. I hate to ask you, Bethan love, but could you lend it to me?'

'There's the money you gave me for Arthur's new clothes. I can delay buying them for a while, will that do?'

'Bethan, you're a marvel. Never complain or criticise.'

'We suit each other, you and me, Griff. Pity is that

150

you're married and we'll never be able to walk out together and show the world how happy we are.'

Voices reached them and they hurriedly separated, each adjusting their clothes. Bethan blew him a kiss, pointed to the drawer where she kept the cash box.

'Take what you need, Griff, and put it back when you can. I've got to go. Love you,' she whispered as she slipped out of the door and ran back down the stairs to the shop. Griff took twenty-five pounds out of the box which he replaced in its hiding place, then he ran down the stairs and into the storeroom where the sacks of potatoes were kept, to wait until it was safe to leave.

He walked in the shadows of the back walls to the end of the row near Amy's shop and, running across the road, went up Sheepy Lane to the distant woods. He walked for a long time setting traps occasionally, studying the ground for likely places to put others, all the time thinking about how he could get the twenty-five pounds back to Bethan. She was good about money, rarely asked him for any, but showed her gratitude in an exciting way when he gave her some to help with the expenses of the boy.

She never pressured him. Knowing how he felt about her, she had not once suggested he divorce Hilda and marry her. He constantly marvelled at his good fortune. He had Hilda for the basic comforts of a home, and Bethan for practically everything else. Bethan was the joy in his life, Hilda was the firm, reliable base.

He walked back home in the darkness of the isolated hills, from where he could hear nothing, and see little apart from the shadowy trees and shrubs along his path. On the air he smelt woodsmoke and as he passed Nelly's cottage on his way down to the village he saw a light in her window. Curious, he crept down the path, hoping those dogs of hers would not wake and start to bark. Peering in through the window he saw Nelly stretched

151

out on the couch, the dogs at her feet, and George snoring gently in the big armchair. The fire was smouldering in the grate and sending a column of grey smoke upwards, rising high in the still, dry air. Griff smiled and retraced his steps. He was not the only man to have found the secret of a happy life. Nelly and George attracted sympathy from people who thought they had nothing. In fact what they had was something so rare that only another contented man could recognise it.

He reached his house without seeing anyone and carefully replaced the money he had taken from Hilda's box. He went upstairs and slipped in beside his wife and dreamed of Bethan.

On Saturday morning Amy's shop was busier than usual. Mainly because she had a fresh supply of locally grown vegetables which attracted even those who normally bought in the town. The pavement display stretched across the window and past the side door which led to the flat in which the Powells lived. In between serving customers, she and Mavis Powell hurriedly tidied up the fallen cabbage leaves and swept up the soil from the potatoes and made the row of boxes and wooden crates as unobstrusive as possible, knowing that if Constable Harris passed, he would come in and complain about her blocking the pavement, as he frequently did.

The arrival of Farmer Leighton and Billie who both had dogs with them did nothing to help as the two women briskly but patiently served the steady flow of customers. When there was a brief lull, she went into the small kitchen and made a cup of tea, sitting down thankfully on the one chair to rest her tired legs. Sian was awake and cooing happily in her cot, which Amy had placed in the playpen Billie had made for her. She picked the little girl up and hugged her.

'You, my lovely, are the most amiable and good-tempered baby anyone could have and I love you.' She played with a bouncing toy, laughing with the child until the whistle of the kettle brought her back to the hubbub of voices, as customers waited to be served. She poured the teas and took one to Billie.

'Amy, would you and Margaret like to come fishing with me tomorrow?' Billie asked. 'We'll ask Oliver too if Margaret would like to.'

'No, I can't. Prue is coming for the day.' She pulled a face, suggesting she would prefer the offered day out to seeing her sister. 'I can't put her off and there's no way she would come with us.'

'Then I'll take Margaret and Oliver. Mary will come with us so they'll be quite safe.'

'Ask her,' Amy said. 'I'm sure she'd love to go with you. Pity I can't come with you. A day away from the shop and everything would suit me fine.' She served Netta with a loaf and added, 'Come to lunch, Billie, and you and the children can go as soon as you've eaten.'

'Great,' Billie smiled.

She watched as he went outside and stood talking to Mr Leighton, Leighton's hand proudly on his new tractor. She guessed they were discussing the various virtues of the different types and comparing both to the horses now retired. She wondered if farming talk could ever be anything but boring to her. Billie was becoming a regular visitor to her home and he was gradually becoming a part of her life. It was to him she turned if things went wrong in the house, he who mended broken windows or wired electric plugs. But, she wondered, if he was becoming a part of her life, could she ever become a part of his? Chickens, milk yields, wool prices, it was all so far from anything she had been involved in she doubted if she could ever be excited by them.

Billie tried to show an interest in the shop, suggesting changes to the layout and offering to add to the shelves and fitments, never minding when she explained how his ideas would not work. He was a calm man, never roused to anger and never upset by the lack of time she had to spend with him. He accepted her as she was and that was flattering as well as restful. When she had washed the cups and saucers she tidied up the muddle of the almost-empty crates and it was nearly half an hour before she realised he had gone.

The trouble with Billie was that he never stayed in her mind for long. While he was there she was happy to be with him, but away from her his presence was never felt. It was not like that with Victor. She thought of him often and when he left her she felt the separation like a cold draught in her heart. She would never have allowed him to go without being aware of his departure, without watching him drive or walk away, looking at his retreating figure until something blocked the sight of him.

The Sunday lunch was not as she planned. Sheila Davies called in at ten o'clock and at eleven thirty Amy felt obliged, by her promise to Freddie, to invite her to stay for the meal. Sheila thanked her and at once began to help with the vegetables. Amy tried not to be irritated by the girl, but even the way she cut up the potatoes for roasting made her want to snatch them from her and throw them in the rubbish bin. She sighed inwardly. She had to admit it, whatever Sheila did or did not do, she could not pretend to like her.

It was a relief when Billie and his sister arrived earlier than she expected.

'Go on in and talk to Mary, will you, Sheila? There's no room in this kitchen for another helper.' Her face a little tense, Sheila dried her hands and went to where Mary was glancing through some magazines. Amy knew she had spoken too sharply but before she could soften the words the door bell went again and Prue arrived.

Leaving the vegetables simmering and the roast potatoes beginning to brown, Amy picked up the baby and handed her to her mother. To her surprise and relief, Prue seemed less afraid of holding the little girl and even showed a glimmer of a smile when she looked down at her daughter. She sat in the armchair and Sheila sat on the arm and Amy felt a pang of compassion as Sheila helped Prue to change the baby's napkin, and later to feed Sian before putting her down near Prue to sleep. It was a surprise to see how well the young girl got on with the older, tight-faced Prue. Amy guessed that Sheila was putting on an act and pretending to agree with the few remarks Prue made but she was grateful to her and, when opportunity offered, she thanked her for her kindness to Prue.

During the meal, Prue changed her attitude to Sheila and even refused to sit near her. It was, Amy guessed, Prue's erratic memory reminding her of Sheila's earlier behaviour and, half remembering, she disapproved. Mary was very quiet. She had only been to Amy's house a few times and whether it was the strangeness of an unfamiliar place or the atmosphere created by having Sheila and Prue present she couldn't decide. Billie sat beside her and managed to appear unaffected by the antagonism. Margaret and Oliver giggled!

It was a relief when the meal was over. Amy had swallowed her food without tasting it, wishing the time away, longing for the moment when she would be alone. The dishes were stacked in the kitchen and although Mary offered to help Amy insisted they set off for their fishing expedition.

'Don't waste the best of the day,' she said with a forced smile of politeness. She felt embarrassed as Mary stood watching Billie kiss her goodbye and thought she saw in the woman's expression a slight anxiety, a fear

155

showing in the sombre dark eyes. Perhaps I would be sentencing her to years of isolation if I accepted Billie as the answer to my own loneliness, she thought.

The children were in the Landrover and Mary settled in the driving seat when Amy had yet another visitor. Nelly came towards the car, both dogs bouncing about beside her in their delight at seeing Oliver and Margaret.

'Out for a walk, Nelly?' Billie asked.

'Come to give Amy a hand with clearin' out the shed,' she shouted. 'If she's goin' ter move back to the flat she's got a lot of clearin' to do, ain't she?'

Billie left the car and walked back to where Amy was standing. 'What's this about moving back then?'

'Just an idea at the moment. It depends on whether I can persuade Mavis and Ralph to move out.'

'You didn't tell me?'

Amy felt that flurry of irritation that Billie often caused. She hated being crowded and even the slightest hint that he was proprietorial towards her made her eyes flash with anger. Billie seemed unaware of it as he went on, 'You should talk to me about these things, Amy. I want to help, you know that.

'It's only an idea, Billie, there's nothing decided.'

'That's the time to talk.'

'Then we'll talk, but not now,' she said and glanced back to where Prue and Sheila were watching and obviously listening in the doorway. 'I don't want the Powells finding out before I have time to tell them, now do I?'

'Amy,' he lowered his voice and bent his head down to hers, 'could you consider moving to the farm instead?'

'Billie, I couldn't consider anything today. There's Prue and Sheila about to scratch each other's eyes out and now Nelly arrived expecting me to start thinking about what to throw out from the shed. I forgot I asked her to come and help. Isn't that enough for a Sunday afternoon?'

'The seed of an idea is planted, now I'll stand back and

let it grow,' Billie whispered. He kissed her lightly and went to where the children and his sister were waiting.

Amy wondered if his words had been overheard. Nelly did not keep her wondering for long.

'Gettin' poetical, your Billie, ain't 'e?' she laughed.

Amy left Nelly happily throwing things out of the shed and sweeping up the dust and oddments that seem to appear on their own in any outhouse or shed. Sheila made a pot of tea and she poured a cup for Amy.

'I'd better get back now, Mrs Prichard,' she said, reaching for her coat, 'I expect you and Mrs Beynon have lots to talk about.'

Amy sighed and looked at the window where Prue stood with her coat on, watching for the taxi that was not due for over two hours. She seemed oblivious to them and apparently did not hear the wailing cry of Sian, who seemed restless as if even she had been aware of the undercurrents in the oddly assorted gathering.

'Lucky you,' she whispered with unexpected candor. 'I wish I had somewhere to go!'

The day after the fishing trip Oliver was awoken early and it was hardly seven o'clock before he had eaten his breakfast and was dressed ready for school. Evie was still in her dressing gown but the kitchen was clear of dishes and the house as neat and orderly as it could be. Timothy was in the spare bedroom, which Evie called his study, preparing his talk for assembly.

When someone knocked at the back door it was Evie's first impulse to ignore it. Anyone who called at such an inconvenient time hardly deserved a thought. Oliver stood on a chair and looked out of the kitchen window and at once Evie pulled him down with irritation.

'Now I'll have to answer, they're bound to have seen you,' she complained in a hissing whisper. She opened the door, tightening the belt of her dressing gown

157

as she did so, and saw Dawn Simmons standing there.

'What do you want so early in the morning?' Evie asked.

'Is Mr Chartridge in?' Dawn said with no sign of being intimidated by Evie's disapproval. 'I've got something to show him.'

'Mr Chartridge is the school headmaster and not on duty twenty-four hours a day. Can't you see him at school?'

'Of course I can, but I thought he'd like to see these.' Dawn held out a packet containing some photographs. 'You and Oliver can look too,' she offered as added encouragement.

Evie took the package and pulled out the photographs with obvious distaste and, holding them at the very edge as if too great a contact might be dangerous, she looked at the pictures Dawn had taken at the Mumbles Railway celebrations.

They were very good, even she could see that, and she nodded approval as she turned the pictures over and examined each one with genuine interest. Then her face showed surprise and puzzlement and she handed the offending photograph to Oliver, who had been trying to see them as she shuffled through the pile.

'Oliver? Is this you?'

'Yes, Mam, er, Mother,' he stammered.

'But what are you wearing?' Oliver did not answer her and she stared at him. 'Oliver? Where did you get these awful, common clothes?'

'I liked them,' he said mutinously, his head down and his ears beginning to redden.

'His gran brought them for him so he could enjoy the picnic without spoiling his best clothes,' Dawn said. 'Thinking of you, she was. All that washing off of sand and icecream if he wore his best.'

'I'll see your grandmother about this.' Evie handed

the photographs back and nodded dismissal to Dawn. 'Very nice. You must show them to Mr Chartridge when you get to school. He's far too busy to be interrupted now.'

'I'm going to show Nelly. You coming?' Dawn asked Oliver, who nodded, after glancing at his mother for permission.

'Don't be long and for goodness sake avoid the mud in the lane. I don't want you disgracing us by arriving at school looking like a tramp.'

'Grandad George was a tramp and his shoes are always shiny-clean,' Oliver whispered to Dawn.

'What did you say?' Evie demanded, but the firm closing of the back door was the only reply she received.

Oliver set off up the back garden and over the fence into the field behind the house. At the top of the field were the woods and he and Dawn followed the edge of the trees until they reached Nelly's gate.

Nelly was sitting outside her door, drinking a cup of tea and feeding the two big dogs with cake. She smiled a greeting when she saw the two children and waved them inside to find a piece of bread and jam. Dawn dropped the photographs on to Nelly's lap as she followed Oliver into the cottage.

After she had looked at them, Nelly shouted her admiration and delight at the excellence of the pictures and laughed at the amusing shots of some of the local people the girl had managed to take: one of Phil reaching over to take a cake, his eyes wide as he tried to do so without his wife seeing him; Johnny concentrating on the sand castle he was building; Nelly laughing, her mouth wide open, her arms spread in abandon; a child crying, his distorted features covered in the remnants of an icecream, sand clearly showing on his bare torso. A story in every one.

'Ere, young Dawn, these are good! Shown my

son-in-law, Tedious Timothy, 'ave yer?' She corrected herself with a wink at Oliver and said ashamedly, 'I means the 'eadmaster. Mr Chartridge. Seen 'em 'as 'e?'

'Not yet,' Dawn told her. 'I called but Mrs Chartridge said he was busy. She looked at them, but all she said was, "Where did Oliver get those clothes?".'

'Blimey!' Nelly covered her face with a grubby hand, her eyes widening with horror. 'Fergot them photographs I did, young Ollie. Cross was she? About us changin' yer suit fer somethin' decent fer once?' Unrepentant, she laughed, her mouth wide and showing her uneven teeth. 'Blimey, I bet she 'ad a shock, seein' you dressed proper summery and not like you was goin' to Buckin'am Palace for a medal!'

Margaret arrived, having walked to the shop early with her mother and the baby, and her face dropped when she saw Dawn with Oliver and Nelly, sitting drinking lemonade and laughing at the old woman's stories. Dawn was an interloper and Margaret wished she would go away.

' 'Ello, Margaret, got time fer a drink of pop, 'ave yer?' Nelly called and frowned as Margaret walked on without waiting for Oliver and Dawn to walk with her.

'Go on, you two,' she said, pulling herself clumsily to her feet. 'Got things ter do, I 'ave, an' you two don't want to be late fer school or I'll get a rocket from yer mum.'

At playtime, while Dawn was proudly showing her photographs to Timothy, Margaret approached Oliver.

'I think we need a secret place. Somewhere only you and I can go,' she said.

'Not even Dawn?' Oliver asked.

'Definitely not her!' Margaret was vehement.

'Gran says we should be nice to her as she hasn't got a mother.'

'I haven't got a father!'

Confused by the logic of this, Oliver agreed. 'All right,

160

a secret from everyone. What will it be, a hollow tree? I know where there's one.'

'No, I want us to have a tree house. I think Uncle Billie would help us make one.'

'Yes, we'd need help. I don't think my father would let me use a big saw,' Oliver said regretfully.

They discussed the project until the bell went, sending them running back to their lessons, having agreed to meet later and explore the woods for a likely site.

Margaret's plan to exclude Dawn was not a success. Billie and George agreed to help them and on the following Saturday, with Oliver explaining what he needed, the two men carried sawn logs into the wood near the small stream to begin the tree house. Both men commented on Oliver's 'good eye' and his ability to guess with surprising accuracy when a piece of wood was needed, without the use of the swivel-hinged measure Billie had brought. The place they had chosen was not very far from the lane and as the men sawed and banged, Margaret watched anxiously for signs of the interloper. The last nail was in place and the ropes all tightly fastened to support the platform with the leafy roof, some eight feet up in an oak, when she heard someone approaching. To her relief it was not Dawn, then she recognised the man. It was Dawn's father.

He turned aside from the path he was following when he saw the group of people, and dragging a sack which he had been filling with fallen branches for his fire, he disappeared down the leafy pathway from which he had appeared. From behind him appeared Dawn and she did not walk away but ran at once to see what they were doing.

'Go away Dawn Simmons,' Margaret hissed. 'This is private.'

'Mr Brown,' Dawn called to Billie, who was testing the

tree house with his strong arms, pulling at the branches to make sure there was no movement. 'Mr Brown, what are you making?'

'It's a secret, or it's supposed to be. I expect, if you're patient, Margaret and Oliver will invite you to come and see one day, but not yet. It's private, see.'

Dawn flounced away, not following her father but down towards Nelly's cottage, and it was there they found her when the tree house was declared finished and they all went for a drink and a rest. Oliver did not go into the cottage. He struggled to reach an apple box which he remembered seeing at the back of Nelly's old shed.

'Gran, can I have this for a cupboard in our tree house?' he asked and, when he and Billie went back to fix it into place, they found that once again Oliver's judgement was good. The box fitted where Oliver said it would, with only a small amount of trimming and a few stout nails.

Billie seemed to fill Nelly's room, sitting in the big armchair and spreading his long legs across the hearth. George sat the other side of the fire, as tall but not as hefty, and even the dogs failed to find a place against the brass fender. Summer it might be, but the warmth of the fire was an attraction. The door was open as always and as Nelly went up the cinder path to refill the sooty kettle from the tap in the lane she saw Tad hovering as if waiting for someone.

'If it's your Dawn you're looking for, she's inside 'avin' a biscuit with Oliver an' Margaret. Go in, why don't yer. The only cup left 'as got an 'andle missin' but the tea tastes just as good without one.'

'I'll wait for her here,' the man muttered. He had the sack of wood at his feet and Nelly shrugged.

'Put that against the gate, no one'll pinch it. 'Ere, you can carry me kettle. I filled it a bit full an' it pulls somethin' awful on me bad 'ip.'

Reluctantly the man threw aside the sack and took the kettle from her, following her down the path but stopping at the doorway when he saw the roomful of people.

'Come on in, why don't yer.' Nelly poured him a cup of tea as George placed the heavy kettle on the fire. 'Dawn, pass the sugar for yer dad. Any biscuits left?'

Tad stood just inside the door, ill at ease, sipping the strong tea. He said nothing, only nodding or shaking his head at any remarks directed at him.

'Blimey, Tad,' Nelly laughed, 'you're worse than Mr Leighton fer bein' quiet. 'E doesn't do nothin' but grunt an' nod.'

The man raised his chin as if about to protest but changed his mind and gave a half grin, the movement animating the thin face momentarily.

Margaret and Oliver were squashed together in a corner, sitting on a pile of blankets which Nelly had intended to wash but had forgotten. When Amy arrived to collect her daughter, Margaret hesitated to rise. Dawn was standing near them and obviously waiting for the opportunity to take her place beside Oliver.

'You're late for your music lesson, Margaret love,' Amy said.

'Mam, I don't want to go. Not tonight. Can't I miss just this once?'

Nelly's sharp eyes had guessed the reason for Margaret's reluctance and said, 'Why don't you go with her, Ollie? I'll tell yer mum where you are so she won't worry about yer. You likes listening to Margaret play, don't yer?'

Squeezing through the forest of legs, both human and canine, the two children left and Amy, with Sian in her arms, found a place next to Billie on the arm of a chair.

'Better than Christmas, this is,' Nelly said in delight. I wonder 'oo else will be calling? Go on George, find that flagon of beer we bought for tonight, why don't yer?'

The dogs pricked up their ears and began to bark and push their way towards the door. Nelly opened it by pushing it with her backside and saw Victor walking down the path.

' 'Ello, Victor. Come just in time fer a beer. Not more than a mouthful but you're welcome to it'. As she said the name she glanced around to see the effect on Billie. The big farmer slipped an arm around Amy's waist and pulled her closer. Nelly's dark eyes gleamed in delight. Billie was better for her than Victor. Best they should both be reminded now and then.

'I've come with a message from Phil,' Victor said as he reached the door. 'Are you coming to the Drovers tonight?'

'We wasn't,' Nelly frowned. 'Why, what's on? Somethin' we shouldn't miss?'

'Only the fourth or fifth meeting called by Bert to arrange the outing,' Victor smiled.

'Shall we go, George? You goin' Billie?' she asked, deliberately letting Victor know he was there. The name made Victor pop his head around the door to see who else was present and, seeing Amy, pushed his way in.

'Hello, Amy. Will you be able to go? It should be a laugh?'

'No, I can't take Sian and there's no one to mind her. I bet half of Hen Carw Parc will be there.'

'Pity. I've persuaded our Delina to go. She'd have liked to have seen you there.'

The impromptu party broke up and Tad took Dawn home. Billie walked with Amy as far as the end of the lane then climbed into the Landrover to drive home. Victor watched them, Billie carrying the baby and laughing with Amy as they reached the road, leaning over to kiss her goodbye before driving off. There was a defeated expression on Victor's face. He was losing her.

He was losing even the dream of her. It was an impossible dream and with a wife who he could not bring himself to divorce it was a foolish dream, but he needed that thread of hope – little more than a fantasy – that one day he and Amy would be together. It was all he had to help him through the lonely days and the interminably long dark nights.

Seeing her sitting beside Billie, with Billie's arm resting on her slim waist, had reinforced the fragility of the dream. Billie was free and wealthy while he was married and, with only the small wage he earned, he had less than nothing to offer. Instinctively his hand reached for the cigarette packet and his lighter, but he had vowed to forgo that comfort. He snapped a twig from hawthorn bush and put it in his mouth to chew.

He walked through the village, up Sheepy Lane towards the council house where his wife would have prepared a meal for him to eat in solitary silence. He envied Nelly and George their poor cottage and their meagre existence. At least Nelly was cheerful and content and showed her love and affection for George in everything she said and did.

How little we really need, he thought as he passed Ethel's cottage with its door standing open inviting anyone who passed to call in and be sure of a welcome. A home where you can relax, someone to call you their love, and enough money to live on without worry. Yes, even George, who had lived for years as a tramp, has more than me. He turned at the beginning of Hywel Rise and decided not to go home. He would go straight to the Drovers and forget his problems in a few hours of friendly company and laughter.

# Chapter Nine

It was almost nine o'clock before Nelly and George set off for the Drovers. Walking along the grassy bank beside the road they saw others heading in the same direction. Billie and Mary were walking ahead of them and behind them, catching up, were Johnny and Fay, Milly Toogood and the 'Pup', Sybil Tremain, and behind them trailing reluctantly, was Milly's husband, Tommy.

Tommy was a quiet man who was rarely seen and who rarely spoke above a whisper. He walked behind Sybil, who walked behind Milly, his head bent, 'as if 'e's lookin' fer mushrooms', Nelly often said. His only and recent claim to fame, was Bert Roberts' insistence that he act as secretary to the committee called to plan the outing for the darts team. Bert needed someone who definitely wouldn't argue or answer back and, after years of being married to Milly, Tommy was just that.

The bar was full and people were standing outside in the warm summer evening, discussing their interests, small groups huddled together as if their subjects were state secrets. Griff was there, taking surreptitious bets on whether Bert would achieve a result from the meeting about to begin.

Nelly pushed her way through to the large, less popular bar room. George and the others followed and saw that the tables had been re-arranged so that the centre of the room now had a line of tables and chairs with, at each place, a piece of paper and a pencil.

At the far end Bert Roberts stood, the light of battle in his eye, irritably trying to get his committee members seated, his little wife tucked into a corner to enjoy the proceedings. Nelly and the rest spread themselves around the edge of the room to watch. George and Johnny went to get drinks from the counter in the other bar and the hum of conversation swelled until Bert banged on the table with a small toffee hammer he had brought for the purpose, and demanded, 'H' order!'

The importance of the occasion and the audience it had attracted gave him an enlarged sense of importance so he added an 'H' and shouted again,

'H'order!'

He shuffled the papers he had in front of him importantly and gestured irritably to Tommy Toogood to sit beside him.

'Now, I'm calling this meeting to h'order,' he said briskly. 'I want to get this matter of the outing settled satisfactorily and if we have time we'll draw for the next round of the darts tournament.' In a voice barely heard, Tommy said, 'I propose we declare the minutes of the last meeting read, so as to save time, right?'

'Just a minute, Tommy.' Bert's voice dropped to low pomposity. 'On a point of order, there's plenty of time for proposals after my opening comments.'

'But you told me to—' Tommy protested mildly.

'Tommy, please, no digressions. Now, the purpose of this meeting is for—'

'Hang on a minute, Bert, you'd better wait for—' Victor began.

'On a point of order, please address all comments through the chair.'

'Who's the chairman then?' Victor looked confused.

'Bert,' someone explained.

'It was Bert I was speaking to!'

'What was it you wanted to say, Victor?' Bert spoke with patient martyrdom.

'I think you should wait for young Gerry and Pete. You remember what happened last time they came late. They insisted on being told all that had happened and by the time—'

'I know,' Bert snapped, 'by the time we'd explained, the landlord had called stop-tap and the committee vanished. Well, they aren't here and I've called the meeting to order. Now, where was I?' He shuffled the papers again.

'It's going to be just like last time,' Johnny whispered.

'I would like, in spite of absentees, to declare this meeting open,' Bert announced.

'I still think we should wait for Gerry and Pete,' Victor said, then added hurriedly, 'Mr Chairman, Griff isn't here either and he sees to tickets and booking the coach and all that.'

'Yes, he should be here,' Phil said, looking around for the approval of the others. He was rewarded by a murmur of agreement.

'Quite right,' Nelly shouted, ' 'E should be 'ere.'

'*Chwarae teg*, be fair, Mr Chairman, Griff should be present.'

'I agree, He *should* be present. I'm not trying to do things in secret, am I? He knows when and where the meeting is to start, doesn't he? He *should* be here, that's all I'm saying and I'm justified in starting without him, am I right?'

'No, Mr Chairman,' Tommy said agreeably.

'What d'you mean, Tommy?' Bert demanded.

'I mean what I say, boy.'

'You saying I'm wrong?'

Billie, who was enjoying the confusion said encouragingly, 'That's what he said, Bert.'

'I said you aren't trying to do anything in secret, Mr

169

Chairman. I answered your first question. You will ask three in a row and you know how it confuses things.'

'All right, I want a vote that we start without Griff, Pete and Gerry.' A few put up their hands and Bert made a half-hearted attempt to count them and called, 'Motion carried.'

'Wait a minute,' Billie called. 'Aren't you supposed to call for those against? Got to do things by the book,' he grinned.

'Yes,' Archie called, 'I want to go down as an abstainer.'

'Yes, Mr Chairman, we're all abstainers!'

'Damn me, that's a laugh!'

At this point, several of the committee stood up and announced their need for further refreshment. Bert turned to complain to Tommy, but he too had hurriedly departed in the direction of the bar.

'Better than the telly, ain't 'e' Nelly shouted to Fay. 'I feels a bit sorry for 'im but 'e's good fer a laugh.'

'I didn't want to come,' Fay admitted, 'but now I wish we'd tried harder to persuade Johnny's mother to come.'

'Watching that telly again, is she?' Nelly sighed. 'It's goin' to ruin everythin' that telly. Netta would never 'ave missed a show like this before she got that thing.' She touched Fay's arm apologetically. ' 'Ere, I'm sorry, you give it to 'er, didn't yer? Very kind an all that, but, well, it's one of the changes in the village that I don't like. People don't get out and meet. Just sit in their own rooms laughing and listenin' to folks 'oo are miles away. It's interestin' but it ain't natural, is it? Soon we'll all be strangers.'

'I think Johnny and I will buy one before the winter, Nelly,' Fay told her. 'It's cheaper than going to the cinema.'

'But not as much fun as this silly sod, eh?' Nelly pointed to where Bert was again attempting to call his

170

meeting to order. He was just beginning his opening announcements.

'—so we have the choice of racing at Newbury on August 13th, or Chepstow on September 18th. Now can we consider Chepstow?'

'What about Newbury then?' Victor asked. 'Just because you've got a sister you want to visit in Chepstow there's no need to force us all to go there.'

Amid roars of laughter Griff, his son Pete, and Gerry Williams walked in.

'Hello, boys,' Pete called, removing his motor-cycling gloves. 'Sorry we're late. Gerry had trouble starting.'

'Trouble with the bike?'

'No, no. Mam wouldn't let me start till I'd tidied my room,' Gerry explained.

'Haven't *you* started yet?' Griff asked.

'Damn aye. We've had a proposal and a vote.'

'Where are we going then?'

'Not a vote on that,' Billie laughed. 'We voted to start without you.'

'But we didn't,' Bert said, 'because someone who shall be nameless announced a break for refreshments.'

'What about going to the races at Newbury on August 13th?' Nelly shouted. Voices were raised in agreement but were finally shouted down by Bert, who insisted on 'H' order', a full democratic discussion, a proposal and vote.

'Good try, Nelly,' Billie said. 'Pity it can't be that simple.'

The only proposal and vote Bert achieved was to decide on a further meeting on the following night. Because of the tormenting and confusion, he sensibly told the meeting he would announce the venue personally on the following day.

'Can't say I blame him,' Victor said as they all pushed their way out into the chill night air. 'We did give him a rough time.'

'Still,' Billie argued, 'it was a simple thing to arrange. All he had to do was ask who votes for Chepstow and the thing would have been decided.'

'Who gave him that rule book?' George asked.

'That Phil, the teaser, and he underlined all the useful bits to make sure we had a good laugh.'

'Poor Bert,' Nelly said, in a maudlin voice. 'But 'e's better than the telly.'

She stood watching the crowd disperse as George called his 'good nights' to Phil and Johnny. The two young boys were at the kerb, their motor-bikes growling, impatient to be off. Billie had got into his Landrover and Victor stood hesitantly, obviously in no hurry to get home.

'Come back fer a cuppa why don't yer?' Nelly called, but Victor shook his head.

'No thanks, Nelly, I'd better get home.'

But she noticed with some displeasure that he set off, not in the direction of the village, but to Amy's house. 'A bit late fer calling, ain't it?' she shouted.

Bert came out and, with Tommy close beside him listening patiently to his complaints, walked bristly off with Milly and the Pup in pursuit. Sidney and Mr Leighton were talking to George and she went to join them.

' 'Ere, I think Victor's gone to see Amy. D'you think we should go too? She might be in need of a chaperone.'

'Home, Nelly,' George laughed. 'I don't think that at her age Amy needs our help.'

Victor increased his speed, leaving the laughing, chattering crowd behind as he hurried towards Amy's house. He knew it was late, and understood her concern about her reputation now Margaret was old enough to be hurt, but he had to see her. His fingers reached for the hundredth time for his cigarettes and he regretted not buying

172

any at the pub. He couldn't go on with this gnawing ache much longer. The need for tobacco made a miserable life intolerable and would continue to do so unless he could see Amy and hear her reassure him that Billie was not going to take her away from him.

There were no lights showing and he hesitated to knock, afraid that she had gone to bed. Yet the curtains were open, and the fire in the living room was still unlit. Even in the summer, Amy almost always lit a fire in the evening. She obviously was not in. He walked back down the drive and looked both ways along the road as if expecting to see her approaching. He remembered thankfully that Billie had been at the pub. At least she was not with him.

He leaned against the gate and, picking a twig from the hedge, began to chew it. There was nothing to rush home for. He might as well wait. Then he remembered how Billie had often gone inside, using the key Amy hid in the garden, to light the fire to welcome her home. It was too late for that. She would not thank him for lighting the fire and giving her the task of relaying it the following morning. He pondered the problem. What could he do to help her? It was after ten-thirty and there would be nothing for her to do except get Margaret settled into bed. Hot-water bottles, he thought at last. He would fill them and put them to warm the beds.

Satisfied he had a reasonable excuse for going inside, he found the key and went around to the back door. To his surprise it was open. A brief glance inside showed him that the place had been ransacked. He ran to the phone in the hall and telephoned for the police. He was breathless with shock, his chest heaved as he waited for the police to arrive. What if they suspected him? The excuse for entering a house belonging to someone else now seemed very weak.

He heard the sound of a car engine and opened the

front door, expecting to see PC Harris. But it was Amy and Margaret and he went to meet them to explain what had happened before she stepped inside.

'Victor? What are you doing here?'

'Amy love, there's been a bit of trouble.' He gripped her arms and went on, 'I'm afraid there's been a burglary.'

'Oh no. Not here?'

'I left the pub and came in the hope of seeing you for a few minutes and, when you were not here, I thought I'd go in and fill the hot-water bottle for Margaret's bed, and the back door was open and . . . Well, the police are on the way. Best we wait here until they come.' He put an arm around them both, making jokes to cheer Margaret, taking the sleeping baby from Amy and cuddling her, whilst they waited in the porch until the police arrived.

Harris was on his bicycle but a police car arrived only moments after him and the uniformed men went in, switched on all the lights and searched the house to make sure the offender was no longer on the premises. Then Amy and Margaret were allowed inside and Victor was questioned about the circumstances in which he made the discovery.

Amy was very shaken. She had never worried about living in the house with Margaret and a baby to care for, but now she was too frightened to go upstairs.

'I'll stay,' Victor said. 'You and the children can go to bed and sleep. I'll stay down here until morning.' He turned to the constable. 'Would you let my wife know, Mr Harris? I'm sure she'll understand, in the circumstances.'

'I think, if Mrs Prichard agrees, that would be a good idea. There's almost no possibility of the person returning, but I'm sure you'll sleep easier if you have someone else on the premises, won't you?'

'Right then. I'll fill those hot-water bottles and get you lot settled. Don't worry about me, I'll sit on the armchair and be perfectly comfortable.'

When the police had finished their searches, Victor made more tea and a few sandwiches while Amy settled the children. Margaret was upset and too frightened to sleep in her own room, so Amy thankfully agreed that they should share. She put her in the double bed, promising to be up soon. The cot was beside the bed; Amy needed to have her dependants close to her. If Victor had not stayed, she would probably have put them all to sleep in the front room, near an escape route through the front door. She wondered how many days would pass before she felt relaxed again and able to go to bed normally.

She went downstairs to where Victor sat waiting for her. 'Thank you, Victor. I don't know what I would have done if you hadn't been here.'

'You'd have coped, like you always do, love.' He stood up and held her. 'You're trembling. The shock hasn't left you.'

'I doubt if it ever will. I thought old Archie was over-reacting when he said he was afraid to leave the house for fear of having to walk back in, expecting there to have been a repeat robbery, but now I can understand. I'm sure I'll feel dread every time I put the key in that front door.

'Amy, how many people know where you keep that spare key?'

'Practically everyone, I should think. I tell delivery men, Nelly uses it to come in and clean, there's you, and Billie and some of Margaret's friends are bound to know. They'd have seen her use it.'

'Then you'll have to give Margaret and Nelly a key when I've changed the lock, and stop leaving one outside.'

'You mean someone used that key?'

'More than likely, according to the police. They thought you were crazy to do such a thing.'

'But there's never been any trouble, here in Hen Carw Parc.'

'Not until now, but things are changing. People aren't as trustworthy as they used to be. And someone in Hen Carw Parc is using local knowledge, like where you keep your key and what time people are likely to be out, to commit these robberies.'

Margaret called and Amy kissed Victor briefly on the cheek. 'I'd better go. Margaret won't sleep before I'm there and who can blame her?' She went up the stairs and Victor pulled the blanket she had given him around his shoulders and settled to rest until morning. He did not turn out the lights, in case Margaret or Amy became frightened with bad dreams. Best they could see that everything was normal.

The night was black with a low cloud obliterating the moon. Victor could not sleep and his wide-awake mind refused to let him rest. He folded the blanket and stood looking out into the darkness, wondering who could have robbed Amy and destroyed her peace of mind. According to her first hurried searches they had taken about fifty pounds in cash and a watch given to her by her mother – no longer working but with a case of gold. Little else was missing although she admitted that her mind was so frozen with horror that she could not think clearly enough to remember.

So many of the local people had been at the pub. And among those who were not, how many could be even briefly suspected of these robberies? Tad Simmons came to mind. He was obviously short of money; you only had to see how that pest of a kid, Dawn, was dressed to know that. But was he the type to break into houses and take from neighbours and friends? On second thoughts, he doesn't have any friends, he reflected. But would he risk prison, leaving his daughter to go into care? But then, people who did these things hardly expected to be caught. He shivered at the prospect of a prison sentence, and reminded himself that the police were far from satisfied with his story about coming into a house with the intention of putting hot-water bottles into beds in the middle of summer!

He heard a sound and concentrated on it. If it were Margaret waking, he could hardly go up. He guessed that Amy was sleeping lightly, if at all, and she would hear the moment either of the children woke. Footsteps crossed the landing and he watched the stairs. Amy came down quietly and walked into his arms.

'I'm too wide awake to sleep and my fidgeting was disturbing Margaret,' she explained.

'As you see, I haven't slept either.'

'I'm jumping at every sound. Every shadow seems like a threat,' Amy said, shivering. Victor put the blanket around her and held her close. 'I'm so glad you're here,' she whispered.

He wanted to ask if she would have felt the same if it had been Billie Brown who had arrived in time to discover the burglary but he daren't. If just anyone would have done to comfort her, he would rather not know.

She moved away from him, looking into the kitchen, touching the bolt that had been pushed into place at the top and bottom of the door. She went to the front door and checked that.

'I've made sure everything is locked, love. The windows are all closed. You have nothing to worry about. In any case, he won't be back.'

'I keep thinking of that watch. It's all I have to remember my mother by. Gold it was, so it will be smashed up and melted down. No value as a watch to anyone but me.'

'I'll buy you another and you can remember me every time you look at it.'

The blanket had slipped from her shoulder and he reached to pull it up and suddenly she was crying, clinging to him and her warm body was moulded against his own. Desire flared urgently and he kissed her tears away, the kisses becoming less to comfort, more to arouse. She sank with him to the floor and he slowly, lovingly slipped off the nightdress she wore and soon they lay naked and oblivious to everything but each other and their need for love. Only briefly did Victor wonder at her need: whether it was for himself, Victor, or whether she was blanking out the shock of the robbery for a few precious moments. She whispered his name and he knew her thoughts were for him alone.

For the rest of the night they sat, their arms around each other and kissed occasionally, hugged frequently, each revelling in the sensation of a shared love. The curtains were pulled back and they watched as a grey dawn suddenly brightened and became first tinged with pink then broke into the richness of a beautiful summer's day. Then, regretfully, Amy returned to her bed so Margaret wouldn't awake and miss her.

Later that day they learnt that there had been more than one robbery. Two houses on the council estate had been broken into and money had been taken. Altogether almost one hundred pounds had been taken, plus a few items of jewellery.

Amy called Margaret and prepared to send her to school as usual. 'There's no point in making more of a drama out of this than necessary,' she told Victor as they prepared breakfast. 'I'll open the shop and Margaret will go to school as if the day is a normal one. The police will know where to find me if they want me.'

'I think I'd better ring them to see if they want to question me any further,' Victor said. 'I'm afraid I'm a suspect, Amy, my love.'

178

'Don't call me that.' She hissed frowning. 'Not with Margaret here.'

But he could not be discouraged after the magical night he had spent in her arms and for once her frown did not affect him.

'My love, my love, my love,' he whispered into her hair. Then, as Margaret came down the stairs, he greeted her with a smile and said, 'Margaret, lovely girl, how would you like to come to the pictures tomorrow night, special treat. And I'll come back here with you to make sure everything is safe and secure before I go home?'

'Oh yes. Please Uncle Victor!' She turned her brown eyes on her mother, 'Mam, can we?'

'I think it's a good idea.' She smiled her thanks at Victor. 'What about asking Delina as well?'

So it was decided and, as Victor set off home, promising to return with tools to change the locks as soon as he had changed, Amy was humming happily, pretending for Margaret's sake that the horror of the previous evening was forgotten.

The news seemed to have reached everyone before ten o'clock. Billie arrived having heard the news early from Mary, whose rounds began before six o'clock with the milking from the previous evening.

'Amy, are you all right?' he asked, lumbering into the kitchen as soon as she released the bolts. 'I was so worried. Why didn't I call last evening? I could have done so easily. I've brought some tools with me. I'll change your locks for a start, then we'll think of what else we can do to make sure you and Margaret and Sian are safe.'

'Hold on, we aren't hurt!' She smiled at Margaret. 'Not even frightened, are we, love?'

'No, Mam, but I'm glad Uncle Victor was there.'

'Victor?' Billie asked.

'He called after the meeting and we were out, at

Ethel's. He discovered the break-in and waited for us.'

Billie said nothing but his disapproval of Victor's late-night visit was evident from his tightened lips.

'He stayed with us all night,' Margaret added. 'Then he helped Mam cook my breakfast and heard my piano piece for church today.'

Amy refused to look at Billie, afraid he would see in her eyes that the overnight visit was not innocent. She put the kettle on the cooker and asked, without turning around, if he would like some tea.

'No thanks,' he said. 'I think, so long as you're all OK, I'll get back and help Mary clear up after the milking. There's bottling to do for the second round and—'

Amy felt guilty at the way she had hurt him. He couldn't know, but something in the way she acted had obviously given him the correct impression of what had happened between herself and Victor. She rummaged in her brain to find a way of easing his suspicions, partly to comfort him and partly because she did not want others to receive the same impression. Billie was slow thinking and he might unintentionally pass on his conviction that she and Victor were lovers. His honest face was utterly readable, especially by people like Milly Toogood.

'Margaret and I slept together last night,' she said brightly. 'And Sian was in with us. At least, her cot was beside the bed. We felt we wanted to be close together.'

'Yes, and Mam fidgeted all night and wouldn't let me sleep!' Margaret added.

'Better than snoring,' Amy laughed. 'Felt safe, didn't we, love, with Uncle Victor downstairs?' She felt that even if she had not completely succeeded, Billie would allow her the benefit of the doubt.

Several people called during the day to ask if they could help. Nelly offered to clean through, her answer to everything that couldn't be cured with a cup of tea. George volunteered to lock some of the downstairs

180

windows, Milly to see what was to be learnt, and Phil puffed up on his bike, furious that he had to be told by Nelly what had happened the previous day. Victor reappeared in the afternoon, with Delina and his eldest son, Daniel, who was almost eighteen. They changed the locks on both doors and gave Amy the new key.

'I'll get you the extra keys tomorrow,' Victor promised. The day was completely disrupted and Amy spent most of it making tea for visitors who had called to offer sympathy and declare their anger. Constable Harris returned and asked if Amy had noticed anything else missing, but in the shock and confusion she had not. When evening came she began to feel frightened. For the first time the house felt threatening and no longer her home.

'Damn the man, whoever he is,' she said to Victor, who had returned alone as she was preparing Margaret for bed. 'How can people like that live with their conscience?'

'I'll stay,' he said. 'For tonight only, I'll stay.' He stared at Amy and in his eyes she saw a pleading as well as a strength. 'You and Margaret can sleep undisturbed. After tonight you'll be able to push the fear aside. There'll be the shop and the dozens of daily irritations to fill your mind and you'll gradually forget, but tonight I think it's best I stay.' Amy nodded agreement. Victor went home briefly to explain to Delina and the boys that he was staying to reassure Amy and Margaret ignoring the accusing look on Imogine's stern face. He wondered vaguely if she really cared where he would be sleeping and decided she probably didn't.

Victor had not slept the previous night and, in spite of his efforts to stay awake, his eyes were heavy, and sleep overtook him within a few minutes of settling under the blanket on the couch. When Amy came down during the darkest hour she stood looking down at him and wondered what it was that made one man so dear and another nothing more than a friend. He did not stir, even when she knelt and kissed him.

She made a hot drink and stood for a while staring out into the blackness of the garden, seeing little but imagining it occupied by men waiting for a chance to enter her home and grab what they wanted. Shivering, she turned to the windows at the front and, her eyes took in the faint light from the distant road, saw a figure standing near her porch. She stifled the scream that filled her throat and shook Victor awake.

'Victor, there's someone outside,' she hissed, a sob of fear echoing in the words. Victor shook off sleep in an instant and went to the window.

'Call the police,' he said. 'Hurry.' He crept to the front door and carefully eased back the bolts. 'If he so much as touches your door, I'll kill him,' he growled.

'Please, Victor, don't open the door, stay here with me.'

He watched as she picked up the phone in the hall and dialled the number, waited until the sleepy voice at the other end said he was on his way, then taking her hand, led her back to the window. The man was still there, but as they watched he seemed to fade from their view. Sliding silently into the shadows until he was nothing more substantial than a false memory. Holding Amy tightly against him, Victor opened the door and stared out. The night was still and silent, until the sudden snarl of an engine broke the eerie quiet. But the sound was not of the approach of the police car but that of a motorcycle being driven away from the village.

When Constable Harris arrived, he searched the garden and the surrounding area diligently but left with assurances that whoever it had been was now safely far away.

'He was probably nothing to do with these robberies,

Mrs Prichard,' he said. 'Probably a poacher. There's plenty of them about. Go back to sleep, both of you and I'll hang around for a bit just in case he comes back this way.' He glanced at the blanket on the couch where Victor had been sleeping. 'Just as well you decided to stay again. Makes the ladies feel secure, having a man about, doesn't it?'

Amy went back upstairs and Victor saw the constable out. The night seemed to take an age to settle; sleep was as far away from him as on the previous night. He lay on the couch watching the staircase, willing Amy to come to him. After an hour he relaxed into sleep, only to be woken by her lips on his. He opened his arms and enfolded her, taking her into his embrace and making her a part of a wonderful dream.

He left early on the following morning, after sharing a romantic breakfast with Amy in the early dawn. He walked home through the lane past Nelly's cottage and the singing woods, his heart swollen with happiness. Amy loved him. There was no doubt in his mind now, only the determination that somehow he would free himself of his soulless marriage and spend the rest of his life with her. Even the need for a cigarette no longer tormented him. He would spend the money he was saving plus the cash, still intact, from his racing success, on buying her a gold watch to replace the one that had been stolen.

Amy's shop was busy on Monday morning, with people coming in to hear the details of the break-in from her. She dealt with them all with more than normal patience, even spending time explaining to Milly Toogood how Victor had been kind enough, on the recommendation of the police, to stay with her and Margaret through the night. By the time the weekend came around again, the talk had faded and Amy's fears were set aside. She walked into the house with only the

183

slightest apprehension and knew that for her, the house was again her home – a safe haven after the busy day dealing with customers and wholesalers and being chivied by the constable to remove her vegetables from the pavement. Thanks to Victor, it was also a place where she could wrap herself in memories of love and shared happiness, even if that happiness was brief and stolen.

On the following Sunday Prue came out of hospital again and for the first time Amy felt encouraged. As soon as Prue came into the room, leaving Amy to pay the taxi, she concentrated on Sian. Margaret was in church and in the afternoon would be at Sunday School, followed by a rehearsal for the concert planned for later in the year. It left Amy and Prue together and instead of the day dragging by on long silences, Amy found to her delight that her sister seemed anxious to talk.

They chatted through the open door as she prepared lunch, adding an occasional word to Prue's remarks, wondering at the volume of words flowing from her sister. Thank goodness her days of total withdrawal seemed at an end.

Rationing had finally ended, with meat being freely available for the first time since March 1940. She put the large beef joint into the oven with a sigh of satisfaction. She would fill their plates with slices of the luxury and over-indulge with the rest of the nation. Contentedly, she began preparing the vegetables.

She had not told Prue about the robbery. It was unlikely the thief would be caught and the talk would have died down long before Prue was home again and living in the village. It was still a shock to her every time she thought about it but she had deliberately not discussed it with Margaret except when her daughter brought the subject up, and had then treated it like an adventure rather than a threat to their safety.

After they had eaten lunch and Margaret had gone back to the church, Netta Cartwright called. She was carrying a bag containing wool and needles and an assortment of patterns.

'Is Prue there?' she asked, as Amy invited her inside. 'I've called for her help.'

Netta was very like her son, Johnny, although she was built like a dumpling while he didn't have an ounce of spare flesh on his body. Nothing ever seemed to put Netta out of countenance and in this Johnny differed from her.

Quick to anger in defence of something unfair, Johnny had been a sworn enemy of Prue Beynon when she lived in the house near Mrs French and had spent much of her time looking out of her landing window watching and observing and, to the dismay of many, reporting and criticising what she saw. 'Nosy Old Bugger' was what Johnny called Prue Beynon.

Netta sympathised with his opinion but had always tried to befriend the woman who few could admit to liking. Now, with Prue ill and in a hospital for the mentally disturbed, Netta had come to try and bring Prue back into the life her illness had forced her to abandon. She opened her bag and handed Prue the soft, fine wool she had brought, and a pair of needles.

'Making for the sale of work we are, Prue,' she explained, 'and someone gave me this lovely wool. Too fine for me to knit. Two-ply and so fine it will knit up like lace in the hands of an expert. Can't attempt it myself. Would you be willing to make something for us? Church Hall Fund it is, as I expect Amy has told you. Best knitter we have in our sewing and knitting circle you are.'

Prue did not respond but Netta handed her some of the patterns she had brought, tapping the top one with a work-roughened finger. 'It's this baby frock I'd like to see made up. Two-ply, and such a beautiful

185

feather stitch. D'you think you could make it for us? Pride of place it would have, centrepiece for the stall. Pinned out on stiff blue paper so the pattern could be admired. Remember we did that last year with a shawl you'd made for us? Lovely work, that was.'

Prue put down the patterns and, ignoring both Amy and Netta, stared down at the baby propped up in the corner of the couch, wrapped in a shop-bought shawl and wearing a plain white dress. She did not say anything until Netta had gone. Then, when it was almost time for the taxi to call to take her back to the hospital, she picked up the wool, needles and the pattern of the fan-and-feather dress and put them in her handbag.

'Going to have a go, are you?' Amy smiled.

'Not for the stall!'

'Oh?' Amy crossed her fingers behind her back and held her breath as Prue said.'

'For Sian. Disgraceful you are, Amy, letting her be seen in shop-bought things and not even a bit of embroidery on her little dress.'

Amy apologised, reminding her sister that she was not as good at handwork as Prue. The complaint, coming from her sister was like a dream come true. It was the first time Prue had shown any sign of returning to normal. Tomorrow she would go and thank Netta and tell her how their plan had worked.

Later that evening Morgan Morgan called to collect Prue's accounts books and she found herself telling the young man about the horrifying events of the evening. He listened with comforting concern, his hazel eyes frowning with distress at her account of the robbery. Morgan Morgan was a quiet, serious-looking man in his early twenties who still had a school-boy look and long thin hands you expected to be covered with ink from writing in exercise books.

186

He was always neatly dressed and wore his brown hair firmly pressed into place with generous amounts of Vaseline Hair Tonic. There was about him, Amy thought with a smile, something of the old and faithful clerk, yet he was hardly more then twenty-two. She compared his old/young face with the more mature face of her son and for a moment wished Freddie were back to that innocence. He muttered the usual clichés, adding nothing that had not been said a dozen times by others and walked away, the books held under his arms in a firm grip that made the slender hands fade to whiteness around the knuckles.

So stiff and formal, and anxious to say and do the right thing, Amy judged. He was in danger of losing his identity altogether. Freddie might be a worry with his adult concern for Sheila, but at least he had a strong character and was not afraid to reveal it.

The horrors of the robbery faded but Amy was still uneasy for the period between turning off the downstairs lights and finally getting to sleep. She knew the likelihood of a repeat was minimal but feared hearing the sound of someone attempting to enter. She allowed Margaret to return to her own room, but wished she had both children within reach of her. The few yards seemed like miles each time a strange sound reached her tense ears and momentarily threatened their safety. Her nerves were on a switchback.

She touched the pillow beside her, imagining what it would be like to have Victor sleeping there. She smiled to herself: making love in the bed would certainly be a novelty. Perhaps marriage would be too tame for me, she mused. Loving in odd places has a certain magic. She thought of the couch and the floor beside the fireplace, and smiled as she drifted into sleep.

# Chapter Ten

Billie Brown was large, very strong and confident that whatever situation life faced him with he could cope. There had never been a time when he had not been able to. Tall, muscular, with broad shoulders and hands that were delicate enough to mend the smallest watch, yet were capable of hauling out the most stubborn tree root, he seemed to most men and women the essence of manhood. The exception to his calm confidence was Amy. She made him tremble inside and feel inadequate and gauche.

He had been distressed by the revelation that Victor had stayed overnight on two occasions and when he had discussed this with Mary, instead of reassuring him, she reminded him of Amy's past affairs with married man.

'Perhaps she prefers the fragility of an affair rather than a marriage that would be a permanent commitment,' she ventured. 'Not all women need the security of a marriage, and Amy has a good business and plenty of friends to help her when needed.'

'Amy isn't like that. She isn't what Mam would have called a "loose woman", Mary, and I don't think you should suggest she is.'

'I'm not saying she's loose but I do think she plays with the idea of marriage and prefers her freedom.'

'I want to marry her,' Billie said, and watched his sister's face to see if the idea worried her. 'You don't have to fear that your life will change, except you'd probably have less to do. Amy isn't the sort to be lazy and she'd soon be finding ways to help around here.'

Mary thought it very unlikely that Amy, with her pretty clothes and smart hairstyle, would enjoy the sort of work that kept Billie and herself busy for most of the hours of daylight, but she did not say so.

'Have you talked to her about living here?' she asked.

'No, no, only hinted, like.'

'Best you discuss it, explain what she would be taking on. It isn't fair not to tell her what you'd expect of her.'

Billie thought of the way he often saw Amy, laughing with Victor, sharing a foolish joke that he failed to see the humour of, Victor going to help her in the kitchen, fitting in with her wishes as if rehearsed. They looked so natural together it was hard to imagine himself in the same situation, although he, of course, would not help in the kitchen: that was woman's work.

It was late morning and a lull in his work gave him the impulse to walk up through the wooded hill overlooking the farm to where Nelly's cottage stood. He followed the stream then strode up through the trees and out at the top of Leighton's field from where he could look down on the village. He stood for a while, idly watching the traffic passing below him, then strolled past Nelly's cottage, where the dogs set up a chorus of barking, and made his dog snarl at them through their gate, then on to the furthest end of the village. Looking down at the toytown scene below he recognised Victor's van outside Amy's shop. He saw Victor get into the driving cab and move off, leaving Amy standing waving at him until the van passed out of her sight.

'This is ridiculous,' he said aloud. 'Today I must start to persuade her that her happiness lies with me.' Determination showing in his jutting chin, he walked briskly down Sheepy Lane and over to the shop. He saw that there were two customers inside and he leaned

190

against the wall, considering what he would say, what impression he wanted to give. It was simple on the face of it. He wanted to take Amy out, have exclusive right to her spare time, be a part of her life and take Margaret and baby Sian into his care. The first move was to take Amy out, just the two of them, somewhere where they could talk, but it seemed an impossible hurdle.

He had done all the usual things like call at the house, give help whenever he saw the opportunity, take her for a drink. It was not enough. If he were not careful he would lose her, if not to Victor, who wasn't free, then to someone else she met, who could appear and sweep her off her feet in a matter of weeks, while he was dithering like a gormless schoolboy.

Customers came and went and, if Amy had seen him standing nearby, she made no move to invite him inside. He stood, his head bent, eyes closed against dust disturbed by passing cars, and his mind drifted to his sister. She must be worried about how his marrying would affect her. She said so little about her thoughts and opinions. Mary only talked about her cows: worrying about fat content and whether the calf to be born would be male or female and what she would name it. The last two had been called Oliver and Margaret which had delighted the children enormously. The cows were Mary's family, but would she accept that Margaret and Amy might be his? And perhaps baby Sian as well? The farm needed children around but would his bringing them there ruin Mary's contentment?

He walked the few paces to the shop steps and saw Amy mopping the floor. He hesitated, looking down at his boots which were covered with drying mud. He stood on the top step and said, 'Hello, Amy, I wanted a word.'

'Come in, Billie, the shop is empty, for the moment at least.' She paused as she looked at his boots. 'Oh Billie, if it isn't your dog it's your muddy boots!'

He grinned and slipped them off, his feet, in their brown hand-knitted socks looking surprisingly large. She realised foolishly that a man's unshod feet were not a common sight for her.

She waited for him to tell her the reason for his call, and tidied up the cheese board and fussed with the stacks of greaseproof paper cut ready to wrap the pieces she sold.

'It's about Sunday,' he said at last. 'I was wondering if you and Margaret and Oliver would come to the farm and have tea. Mary makes lovely cakes.'

'Thank you Billie. Any particular reason? A birthday or something?' It was not an unusual occurence so she was curious to know why he had waited so long for the shop to be empty before coming in to invite her.

'No, no. Just I'd like to see you, and Margaret of course, for a chat.'

'Will you come and fetch us or shall we walk down?' she coaxed, sensing he wanted to add something more.

'I'll call and we can walk down through the fields. Margaret will like that, and young Oliver. I'll carry Sian, no trouble. All right?'

'All right,' Amy smiled. 'Was there something else?' He seemed quite ill at ease.

'No, no. Look, there's Netta Cartwright coming. See you on Sunday then, right?'

'What time?' Amy asked but he had slipped his feet into his boots and was already striding back across the road.

Amy was serving Netta with some knitting wool when she heard footsteps coming down the stairs from the flat above. The side door opened and Mavis and Ralph stepped out. They waved at Amy and, as they passed the shop door, Mavis called, 'We're going up to see Sheila. I'll be back to open up after lunch.' They crossed the road and walked up Sheepy Lane.

'I bet Sheila won't be pleased to see them. She's avoiding them. She knows they want her to come back to live with them.'

'I can't see why she doesn't, ' Netta said with a frown. 'Living up on the council houses with only a grandmother for company, it can't be much fun for a young girl.'

'I should think she's had enough fun for a while!' Amy said sharply.

'Young, she is,' Netta said gently, 'and having to face troubles most adults would find daunting.'

'You're right,' Amy admitted, 'but no matter what problems she's had, I still think she's brought them on herself. Tried to involve my Freddie in her disasters, didn't she? And what's more, she still is. D'you know he spent a week's leave with her and didn't come to see Margaret and me? No, it's no good, Netta, I can't feel much sympathy. I think she's one of those girls who'll go through life sliding from one mess into the next. My only fear is that she'll take Freddie with her.'

'He's a long way off most of the time and he'll probably out-grow her.'

'Perhaps, but not while she writes and pleads for his help. He got a twenty-four-hour pass and came home on compassionate grounds. Asked me to treat her like a daughter, would you believe? Me, befriend that one!'

'We all have times we don't want to look back on, or live through again.' Netta spoke in her whispering voice, but glancing at her Amy knew that although her rosy face was gentle and calm she was being reminded that she too had made mistakes.

'It's easy to forget our own mistakes, Netta, and pretend they were the fault of someone else. But when your children are involved it's different.'

'Give it time and see what happens. Freddie's so young.'

'So was I once, and like I'm sure you must, I wonder where the years have gone.'

Mavis and Ralph walked up the steep hill towards St Illtyd's Drive. The gardens were mostly planted with privet hedges and Mavis hoped these would shield the two of them from Sheila's view as they approached. She guessed, although she would never have admitted it, that if her daughter saw them coming, she would slip out of the back door, down the garden and across the fields.

It isn't as if we were forcing her to do anything, Mavis complained silently, we only want what's best for her like we always have.

Sheila had been a difficult child and Mavis and Ralph had tried to protect her by restricting her going out. They refused to allow her to join Youth Clubs or even go out with the girls with whom she worked except after they had been thoroughly vetted in a tense teatime interview. The result was that Sheila had been forced into lying, which she found enjoyably easy. She had invited only the most boring and well behaved girls home and had spent the rare evenings out with others who were more inclined to have fun. For Sheila, fun was synonymous with men.

Leaving Ralph to knock formally at the front door, Mavis did an undignified dash around the kitchen door where she found her daughter, a coat around her shoulders, about to leave.

'Hello, Mam, I can't stop. I've got to go to the shop for Gran. She wants some Aspros.'

'We'll go together, later,' Mavis said firmly. 'We want to talk to you. Now.'

'Oh, no. Is Dad there too?'

'Of course. We both want to help you decide what to do next. Now the sad episode of the baby is over, you must start making plans for the future.' As she spoke,

194

Mavis walked forward, forcing her daughter to walk out of the kitchen and into the hall, where Mavis opened the door and let Ralph inside.

'Sheila, glad we've caught you at last,' Ralph said. 'Is your Gran here?'

'Still in bed. She's got a bit of a cold. Call her, shall I?'

'Not yet,' Mavis said firmly. 'Come and sit down in the kitchen.' She pulled a chair from under the table and pressed Sheila down into it.

'When are you going back to work, Sheila?' Ralph asked. 'Best for you not to be idle for long.'

'What work? I gave up the job in the gown-shop when I left to have—when the baby was due.'

Ralph was embarrassed to see tears in Sheila's eyes and he turned away, defeated.

'All right, go and see the manageress. See if she'll have you back,' Mavis persisted. 'Sheila, you have to work. You can't hang around here looking after Gran. You're young and you want a career.'

'I don't want a career. I want a husband and a home of my own.'

'Well, you had a husband and see how far that got you!' Mavis was determined to make Sheila face facts and, unlike Ralph, was undeterred by their daughter's tearful face. 'Gone he is, that Maurice Davies, and you won't be seeing him again or I'm very mistaken. Bad lot, he was. Best for you to be clear of him but until you can end the marriage you'll have to get on with the rest of your life. Now, what would you like to do?'

Sheila shrugged and stared wistfully at the back door wishing she could get up and run out through it leaving her parents to pick the bones of her life over without her having to listen.

'What your father and I would like to do is either come back here where we all lived so happily, or persuade you to come and live with us at the flat. The choice is yours.

195

Working at the shop, I find the flat very convenient and your father's bus stop is only across the road, but you say what you want. Will you come to us, or shall we come back here?'

'Neither. I'm going away.'

It was an instantaneous remark. Crowded in by her parents, with the prospect of becoming their little girl once again, and with Gran there to guard her when both parents were out of the house, there was nothing else she could do. To her startled parents, she repeated, 'I'm leaving Hen Carw Parc and won't be bothering either of you again.'

'No you aren't,' Ralph began, rising from his chair.

'Hush, Ralph,' Mavis said, then, turning to Sheila asked, 'What will you do? Where will you go?'

'I'll tell you when I've decided.'

'Not going to Australia to find that Maurice Davies, are you?'

'Of course not, I'm not a fool!'

'Don't talk to me like that,' Ralph protested, but Mavis hushed him with a scowl.

'Tell me where you're going. Perhaps we can help if we can't persuade you to change your mind.'

'You won't change my mind.'

'Then come back home for a while, just till you decide.' Mavis pleaded. 'Shamed we'd be, if you went off and us not trying to persuade you different.'

'Mam, I really have to go out. Gran wants some Aspros and Amy shuts for lunch.'

'We'll walk down with you. Come back and have a bite of lunch with us before I open the shop. I've got a nice tin of salmon and we could have a bit of salad.'

'No thanks, I'll come straight back. Go and talk to Gran while I get ready.' She put on the abandoned coat and brushed her hair while Mavis and Ralph went in to see Mavis's mother. When they returned to the kitchen, Sheila had gone.

Sheila ran down the garden and out into the fields. Without any idea where she was going she turned down towards Sheepy Lane and was soon behind Ethel Davies's house. She was about to pass it, not wanting to talk to anyone but the thought that Ethel might have received a letter from Maurice persuaded her to call and so she went through the weakest part of Ethel's hedge, where, as boys, Maurice and his brothers had pushed their way through to play in the fields.

She called as she approached the house, watching the door to see if Ethel was about, unaware of the beauty of the long narrow garden with its beds of annuals filling the air with sweet perfume. Paeonies and petunias, sweet williams and sweet peas were all in organised displays between neat patches of grass. Marigolds and nasturtiums had taken over the odd corners and grew in wild profusion and, even from the walls, flowers sprouted and added to the richness of the exhibition.

Although she was unable to work in the garden because of her arthritis, Ethel's sons helped to keep it filled with flowers and free from weeds, but Sheila saw none of it: her eyes watched the door and her feet trod the only straight and orderly thing in the garden, the stone-flagged path between the clothes-line posts.

Ethel sat in a chair near the sink, peeling potatoes. She smiled a welcome as Sheila appeared, pushing the door wider and offering her a chair. 'There's lovely to see you, Sheila. Staying for a while, are you? What about some lunch. There's some cheese, onion and potato pie with salad, how will that be?'

'Thank you, I'd like that.'

Sheila sat down and watched as, hardly moving from her chair, Ethel expertly reached out to shelves and

197

drawers to set the table before asking Sheila to take from the oven the freshly cooked pie.

'Meat off ration at last, and there's me still making do with old cheese and onion pie. I can't get used to the idea that we can order as much meat as we want.'

'Free of ration, we are, but the price still restricts it as far as Gran and I are concerned,' Sheila said.

'Have you thought what you'll do, love?' Ethel asked as Sheila finished her simple meal. 'About working I mean. Going back to the shop, are you?'

'The salon, you mean?' Sheila asked. Why did these people always reduce everything to the ordinary? It was a gown-shop or a salon. To call it a shop made it sound like a place to buy groceries, like Amy's.

'The gown-salon, yes,' Ethel said patiently. 'Saleswoman you were and that's a good position for someone as young as you to have achieved, for sure.'

'I think I'm moving away.'

'Oh? That's nice, so long as it's somewhere comfortable. Living on your own is very expensive if you want somewhere decent, and I'm sure you would.' Ethel's deep-set eyes watched the girl, wanting to help but afraid that a wrong word would send her out through the door faster than she had entered. Touchy she was, easily offended. She thinks us a lot of idiots. She smiled to herself. She thinks us incapable of doing anything but what our mothers told us, slipping back to how things were in 1939. If only she could be persuaded to relax and talk.

'Tell me what you hope to do,' she coaxed. 'You don't want to leave here before you have somewhere nice to stay.'

'I'll be all right. I—'

The sound of the front door opening wider on the flagstones made Sheila stop talking and look up in relief. She had been saying too much. The less her parents got to hear about her plans the better. Not that she had anything definite in mind, but news spread in this village like a puffed dandelion clock. She stood to go, taking her coat from the back of a chair as Ethel's son came in. Phil-the-Post took off his hat and bag and threw them on to a chair.

'Cup of tea, Mam. I'm gasping!' Coming in from the sunshine, he failed to see Sheila for a moment, then he grinned and added, 'Unless young Sheila's drunk it all.' He placed a letter on the table. 'Letter here from Australia, Mam, perhaps Sheila ought to—' Too late he saw the frown and the shake of Ethel's head.

The letter lay on the white cloth, temptingly close to Sheila, who waited in the hope that Ethel would let her see the contents.

'If there's an address,' Sheila said, 'just so I could let him know about the baby and how I am, he might like to hear—'

'There's been no address, love. Just a note telling me he's alive and still looking for work. He doesn't know about the baby. We haven't been able to tell him.' She reached up to a teapot behind which were several envelopes. 'You can read them if you like, just so you know we aren't keeping anything from you.' Ethel opened the new letter and handed them all to Sheila. They would hurt her, not having a word about her or a request for news of his baby, but she had to show Sheila that she was not lying to her, she had to try and persuade the girl to trust her, treat her like a friend.

Sheila was so excited and tense she hardly took in a word and had to begin again. She really needed someone to read the letters to her so she could concentrate on the words and not have the thought that the paper had come from Maurice's hands affecting her mind. And then there was the realisation it had been sent not to her but to his mother. That thought hurt her and made the thin paper quiver in her hands.

The newly arrived letter was brief: only two short paragraphs telling Ethel Maurice was well and at last working in a garage but hoping for something more interesting soon. He sent love to his brothers and to his mother but did not mention Sheila at all. As Ethel had said, there was no address, only the promise that as soon as he was settled in a permanent place he would let them know. Sheila dropped the flimsy note on to the table and walked out.

She walked towards town without any particular goal in mind but a bus passed her and, although it was not an official stop, Johnny was driving and he drew to a halt for her to get on. In Llangwyn she walked away from the shops and, when she reached the school where Delina Honeyman lived, she paused. A glance at her watch told her there was little more than an hour before school closed and she decided to wait.

A cafe helped her to pass the time and a brief visit to the library where she wrote a letter to Freddie. She posted the letter and stood outside the school to watch as the children ran out, shouting their delight at the freedom, some carrying paintings they had done that day, others hurriedly stuffing cardigans and coats into satchels and small cases.

Delina was almost the last to leave and Sheila had almost decided that she was absent from school that day, when she saw her wheeling her bicycle out from the rear of the building and walking towards her. She was pretty, Sheila grudgingly admitted. 'Her hair a golden mane and eyes of hyacinth-blue': she had read the description recently in a magazine story and remembered it.

'Delina, can I have a word?' Sheila said when it was obvious the girl was going to pass her without a glance.

'I don't think so,' Delina said politely. 'There's nothing I want to hear from you.'

'I wanted to tell you how sorry I am for what happened,

200

now the baby is dead and I'm all alone. It seems so cruel, me having to marry a man who didn't love me and only used me, and you being all alone, like me.'

She had chosen her approach well and Delina moved closer. 'I'm sorry too, Sheila, but you aren't the cause of me being alone. Maurice was completely to blame. After all, you were very young.'

'And with no experience of men.' Sheila was glad she had come out in a hurry and not changed from the dowdy brown skirt that was too long and the loose blouse which disguised her large breasts.

'Have you heard from him?' she asked as Delina pushed her bicycle alongside her to the curb. 'Maurice, I mean.'

'No.' Delina said firmly. 'At least, yes I have in a way. There was a letter arrived yesterday but I put it straight into the ash-bin.'

'Best place too.' Sheila began to walk away. 'Well, that's all I wanted to say.' She looked back as Delina mounted her bicycle, then wandered off to get the bus home.

Later that night, when it was dark enough for her not to be easily recognised, Sheila crept around the side of Delina's house and carefully lifted the lid off the ash-bin. She found the letter in a puddle of baked beans and, wiping it off on the grass, joyfully took it home.

Delina was restless after Sheila had spoken to her. The brief conversation had brought the memories flooding back. She had deliberately pushed all thoughts of the fiasco of their wedding plans away from her. But the wedding dress her family had bought for her was still wrapped in blue tissue, hanging in the wardrobe with the white sandals, and the apple-blossom head-dress was still tucked away in a drawer. She took them all out and looked at them, running her fingers across the beautiful material, placing the head-dress on her soft golden hair. Would she ever feel the same about someone else, or had the experience frozen her for ever?

After she had helped her mother clear away the dishes, she went to where she had parked her bicycle. She was restless and, although she had preparations for school to do, she wanted to ride for a while to try and clear any thoughts of the marriage-that-nearly-was out of her mind.

She free-wheeled down Hywel Rise, enjoying the breeze on her body cooling her, feeling it cleansing her of the day's rush and emptying her mind of worries. She saw the cat as a blur of black rolling across the road and before she could react a child ran out in pursuit of it. She shouted and pulled on her brakes at the same time, but the gravel on the road succeeded in unseating her and she fell beside the bicycle, the wheels still spinning. She jumped up and began to shout at the girl who stared back defiantly and began to shout for her father.

'Oh, it's you, Dawn Simmons. Don't you think you should look before running out into the road?' Delina said, her voice restrained, her eyes darting anxious looks at the door of Dawn's house, dreading another encounter with the ill-mannered Tad.

She picked up the bicycle which was scratched and twisted, and straightened it out by holding the front wheel between her legs and tugging on the handlebars. Dawn had disappeared and as Delina remounted and tried out the machine for damage, a shadow covered the road in front of her and Dawn's father stood there.

'You careless, unfeeling woman. Not only almost running my daughter down, you don't even ask if she's harmed. What d'you think this is, a race-track?'

'I assure you I was not the one at fault, Mr Simmons,' she said hotly. 'Your daughter ran out after a cat and gave me no chance. It was fortunate for her I do *not* use the road as a race- track or she might have been hurt. As it is, I am the one to have been hurt.' She looked down to where a trickle of blood was moving slowly down her shin. Tad appeared not to see.

'A cat?' he said. 'We don't have a cat. Dawn? Did you see a cat?'

'No Dad, we haven't got one, have we?'

'But she did!'

'Was there a cat, Dawn?'

'No, Dad.' Dawn did not even blush.

'So, if you come this way again make sure you ride with care and consideration for others.' Tad turned sharply away from her and walked back inside, leaving a grinning Dawn watching her. Delina burst into tears and, pushing hard on the pedals, rode off down the hill, leaving a gathering of interested onlookers to discuss the affair with few facts and lots of imagination.

Sheila read the letter Maurice had written to Delina with dismay. He really had loved Delina, she thought, as she read his pleading request for her to join him in Australia. There was an address, something he had not given his mother, believing no doubt that Ethel would have felt obliged to pass it on to Sheila if she had asked. But the crumpled, bean-soaked paper was easily read and Sheila sat down to write to him.

She wrote first about the baby, long sentences about the loneliness and the devastation at losing their child. She went on to remind him of the sex they had shared, the skills he had taught her and which she missed so very much, there being no one else with whom she wanted to share such bliss. She implied that she and Delina were friends and that it was Delina who had given her his address. Then she explained that Delina had found someone new and it was she, Sheila, who held for him undying love. She pleaded and grovelled and begged him to send for her and told him repeatedly that she forgave him for running out on her, insisting she understood how devastated he had been.

'Put it all in the past where it belongs,' she pleaded. 'Let me come out to share your life,' and she signed the letter 'your ever devoted and loving wife, Sheila.'

She closed the envelope quickly before she changed her mind about sending it. Childish it might be and with sentences that wouldn't be out of place in some of the romantic stories she enjoyed reading, but he surely could not fail to be roused by it. The next day, she posted the letter in Llangwyn, in case Phil-the-Post noticed the addresses when he emptied the post boxes.

In Hen Carw Parc in 1954 it was frowned upon for a woman to go into a public house alone. To appear respectable, a woman needed to be accompanied by a man. Amy frequently broke the unwritten rule and Sheila was about to do the same. She was restless after writing to Maurice, wondering how long she would have to wait for a reply, if he ever did respond to it. Surely he wouldn't ignore the news about the loss of the baby who, unknowingly, had caused so much trouble? Ethel had heard from him but had been unable to write to tell him what had happened. It was fitting, Sheila thought, that he received the news from her, his legal if unwanted wife.

She had gone over in her mind the words she had used and wondered if she could have made it more dramatic. She had tried not to sound accusing but intended to make him feel a sympathy for her and admiration for the way she had coped, alone. She daydreamed about how she would casually mention hearing from him, showing the letter to Delina and to Ethel, without allowing them to know the contents. Whatever tone he responded in, she would let it be known that he had contacted her. That was a pleasure in store even if his reply was cold and brief. They would see the envelope and know he had written to her.

She ordered a shandy and sat down near the empty grate to sip it. It was lunchtime and there were few customers except those waiting to see Griff to hand him their bets and for the lucky ones to receive yesterday's winnings. A bunch of flowers in a copper bucket filled the stone hearth and dropped yellow pollen on to the dusty surface of the grate. She pulled out a marguerite daisy and began pulling out the petals as a child would: he loves me, he loves me not. But who, she wondered, loved her best? Maurice who had flown from her bed rather than become her husband, or Freddie Prichard, who in spite of his youth, loved her deeply enough to ignore her past mistakes?

Two of Freddie's friends came in and she called across to them. 'Hello Pete, hello Gerry, where are your bikes? I didn't hear you drive up in your mad-cap way.' She would not normally bother to talk to them, for they were almost as young as Freddie but far too immature for her taste. They were red-faced with black hair which they plastered down with grease, bristles showing uneasily amid spots. She shuddered: how could they step outside their door looking like that? But she was in need of company and did not object when Pete Evans came to sit next to her. He pulled put a flat, folded roll of pound and ten-shilling notes which he waved in front of her eyes.

'Want a drink?' he grinned, then, as Sheila opened her mouth to ask for a vodka, which she thought sounded mature and worldly, he pushed the wad back into his pocket and, standing, said, 'If you want one you can get your own.' He laughed and rejoined Gerry at the bar.

Sheila gave them both an icy stare and looked around the room for someone with whom she could share her disgust. In the far corner, half hidden by the flowers, she

205

saw Constable Harris and as he looked at her, she raised her eyes skywards in a gesture of disapproval. Constable Harris just nodded and went back to the paper he was reading.

Archie Pearce left Griff and stood near the two boys, accepting the pint they offered him with surprise.

'Were you two boys out late last night?' Archie asked, his lips rimmed with foam. 'Don't sleep too well these nights and I thought I heard a couple of bikes like yours zooming around the lanes and down the main road. You two, was it?'

'No, man, our bikes is out of service and have been for a week or more.' Pete leaned over so he could see the policeman and said, 'Hear that, mate? Mystery bikes roaming the countryside and at night too. Perhaps they're the burglars you're supposed to be searching for, looking for likely places to burgle. Should be looking for them, shouldn't you mate?'

'Damn, I wish I hadn't mentioned it now,' Archie said with a groan. 'No sooner than I start to feel better about going home, someone mentions burglars and I start to shake.'

'Don't worry, Pop, we'll walk home with you tonight, won't we Pete?'

'Don't call me Pop,' Archie said, hanging on to his glass in case they took it off him.

'And don't call me mate!' Constable Harris closed his paper. 'Now, what's this about a late night motor-cyclist?'

'We've heard them too,' Gerry said, his urgent expression making him look even younger than his sixteen years. His face was redder than normal, the dark eyes staring and wide. Here they were, talking to the police, and them under the legal age for drinking.

'I'll call over later, after you've finished work and have a look at those motor-bikes of yours,' Harris said slowly. 'Yes, and perhaps glance at your birth certificates while I'm there.' He stood beside them threateningly as they finished their drinks and disappeared around the door. He chuckled and leaned on the bar beside Archie.

'They aren't bad kids, Constable,' Archie said. 'Bought me a drink and offered to go back with me tonight if I was worried. Still half expecting another burglary, I am.'

'Mrs Dorothy Williams wasn't expecting one but an hour ago, when she got back from the sewing circle in the church, she found her house open and all the cash she had missing.'

'Damn me, another one!' Archie spluttered. 'I'll be too afraid to go to work soon!'

'Mrs Williams,' Sheila said, 'well, she's got plenty. Not as bad as taking from Archie the little he had.'

'It's all stealing, Sheila,' Harris said. 'And I only hope we catch them soon. It's getting to be a real worry.'

'Them? You know who it is?'

'No, but I'm beginning to get a picture of them. I believe there's at least two, and talk about motor-bikes in the night makes me think I know how they get about. Easy to ride and they can even cross fields if they need to. Now, not a word, Sheila, or you, Archie. But if you hear them bikes again, just let me know. Right?'

The constable went out, his slow stride clearly heard as he crossed the concrete forecourt, until he reached the place where he had left his bicycle leaning against the wall. Then he gave a shout of rage and came running back inside.

'Someone has stolen my bicycle!' he stormed.

Sheila ran out with others in time to see Pete riding the constable's bike with Gerry sitting on the cross-bar.

'It's all right, Constable, only a joke,' they laughed.

'Perhaps it was to take your mind off their motor-bikes,' Sheila whispered to Constable Harris as he waited for his property to be returned.

# Chapter Eleven

Constable Harris walked along the lane behind Amy's shop, almost to the back of Milly's daughter's fish-and-chip shop. He stopped at the gate of Griff Evans's house and went in. It was quite early and the streets were quiet, with the children not yet leaving for school. There was something about an early call that put people off their stroke, he always thought. Maybe it was the unwashed breakfast things and the crumbs on the table cloth, or the hair not yet combed and the apron covering the work-skirt used to clean the grate of the previous evening's ashes. Whatever the reason, Harris knew it had happened again when Hilda Evans opened the back door to his knock. She glanced back into the house as if deciding whether it was possible to invite him in and avoid him seeing the mess in her kitchen.

'Come in, Constable.' Hilda pushed ineffectually at the hair just removed from Dinkie curlers and in small tight rolls around her head. 'There's early you're calling. No trouble, is there?'

'Trouble? No. I just want to have a look at your son's motor-bike, see if he's got the lights working. Had a complaint about a bike being ridden without lights, that's all.' He shook his hands, palms up as if to say it was a trivial thing and not his decision, but he was simply following the instructions of less acute men.

'Lights not working?' Mrs Evans laughed, showing her white artificial teeth, incongruous in her dark and wrinkled face. 'Damn it all, Constable, nothing's working! Them two boys, my Pete and Gerry, they've never finished working on those bikes. Always a pile of pieces on the shed bench, those bikes are, and that's where you'll find them now.' She laughed again, relief that it was nothing more serious making the laughter unnecessarily loud.

'Do you mind if I look?' Harris asked politely.

'Of course, come and look!'

She led him down the garden where rows of cabbages, potatoes and runner beans and an assortment of salad vegetables grew in orderly rows.

'Not much for flowers, your Griff, is he?' Harris remarked.

'Saves a lot of money, growing food. Not much pay at the forestry,' Hilda explained. 'But it's me who does most of it, mind.'

The shed was half hidden by a screen of honeysuckle growing along a trellis fence. Flowers were faded now but still with a hint of scent on the air.

'I won't let Griff pull this down,' she said proudly. 'Brought it with me when I married and kept it through three moves, I have.' She opened the door of the shed and ushered him inside. 'There they are, look. Lights working? That's a laugh! Griff says they should sell the bikes and buy a Meccano set each. That's what they really want, something to fiddle with and pull about every five minutes.'

The building was large and in poor condition, its corrugated iron walls showing rust and, in places, holes, where the weather had defeated it. But at the furthest end, near the double doors which led out into the lane, was a huge bench on which Constable Harris recognised the pieces of an engine. Alongside the bench, on cardboard boxes opened flat were the wheels and mudguards and other more complicated parts of the two machines.

210

In an old biscuit tin, soaking in what he guessed was paraffin, were the chains. He laughed.

'I see what you mean about wanting a Meccano set! How often are the bikes like this?'

'How many months in a year?' Hilda sighed. 'All their working days in a garage and all their spare time messing about with these. Can't understand the attraction myself. They do get them going sometimes, mind, but most of the time this is where they are, spread out like a jigsaw puzzle over the shed and even the garden. Griff gets mad and tells them to get the place cleared, but you know what boys are like, Constable. Never take a blind bit of notice, do they?'

Constable Harris scratched out the boy's names from the list he had written in his notebook and left. Too bad the slight suspicion he had nurtured since seeing that money in Pete's hand had come to nothing. He had learnt at the garage where the boys worked that they had been delivering motor-bikes to a customer and had collected the payment.

He wouldn't have really wanted it to be a couple of the local boys who were carrying out the robberies. Best if it was someone from outside the village. He never had a moment's trouble working among these people and a local arrest might changes things. Getting on his bicycle, he went home to make himself a bacon sandwich. Butter he'd have on the bread. Now it was off ration, he would spread it till it dribbled out and on to the plate in golden splashes.

The farm run by Billie and his sister Mary was not large. The buildings, apart from the new and splendid cow house and milking parlour, were whitewashed ex-cottages and stone-built sheds from over a hundred years before. There was a huge woodpile against one of the out-houses and an axe sticking out of a piece of wood ready for Billie to use.

The farmhouse itself was very large, a rambling building with windows looking out over the hills which rolled up on all sides. The stream ran close by and, in the distance, looking towards Hen Carw Parc, the ruins of the old castle could occasionally be seen. When the trees in the woods lost their leaves and the grasses and wild flowers fell back into their winter rest, the ancient stones stood out, a sombre grey amid the yellows and greens.

Billie walked up through the fields and called for Amy and the children at two o'clock, while Amy was putting the dishes away after their Sunday lunch. She was flushed from the kitchen heat, her blonde hair a little awry. Billie thought she had never looked more beautiful, or desirable. She wished he could have told her so – he even tried – but with Margaret and Oliver asking question about the various activities of the farm he could not. Instead he mumbled about the beautiful day and how nice Margaret looked in her new green print dress.

He waited while Amy went upstairs to change from the beige skirt and sleeveless blouse she had worn to do her weekend housework, and smiled his pleasure as she returned. She wore a cap-sleeved dress with a low vee neck, a tight waist and a full skirt. The small belt in the same coral linen as the dress made her small waist look even tinier and Billie imagined he could span it easily with his hands. He was fascinated by her small waist. The rest of her was curvy, yet she had this smallness that made him feel protective. He straightened up to his full height and smiled to himself. He was beginning to act like a man about to charge dragons in defence of his love.

His large hands cradled the baby against his chest and his dark eyes looked down at her with such gentleness, that Amy, as she went to take Sian to dress her, was overcome with affection for him. He really was a gentle giant of a man and if she married him he would care for them all with devotion. The thought made her light-hearted and as they set out they were all chattering gaily, Margaret and Oliver hand in hand in front and Amy beside Billie, who carried Sian.

Billie's heart was swollen with happiness as he strode out with them. He imagined how wonderful life would be if he were a part of this group every day of his life. He had to make her forget Victor. He *had* to, He needed to wake each morning and see Amy's fair head beside him, her blue eyes watching him – or perhaps she would still be sleeping and he would go downstairs and bring her a cup of tea which she would drink while he sat beside her on the big bed. He did not realise he was smiling, until Margaret asked, 'What are you laughing at, Uncle Billie?'

Billie turned to see that Amy was smiling too. 'It's a lovely day,' he laughed.

'It isn't,' Margaret said. 'It's cold and the sun won't wake up.'

'A lovely day because I'm enjoying myself,' Billie explained with a shy glance at Amy.

They walked along the banks of the river, wandering without any hurry towards the farmhouse where Mary had prepared tea for them all. When they reached the front door, she opened it for them and smiled a welcome.

'Lovely to see you all,' she said, taking the baby from Billie and putting her on the big settee. 'I hope you're hungry after your walk?'

The table was spread with a white cloth and, on large blue-rimmed plates, Mary had set out an assortment of sandwiches, pasties and scones as well as jellies and blancmange, which she knew Oliver and Margaret loved. The children wanted to begin at once but Mary had other plans.

'Before we eat I want to take you to see the lambs, show you how they've grown,' she said. 'We'll leave Sian here with your mother, Margaret, and you and Oliver can help me bring them down from the top field for Uncle Billie. He wants to make sure they're all marked,' she explained as she led them out. 'Won't be long, you two. Why don't you show Amy the house, Billie?'

It was so contrived that Billie felt embarrassed. But he picked up Sian and said, 'Might as well have a look at the old place while you're here.' He waited until Amy followed, then led her up the long staircase to the first floor.

To Amy, the place seemed to be a warren of corridors and odd spaces which made the place more like a film set for an historical story rather than a place where two people lived. Corridors opened out on to wide landings on which a piece of furniture had been placed to fill the emptiness: a chair, or a small chest of drawers and even in one place, a small *chaise-longue*.

'I have to keep looking out of the windows to see where we are,' Amy laughed. 'All these long passageways makes me lose my sense of direction.'

Most of the rooms had furniture although they did not feel as if they were ever used. She wondered, as Billie explained about his ancestors, what it would have been like to have been born into a large family such as the one this house had been originally built for.

'Seventeen children they had, the couple who built it, but it goes back even further than that, as they used an older house to start with, building on and adding room after room as the family and wealth grew.'

'It's facinating. I can see that a place like this would soon grow on you. Be like wearing a well loved coat,' Amy laughed. 'But, being practical, who does all the work?'

'Mary mostly. We have someone in a few times a year to go through it all, and when it comes to decorating, well, I do that.'

'But it's so much to look after.' She thought of how much time it took to keep her own small house clean and shining.

214

'Not really. In fact, if someone came here, they wouldn't have to do anything they didn't want to.' His eyes slid away from her and he added, 'It can be what ever you wanted it to be, a house like this. A burden or a joy. We can afford for someone to do all the work if necessary. I can't imagine it being a burden, not ever. And it's a happy house. I don't think anyone living here has been anything but happy.'

'I can believe that,' Amy said.

He went ahead of her again, opening a door on a big, sunny room which, facing south must, Amy decided, have a warmth and light that some of the other, back rooms, might lack. The furniture was heavy but as there was not too much of it, the dark polished wardrobe and chests did not fill the room and hide its beauty. It was a beautiful room, with three tall narrow windows covered with casement lace and chintzy gold, cream and blue floor-length curtains.

Amy felt the atmosphere thicken and Billie stood closer to her as she stood looking out of the window to where fields rose towards the woodland. It was so still, not even a tree-top moved in the late afternoon. The sounds coming from the children below, whooping and playing were cut off, distant, leaving Amy with the sensation of being alone with Billie in an isolated world into which they had intruded. She became conscious of Billie breathing faster than normal. His eyes were upon her and she moved, only a fraction, but he reached out and held her arm, the baby still cradled contentedly in the other.

'Amy.' He reached out clumsily and, startled, she turned so the intended kiss touched her cheek. He's an amateur and so am I! she thought foolishly as he tried once again to find her lips and, for a moment his mouth trembled against hers, a slight pressure but no conviction making it little more than a feathery salute

215

such as a stranger might give at some silly party game.

'Amy, could you live here with me?' She stopped his words with a kiss that was sweet and full of promise. She knew what he had been about to say and she was not ready to reply. She forgot Victor and everything else in the demands of his kiss, surprised at his new-found strength. He forced her head back, his lips moving against hers in sensual rhythms that spread to her body and made her want to sway, and press herself against him. Sounds from below ceased and there was nothing except the two of them. She brought herself back to earth with a stunned gasp, with the baby separating them and his hand just resting on her waist. How could she feel like this? It was Victor she loved.

'We'd better go down,' she said breathlessly. She was confused and needed to clear her mind.

'I want to look after you, Amy. You and Margaret and Freddie. We'd be such a happy family, living here.'

Amy slipped out of his one-handed embrace and sat on the edge of the over-stuffed bed. 'I don't think this is something we can discuss now. Let you and me meet one day soon and talk about how we feel. I – I don't feel free to promise anything. I have to be honest with you, Billie.'

'Victor, isn't it?'

'Victor, and the fear of such an enormous change in my life.'

He bent down and lifted her to her feet and tried again to kiss her, his arm holding Sian, the other hand on her shoulder. Amy found it very unsatisfactory and in a sudden impulse wrapped her arms around him after placing the baby on the floor at their feet. She wrapped her arms around his broad shoulders and pressed her body tightly against his and kissed him as she expected to be kissed.

She felt him react sharply, jerking himself away from her before surrendering with a low groan and slipping

216

into the exciting sensation of two people coming together in love. She rolled against him, and felt his body responding before she breathlessly eased herself away and stared up into eyes that were dark with passion. She knew that once he had been released from his inhibitions he would be an impossible man to hold back. The thought did not greatly displease her.

They went downstairs, Amy laughing as she constantly went along the wrong corridors, looking out of every window they passed, running briefly into each room to look out and check on their progress, and making both Billie and Sian laugh. They reached the kitchen where Mary and the two children were preparing the big teapot and setting out the sugar and milk in the blue bordered china.

Excusing herself she went back up the stairs to the bathroom. She had been excited by Billie and the thought of teaching him about love made her want to spend a few moments by herself before she went down to face Mary and the others. She must take things slowly. Impulse and the desire for love had brought her little happiness in the past and she had recently broken a promise she had made to herself never to start another affair with a married man. She must not let her body dictate to her. Billie was a temptation, but was he a man she could spend the rest of her life with? The corridor was dark and chilly and she shivered as she thought how easy it would be to succumb to the needs of her body and ignore the warnings of her mind.

The bathroom had been a bedroom, with little done to change its appearance. There was a white bath on curled feet against the far wall, a wash-basin and toilet against another and a large tiled fireplace, still open and obviously used to heat the room against the chill of winter on a third. The window was near the wash-basin and had curtains, not frosted glass, with towelling curtains decorated with pictures of fish and boats and sea-shells. This would have to be changed, she decided, shivering in the sunless room. It was at the back of the building and would probably be like a refrigerator for half of the year. Yes, she would change – she stopped her thoughts with a groan. Once again she was rushing into something without careful thought, her body deceiving her into believing she had found her future love. She washed her hands and sighed. If only Freddie were home. She would be able to discuss it with him and, although he was only sixteen, he would understand her dilemma and make her see all sides of the situation. She reapplied her makeup and returned down the stairs to the welcome fire.

Billie was sitting in the wooden settle and the children were already at the table. She sat where Mary gestured, beside the place set for Billie. Mary sat at the furthest end of the big table, near the teapot and the loaf of homemade bread, ready to replenish when necessary.

Amy did not eat much. She was tense, and guilt at leading Billie on, and even at allowing her own thoughts to race towards a commitment, washed over her at regular intervals. She sensed his eyes on her and across the table she knew that his sister too was watching her, trying to read the signs and know what had happened during the time she had taken the children to see the lambs.

Mary's face remained impassive, trying to guess from Billie and Amy if the big ungainly house had discouraged Amy from thinking of it as a future home as she desperately hoped, or whether Billie had persuaded her with talk of the money available to modernise it that the place was a perfect place for her to bring her children. A farm, especially on a pleasant summer's day, was deceptively beautiful and peaceful. She smiled and laughed with Billie as he talked to the children, and hoped she did not show that she was chilled by the thought of the upheaval and eventual banishment that Billie's marriage would bring her.

218

Billie drove them all home, dropping Oliver off before driving out of the village to Amy's home. 'Shall I stay while you put the children to bed?' he asked, but Amy shook her head.

'I still have work to do. Morgan will be calling in with Prue's books, which I'm supposed to look through every weekend but never do. And there's the orders to write out and the accounts not yet done. I'll be busy till eleven o'clock as it is. Best we leave things for today, Billie.'

'Won't you let me help?'

Again she shook her head and he saw the determination in her eyes and lowered his shoulders, accepting defeat. 'Perhaps you're right.' He stood for a moment, wanting to say something more, wanting to end the afternoon on a positive note but unable to find the words. To take the steam out of the situation, Amy asked lightly, 'Who made your pullover, Billie?'

'Mary.' The mundane remark startled him, then he seemed to guess her intention and added, 'Looks after me well, Mary does. But Amy, it isn't enough. I want a wife and a family to work for and plan for. Don't try to talk about pullovers when I'm asking you to marry me.'

He left soon after, with Amy's promise to meet him soon and discuss how they felt about each other. As soon as the sound of his car faded, there was a knock at the door and Victor stood there.

'Where have you been, Amy? I've tried ringing you and now I've waited two hours.'

'Is something wrong?'

'Yes, there is something wrong. You've spent the day with that rich farmer, Billie Brown, that's what's wrong.'

She was angry. 'What business is it of yours?' she demanded. 'I go where I like and with whom I like. You haven't the right to ask me where I've been or criticise my friends!'

'I can't help hating it when you go off with that farmer. Amy, love, I know I can't offer you anything yet, but don't give up on me, please.'

Amy's blue eyes darted from his face to the kitchen door, warningly. 'Margaret is in there,' she hissed. 'Now go, I don't want to stand here arguing with you. I've got work to do.' She closed the door before he could add anything more.

She had not got any further than the end of the hall when the door bell went again. She jerked the door open, intending to give Victor a firm telling-off, and the man who stood there took several paces backwards.

'Oh, it's you, Morgan. Called for the books have you? I haven't done more than glance at them,' she apologised, handing them to him. 'But I'm sure everything is fine in your capable hands.'

'Thank you, Mrs Prichard.' He backed nervously away and almost ran down the drive, causing her to smile. 'Getting to be an old nag, I am,' she said to Margaret. 'Shouting at poor Uncle Victor just because I've got a lot to do.'

Amy did not sleep well that night. She was restless and wide awake, trying to read, trying to think about the following day's work, and making imaginary lists of things she should do. Then, at three o'clock, she rose and made a cup of tea. She sat looking out of the window and watched dawn break, the trees in silhouette at the top of the hill behind the house, the sky changing from grey to yellow to pink and finally to blue as she sat there.

Sian woke and she took her downstairs to feed her, sitting in the semi-dark, with the window wide open and the chill clean air of the morning flowing around her. Sian, wrapped in a soft, fluffy woollen shawl was cosily pressed against her, but the fresh air made the little nose red and Amy reluctantly put her back in her cot. She felt the need to cuddle the baby, the need to feel someone

220

close and dependant. The phone was in the hall and for a while she was tempted to ring Billie, to talk to him and hear his voice telling her he loved her, but she did not.

She sat back in her chair and allowed her thoughts to drift luxuriously. First to the big farmhouse and the image of living there with no accounts to do and no orders to write out. The remainder of the order, which she had not done on the previous evening, brought Victor to mind. Sadness filled her. How could she think of marrying Billie when there was Victor?'

They had spent so little time together, with nothing but a few brief stolen kisses and a touch of hands when they were certain of not being observed, then the breathlessly wonderful nights together after the robbery. She wondered if it was the illegality of loving Victor that made him so much more exciting than Billie. The kisses she had shared with Billie had been disappointing until she had brazenly shown him how. The remembered kiss from Victor at Christmas, with half the village in Ethel's house looking on, had given her more of a thrill. Something had grown between them, unbidden, unwanted but undeniably strong. Some wicked fairy must have been present at my birth and mixed up love and passion so I'll never straighten out my love-life, she thought wryly.

Sian cried and she remembered how gentle Billie was with her, taking the tiny child in his huge hands as carefully as he would hold a butterfly wing. She pulled at her hair in frustration. Why couldn't she accept what Billie was offering her? In many countries women were not allowed a choice but told who they would marry. If that were the case, Billie would be the choice in place of Victor on all counts; availability and prospects, and, she realised honestly, for his great and genuine love for her.

After she'd settle Sian, she ran a bath and as she scrubbed her legs and arms with a small brush, she enjoyed the punishment, and then the soreness and the glow when she finished. She compared her small warm bathroom to the chilly barn of a place in the farmhouse, and the thought of decisions to come still troubled her when she and Margaret set out for the shop an hour later.

Later that day, while she and Mavis counted the takings and tidied the shop before leaving, there was a knock at the shop door. 'Milly Toogood I bet!' Amy groaned. 'Go and let her in, Mavis. She'll bang the door down else!'

But it was not Milly. Mary stood there, in brown overall and wellington boots, a battered hat on her head. She smiled at Mavis and asked if Amy was in, and as Amy stepped forward and invited her inside, answered, 'No, I won't come in, but I'd like to talk to you sometime. How about lunchtime tomorrow? I'll be finished with the milk and there's a break before the second milking.'

'Of course. Shall we go to my house, or would you prefer somewhere in town?'

'The Drovers will be all right. We can have a drink there.' Puzzled, Amy agreed. It was odd for a woman to suggest meeting in a public house, but perhaps it was simply convenient. She turned to Mavis as they re-closed the door. 'Now I wonder what she wants to talk to me about?'

'Billie?' Mavis said, her head, birdlike, on one side.

Nelly cleaned for Mrs Dorothy Williams a friend of Mrs French once a week. The Williamses lived in a large house on the outskirts of the village and when Nelly arrived to begin her work she found the distraught woman pulling out the contents of the drawers and cupboards as if she were searching for something. The grey hair, usually held back in a neat bun, was straggling out from her head and the dress of grey wool was stained and streaked with dust.

'Whatever are you doin'?' Nelly asked, as she tied the dogs to the fence and went through the back door, removing her coat as she did so. 'Why didn't yer tell me we was spring cleanin'. I'd 'ave come earlier.'

'Not spring cleaning, Nelly. I want to scrub everything and get the taint of intruders out of my house.'

'Yes, I 'eard about the burglary. Any clues to who done it?'

'None so far, except that they probably came through the garden.' She threw a pile of tableclothes down to join the pile already on the floor. 'The police found a few leaves that they thought must have come from the hedge.' She shuddered as she tipped out some tea towels from a drawer. 'I can't bear to think of a stranger's hands rummaging through my things. I spent these past days at my sister's, waiting to have the courage to do this.'

'Should 'ave called on me, I'd 'ave seen to it while you were away.'

The two women spent the day sorting out the contents of the kitchen, scrubbing the shelves and replacing the washed items in their respective places. The living room was cleaned and polished as well as the small study used by Mr Williams for his hobby of stamp-collecting. These were places where the thieves looked for the money which they eventually found in the sideboard under a pile of papers.

'*Ach y fi*,' wailed Mrs Williams, 'I can't bear the thought of them touching all my things. How will I ever feel safe again?'

'Thank Gawd they didn't go upstairs,' Nelly said as she straightened the last rug.

'Oh, they wouldn't, would they? The money was downstairs and the police thought they would have looked here first.'

Nelly thought it highly likely that the intruders

searched the bedrooms but denied it, thinking it pointless to worry the woman any more.

'Too risky to go upstairs,' she said authoritavely. She was glad she had hidden the clump of mud from a man's shoe that she had found in the small bedroom.

The result of all their labour was a house smelling of soap and lavender polish and two very tired people who, when Mr Williams came home from his office, were invited to have a drink and relax before Nelly caught the bus home.

It was almost five-thirty when Nelly and the two dogs walked up her lane. She limped rather badly, her hips an almost constant source of pain. They had been made worse by the kneeling and rising, bending and stretching deep into cupboards and high up walls to wash the picture rails and pelmets free imaginary finger marks. She could understand the distress of finding the place had been entered by unknown people. Like poor old Archie, it would be a long time before Mrs Williams felt at ease again in her home. Over Nelly's arm were two coats, given to her by Mrs Williams before she left. They had been in the hall cupboards and would never be worn by their owner again, who swore they smelt of a stranger's touch.

At the bend in the lane, Nelly heard voices and for a moment her heart leapt at the thought that she too had unwelcome visitors, but the sight of a lorry reassured her and she hurried to see who it was. The dogs ran ahead of her, barking, their tails wagging enthusiastically.

'Fat lot of good you are, Bobby an' Spotty,' Nelly laughed to let whoever it was know she was coming.

'Come on, Nelly, I want your autograph,' a voice called and she saw that the lorry bearing the name of a local builder's merchants had begun to unload the materials needed to install her new bathroom. A bath lay on the path near the back door and a toilet was standing under the apple tree with an assortment of pipes and fittings spread around like futuristic flowers on the lawn.

' 'Ang on, I'm comin'.' She pushed her way with difficulty past the lorry and went through the gate, leaving the dogs fussing around the driver and his mate who were trying to lift a door and carry it down the path.

Nelly turned her back to her door and gave it a shove, and she was catapulted into her living room and sent staggering across to the couch.

'I keeps fergettin' that George 'as fixed that damned door,' she explained to the startled men. 'Stay an' 'ave a cuppa, why don't yer?'

'Thanks.' The two men sat down at once on the chairs outside the back door.

She stirred the fire into a blaze, throwing on a few sticks to liven it and turned the swivel carrying the black kettle over the heat. As it began to hum she set out cups and saucers and took a fruit cake from a tin. She went out and released the chickens from their run to wander around the garden, and while the kettle boiled, chatted to the men.

George arrived as they were about to go inside and help themselves to the cake she offered, delaying them further. When they finally went in the men stopped in the doorway and stared at the table. The cake was rapidly disappearing as two hens packed furiously at it and the two dogs stretched up and rolled their tongues around the table, reaching the spillage and leaving a pattern of wet curved licks on the wooden surface.

'What about a biscuit instead?' George said calmly, lifting the hens off and throwing them, complaining, out of the door. The dogs looked guilty and ˜ettled in a corner, rolling their eyes in a pleading way thaɪ made them all laugh.

'Always like this, is it?' the driver asked and Nelly nodded.

'Ain't never dull, is it George?'

The gate opened and clacking heels came down the path. Nelly looked out and saw Evie coming, intent on a quarrel, her head bent, her eyes frowning in anger.

'Bloody 'ell, what 'ave I done now, George?' Nelly whispered.

'I might have guessed it was you, Mother,' Amy said.

' 'Course it's me. Who else d'you expect?'

'I mean causing chaos. I'm trying to drive around to the council houses and the lane is blocked. You giving the workmen tea is why.'

The driver stood up, his cup rattling against the saucer in his haste. 'I'll shift it at once, Mrs.'

'Fer Gawd's sake, let 'im finish 'is tea, Evie,' Nelly grumbled. 'What's so urgent you can't spare a minute?' She turned to the driver. 'Finish yer tea, gives yer indigestion, she does.'

'I don't know how you can find time to waste, I have plenty to do.' She turned to the driver who was hesitating, wondering which woman to obey, changing the weight from one foot to the other as he decided to stay, then go. Seeing the look on Evie's face he decided to go.

'Just give us half a minute and we'll be out of your way, Mrs.' He handed the cup to Nelly, 'Pour me another while I move the lorry, will you? Lovely that was.' He winked. 'Especially the cake.' He left with his mate to guide him as he manoeuvred the lorry in the confined space.

'While I'm here, Mother,' Evie said, 'will you have Oliver to sleep here next week?'

'Sleep here?' Nelly was surprised. It was difficult to persuade Evie that the place was sufficiently clean to allow the boy to eat something, but to sleep here? Nelly slowly moved in the hope of Evie not noticing the mess of cake where the hens had held an impromptu picnic. 'Of course 'e can sleep 'ere. But why?'

'Timothy and I have to attend a dinner. It's council

226

business and we'll be back late. Amy usually helps but she will be out that evening and Netta Cartwright will be going to see Prue Beynon, so—'

'So I'm yer last 'ope?'

'I'll have to come and see the room you're giving him first, of course.'

'Of course.'

'Make sure it's clean enough and that his bed covers are sufficient.'

'Of course.' Nelly's dark eyes glittered with anger. When it suited them Evie and Timothy didn't mind the boy coming to the cottage, but when it could be avoided Evie made it quite clear to everyone that her mother did not reach her very high standards.

'Want the police to check, do yer? Make sure we ain't harbourin' no criminals or makin' illicit booze in the shed?'

'Don't be ridiculous, Mother.'

George, who could see how the anger was rising in Nelly, intervened and said,

'We'll be delighted to have him. Nelly and I will make sure everything is just as you want it. You won't have to worry about a thing.'

'I don't expect miracles!' Evie snapped. 'I just want to know he'll be safe.'

George put a restraining arm on Nelly's arm as Evie walked back up the path but he couldn't gag her.

'An' you shouldn't be drivin' in daft stiletto shoes like them, Evie. You ain't even passed yer test yet!'

'Timothy is in the car with me, Mother. You know I wouldn't disobey the law.'

'An' where's young Ollie now then? Who's with 'im this time? Sure 'e's safe, are yer?'

George was thankful that the men stayed a while, allowing Nelly to calm down a little and forget her daughter's rudeness.

Later, when they were alone, he said, 'Exciting, isn't it, Nelly love?'

'What, 'avin' young Ollie to spend the night? Yes, we'll get 'im a real good supper, shall we? Now, what d'you think 'e'll fancy?'

'I wasn't thinking of that, but the fact that he'll have to have my back bedroom and my single bed. One of us will have to sleep down here, which he might find a bit odd, or I will have to share your bed.'

'Ooh, George! Yer right! It is excitin'. 'Ere, you going ter buy me a new frilly nightie, are yer?'

'Are you going to bring me tea in bed?' he chuckled.

Their marriage had been one of convenience and had taken place to prevent Evie from persuading the local doctor that Nelly was unable to care for herself and should leave her cottage. They had never shared the same bed, George sleeping downstairs on the couch or in the big armchair until they had cleared the back bedroom sufficiently and bought him a secondhand bed. Now, with Oliver coming, they might have to share the big feather bed in which Nelly had slept since she had bought it from Clara, her gypsy friend who had made it from duck and chicken feathers.

The bed cover had also been made by Clara. She had washed the sheep's wool gathered from the hedges around the fields and after washing it had sewn it between two layers of cotton, and quilted it in a curved pattern of small running stitches during the winter months, with only an oil lamp to work by. Nelly was very proud of it and decided that, for this special occasion, they would both be put outside for a 'blow'.

The following morning she struggled down the stairs with the feather bed and dragged it out on to the lawn. Lowering the clothes line she threw it across and tried in vain to raise it up and allow the wind to freshen and cleanse it. It was not until Phil came and offered to find a

228

few willing hands to help that she had any hope of success.

'I'll round up a few men as soon as I can,' Phil promised, puffing over his attempt to raise the heavy mattress. When George came home from the farm, it was to see Johnny, Phil, Bert and Victor all swinging on the line and hauling up the bed.

'I ain't got the 'eart to tell 'em,' Nelly whispered to him, 'but it's almost time to drag it back in again.'

# Chapter Twelve

When Amy arrived for her lunchtime appointment with Billie's sister, she paused in the doorway of the Drovers and combed her hair and touched her cheeks with a powder puff to calm herself. She looked at herself for a moment or two in her compact mirror, assuring herself that she had done her best to look attractive. She had dressed and made up with great care before leaving the shop but waiting for the bus then the short walk had ruffled her and she needed to feel utterly confident for the interview to come.

She wondered what Mary would say. Would she try to discourage the relationship between her brother and herself? She thought that very likely, considering what Mary had to lose. Or was she going to tell Amy how pleased she was that her brother was facing a happy future? She considered the former the most likely and she took a deep breath and walked into the bar.

Mary was sitting at a corner table and she smiled a welcome and stood to order a drink. Amy asked for a tonic, not wanting to be anything but sharp, while the woman told her what was on her mind. There was a defensive tilt to her chin as she accepted the drink and settled beside Mary.

Billie's sister was not tall and her plumpness made her appear even shorter. She had on the overalls she wore for the milk round and on her feet were a pair of scuffed and worn black shoes, low heeled and practical rather than smart. Amy wondered if the woman was deliberately making a point. A farm did not go with fashionable clothes. She wished she had not dressed with quite so much care, then realised that she should never pretend to be something she was not. She never had in the past. Why should she now?

'It's about you and Billie,' Mary began after a brief silence. 'I want you to know how I feel.'

'There's no need,' Amy said quickly. 'What Billie and I feel is what counts and so far there is nothing but affection and friendship between us.'

'If it develops into something more,' Mary continued, 'I want you to know that I would welcome you and do everything to make you and your family feel at home in my home.'

Amy did not miss the slightly emphasised 'my home'. 'Thank you, but—'

'I've looked after Billie for years. He's younger than me and I've treated him like my child in some ways.'

'He's looked after you too,' Amy defended.

'Of course. But if he should marry and bring a ready-made family back to live at the farm, I would be glad to retire from the role of mother and housekeeper and develop my own life. The house is huge, as you know, and I'm sure we can all fit in without treading on each other's toes. I wouldn't need more than a couple of rooms. The rest would be yours.'

'I'm not sure I want it,' Amy muttered. The thought of taking on the enormous house and the work it must surely entail was daunting, more daunting now the subject had actually been broached in a definite way. 'I run a shop and even that, together with the small house Harry Beynon left me, is more than I can cope with at times.'

'But you'd give up the shop, surely?'

'Mary, I hadn't thought this far into things. I get very

232

fed up with having so much to do, but I like my life and I'm not sure I want to change it so dramatically.'

'Oh, I thought you and Billie were—'

'Billie and I might eventually think along those lines but not yet. Perhaps never. And to give up my shop, well, that I would never do. There might be a time when Freddie or Margaret would want to take it over. No, Mary, I think you're running too far and too fast.'

'I'm sorry. I wanted to reassure you, let you know that there wouldn't be any problems from me. I'd willingly let go of the house and hand it over to you.'

'Do you want to be free? Is that it?'

'I'm past fifty. It's rather late for frolicking, but yes, I would welcome a bit more time to call my own. But you won't tell Billie, will you? He'd be hurt if he thought I was less than happy looking after him and the old farm-house.'

'Not a word,' Amy promised. 'Now, will you have another drink before we go? Mavis is at the shop but I have some things to see to and I'll stay there until Margaret comes out of school.'

They chatted amiably for a while, each with their own thoughts under the surface of the polite conversation: Mary convinced she had given Amy plenty of doubts about the possibilities of a marriage to Billie, who, she had reminded her, was well set in his ways; Amy wondering how Billie could have believed for a moment that she would give up the shop and become a farmer's wife in wellingtons and the dreaded brown overalls? Amy was surprised at how friendly and interesting Mary was, having had very little to do with her previously. Mary worked hard with her cows and her milk round and rarely had time to stop and chatter, giving the impression that she was a surly misery. She wondered how many lost chances Mary's life had held, loves she had let slip away because of her duty to her brother and the property they had inherited.

233

Fay was nervous. She knew the sensible thing to do was to stay well clear of the hotel in Llangwyn where she had met the man, whose name she had not learnt. He had said she would find him there every Tuesday and every moment since she told herself that if she did go he would not be there and she would feel disappointed and a little foolish. But the day and the face of the man stayed in her mind and, as she tore off the day on her kitchen calendar, the word 'Tuesday' seemed to leap out at her and urge her on.

She looked at her diary and made a mental note of her route round the shops at which she had to call. Her stomach lurched as she noted that, consciously or not, she had planned a morning that would bring her back to Llangwyn by twelve-thirty. She set off on her round, the back of the car and the boot filled with samples of the late summer and autumn models she hoped to sell.

An excitement filled her. She was more aware of everything around her and an expectancy of something wonderful made her step light, her eyes sparkle. The morning was an exceptionally good one, her confidence helping her to persuade her customers to buy more than they intended, and she drove into Llangwyn at twelve-fifteen with an order book filled and the conviction that she deserved a treat. She needed to sit and drink a coffee and eat a sandwich, to sort out her orders, didn't she? Her footsteps took her to the hotel, where she repaired her makeup before finding herself a seat, quickly, without looking around the room to see if he was there.

Still not looking up, she delved into the capacious bag, in which she carried illustrations of the hats she was unable to carry, samples of fabrics, boxes of assorted feathers and veilings with swatches of dye samples. Pulling out her order book she began to fill it in with her usual neatness, reading the impatiently scrawled notes

234

and crossing them off as they were transferred to the book.

The man came silently over the carpeted floor and asked if he might join her. She looked up and found with warm pleasure that he was as attractive as she had remembered. She moved her things hurriedly and made room for the cup and saucer he had brought with him.

'Are you sure I'm not disturbing you?'

That, thought Fay, he was most certainly doing! They talked about their day, his eyes with the golden specks showing deep interest in all she had to say. He had a ready laugh and she found herself relating incidents that she had previously told Johnny, but which gained a far greater response from Dexter. She found even the newly discovered name exciting, and repeated in silently to herself. When there was no further excuse to stay, he suggested a walk.

'We could walk beside the river?' Dexter suggested with a warm smile. 'I don't think I could bear to let you go just yet.'

They crossed the road to go through the arcade of shops and came to the river-bank. The seats along the path which followed the river for a while were mostly filled with people sitting enjoying the watery sun and watching the water flowing gently past, but they found one finally and sat for an hour exchanging details of each other and finding they had a great deal in common. They both loved the theatre although went only rarely, their tastes in music and books coincided, and when they stood to walk back to their respective lives, Fay was flushed with happiness.

She did not see the bus which passed close to them as they stood on a corner on their way to the car park. But the driver of the bus saw them and he slowed the bus, to the consternation and annoyance of several motorists, and watched the couple cross the road, laughing and

235

obviously enjoying each other's company. He picked up speed again and his heart was weighed down with dread. His Fay, his lovely Fay. Surely she hadn't found someone else?

Johnny did not know whether to mention seeing Fay or to try and forget it. The man was probably one of her customers, although he knew that for a man to run a hat-shop was rare. He watched as Fay prepared the fish and salad for their meal and saw she was in excellent spirits. When she told him that her morning had been very successful he tried to put her bright eyes and excited smile down to that. Although he was longing for her to tell him about meeting the man, to pull him out of his misery of suspicion and doubts, she did not mention him at all.

He had never dreamed he could be so suspicious and jealous and believed that if it had not been for Fay's ex-fiancé turning up unexpectedly to ruin temporarily their wedding plans, he might never have become so. He knew Fay was not completely happy but thought that as time passed and they settled into the easy companionship which most of the time they enjoyed, they would both forget any doubts. When they had a baby and Fay stayed at home to be a full-time wife and mother, that, he was convinced, was when everything would be perfect.

She seemed to have given up thoughts of buying a house and moving out of the village: the council house they rented was comfortable enough and not far from his mother's home where they had begun their married life. If she gave up her job – he could not bring himself to call it a career – then his wages would not give them any luxuries. But he wanted very little, and, if Fay was really restless, then perhaps, after a while she could find something else to do, something which did not involve her spending so many hours away from home and, he thought

236

with sudden guilt, a job where she would not come across so many interesting men.

'Meet anyone interesting today, lovely?' he couldn't resist asking when they were getting into bed.

'No one more interesting than you, Johnny,' Fay smiled contentedly as she opened her arms to him.

And with that he had to be content.

The following Tuesday, Johnny was off work. But instead of going to his mother's house to see if there were any jobs needing doing, or spending the day in the garden, he rode into town on the eleven-thirty bus and stood where he could see the hotel where Fay had told him she often had a lunchtime snack. It was nothing to go on, he knew that, but his day off, coinciding with it being the same day he had seen Fay with the man, made it irresistible.

He stood for a while, feeling foolish and rather guilty, wanting to see her but dreading finding her having lunch with the stranger. Why couldn't he trust her? Since their wedding he had never thought her capable of cheating on him. What was there about seeing her laughing with a man as they crossed the street in full view of the town that distressed him so much?

She went into the hotel at twelve-thirty and he decided to wait for her to re-emerge. He could make the excuse that he missed her. She would believe that for sure. He was always showing her how much he wanted her company. Perhaps he would buy a few pairs of socks as an excuse for coming into town. The thought of how involved the incident was becoming was frightening. Was he going to ruin everything by becoming pathologically jealous? He ought to go home, now, at once.

He hurried to the bus stop but changed his mind again and quickly bought two pairs of short summer socks and a bunch of flowers. Then he returned to wait, his eyes never leaving the hotel entrance. At one-thirty she came out, alone. He walked across the road and handed her the flowers.

'Fay, my lovely, I was in town and thought I might see you. Never miss a chance of a moment with you, do I? Glad are you? That I love you so much?'

He saw at once that he had done the wrong thing. She tensed up, her beautiful face a pale mask of anger.

'What are you really doing, Johnny? Checking up on me?'

'*Duw annwyl!* No! What gives you such an idea, lovely?'

She knew she had over-reacted to the sight of him, when she had just left Dexter, but she had to continue. 'How did you know where to find me then?'

'I didn't,' he lied frantically. 'I saw you going in there by chance, and I wouldn't follow you in case you were lunching with a client. I waited for you to come out, that's all. Finished for the day, have you? We can go home together.'

'No, I haven't finished for the day. I have several calls to make.'

Still showing her irritation, she walked back to the car park with Johnny beside her, the flowers held under her arm like a brolly. As they crossed the road, Dexter stepped out of the hotel entrance and walked off in the opposite direction.

If Timothy did not give his son homework, then Evie did. Every evening Oliver had some reading and writing to do and he got into the habit of taking it round to his grandmother's cottage where he knew he would have the attention he needed to make sense of the tasks. It was usually Nelly who helped him and on that evening she was pointing to the odd word on the page with her dirt-engrained fingers and praising him as he called them out.

When he hesitated, she coaxed.

'Come on, Ollie, you know what that is. Start with the first bit of the word like I showed you.' She covered all but the first part of the word with her finger.

'It's – a dirty finger!' he joked, and laughingly jumped out of his chair.

'Cheeky little devil,' Nelly laughed. ' 'Ere that, George? Our grandson's gettin' above 'imself.' She eased herself up, and picked up the dogs' leads. 'Come on, let's take the dogs fer a run.'

They walked up the path and across the lane where a well-used path took them through the trees towards the stream. The dogs drank and paddled, swishing their feet like children enjoying the sound and the sensation of the cold water.

'Been to yer den lately?' Nelly asked. Oliver shook his head.

'Margaret isn't so keen now. Dawn keeps coming and she and Margaret can't be friends.'

Their feet unconsciously wandered to the clearing where the tree house was situated and Oliver pulled down the rope-ladder he and Billie had made and he climbed up.

'Come on up, Gran,' he teased.

'No, you bring it down 'ere!' she retorted.

As he was climbing back down, Dawn arrived and the first they heard of her approach was the clicking of her camera in the still evening air. She took a notebook out of the pocket of her dress and meticulously marked down the time and place.

' 'Ello, Dawn. You still takin' snaps fer the competition?' Nelly asked.

'No, I've already entered three taken at Mumbles, and three of people in the village.'

239

'Six? That'll be an exhibition of yer own!'

'Pity is, Mr Chartridge won't allow me to enter more than three. He'll have to chose the one he thinks is best. He might chose the wrong one.' She moved closer to Oliver. 'I was wondering. Could you enter one of mine? There's money offered for prizes and my dad would be pleased if I won it.'

'My dad would know,' Oliver said.

'Not if you said I'd lent you the camera. Go on, Oliver, be a sport.'

'I've a camera of my own. Why should he believe I used yours?'

'Don't bother then!' Dawn ran off, ignoring Nelly's entreaties to wait.

Oliver went home and Nelly paused, listening for a while with concentration to make sure all was quiet. Then she squatted behind a clump of bramble bushes and slipped her knickers down. She groaned as she heard the click of Dawn's camera.

Dawn ran home grinning widely and took out the packets of photographs she had taken so far, selecting a few to show her father and hiding the rest under her pillow. It was very expensive, this photography lark, and she didn't want him to ask where she found the money. A few shillings she had found on Ethel Davies's back-kitchen table, and the milk money left out along the road, had given her sufficient to continue for a while. She rolled up the completed film ready to take to be developed and licked the fixing label.

Sheila watched for the postman every morning, although she knew it was far too soon to hear from Maurice, even if he had written back immediately. She daydreamed about the reply she would eventually receive, how impressed he was at the idea of her and Delina being friends, and how he regretted leaving her like he did. He

240

would ask for her forgiveness and promise to love her for ever.

Despondently she left the dream and watched as Phil went into the garden next door, his bicycle propped against the privet hedge, the bag hanging on the handlebar. Voices reached her across the dividing hedge and she watched for him to pass her gate, pushing his bicycle, hating him for no other reason than that he could not possibly have the letter she longed to received.

Her hopes rose ridiculously as he came up her path and popped a few envelopes through the letter box. She ran to pick them up off the coconut mat and her hopes, foolishly risen, plummeted. Of course there was no letter from Australia. But did there have to be one from Freddie? Irritably she tore it into several pieces and threw them in the bin.

Really, she thought, I'm as silly as Delina, not opening Maurice's letters. But she refused to feel regret at the loss of the boring chatter that Freddie would have written. She went on with the housework she had set herself. At eleven o'clock, when she and Gran usually had a cup of tea and a biscuit, she thought again about the letter. Could this one be different from the others? No. She pulled the morning paper towards her and resolutely refused to think of the torn and unread letter in the bin. She had wiped the baked beans off the letter from Maurice, but there would be nothing in the scribble from Freddie that would make that unpleasant chore worth while.

At lunchtime, when she took a poached egg and some bread and butter in for her grandmother, she sat with her meal, feeling so bored that the temptation to throw the plate across the room was almost worth the mess she would have to clear up. Instead of throwing the egg, she went out to retrieve Freddie's letter. What she read made her sit up in surprise.

241

'I am being moved to a camp in the West Country,' it said. 'Why don't you join me?' The letter went on to explain how easily he could find her a room and a job. 'I'll be able to spend some time with you and we'd be together, you wouldn't be on your own ever again, and I would be able to look after you.'

The idea was so surprising that she spent the rest of the afternoon contemplating the image of having a room of her own, free from interference and the criticism of her parents, who were still complaining about reports of her being in the Drovers on her own one lunchtime, and without having to look after Gran. Even with visits from Freddie to suffer, it sounded like heaven.

She was tempted to write straight back and agree to go, but she didn't have a stamp and there was no way she would buy one from Amy and let her know she was writing to her precious son. Tomorrow she would decide. She would sleep on it and answer him tomorrow. She would go into Llangwyn and buy the tuppenny-halfpenny stamp from there.

She was restless and at six o'clock, when they had eaten and the dishes were draining beside the sink, she slipped on her coat. The evening was not very pleasant but she had to get out. At least it was not raining. Calling to her gran to tell her she was going for a walk, she went out of the front door and down the hill towards Sheepy Lane.

Where could she go? She couldn't discuss this with Ethel, and her parents would be horrified at the suggestion of her joining Freddie, a sixteen-year-old boy, while she was still married to Maurice. His desertion of her seemed less important to her parents than the opinion of the local people, she thought resentfully. No one puts me first. Except Freddie, she had to admit. She sighed. In all the world he was the only one to care.

Reaching the junction of Hywel Rise and Sheepy Lane

she walked up to the woods. The trees were in full leaf and very beautiful, but she was unaware of them. She recalled with half-remembered fear as well as excitement the place where Maurice had first forced her to make love. Why had it all gone wrong? Why couldn't it have been a real love story like in her magazines, instead of a closeted passion which had been forgotten the moment Maurice had met Miss High-and-Mighty Delina Honeyman?

She stood silently under the trees, listening to the sounds of the birds and wishing Freddie were with her. Better Freddie than being alone, despised by all the village for ruining Maurice's life and sending him away from his home and family. She sighed again. Why did everyone side with Maurice? It was her who had suffered most. A husband thousands of miles away preventing her from finding someone else, the agony of the baby's birth and death. What had Maurice suffered compared with that?

Disconsolately she wandered to where the marks of a motor-bike could be clearly seen heading for the hill below which was Billie Brown's farm. She looked down at the farm nestling in the fold of the hills, then detoured to climb over the castle ruins before wandering back home.

The following morning she went into town on the nine o'clock bus, the letter from Freddie in her pocket. She had debated the pros and cons of going to live near him through much of the night and at first the idea had seemed perfect. No interference and no over-anxious parents were the main things in its favour. But then she had begun to think about Freddie in uniform and with no money. His friends, all in uniform with no money; herself, stuck in some boring job in a small town with no new clothes and no fun.

243

There had had very little fun in her life and it seemed ridiculous to walk into a situation where she would have little chance of an escape to better things. She did not really know what she meant by 'better things', only that Freddie was not the way to find them. She put the letter, telling him she would not be coming, into the letter box and listened to it fall with a sigh of relief. How nearly she had fallen into a trap, taking a slight security and giving up her freedom for it.

She had dressed with care, making the best of the few decent clothes she had. The iron had thumped away for an hour before she was satisfied that the black slim-line skirt and the polo-necked silky blouse were as neat as she could make them, her stiletto heeled shoes polished and the single run in her nylon stockings carefully and neatly repaired.

A pleasant hour was spent at the hairdresser's where her hair was washed and set in a loosely waved style which she knew framed her face attractively. It was money she and Gran could not easily afford but, by economising for a few days on food, she would be able to cover its loss. After a cup of tea in the local hotel (the smart new Sheila would not consider a cafe) she spent a while repairing her makeup, adding a little more mascara than usual and stepped out with confidence to get her old job back.

There had been a new girl taken on in her place, but seeing Sheila, dressed, made up and so obviously returned to her usual good health, the manageress was tempted. Sheila had not been well liked by the rest of the sales staff but she had been very good at her job and customers still asked for her when they came to buy for a special occasion. Sheila came out after twenty minutes leaving a guilty manageress and a sobbing, sacked, fourth sales girl. She had started to pick herself up again and had no one, not even Freddie Prichard and certainly not her parents, to thank for helping her.

At the bus stop she pushed herself to the front of the queue, the women with their bags of shopping seemingly too surprised to stop her. The first bus that came was for Hen Carw Parc, and she ran up the stairs to the front seat, still smiling over her success. The conductor, with a fully loaded bus to attend, failed to reach her and ask for her fare and she pocketed the money with satisfaction. Another good augury. Things were definitely going her way.

She was so delighted at the way her day had gone she hardly glanced along the road when she alighted, and a tractor, about to overtake the parked bus, which was still spilling out its passengers, had to stop with a suddenness that made Billie shout, 'Damned fool! What d'you think you're doing,' Billie glared at her. 'Look where you're going, you idiot!'

'Travelling too fast, you were!' Sheila looked at the other passengers for support. 'Could have killed me. Shaking like a leaf, I am, and me with the hill to walk up.'

The bus moved away and people began to disperse as Billie climbed down from his tractor. He walked up to her, towering above her, his brown dungarees and the cowboy shirt blocking her view of the road.

'All right, are you?'

'No thanks to you!'

'If you want, I'll walk up and see you safe home, or will you go to your parents? Not far, are they? Only in the flat above the shop.'

'No, I'm all right.'

She began to cross the road, looking ostentatiously right and left several times. As she reached the other side she called back. 'You want to watch out for burglars, by the way.'

'What d'you mean?'

'I was in the woods yesterday and saw the marks of motor-bikes, stopped where they could look down on your place.'

'Told the police, have you?'

'No,' she admitted. 'I'd forgotten until you nearly ran me down.'

'Can you show me?'

'If you like.'

She walked up Sheepy Lane and Billie went to the tractor and drove slowly past her, waiting at the point where the lane turned westward to pass Nelly's cottage. He stopped the noisy engine and walked with her to the furthest edge of the trees where she had seen the tracks. Close beside him, she bent down and pointed a varnished finger-nail to where the tracks could be seen. Looking up at him, widening her eyes in a way she knew excited men, her face admiring, she said, 'I expect you can learn a lot just by looking at these silly tyre marks, can't you? They don't mean a thing to me. I just thought you ought to know.'

She slipped on an imaginary stone and his arms reached out to save her from falling. Laughing, she moved away from him, inwardly amused at the sudden interest in his dark warm eyes. Really, men were so predictable. A bird, frightened into flight by the sudden movements, squawked in alarm and obliterated the sound of a camera shutter.

Leaving Billie to study the tyre marks, Sheila walked home, well contented with her day. She had a job, she was still able to attract men and what was more important, she still enjoyed the sensation. Even the reactions of an ugly old man like Billie, who was forty if he was a day, made her feel more alive and reminded her that life was potentially full of exciting things.

She wondered if Gran would mind having fish and chips tonight. She didn't feel like cooking and the walk down to the village would show people her newly recovered confidence and make them realise that Sheila Davies was fit and well and raring to go.

The school was so quiet that Timothy felt a strange unease as he worked at setting up the display paper for the children's photographs. The windows were open and the soft evening breeze touched the papers on his desk and made them dance. A sparrow settled on the sill to watch him work, with its head on one side as if questioning the display. Timothy watched its jerking movements and smiled. That would make an interesting photograph, he thought.

He covered a length of recently denuded wall, the pictures he had taken down all in a neat pile for the children to claim and take home. In every classroom the teachers were preparing displays ready for when the parents came to see the photography competition: there would be a representation of work from every child. The hall Timothy had wanted to do himself.

The blue backing paper was almost fixed and he picked a photograph up from a pile on the desk, holding it against the paper to judge the effect. Footsteps sounded hollowly in the empty building and, still holding the photograph at arm's length, he smiled as Mrs French came into the hall. 'Do you think this colour will be suitable, Mrs French?' he asked.

'Perfect, Mr Chartridge,' she smiled, 'but I hope you have enough room for them all. It seems that every child in the school has entered the competition.'

He turned over a few of the entries and held up some of his favourites for her to see.

'Lots from Dawn. A number taken at Mumbles, but none of the trains, or even the horse-pulled coach. They're all of people. Very interesting.' Then his face froze and he hurriedly screwed up the picture of Nelly peeing in the woods and threw it into the waste-paper bin. He must remember to remove it when he left and make sure, once he got it out of school, that Evie didn't see it. He was tense as Mrs French looked through the rest of Dawn's entries.

'She does have an eye for a picture,' she said and he agreed lugubriously. 'This one of a child staring down with disbelief at his fallen icecream,' Mrs French went on, 'and this one showing laughing, dancing children. And this—'

Timothy started with alarm, wondering what she had found and was only partly relieved to see it was a picture of a child with only one shoe on, crying for attention, only his mother's lower half in view, dragging him behind her, unaware of his distress.

'I have an hour or two. Shall we make a start on the display?' Mrs French offered and they began sticking the photographs on to the paper, grouping them into subjects. The name of the photographer was written on the back of the pictures and Mrs French noted that he only used three of Dawn's, putting the rest aside.

'A pity they can't all be shown. They're very good,' she said, but Timothy tightened his lips and did not reply.

'How is Dawn getting on at school? Is she settling down now?'

'Not really. She's a difficult child who revels in causing embarrassment and irritation.'

'Her attendance?' she coaxed.

'Poor. She's out of school more than she's in. Every week there's at least one note saying she has a cold or a cough or is "unwell".'

'The handwriting, it is her father's, isn't it?'

'You're wondering if she writes them herself? I wouldn't know. The writing is small and a bit childlike and there are spelling mistakes but her father is only a

248

factory hand, with no education. It would seem unremarkable that he does not write a good hand,' he said pompously, unaware of how wrong he was. 'I do see rather a lot of notes and you'd be amazed at the number of children who try to outwit me.'

'I have them too, for music lessons,' Mrs French laughed. 'When the weather is good there are enough colds and coughs and sprained wrists to constitute an epidemic!'

While Timothy went to the cupboard for more drawing pins, Mrs French took out the crumpled photograph and, recognising Nelly and what she was doing, found it impossible not to smile. When Timothy returned, she held the photograph out to him and offered, 'Shall I take this and dispose of it for you? I think we ought to make sure Mrs Chartridge doesn't see it, don't you?'

The children began to arrive for the concert rehearsal and Mrs French sat at the piano. She felt so merry that she found herself searching for an excuse to laugh, and the rehearsal was one of the most enjoyable the children remembered. She thought the photograph of Nelly in the woods might be worth keeping to look at just before the concert, for its cheering effect. Her jolly mood had certainly added a sense of fun to the singing.

# Chapter Thirteen

Amy was haunted by Victor. He appeared at the shop and at the house more regularly than ever before. Wherever he was delivering he managed to pass through the village and spend a moment with her, his eyes full of reproach if she mentioned Billie or the farm. He was unable to say or do anything to persuade her to refuse the farmer's proposal: he had nothing to offer, not even his freedom to love her. No money, except what he was secretly saving, and that was for the gold watch he had promised her, to replace the one that had been stolen. How could he ask her to love him and not Billie?

The evenings were long and it was rare that a day passed without him calling at the house, usually on the pretext of weeding her garden, but, as Billie made sure there was nothing to do in that area, he would just pick idly at a few recalcitrant daisies and talk to Amy or Margaret. He knew Amy wanted him and also knew she had meant it when she had told him the brief affair must end. One day, he threw down the trowel he was using and stormed into the house. He flopped into a chair and muttered, 'Why don't you marry Billie and put me out of my misery?'

Startled, Amy asked. 'Is that what you want?'

'You know it isn't!'

'Then why—?'

'I hate every moment of my life when I'm not with you, Amy, and I dread every moment when I *am* with you, expecting to be told to go. I survive each day on the crazy hope that Billie will drop dead, or you'll find out something about him that will make you forget the idea of being his wife.'

'Mr and Mrs Brown,' Amy mused. 'Amy and Billie, yes, I must confess I like the sound of it.'

'And I can't blame you, love,' Victor said sadly. 'Why waste your youth hovering around when you can have a man, a decent man, damn him, who wants to give you everything. A home, a loving husband, a place of comfort for Margaret and Freddie. But I want you to know that I love you and as soon as the boys are eighteen, I'm leaving Imogine, whatever you decide now. You aren't breaking up my marriage. My marriage ended when I was in court for stealing. Since then my life has been nothing, apart from loving you.'

He picked up the trowel from the lawn where he had thrown it and continued to attack the daisies.

'Going to the darts match tonight?' Amy asked later, when she went out with some tea. She had kept away from him, afraid that she would be persuaded by his wretchedness to allow the affair to continue.

'Are you?' he asked hopefully.

'No, I've had enough of darts for a while. They've fixed the outing at last. Are you going?'

'I might as well. There's got to be something to break the monotony.'

'I'll pack you a snack box,' she promised. 'Call in the shop before you get on the coach and collect it.'

'Is Billie going?'

'He has to. Catrin won't let Phil go without someone to keep an eye on him. He got lost last time and didn't turn up till the following day! Too much beer on the coach, if you ask me.'

'I'll call at the shop about eight, then,' Victor said. He looked thoughtful.

Constable Harris was asking questions about motor-bikes. He had gone three times to ask Griff's son, Pete, if his was working and was proudly shown the bike, shining and, for once, in perfect order.

'Me and Pete had a puncture last week and we stripped the bikes down and gave them a good greasing and now they're ready for anything,' Pete told him. 'Want a ride, do you?'

'No thanks, I'll stick to pedal power. More peaceful,' Harris replied.

It was Sheila who mentioned Griff's own bike and when Harris saw the man calling at the fish-and-chip shop he asked to see it.

'Hang on till I finish work, and I'll show you,' Griff promised. 'Bit of a mess, mind, the exhaust has gone.'

'I'll call and ask your missus to show me,' Harris said and, doubtfully, Griff agreed.

'She doesn't know much about bikes, mind,' he said.

'Me neither,' Harris told him.

Catching Hilda as she finished chipping the potatoes for the evening's frying, Harris went with her through the garage doors to where, in a corner, hidden by old mats and some ancient blankets, Griff's motor-bike was found and brought out into the daylight. The exhaust was hanging off, and, after moving it and hearing an unpleasant sound of scraping, Harris pushed it back and re-covered it. It didn't seem likely that it had been used lately. Best he looked somewhere else for the mysterious night-rider. Thankful once again that his enquiries led him away from the village inhabitants, Harris went on his way.

On the day of the darts team outing, Nelly took the dogs and walked to the end of the lane to see them off.

'Men only!' she laughed with Constable Harris. 'A lot

253

of babies without the women to look after them!' Most of the men carried parcels of food. 'I bet most of that grub'll be thrown into the first rubbish bin they pass,' she prophesied. ' 'Alf the fun of an outing is finding somewhere to eat. Enjoy yer fish an' chips!' she shouted as Phil was handed a paper-wrapped package with an apple and a banana. Catrin smiled at her.

'You're probably right and they'll find something more interesting, but you've got to make them feel cared for, haven't you?'

Nelly watched Billie standing behind the coach, overseeing the loading of the beer crates into the luggage department. Head and shoulders above most, she saw him constantly turning to look towards the shop, which was still closed. She screwed up her eyes and peered at the darkened window. There was someone inside, probably Mavis getting things ready for opening, she thought, then she stepped closer. Standing at the kerb she concentrated and recognised the two people inside. One was Amy, clearly recognisable with her fluffy blonde hair and the other was Victor. No wonder Billie looks sick, she thought.

She waited to see if Victor was going on the coach but, as Billie stepped on to the coach beside Phil and the driver began to rev the engine warningly, the shop door did not open and Victor did not appear. Inside the coach men were changing seats, arguing about who would sit where, whilst the driver asked Billie to close the door.

Bert was about to be locked out and he banged furiously on the door and called irritably, ' 'Ang on a minute will you! Archie Pearce isn't here yet!' He ran his finger down his list as, with a groan, the driver reversed the coach back to Archie's door with Bert running after it shouting abuse. Archie came out carrying the tuck box he used for work.

'Been ready ages,' he insisted as the driver began to

complain. 'Just waiting for you lot to sort yourselves out. Damn me, you're more fussy about who you sit by than a pack of school-kids!' He was hauled on to the bus and, with Billie bending to take one more look at the shop, the bus struggled off. Faces at the bus windows were grinning and arms were waving at Nelly and the others who had come to see them off, stretching for a last glimpse as the women dispersed. Nelly stood after they had all gone, watching the shop which was still in semi-darkness, the two figures still visible. She sighed. It seemed that Amy had chosen between Victor Honeyman and Billie Brown and made the wrong decision as usual. She sighed again and went back to the cottage.

Amy watched the coach go, its exhaust issuing a gust of smoke that all but obliterated it as it turned the bend into the road on the way to Llangwyn to pick up the rest of the passengers. Then she turned to Victor.

'So you aren't going and Billie knows you are here with me. What are you trying to do to me, Victor?'

'Stop you making a mistake, love.'

'I wish people would let me make my own mistakes and not think they know better than me what I need! I've made plenty of mistakes and I've always coped. What gives you the right to try and protect me?'

'This.' He handed her a photograph. It was not clear but it was easy to see the woodland scene and the two people, close together, looking into each other's eyes. Billie's large body almost hid the small, delicate figure of Sheila Davies, who was looking up into Billie's face with obvious admiration.

'Where did you get this?' she demanded.

'Dawn gave it to Delina when they met in the lane. She threw it at her actually. This and others. She's been going around with that damned camera of hers and taking snaps of everyone she sees.'

'But not many in such an interesting position,' Amy said harshly. 'What's Sheila's game I wonder? Surely she isn't after Billie? I doubt she's so desperate that she'll want a man of his age.'

'Not likely is it? He's too old for *you*!'

Amy ignored him and concentrated on Sheila. 'I've always known that girl was trouble. I've said it often enough.'

'Who, young Dawn? I agree with you there.'

'No, Sheila Powell.'

'Davies,' he corrected. He watched her as she efficiently sorted out the vegetables ready for the outside display. 'What are you going to do about the photograph?' he asked.

'I don't know. I *do* know that I can't stay in the shop today. It's a long walk I need. Something to get the steam out of me before I burst! Why should Billie want to bother with Sheila? In all the years I've known him there's never been any harsh gossip.'

'There's dull!' Victor smiled. 'They can't say that about you or me, can they, love?'

'It must be one of Sheila's tricks. Perhaps she and Dawn arranged it between them.'

Victor could see she was upset and knew it was not only the photograph. 'There's no use speculating. But I suppose we have to give the man the benefit of the doubt, seeing that it's Sheila involved.' There was no point trying to blacken Billie any further. He guessed that a wrong word and she would tell him to go.

'What's troubling you, love?' he asked after a few moments' quiet. 'I know you well enough to be able to tell when there's something on your mind.'

'It's Margaret,' she told him. 'Mrs French has offered to pay for her to go to a private school, where she will be able to concentrate more on her music.'

'There's no trouble making a decision on that one.

256

You wouldn't want her to leave you at her age, surely?'

'But if it's best for her?'

'Trouble is, with those decisions you never know until it's too late. No, Margaret's place is here with you and Freddie, when he's home. How could it be best to put her in among strangers? Growing up away from her home, changing her so she won't belong anywhere. No. Imogine's family wanted to do that for Delina and the boys, but that was one time I insisted on having my own way, and none of us have regretted it.'

'But Margaret is very talented.'

'According to Mrs French. Get someone else to look at her, and see if they agree.'

She half nodded, her mind distant. He saw her look again towards the photograph of Billie and Sheila.

'Billie wouldn't do anything with a kid like Sheila,' he said quietly. 'He's too fond of you to risk losing you.'

He helped her to carry the vegetables outside and arrange them under the window. She was angry and hurt and her fingers worked quickly as she untied strings of cabbages and pulled onions free from their net sacks. Her face was flushed slightly and he thought her the most beautiful and desirable woman he had known. He had to play fair with Billie, to the point of not accusing him of something he was certainly innocent of, but he would not be noble enough to help him, or be stupid enough to miss a good opportunity.

'Ask Mavis to do the morning shift for you,' he said eagerly. 'It isn't often you have a Saturday off.'

'I couldn't, Victor. But I must admit I don't feel like being pleasant to customers today.'

'Then ask. She can only say no.'

Amy went to the side door which led up to the flat and knocked. Mavis had her hair in curlers and still wore her dressing gown when she opened the door but she agreed

257

at once to manage the shop in the morning as well as the afternoon.

'Saturday morning isn't too bad and I'll be able to catch up with my work tomorrow, but don't tell the vicar,' she joked.

'Right then,' Amy said, her hands on her hips. 'Now, what are we going to do with the day?'

'Fetch Margaret and Oliver and ask them to come with us. Where, is up to you.'

'They're already going out. Nelly has invited them to have a picnic up at the old castle ruins. Dawn as well.'

A smile lit Victor's face, his blue eyes glowing with pleasure. 'Lovely. I'll have you all to myself for a whole day.'

'But—'

'Definitely no buts! There's nothing you can do about it. Fate has played straight into my hands.' He gave a huge wink and handed her the coat she had thrown across the counter. 'As soon as Mavis gets her hair out of them old tin cans, we're off.'

'I'll have to go home for Sian's food first. I didn't bring enough for the whole day.'

'Lovely,' Victor said again.

They walked down the road to the house, the baby propped up a little so she could see something more than the sky above, Victor talking to her all the way, pushing the pram in sudden bursts of speed to make the child laugh.

'She's too young for games,' Amy laughed.

'You know that, but does she?' he replied, watching the little face show a wide toothless grin of delight.

The plan was for them to take the food Amy had packed for him, plus extra she had brought from the shop, and walk along the lanes towards Llangwyn, but in fact they did not leave the house.

Amy prepared the food for Sian and made them a cup

of tea. Victor seemed in no hurry to start and at twelve o'clock he amused Amy by spreading her seersucker tablecloth on the carpet and setting the food out on it.

'We'll have our picnic here,' he said with a grin. 'Then we won't have to bother carrying it.'

Amy chuckled and sat down beside him but as his arms wrapped around her and he pulled her gently to him, the smile faded and tears came instead.

'Amy, what is it? I won't touch you if you don't want me to, although how you expect to smile at me like that and me not go to pieces I don't know.'

'I'm crying because you're such a fool and you make fun out of simple things and I love you and I can't see any point in even starting to think where it will all end.'

He kissed her then and the tears dried as need of him overcame her despair. Leaving the baby sleeping peacefully in her pram, he carried her upstairs. She guided him into her bedroom where the bed lay temptingly smooth and icily cool, its satin cover creaseless and untouched.

They kissed, resting on the soft bed, exploring each other until their clothes became impossible to bear. He undressed her slowly, kissing each newly revealed splendour with reverence and with wonder on his face at the perfection of her skin. His kisses began on her shoulder and gradually encircled her throat and face and down over her warm body. When they had finally made love they relaxed and slept.

Amy woke first to hear someone knocking at the door.

'Victor,' she whispered and he was awake in a moment.

'Let them knock, love, there's nothing that will get you fit to open the door in less than three minutes and whoever it is will have long given up.' He put an arm around her, pressing her against him, his lips touching her eyes. He felt her lashes flutter.

'Hush, love, there's nothing we can do,' he whispered

259

as the door knocker went again, this time with so much force that Amy jumped up. 'They'll wake Sian.' Amy's eyes were wide with anxiety. 'Best I go and see who it is.'

'Go down looking like this?'

'Well at least look through the window! The alarm was rapidly turning into laughter.

'All right then,' he crawled off the bed and along the floor to peer through the lowest part of the window, wishing it was not mid-summer and bright daylight. He saw a woman walking away to where a taxi growled good-naturedly at the roadside.

'It's your sister,' he reported, ducking low as he crawled back. He put his head on one side, listening, then added, 'and no, she didn't wake Sian, so we might as well make the most of it.' He began kissing her again, this time starting at her toes.

Prue instructed the taxi driver to turn around and take her to Netta Cartwright's house in the row near the school. Instructing the driver to wait once again, she knocked and this time had a response.

'Went to see my sister but she was out,' she said without preamble. 'Give this money to the driver, will you?' She walked in to sit on the armchair near the fireplace. Putting down the small leather bag she carried, she took out some knitting. 'I can't seem to concentrate long enough to get this pattern started,' she said, handing it to Netta. 'Sort it for me will you?'

Used to Prue's rude manner, Netta took the knitting, undid a couple of rows and gently explained to Prue where she had gone wrong.

'Now we'll have a cup of tea, shall we?' she said to her uninvited visitor, but Prue's head was deep in the pattern book and did not answer.

'Prue, why don't you come back to the knitting circle?' Netta asked, returning with the tray. 'Good you are with handwork, and we need a few to get the others started.'

'There's no chance of me returning to this village,' Prue announced firmly, in between counting stitches and glancing at her pattern, 'and that is definite.'

'Best not to be definite about anything in this changing world,' Netta replied mildly. She watched as Prue finished a few rows of knitting and seemed satisfied that she had now mastered the intricate lace-like design. Prue was looking much better. The fact that she was grumbling and back to her usual off-hand and thoughtless ways was encouraging. She thought she would try a different tack and said quietly, 'Shame about your house, isn't it?'

'What's a shame?' Prue asked quickly, her thin hands stilled.

'Well, it can't be as clean as when you were there, now can it? Nelly does her best, in fact she does more cleaning than you pay her for, but it isn't the same without someone to keep an eye on it. Last week I went there myself to brush out a lot of mud from the front porch. Courting couple someone said it was, standing there and marking your lovely red porch tiles scuffing their heels. Shame it is.'

'Perhaps I'll just go and look, before the taxi comes back. You can take me.'

Netta picked up a coat and they went out. Prue stared ahead of her as if determined not to see or speak to anyone who passed, but no one did. Saturday was a day when many of the villagers went into town for a look at the shops. Only Johnny in his bus saw them and he tooted enthusiastically at his mother, not recognising Prue at first. Then he slowed down and called, 'Back in the village, are you? Best for you too.'

Prue did not reply and he waved and drove on. He had always disliked Prue but, knowing how ill she had been, he was genuinely pleased to see her back. Something to

261

tell Fay, he thought, as he turned the bus gently into the curve in the road and the two women were lost to his mirrored view.

Prue was surprised at how neat the house looked after her long absence but she said nothing of this to Netta. Instead, she rubbed a finger over the surfaces and tutted.

'I don't know what I pay Nelly for. She was always too busy chattering to get on with her work.'

'For five shillings you get good value, I'd say,' Netta admonished gently, her soft voice hardly loud enough to be heard. 'She's a good, kind sort and I think there's a lot of people undervalue her.' She was surprised at the effect of her mild criticism on Prue.

'I didn't mean to criticise her,' Prue said. And Netta turned to her as her voice shook with anxiety.

'I know that. It's a habit with you and we all know you don't mean it,' Netta soothed. But Prue was still upset.

'Don't tell Nelly I was dissatisfied, will you?'

'Indeed I won't. Tell her you're pleased, shall I? It does look as if she's worked hard and she didn't know you were coming to look, did she?'

'Tell her that. Tell her I'm pleased.'

Prue had always been thin but now her eyes seemed too large for her face. Deep-set and shadowed, they aroused Netta's pity.

'Come on, Prue, I don't think you should stay too long, not the first time. Come back in a day or so and we can have a proper look to see if anything wants doing. All right?' She guided Prue back to the front door but in the hall Prue pulled away and opened the door of the small room leading off the hall that had been Harry's office. Prue stared for a while, seeing in her troubled mind's eye the man who used to sit at the table and pour over the books, night after night. The man she had destroyed. Tears filled her blue eyes and trickled down her cheek as she allowed herself to be led back to Netta's

262

house to wait for the taxi that would take her back to the mental hospital which was now her home.

Later that evening, Netta walked up the lane to find Nelly, who was unpacking the debris of a day out with Margaret, Oliver and Dawn.

'I promised I wouldn't say,' Netta said in her quiet voice, 'but I couldn't fathom why she was so upset. First of all she seemed pleased with the look of the house. You really are keeping it looking nice, Nelly. Then, she seemed unable to say how neat it was and began to accuse you of being lazy. Went to pieces she did then, crying, and asking me not to tell you she was criticising you. It's so strange, her not wanting to upset you. She did plenty of upsetting people before she was ill.'

'Per'aps them doctors is tellin' 'er to be nice to people – what an 'ope. Don't worry about it, Netta. Illness like she's got 'as complications. I expect that's what it is, complications.' She looked thoughtful for a while, then added, 'Put 'er mind at rest, will yer? Tell 'er I bears 'er no malice, none at all, an' say I wishes 'er well.' She continued to look thoughtful as she gathered the remnants of cake for the hens at the door. 'Impatient fer their share of the picnic,' Nelly explained as she threw the crumbs down for them.

'The picnic a success, was it?' Netta asked.

'Yes, the kids enjoy a chance to run around and climb an' explore. Funny what kids say though. Dawn said Victor asked her to suggest we went on a picnic today. She said 'e gave 'er money fer icecream, an' all.' Nelly chuckled. 'Couldn't bring herself to ask right out for 'erself I expect. As if Victor cares if me an' the kids go on a picnic or not!'

On the day Sheila received her first pay packet she felt the last scale of depression peeling away from her. Having money in her purse and being able to consider buying some new clothes made her feel human again after the months of ungainliness followed by the distress of losing the baby.

Since the disaster of her marriage and the birth of her child she now felt, with her returned confidence, worldly-wise. She walked from the staff door of the gown-shop and headed towards the bus station, fingering her wedding ring, loose on her finger now she had lost so much weight. The sense of liberty given by the return to her job and the feel of the crisp pay-packet in her hand made her reluctant to go home.

She deliberately missed the bus she had caught every evening that week and wandered instead along the main road of Llangwyn, gazing into shop windows, admiring the clothes adorning the models in the more exclusive fashion shops at the far end of the shopping centre.

Dreaming of the new outfit she would buy for the autumn, she returned to the bus stop on the opposite side of the road, taking in the new hat-shop where Fay had recently started an account, gasping at the prices of the sparsely decorated hats. Clothes she loved but hats, she decided firmly, she could do without. She brushed her hair back from her shoulders as if defying the owner of the shop to think anything was needed to cover its beauty.

The pavements were crowded as she approached the entrance to the bus station, with its metal bars partitioning off the various queues, the floor grease-stained and shining. Sheila frowned with distaste as she tip-toed through, thinking it looked more like a cattle market than a place for people to wait. It was a wonder her shoes hadn't softened and melted in the mess of oil and petrol. She looked along the row of benches against the far wall where a few seats were still vacant. Most refused to leave their place in the queues for the dubious comfort of the wooden benches.

She walked across and found a seat near the corner, but left almost immediately as the man sitting next to her took out a bottle of cider and began to drink noisily. She gave him a frosty glare which worried him not at all, and went back to the queue to lean over the metal rail. Overhearing someone talk about Hen Carw Parc, she realised she had missed another bus and again left the queue and went to find a cup of tea.

Half an hour later, when she was once again heading for the bus station, she heard motor-bikes approaching. She turned and screamed in fright as two bikes seemed to be heading straight for her. They swerved at the last moment and she saw the laughing faces of Pete Evans and Gerry Williams.

'Move your arse, Sheila Powell.' Pete called back. Sheila stood glaring after them but could only manage, 'Oh, oh, you, you pigs!'

A voice at her side asked anxiously if she was all right and a hand steadied her elbow in a comforting way. Shaking, her eyes wide with fright, Sheila turned to see a young man, about twenty-four, staring at her, concern showing in his hazel eyes. His eyes were deep-set above a long thin nose, the mouth pursed slightly in disapproval as he stared after the disappearing bikes and murmured, succinctly, 'Idiots.'

'I agree,' Sheila said in her high voice.

'Will you come and have a cup of tea to calm your nerves? I'm sure you shouldn't go on with your journey until you've recovered from the shock. Hooligans, they were, and not old enough to have machines like those.' His voice was low and soothing and Sheila nodded agreement and moved with him towards the exit.

'Yes, I would be glad to sit for a while.'

'I know a small place just around the corner. Take my arm,' he added. 'You've gone very white.'

Solicitously he guided her to a small cafe that called

itself the Copper Pan and justified the name by having a copper kettle in the fern-filled window. Inside, the place was clean and obviously very expensive. There were several more pans and kitchen utensils around the walls, which were decorated to look like an old fashioned timber-framed room.

They sat in a corner near the window and waited for the waitress to come and take their order. To her relief Sheila did not have to think about what she wanted. The man ordered for her in a masterful way that warmed her heart and made her look at him with undisguised admiration. This was more like stories in magazines. She felt her confidence growing in the presence of this sophisticated and mature man. Maturity was something Sheila admired in a man and she immediately compared him with Freddie, remembering his gaucheness and enjoying the encounter even more.

The waitress brought tea, to which the young man added two heaped spoonsful of sugar before offering it to her. There were cream cakes on the two-tier plate but again he chose for her, selecting an iced, cream-filled doughnut.

'Now, sip the tea while it's hot,' he instructed and, wide-eyed, Sheila did as he asked.

'Very kind of you,' she murmured as she brought the cup to her lips. She closed her eyes and drank the tea which she did not want or need, smiling at him over the cup when she had taken a few sips, before lowering the cup, holding his gaze as she did so.

'My name is Nigel Knighton,' he said, as he coaxed her to take more of the over-sweet liquid. 'I'm an accountant working for a small builders near here. Please tell me who you are?'

'Sheila Pow— Davies,' she corrected. 'I work as first sales in a gown-shop. I live in Hen Carw Parc – for the moment,' she added quickly, for she hated admitting to this handsome and sophisticated man that she lived in a small village.

'Do you? Lovely place Hen Carw Parc,' Nigel said. 'I have to live in town and would love to live in the country. The air is so much fresher and cleaner.'

'You would? I can't get away from it fast enough.'

'Your husband—' he hesitated, glancing at her hand and the shiny new gold band. 'Perhaps he's the one who loves the country?'

Sheila bent her head and whispered, 'Not really. I haven't a husband.' She did not explain, thinking it would be fun to leave him with an air of mystery. He took her hands and rubbed them, wanting to comfort this pretty little thing who had obviously been badly treated by life.

Half an hour later he saw her on to the bus and stood waving until it disappeared from his sight. Sheila sat in her seat, well pleased with her day's events, already planning what she would wear on the following day when they would meet in the same cafe for tea, after work. She glowed with excitement and anticipation. Meeting someone like Nigel, who was an accountant and therefore brainy, was such wonderful luck and how romantic it had been! How wise that she had refused to go to live near Freddie and be escorted around with someone wearing dreary khaki.

She was not even deflated when she stepped off the bus to see her parents waiting for her, their faces dragged down with worry, the recriminations as easy to read in their eyes as the signpost to the council houses on the corner.

'Frantic we've been, Sheila,' Her mother said as soon as they were within hearing. 'We didn't see you getting off the usual bus and then the next one sailed past without stopping.'

'I went for a cup of tea, Mam, that's all! Surely I'm allowed that?'

267

'Of course, just in future phone the shop. Amy will give me a message if I'm not there.'

'Just a bit of thought, that's all we're asking for, Sheila,' her father said disapprovingly. 'Just a bit of thought.'

'Mam,' Sheila said, ignoring her father completely. 'I'm twenty-one and married. I know I haven't got a husband on hand, but I am married and twenty-one. I don't have to tell you everything about my day, now do I?'

'It's just that we worry about you.'

'Then don't!' She flashed them a dazzling smile and ran across the road and up Sheepy Lane without looking back.

# Chapter Fourteen

Johnny was unable to resist looking in on Fay on the following Tuesday. He had changed shifts without telling her and felt like a criminal for the deceit. He stood watching the hotel, dreading seeing her, yet unable to move away. Several times between twelve and twelve-thirty he shifted a few paces, as if heading for the bus stop and home, the guilty feeling that he was spying on her increasing but not stopping him. At a quarter-to-one she came, looked briefly around and walked inside.

Even then he hesitated, afraid that he would learn something he would rather not know. Childish I am, he thought, but childish or not I can't go on imagining the worst without tackling it and getting the truth, however painful. There was fear too, that he would make her angry by appearing during her working day. He knew she liked to forget everything and concentrate on her job while she was away from home, cutting off everything except the knowledge of her stock and the information she had on the latest fashion trends.

If she suspected the real reason for his being in town when he was supposed to be driving his bus – that he did not trust her – there was a risk of damaging a relationship that was already shaky. He stood at the grand carpeted entrance for a moment. There was still time to turn back, go home and try to forget his suspicions. Then, straightening his shoulders he walked in, going straight to the staircase and up to the restaurant.

He saw her immediately and again stopped to consider if he should continue. She was sitting at a corner table, facing the wall and opposite her was a man. He was leaning forward and they were both laughing. Johnny wanted to run away, again like a child, he thought as his legs shook with panic. If he walked away now, gave her time, perhaps she would come to him and tell him about the man, explain how they had met and become so friendly. But his legs refused to work. He was incapable of running anywhere. His eyes were transfixed by the couple at the corner table, wondering what it was that they found so funny when he was crying inside.

A waiter approached and asked if he wanted a table.

'No thanks, I'm joining my wife.' He spoke loudly and saw the couple he was watching jerk apart as Fay recognised his voice. Fay turned a startled face in his direction then gave him a dazzling smile, a slight blush adding to her loveliness. Forcing a smile, he went across and kissed her.

'Shopping, I was, and I thought I'd surprise you, my lovely,' he said. He looked at the man, still chewing, and brushing his mouth with a napkin.

'You must be Johnny?' the man said. 'My name is Dexter, Dexter Lloyd-Rees.

The man spoke with an educated voice, loud and confident and Johnny felt himself shrinking.

'I'm Fay's husband. Lucky man, aren't I?'

'Darling, what are you doing in town?' Fay asked.

'More to the point, what are *you* doing in town?' Johnny asked, embarrassment rapidly turning to anger. 'Why are you spending time with him, when you're always too busy for us?'

'I have to eat, darling,' Fay admonished gently. 'This gentleman only shared my table as the place was beginning to fill up. We have met here before,' she added, 'purely coincidentally, of course.'

'For sure. That's why you and he are sharing the pot of tea and the sandwiches are on one plate and not two! You must think I'm thick!' Johnny's voice was rising and the manager glided silently across the red carpet to intervene.

'Is something wrong?' he asked in a low voice, hoping that the troublemakers would lower their voices too. 'If you would prefer a different table?'

'Yes, there's plenty of room, isn't there? Plenty of choice!' Johnny snapped. 'But no thanks. I don't care much for the company!' He walked briskly out, the pain in his heart a tight band around his chest, stifling his breath and making him want to stand and scream his distress to the world.

Outside he stopped, breathing heavily, wondering what to do. Should he go home? Or would it be best to stay away from everyone for a while and allow time to cool off? For the first time in his life he had nowhere to go. Always in the past, whatever difficulties he had encountered, there had been someone in the village to talk to. He had never faced anything so bad as this. Not even when Fay had failed to turn up for their wedding had he felt so completely alone.

The street was full of hurrying people, all intent on some destination and ignoring him, apart from the few who brushed against him and glared their disapproval of someone who could stand still amid the moving sea of busy bustling people. Fay touched his arm and he shrugged her off. She called his name as he moved away but he darted through the crowd, wanting her, needing her but unable to even look at her face.

How could she seek someone else? Hadn't he loved her enough for ten men? Wasn't he as thoughtful and considerate as any woman could expect? He had agreed with everything she wanted, even leaving the village to go and live up on the council houses isolated from his friends. He hurried on, not aware of where he was heading and finally found himself on the road to Hen Carw Parc. He walked along the road, glancing back occasionally until he saw a bus approaching. The driver recognised him and slowed down while he mounted the platform, smiling and joking with the conductor while his heart bled.

Fay was already there when he reached the house. He walked in and hushed her attempt at an explanation.

'Tonight we're going to the concert at the church hall,' he said coldly. 'We're going together, right? And we won't show by the smallest lack of affection that there's anything wrong between us, right? Even if it is all a farce!'

'But Johnny it *is* all—'

'Just be quiet, Fay. Let's get today over with, then we'll see about tomorrow. For now, I want us to go to the concert, sit next to Mam and enjoy being a part of the village.'

Fay gave up her attempt to appease him. She had worked out a story on the drive home that would cover the meeting of herself and Dexter. She would tell Johnny he was married and that they were waiting for Dexter's wife to join them. The fact that Dexter had hurriedly asked her to meet him the following week in a small village on the coast a few miles out of town, where no buses passed, she tried to forget.

She tried to understand what it was she lacked that made constant reassurance, like the mild flirtation, so necessary. Very many invitations came her way: she was constantly eating out and having new people entering her life and, dressed as attractively as she was, there were often misunderstandings. On three occasions, seeing her sitting alone in an hotel lounge, men had presumed that she was a prostitute and those times were very upsetting.

There had been nothing like that about Dexter. He

272

seemed simply to enjoy her company and she had warmed to the sensation of being flattered and thought interesting as well as beautiful. For Johnny, her being beautiful seemed sufficient. He did not want to know about how she felt about world happenings, or whether the latest book from the travelling library was a good or a bad read. For Johnny, she filled his life completely just by being there. He did not treat her like a person at all.

Watching him getting dressed in the suit he had bought for their wedding, ready to go to the village concert, she felt a surge of guilt at her rebellious thoughts. He really was a good husband and she did love him. If only he would let go of the village and its smallness they could be happy. He deserved better than she gave him, she knew that, but why didn't he try to understand her a little more? Battling to and fro, her thoughts made her frown and caused a headache, which Johnny, refusing to talk, did nothing to alleviate.

She put on a summer dress of white linen with a pattern of yellow poppies and a sash of the same rich yellow which she knew Johnny liked. For once she did not wear a hat, but left her blonde hair falling about her shoulders in a long under-roll which shone with healthy cleanliness. Her eyes were calm and a little sad as they walked down Heol Caradoc and Sheepy Lane, where they met Ethel who was waiting for Phil and Catrin to escort her.

'Tell that son of mine to get his skates on if you see him, will you?' Ethel called as Johnny waved, '*Duw annwyl* – there's slow he is.'

'Take my arm, Fay,' Johnny instructed. 'I want us to look like we're happy when we meet Mam. Eyes like an eagle, Mam has, and would know in an instant if we don't put on a good act.'

'It isn't an act, Johnny,' Fay said. 'I want to take your arm. I love you and want everyone to see how proud I am to be your wife.'

'Peculiar way of showing it, going out with other men!'

'I wasn't going out with him, just sharing a pot of tea!'

'Don't talk about it now. We'll get this over with first. Like I said, everyone'll be here tonight. It's village fun and I want to enjoy it.'

'I might have to pretend about that,' she admitted, 'but not about us.'

There were several people uneasy in the hall that evening. Evie found herself near Nelly, who shouted enthusiastically when Oliver trooped on in the third row of the choir. Nelly's voice was never low and even with the rumble of a hundred conversations, it carried and made people turn their heads to smile. Evie moved. She explained to Timothy that 'with the best will in the world, I cannot sit beside my mother for two hours.'

Timothy brought an extra chair and sat her in the row reserved for the Board of Governors, which was where Evie had wanted to sit in the first place.

Delina sat at the end of the row just behind Evie and to her consternation, as the time to begin approached and latecomers took possession of their seats, Tad walked in. Seeing there were no spare seats he approached Timothy, who rather than offend the short-tempered man, brought yet another chair and placed it beside Delina, who stared stonily towards the stage. Tad smelt of oil and his hands were stained. He had obviously come straight from work.

They had been given programmes and, being the last, there was not one readily available for Tad. When he asked where he might obtain one, with teeth tightly clenched and an artificial bright smile on her face, Delina offered to share hers. She really must not allow this unpleasant man to make her as difficult as himself, she told herself, but it was hard to stand, hearing his rather pleasant voice sing the national anthem and the introduc-

274

tory hymn so close to her and see his dirty but perfectly shaped hands holding the furthest edge of the programme. She was both repulsed and attracted to him and tried to convince herself the attraction was only sympathy.

For the first part of the concert he did not speak but sat listening to the singing and sang when the audience was invited to join in, applauding the soloists with enthusiasm. She saw him wave to his daughter who was at the back of the choir, having been at too few rehearsals to merit the front rows, small as she was. Delina found her own eyes drifting back time and again to the little girl who seemed to be happy joining in the songs.

'Dawn looks to be enjoying herself,' she risked during the second half.

'Yes, she likes singing. Not very good though, between you and me,' he surprised her by admitting.

'But if we all did only what we were good at, there wouldn't be much done, would there?' Delina agreed.

Margaret sang a solo and again Tad spoke, this time in admiration of the girl's lovely voice.

'Now that is a voice!' he whispered as the audience applauded. 'She plays the piano as well, I hear? Does she take lessons with Mrs French?'

'Yes. Mrs French taught her for nothing for a while, and allowed her to go to her house to practise as Margaret didn't have a piano.'

'No piano, with a talent like hers?'

'Not at first. When her mother Amy moved into the house at the end of the village, she bought her one. She was convinced by Mrs French that her daughter had real talent.'

When it was time for the piano solos, Delina noticed that Tad listened attentively, absorbed in the delicately played Schubert melody followed by the difficult fingering of a Chopin Etude.

275

'You like music?' she asked, curious about the man who seemed to have two faces; one the over-protective father with a foul temper, the other this sensitive and quiet man now sitting beside her and sharing her enjoyment of the music.

'I used to play once, but like many other things I had to give it up when war began to go and fight,' he said and at once she saw the change in him. The bitterness stretched his mouth out of the small fullness into a tight, thin line.

'Why don't you go back to it? Thousands of people have had their lives disrupted and yet managed to pick up the pieces.'

'How, with Dawn to look after? I can't even find a proper job. I only work part time so I can be home when she gets in from school. I don't always manage that, but I try my best.'

'I think your best must be very good,' she smiled, 'but—'

Again the change came in him with startling suddenness. 'You do, do you? Nice of you to think so. What is it about you people? You're so condescending and smug. I wonder if any of you would cope if everything in your safe little world fell apart? Not so smug then. Not so self-satisfied and not so sure you know it all, Miss Honeyman!'

Not waiting for the results of the competitions to be announced, he left the hall, bent double as if to avoid interrupting the view for the rest of the audience.

Trying not to be seen, Delina thought sadly. He must constantly feel foolish, she decided, unaffected by his stupid outburst. He always takes offence at the most innocent of remarks and friendly overtures. He must lie in bed at night going over and over the stupidity of the day's events, angry at himself and not at the people he offended.

276

She stared up at the stage, decorated by the women of the village with all the flowers of glorious July. Her mind wandered, trying not to think of the empty chair beside her, wondering if she would ever persuade Tad that the local people were willing to be his friends. She noticed that Dawn was missing from the back of the choir, still on the stage, and guessed that she had seen her father leave and had run after him.

Forcing herself to concentrate on the happenings in the hall, she listened as Timothy announced the presentation of the prizes. The first was the trumpet solo and the boy who had won went to stand beside the headmaster to receive his money.

'The prize money, Mr Evans,' Timothy said, holding out his hand to the school caretaker. But Mr Evans shook his head.

'They've gone, sir, everyone of them. Someone must have taken them. There's not even an envelope to be seen!'

Constable Harris stood up in the back row. He hushed them all and asked that everyone stayed in their seats. Delina dreaded someone shouting that Tad had just left the hall, stepping through the entrance where the prizes had been stacked. She thought someone was certain to mention his swift departure but knew that if he were innocent it would be yet another reason for him to feel that the villagers were against him and his daughter. She responded to the atavistic need to cross her fingers and hope that she had been the only one to notice him leaving.

'That Tad Simmons, he crept out on the quiet, crouching low so as not to be noticed,' someone shouted. The way it was said gave everyone the image of a man guiltily creeping out, bent on robbing the children of their prize money.

A strong desire to defend the man rose in Delina but

277

when the constable questioned her, she only said, 'He was sharing my programme and spoke once or twice. One moment he was there, the next he was gone.'

Her eyes were drawn to a movement and she saw that on the front row Mrs Norwood Bennet-Hughes was rising to her feet. She wore a fur coat although it was a warm July evening and carried a large leather handbag. She beckoned Timothy across. There was a whispered consultation and Timothy, smiling his thanks, made an announcement.

'Thanks to the generosity of Mrs Norwood Bennet-Hughes and other members of our Board of Governors I can announce that the prize money will be given as planned.'

Mrs Norwood Bennet-Hughes opened her large bag and others among the row of dignitaries did the same. Handing a fan of one pound and ten-shilling notes to Timothy, they sat down amid applause and waited for the interrupted proceedings to continue. After handing the prizes to the musicians, in which Margaret's name predominated, Timothy prepared to read out the winners of the photography competitions.

'First prize,' he said slowly, opening the envelope inside which the names were hidden, 'goes to Dawn Simmons.' He glanced around and the choir shuffled as the children looked for her but she did not appear. Timothy had a brief word with the constable and went on. 'The second prize goes to Arthur Toogood, for an interesting view of the nature garden we planted last Spring. Third is – er – Dawn Simmons again, this one a study of two little boys eating a very runny icecream and trying not to waste a drop of it.' He led the clapping for the absent prize-winner then added, 'All the entries are on view in the school hall and if you would like to proceed there as soon as the constable has completed his enquiries, the ladies of the sewing circle will have tea and biscuits available. Thank you all for coming.'

Constable Harris, assisted by Phil and Bert, made a list of everyone who had attended the concert and the crocodile of people made their way across to the school. Timothy stopped Delina as she approached the door in the slowly moving queue.

'I realise this is an imposition, Miss Honeyman, but do you think you could deliver these prizes to Dawn on your way home? You might also tell Mr Simmons what happened after he left us, to explain the absence of the card that should have been with it. I thought as you pass his door and you seem to be on friendly terms with him, you wouldn't mind my asking,' Timothy added.

'I'll put this through the door, certainly,' Delina said taking the money from him, 'if you would write a note of explanation. But, far from being on a friendly basis with Mr Simmons, I have no wish to talk to him, or explain the reason for the lack of a card!' She walked towards the diminishing group waiting to give their names to the policeman and, pushing her way through, hurried over to the school.

There was an anxiety about the crowd as they walked from the church hall. The reminder that there were burglars active in the area made them impatient to get home and reassure themselves that their property was safe. Nelly and George were among the last to leave the hall and George stopped to have a word with his employer, Mr Leighton. Billie was there too and he made his way over to the two men.

'This is worrying,' Billie said. 'I didn't tell the constable – I might have been mistaken – but that Sheila Powell, as was, she told me there had been motor-cyclists watching my place from the woods up near the castle ruins, and I had a vague impression that someone other than me and Mary had been in the yard a few mornings ago. The dogs didn't bark so I might have been wrong, there was no damage done so it seemed daft to mention it. Only a feeling it was, nothing for definite.'

'I think you should tell Constable Harris,' Phil's brother Sidney said. 'He needs to know everything if he's to catch the bugger.' He nodded to where Harris was talking to Timothy in the corner of the almost-empty hall.

'Come on, George, I want to see the rest of the photographs,' said Nelly pulling on George's coat, and he laughingly went with her. When they reached the school, the place was in uproar. Laughter and shouts of anger mingled and it was some moments before Nelly and George could find out the reason. Then they reached the wall where Timothy had made his display and understood what had happened.

Someone, and they could only presume it was Dawn, had added about twenty new pictures to the ones chosen by Timothy. There was Nelly in that embarrassing position in the woods and Sheila apparently about to kiss Billie Brown. There was one of Griff Evan half-crouched as he slipped out of the back gate of the fish-and-chip-shop looking very sly, with alongside it a picture of his wife Hilda in her curlers and without her teeth. Milly, closely followed by Sybil Tremain had a lead and collar added as a caricature of their nickname, and there was one of Evie, stepping out of a car, with her skirts blown up by a gusting wind. Another showed a figure in the woods, clearly identified to many as Griff. He had a gun across his arm and a bag over his shoulder. 'No wonder young Dawn ran off before the fun started!' Nelly laughed. 'I bet there's a few here who'd like to get hold of her.'

Dawn was hiding up in the den made for Margaret and Oliver and, as the early morning light showing across the hills and giving the village a touch of gold, she crept out

280

and climbed down the ladder. It was still early and in the distance she could hear Mary-Dairy's bottles rattling against their crates. She walked around to the top of the estate, behind St Hilda's Crescent and walked through one of the gardens to the front of the houses. She found milk money left out at three of the houses and put the coins into her coat pocket. At the third house, she had hardly reached the gate when her shoulder was held in a tight, painful grip and although she struggled, she could not escape.

It was Phil Davies who held her and from the porch his brother Sidney appeared, having stood there for several hours.

'Got you proper this time, Dawn, and with a couple of witnesses too, so there's no pretending you didn't take the money.'

Dawn threw the coins on to the payment and watched them scatter. 'I didn't touch any money!'

'Sorry, but we both saw you and the people who live in this house saw you go to three other places and pick up money that was put out for Mary.'

'What you going to do? Don't tell my dad, will you?'

'It's your father we're taking you to first and it's up to him, depending on how he behaves, that will make us decide what else we'll do with you. Now, *march*!' The solemn little procession walked along the crescent which joined Heol Caradoc and Hywel Rise at the top of the estate, both men holding on to Dawn to prevent her running away. This time Tad Simmons would have to face facts.

Tad had just woken and gone in to call his daughter, whom he had found sleeping, curled up under the covers on his return from the concert. He had looked in through the bedroom door but had not disturbed her, thankful that she was there and he did not have to face searching the street for her as he often did. Now, he smiled as he

281

saw that she had hardly moved since the previous night. She must have been very tired. He touched the covers, called her and then shook the heaped up blankets before realising to his horror that she was not there.

He had dressed and was just leaving the house when he saw Dawn firmly held by Sidney and Phil, and followed by the owner of the last house she had robbed. 'What's happened?' he called, running to hug Dawn. 'Found her wandering again?'

'Not wandering, taking money left out to pay for milk!' Phil said. 'Now before you start denying that she's a thief' – he emphasised the word deliberately – 'both Sidney and I have been waiting to catch her, and these people saw her too, so let's not waste time arguing, all right?'

Tad was shaking with shock.

'Dawn? Is this true?'

'I wasn't going to keep it, Dad. I was teaching them a lesson for being daft enough to leave money outside like that.'

'Dawn! If this is true then say so. You're in enough trouble without adding lies to the list.'

Dawn puffed up as if to bluster but suddenly her face seemed to collapse and she began to cry, softly and deep inside herself so the sound was little more than a moan. Tad did not move to comfort her.

'You'd better come inside.' He led them to the front door and they all trooped in. 'Now, what are you going to do? Tell the police? She's only a child, and if she starts with a criminal record at her age – I don't suppose I'll be allowed to keep her, she'll go into care.' Tad seemed to be speaking more to himself than to Phil and Sidney.

'Trouble is, Tad, there's more than just milk money being taken and if Dawn is involved in those thefts as well, then we have to report what we've seen,' Sidney said.

'No way that she's broken into houses, man!' Tad said.

'If you could believe a word she says, that would be enough for us, but she's such a little Tom Pepper,' Phil said. 'Tells lies for the fun of it, she does.'

'I'll give up my job and manage on the dole,' Tad said. 'I'll be here all the time and I'll keep a tight rein on her, I promise.'

Dawn stood white-faced and looking far younger than her ten years. Her eyes never left her father and she wiped an occasional tear from her eyes. It was Phil who noticed she was shivering.

'Best get her warmed up, she's cold and probably hungry.'

Tad nodded, he did not tell them she had probably been out all night, he was too ashamed for allowing it to happen.

They agreed to do nothing, but threatened Tad that if Dawn stepped out of line again, the constable would be given the full facts. 'Even if it means we're in trouble for keeping them from him, we'll tell him everything, you can be sure of that,' Sidney said. 'Mam had money taken from the kitchen and I'm sure that went into Dawn's pocket as well, didn't it?' he asked the girl, who nodded.

'I'll pay it all back somehow,' Tad said.

'Just keep her out of trouble in the future and don't make us regret giving her this chance.'

When Phil and the others had gone, Tad put Dawn over his knees and slapped her until his hand stung. She did not cry, but went up to her room and dressed for school. Strangely, the violence was a release for her: she could stop stealing now her father knew. Now he would be there, like other children's fathers. She wouldn't have the lonely hours to fill with mischief, wouldn't have to do things to prove to the other children that her life was more exciting than theirs.

'You know I'll have to give up my job at the factory now, don't you?' Tad said when he went to fetch her down for breakfast. 'I tried to work so we'd have a bit of extra money but now it's finished. I gave them my word I'd watch you, so we'll have to manage on the dole money.'

'Sorry, Dad.'

'No you aren't, Dawn. But you will be. There'll be no money for anything except food, I'll have to buy what clothes you need in jumble sales, and you can forget about money for films and developing.'

'But you'll be here all the time,' Dawn said, thinking of the joy of not coming home to an empty house.

'Oh yes, unfortunately I'll be on your tail every moment of the day and night. Dawn, I haven't asked much from you. I tried to make sure you weren't made to grow up before your time, by being expected to do the shopping and the ironing and cooking. I've dealt with all that and I'm shattered to think that you repaid me by stealing from our neighbours.'

Dawn began to see that the changes were going to be less exciting than she first thought. Having Dad home all day was fine, but without pocket money how would she manage not to steal again?

'Do you think that if I promised not to touch the milk money again, they would let you stay on at the factory?' she asked in a small voice. 'I don't think I'd like being dressed at jumble sales, everyone would know and—'

'I don't think they – or I – can trust you to keep your word.' Tad's eyes were sorrowful and he crossed his arms over his chest and clasped his shoulders tightly, walking up and down the room in his distress.

'You can. I know they meant it when they said they'd go to the police next time.'

Her face was so drained of colour and her eyes red with crying and Tad's heart turned over. He had to take most of the blame for how she behaved.

'I'll ask them,' he replied gruffly. 'But if I ever even suspect you of taking anything belonging to someone else, I'll take you to the police myself! It'll mean you going into a home, then. Understand?'

Dawn ate her breakfast and thought about finding the money for her photography. For her, the camera given to her by Nelly was the only thing in her life that gave her pleasure. It would all be so different if she had a family like the children at school had, she thought wistfully. Then she would have so much to do that she wouldn't need to do things for a 'dare'.

On the day when Oliver was to spend the evening and night with Nelly and George, Evie came to inspect the room he would use. She came to the house with her usual wariness, even holding up her skirt to make sure it did not rub against the walls as she went up the curving staircase and into the back bedroom, recently vacated by George. She lifted the green candlewick bed-cover which Nelly had borrowed from Amy, looked at the white sheets and nodded approval.

'Disappointed, are yer?' Nelly couldn't resist asking. 'Expecting the bed to be full of fleas? Or—'

'All right, Mother. Don't go into details. I know I'm fussy, but he's my son and very precious to me.'

Nelly could have found a sharp reply to that but she bit her tongue.

They went back down the stairs and Evie declined the tea her mother offered, although Nelly had put out her best cups and saucers on the polished tray that George and Oliver had made.

'I really don't have time, Mother, but thank you,' Evie surprised her by saying. 'You have clearly made an effort to make things nice for Oliver.'

'I love 'im too, yer know.'

The dinner Evie and Timothy were to attend began at

eight o'clock and Oliver was sent to the cottage before five.

'Mother needed time to calm down,' Oliver explained seriously.

'Good, you'll be here when George gets in from work. We've got time for a walk before 'and if you like?'

They wandered through the trees and Oliver climbed up into the tree house, looking down at Nelly and telling her all he could see from the extra height. The day was a dull one with a mist lying over the wood making it secluded and private.

'I bet I could see as far as Billie's farm if the sun was shining,' Oliver boasted.

They arrived back at the gate at the same time as George, who was carrying a sack of logs across his shoulders.

'Glad to see you, Oliver. You can help me stack this wood.'

Leaving the man and the boy busily arranging the wood against the side of the shed, Nelly went in to take the casserole from the oven. The potatoes were simmering gently on the fire and, when they were soft, she strained them and called them in for their meal. Bobby and Spotty sat, tails wagging, tongues lolling and dribbing, beside Nelly's chair.

'Oh, Gran. I thought we were having potatoes baked under the fire!'

'Them's fer supper.'

'Mother doesn't let me have supper—' He was so clearly disappointed that Nelly laughed.

'That's why Gawd gives us grans as well as mothers. Grans 'ave different rules, Ollie. Supper is at eight before you get ready fer bed at nine.'

Oliver ate contentedly.

'This is ridiculous, George,' Nelly said much later when Oliver was asleep and they sat near the open door watching the dying day.

'What's ridiculous, love?'

286

'Me, gettin' all excited at sharin' a room with me 'usband.' George laughed and stood up, his tall figure bending to help her from her chair.

'Come on, I think it's time we went to see if we can both fit into that bed of yours.'

It had begun to rain soon after Oliver and Nelly had left the woods and now it fell steadily and without haste, shushing on the leaves and falling dully on the grass. It hissed on the water of the stream and squelched under Nelly's wellingtons as she marched into her part of the wood to attend to her late-night routine.

She was so still that a man passed within a few feet of her without knowing she was there. He was dressed against the weather in dark concealing coat and hood and Nelly did not recognise him, although she thought at first that it might be Griff after a few rabbits or a pheasant from the estate further on. Was he a tramp, she wondered sorrowfully, wishing she could invite him to stay with her and George, if he was wandering. But he was more likely to be a poacher, like Griff. She saw no gun, but a poacher would have it broken and hidden under his clothing anyway. For a moment nervousness made her shiver as she thought he might be the mysterious prowler who had robbed so many houses in the village. She waited for a few minutes before adjusting her clothes and returning to the cottage.

She closed the gate and fixed the latch firmly and smiled at the stupid precaution and the fear that had instigated it. As if a wooden gate would keep anyone out! She undressed by the low fire while George went into the trees and then let the dogs out for their final run. The dogs were restless.

'There's someone about out there,' George said.

'Poachers, I expect.' Nelly banked up the fire with small coals and ashes and lit her candle to go upstairs. 'Lock the door, will yer?'

George did so, using the large key from the mantel-piece, surprised at her request. The cottage door had never been locked since he had known Nelly. Perhaps, he thought, it was the responsibility for young Oliver. Taking a second candle, he lit it with a taper of newspaper and followed Nelly upstairs.

Nelly was in bed and her candle snuffed out. He undressed and put on pyjama trousers and hesitated. Nelly pushed back the covers and snuggled up to him as he slid in beside her. He put an arm around her and enfolded her tightly.

'We've never had a cuddle before,' he whispered, 'not like this.'

'You're 'ere George, that's what matters, no matter 'ow we live, you're 'ere an' I'm glad o' that.'

'I haven't spoilt things for you, have I? Staying here I mean? I married you so Evie would leave you in peace. I didn't intend to stay. I was determined not to, in fact. There was no sense saving you from Evie and spoiling things for you in another way.'

'She's a dragon, ain't she, my Evie?' She laughed and happiness seemed to burst out of her like bubbles. 'George and the dragon!' she laughed.

'Henry,' he chuckled, his white beard tickling her face.

'Yes. Henry. I'm sorry, but I can't think of you as 'Enry Masters. To me you're George an' always will be.'

'George is good enough for me, my dear Nelly.' He kissed her and she laughed again.

'I likes yer beard. People thought I was daft buying you a razor for a present last Christmas. Thought I was wanting you to shave it off. They don't know how fussy you are about keepin' it neat.'

'You'll tell me if I ever make you less than happy, won't you?'

'O' course. Not that you ever could. Now, shift yer

288

arm or you'll wake up as stiff as a yard of frozen pump water in the mornin'.' Holding hands they settled to sleep.

Nelly had just reached the drowsy stage when everything was pleasantly hazy when she heard Oliver calling.

'He might be frightened in a strange room,' George whispered.

'Come on in, Ollie,' Nelly yelled.

The small boy came in beside her. He was cold and grateful for the warmth of her. He tried to think of a reason to justify leaving his room, where trees near the wall were making strange sounds as the rain dripped from the leaves and a branch would occasionally touch the window with whispered tapping. The symphony of the night hours was more noticable here at the edge of the wood, and imagination gave the innocent sounds an eeriness Ollie found disturbing. But as usual, Nelly did not expect explanations.

'There were ten in the bed and the little one said roll over,' Nelly began to sing. 'They all rolled over and one fell out; there were nine in the bed and the little one said roll over—'

Nelly still had the tune running through her head long after George and Oliver had fallen silent. She closed her eyes until the light of the new dawn streaked the walls with light, and the birds announced the arrival of a new day.

# Chapter Fifteen

Constable Harris talked to several people to find out who was where at the time of the concert. Several mentioned the late arrival and early departure of Tad Simmons, and with some trepidation he went to question the man.

'I'm just preparing a plan of where people were on the evening in question,' he explained and to his relief Tad answered crisply and without apparent anger.

'I left work a bit late. I work odd shifts at the factory, brushing the floor and cleaning machines. There had been some spillage and I stayed to clear it up. I got to the concert still in my working clothes – a neighbour had got Dawn ready for her part in the choir. I came home early to cook Dawn's supper. All right?'

'Thank you for your co operation—' Harris was suddenly talking to a closed door. 'Miserable old cuss!' he exclaimed. Later, he walked to the village, passing Nelly's house. It was always a good idea to talk to her. Sharp eyes she had, old Nelly. She was overlooked by many; her being so much a part of the scene, people were hardly aware of her presence sometimes.

The garden of the cottage was a shambles. Workmen and their clutter covered the lawn, the chickens were locked in their pen and grouped around the door chortling anxiously at the unusual confinement. The dogs were sniffing at the tools and the workmen's jackets, in the hope of something edible. Nelly was in her kitchen.

'Blimey, Nelly, it's like World War Three out there! Come to start your drains, have they?'

'Drains, taps *and* a bleedin' bath!'

'That's great.'

'Glad you think so! Look what they've done to me garden. An' me poor 'ens don't know what's 'appening. Fed up they are, but I daren't let 'em out fer fear that they'll wander. Still, I suppose it'll be worth it, though what all the fuss is about I don't know. Managed without a bathroom all me life an' never missed it.'

He asked her who was at the concert and who left early. 'You didn't see anyone you weren't expecting to, or not see someone who should have been there?'

'Well, them Evanses bought tickets but they weren't there. I expect she was working. Hilda 'elps Milly Toogood's daughter in the fish-an'-chip shop.'

'Why is it, Nelly, that Milly Toogood's daughter doesn't have a name? Whenever I mention her she's always "Milly Toogood's daughter".'

Nelly moved closer, confidentially. 'Seems it's on account of 'er marriage. Says she married a Yankie soldier just before the end of the war, but none of us 'as ever seen 'im. Embarrassin' not knowin' what to call 'er. Can't shout "Morning Mrs Yank" can we? And Milly ain't the sort to confide in anyone. So, she's Milly's daughter. Bethan to some.'

'I'll go down and ask about Hilda. Thanks Nelly.'

'Ask about that 'usband of 'ers too.' She was tempted to tell the constable how Griff had diddled her out of a thirty-three to one winner but remembered in time that bookies runners were not smiled upon by the police. 'An' that son of theirs with 'is motor-bike.'

'Yes. Thank you, I will.' Constable Harris nodded to the workmen, now knocking a hole in the side of the cottage, and departed.

Nelly, her hands covering her ears against the noise,

shouted to the men and asked if they wanted food.

'We've all brought sandwiches, thanks,' a young boy shouted back.

'I'll bring you back some chips if you like,' she yelled. Taking the money and orders for several bags of chips, she went down to the village with the dogs. There wasn't anything she needed, but the mess and the noise forced her out. Netta Cartwright was out too but she found her in Amy's shop.

'I'm rising the last of the wool Amy has put away for me, for the dress Prue is making.' Netta paid Amy for the last two balls of fine white wool.

'Still at it then, is she? Well done, Netta. Gettin' 'er interested was a clever move.'

'You've helped Prue a lot,' Amy agreed. 'She was so lethargic I thought she would never recover.'

'Yes, she was coming on well and had started to talk quite freely – the old Prue, disapproving of everyone as always. Then the police went to interview her about the robbery and that upset her something awful. It was a young constable,' Netta explained, 'and he wasn't to know about the other burglary, when someone broke in and killed poor Harry.'

'I hoped she wouldn't have been told, her being so ill,' Amy said. 'It's bound to set her back, isn't it?'

Nelly said nothing. She remembered with painful clarity the moment she had seen Prue and her husband fighting. She saw again the poker in Prue's raised hands coming down on Harry's head. She'd known something terrible had happened, and she'd been right. She had never told anyone what she saw, deciding that Prue had not intended to kill Harry but had lost her temper, probably finding out about Harry and Amy's affair. She did not want the story to come out and bring embarrassment and disgrace to Amy and her children.

'Don't you think so, Nelly?' Netta was saying in her

quiet voice, and Nelly jerked herself out of her daydream to join in the conversation about the improvements in Prue's health.

The constable was going into the chip shop as Nelly reached the door and stood back for her to enter.

'You'll find Hilda Evans around the back,' she whispered as the sizzling of frying chips greeted them. 'Doin' the spuds in the yard, she is.'

'Thank you, Nelly,' the policeman smiled.

Nelly's grubby finger beckoned him closer and she added, ' 'E gambles, 'er 'usband does. Works at the forestry and spends a lot on the 'orses and that's why she 'as to work out there peelin' spuds.'

Harris repeated his thanks.

Nelly took her time joining the small queue for her order, hoping to overhear what was said between Bethan and the constable, but she saw him laugh, take the bag of chips Bethan insisted on giving him, and walk out. 'Come on,' she then grumbled loudly. 'Invisible, am I? I ain't got all day, you know!'

When she reached home there was far less noise. The men had disappeared, tools had fallen silent and the hole in the wall was being neatened by a young boy.

'Ain't finished already, 'ave they? I've brought their chips.'

'They won't be long. Gone to put a bet on up at the Drovers,' the boy told her.

'Blimey, I'd 'ave done that for 'em. Don't tell PC 'Arris about the Drovers, will yer?'

'He probably knows already. It's hardly a secret,' the boy said, throwing a discarded stone on to a pile at the edge of the lawn.

'Ere, watch where you're throwin' them stones!' she shouted as the last one rolled towards the door.

She went inside and put the parcels of chips to keep warm in the fire-heated oven and began to make tea. She felt guilty at her lack of friendliness towards the work-men. She had offered them food – anyone would do that – but she showed by her attitude that the mess they were making to give her a bathroom that she didn't really want was unwelcome. She always enjoyed company but the thought of them knocking through the wall to put a bathroom in the small room beside the back door made her uneasy.

She was used to bathrooms, having cleaned for various ladies over the years, but did not remotely feel the need for one. 'Damn that Evie,' she muttered as she put the kettle over the heat. 'Always interferin' an' messin' things up.' She had walked into the woods first thing every morning for as long as she had been in Hen Carw Parc and, well content with every aspect of her life, feared change.

When the workmen came back she offered them tea and forced herself to join in their conversations as they sat and ate their food. The subject was racing, one dear to her heart and the friendly approach ended up an enjoyable hour, after which the men had to make haste to get their alloted tasks completed.

That night, she and George went to the pictures to see a Cinemascope offering, 'King of the Khyber Rifles' with Tyrone Power and Michael Rennie. They stopped at the Drovers on the way home and when they went to bed George did not go to his own bed, where the covers were still thrown back as Oliver had left them, but joined Nelly in hers.

Delina stayed in town one evening after school and went to the library. She looked through illustrations for a project on 'Travel Through The Ages' which she wanted to use for her class. To her surprise, when she came out Dawn was there, standing outside the building, looking tired and unkempt.

'Dawn? What are you doing here?' Delina asked, stiffling angry thoughts about Tad allowing his daughter to wander in the town with so little regard for her safety.

'I was to have met Dad,' Dawn explained, 'but he hasn't come and I'm cold. Can I have a lift home on your bicycle, Miss?'

'Certainly not. That is against the law without a proper seat.'

'But there's room on the carrier, Miss. I've done it before.'

'Sorry, but no.' Delina was firm. 'It wouldn't be safe and in any case it's not allowed.

'Better just wait then, Miss, hadn't I?'

'How long have you been here?'

'Since three.'

'You haven't been in school?'

'Sore throat, Miss.'

'I see. Well, I think you should go straight home. Do you have your fare? I can certainly help you with that.'

'Return ticket, Miss.'

Delina hesitated. 'Are you sure you'll find your way back all right?'

'Done it lots of times, Miss.'

'I bet you have,' Delina muttered angrily. 'Well, would you like to borrow a shilling for an emergency?'

'No thanks, Miss.'

'Then don't stand around here any longer. Off you go.'

'Right, Miss.'

Delina glanced back as she rode around the corner and saw that the girl was slowly wandering in the direction of the bus station. She wondered if she should have walked with her and seen her safely on the bus, but decided that Dawn was not the sort to appreciate such fussing.

All the way home Delina dreamed of what she would like to tell Tad Simmons. How could he allow a ten-year-old girl to wait for him in town, and then not bother to turn up? She fumed as she peddled along the quiet country road between Llangwyn and Hen Carw Parc, and still felt the gushing anger tightening her jaw as she dismounted and walked up Heol Caradoc.

She could not face using Hywel Rise and having to pass the Simmon's house where Tad was probably sitting reading a paper, and feeling no concern for his daughter wandering around alone. She almost wished she had risked giving the girl a lift on her bicycle. Illegal or not it would have given her the opportunity to tell Tad what she thought of him.

Delina had eaten her meal and was helping her mother to wash the dishes when there was a knock at the door. She removal her apron and went to answer it. Tad stood there, and each glared forcefully at the other.

'You should be ashamed—' Delina began, but she was out-shouted by Tad.

'I should? What sort of a teacher you are I daren't think! Fancy seeing a child stuck in town, having lost her bus fare, and refusing to help her!'

'What?' The unfairness and the untruthfulness shocked her and rendered her speechless. She stood there while he told her what he thought of a woman who would turn her back on a child in such danger.

'She had her return ticket and I offered her money to get home,' she said at last. 'What I did refuse to do was let her ride home on the carrier of my bicycle.'

'That's a very different story from the one my daughter told! Damned good mind to report you, Miss Honeyman!'

'Feel free to do so!' Delina slammed the door so hard that her mother came to see what had happened.

'Just a parent being bloody-minded,' she shocked her mother by saying.

'Really, Delina, you must control your temper.'

297

It had been a bad day for Sheila and she was ill-tempered as well as anxious that she would meet Nigel the accountant when she was looking far from her best. It had rained during the night and continued throughout the day. She had stepped in a puddle on her way to the shops at lunchtime and had to buy a new pair of stockings before going back to the salon. She was angry about the added expense when she was putting away every spare penny towards buying her new autumn outfit.

The school holidays had begun and her customers had been dragging weary children with them when they came to try on new clothes. The children, running in and out of the rails holding expensive dresses and costumes, had worn Sheila to the point where a headache was threatening. She hated the school holidays and the noisy, ill-behaved children and distraught mothers who were far less amenable to spending money on an expensive item with their offspring creating havoc in the salon.

The hem of her skirt was damp and beginning to wrinkle and her feet were still cold from the soaking she had had at lunchtime. Her fair hair was lank and untidy and she had not even bothered to repair her makeup before leaving the shop. The day was a dreadful one and the sooner she could get home and forget it the better.

Wind was gusting and, as she turned a corner near the cafe where she had taken tea with Nigel, her umbrella was blown inside out and she had to battle with it for ages before being able to fold it. She eventually gave up in temper and threw it into a corner of a shop porch. Tightening the hood of her plastic mac around her neck, she scurried to the bus station.

Concentrating on getting the early bus, and fearing to meet Nigel, she was careless of where she stepped. Too close to the kerb, she was suddenly drenched in a wave of icy cold, dirty water which filled her high-heeled patent-leather shoes and left a ridge of mud on her ankles. She looked up with a squeal and recognised that the driver of the car, now slowed by traffic further on, was Evie.

'Thoughtless, careless drivers,' she wailed as people saw what had happened and gave her glances of sympathy. Feet squelching in ruined shoes, she walked to the bus and joined the queue. She was desperate to tell someone how badly Evie had treated her and was even glad to see Amy waiting in the queue, holding Sian, and supporting the pushchair against her knees. Amy was a lot further up the queue, so Sheila joined her, ignoring the muttered complaints of others.

'That Evie Chartridge,' she began, as if continuing a previous conversation to disarm those about to complain of her queue-jumping. 'Soaked me from the knees down she did. Look at my shoes, ruined! Shouldn't be driving at all if you ask me.'

'Evie? Driving? But when?' Amy asked in alarm.

'Now just. I was hurrying to get to the bus stop and she passed me at the end of the road. Shot through a puddle without even trying to slow down, and she soaked me. Look at me feet.'

'But she should be minding Margaret! She promised she'd be there all afternoon.' Consternation made Amy confide in the girl she did not particularly like. 'I do plenty of minding for her. Oliver is always with me, yet the moment I ask her, she forgets!'

'Typical,' Sheila said. 'Always on the take, some people, never prepared to give.'

Sheila saw Delina join the end of the queue and gave a vague wave of recognition before turning back to Amy. She helped her on the bus with the baby and her shopping and found a seat for them both. The conversation soon turned to Freddie.

'He's been so kind to me, your Freddie,' Sheila said as she brought out some photographs he had sent her.

'He was really cut-up about me losing the baby, wasn't he? Dreamed of helping me with her, me being left to cope on my own.'

'He's a thoughtful boy and would help anyone in trouble,' Amy said, tight-lipped. She wished she had caught a bus sooner, worrying about where Margaret was. Now, having to listen to Sheila for the whole journey was too much.

'He still wants to marry me, you know,' Sheila went on.

'But you aren't free to marry anyone, are you?'

'No, but he'll wait.'

Amy found herself leaning forward as if trying to hurry the bus or perhaps to escape the conversation with Sheila. Sheila soon realised that the talk of Freddie was antagonising Amy and began to talk instead of some of the customers she had served, including amusing stories in the hope of making Amy smile.

'I'm worried about Margaret. I don't like her to be on her own,' Amy explained when Sheila paused, waiting for a response to a particularly funny anecdote.

'Yes, I can understand that. Working and mother-hood don't really go together, do they?' Sheila said, and to Amy's relief, she sank into silence.

At the stop near Sheepy Lane Sheila and Delina alighted and paused to exchange a few words about the dreadful weather before crossing the road. Then Sheila pointed and asked, 'Who is that? She looks like a gypsy child.'

'It's Dawn Simmons,' Delina said angrily. She strode across the glistening road and demanded to know what Dawn was doing standing in the rain.

'Waiting for Dad,' Dawn said, shivering.

'Go home at once and change out of those wet clothes,' Delina said firmly. 'No dawdling. Go now, understand? And don't distort my words when you tell

300

your father, like last time. I'm telling you to go home out of the rain and get warm and dry, right?'

Delina watched as the little girl stepped out of the hedge that had given her scant protection from the rain, and walk slowly up the lane in front of them.

'Poor dab,' Sheila whispered. 'No mother, and a father who doesn't seem to care.'

'I think he cares but can't cope. He's probably too proud to accept help,' Delina said sharply. 'A foolish and bad-tempered man who deserves to have the child taken into care.'

A few yards in front of them, the hissing rain did not prevent Dawn from hearing what was said.

'Best for her too!' Sheila said.

Billie Brown did only the routine jobs. There were so many things he intended to do but the continuous rain stopped him doing them. He helped Mary with the milking and bottling and, when she returned after delivering the first round, washed bottles in the open-sided shed before going in and finding the meal Mary had left for him. The fire was bright in the dull room, reflecting on the windows and making everything inside warm and safe. He sat in the wooden settle and dreamed of Amy. A smile stretched his features as he thought of her. He had been puzzled by her coolness for a few days, then she had mentioned the photograph of himself with Sheila and he was delighted to realise she was jealous. The thought of her being upset by thinking he could be interested in a girl like Sheila Davies was ridiculous, but knowing she cared was wonderful.

He did not know that it was dislike of Sheila and not jealously that had caused Amy to be angry. Amy had received a letter from Freddie in which he told her he was moving to the West Country. She had told Mavis, but Mavis already knew, having been told by Sheila some

301

days previously. The picture of Sheila and Billie had angered her. Sheila seemed to taint everything in her life and spoil it.

After the evening milking and the bottling that followed, Billie rang Amy and invited her out. As he was putting down the receiver he heard motor-bikes entering the yard and at once prepared for trouble. He had not reported the fact that there had been someone around the farm when he and Mary had both been out but he wondered if he should ring the constable now, before he went to see who it was. Then he felt foolish. Someone intent on breaking in would hardly drive up on a noisy motor-bike, and he had not seen any sign of wheels other than their own after that night. He opened the door to Pete and Gerry.

'There's a ewe down in the stream,' Pete told him as he opened the door. 'Thought we'd better tell you, like.'

'It seems to have slipped into the water and now it can't get up again. The water's flowing fast, see,' Gerry added, 'and the banks are very slippery with all this rain.'

Billie put on his boots and heavy raincoat and walked with them to where the stream flowed through his land. It was not far away that they found the ewe, who was standing exhausted after trying repeatedly to climb the steep bank. The river had underscored the bank and a once overhanging turf had fallen, Billie guessed, with the ewe standing on it.

A fully grown sheep with its coat soaking wet is a very heavy animal and it was a long time before the three of them got it safely on to the bank. Billie removed his raincoat and his boots and went into the fast flowing stream to persuade the frightened animal to walk further along the stream to where the bank offered an easier prospect of rescuing it. Even then it had taken more than two hours of heaving and pushing to get it up on to

302

the bank. The men as well as the sheep were exhausted.

'You'd better come back to the farm for some warm dry clothes,' Billie panted. 'Grateful I am for your help.'

The boys washed themselves and drank some tea, helping themselves enthusiastically to Mary's cakes before dressing in some of Billie's spare clothes to drive home. Billie's clothes hung on the smaller boys but they were unable to resist the opportunity to look inside the farm house.

They had seen it from the woods and with binoculars had sometimes watched Billie and Mary about their tasks. They told Billie how interested they had been to look inside the building.

'Watched it from the woods, have you?' he asked curiously. 'I saw tyre tracks up there once.'

'We weren't watching your house,' Gerry grinned.

'Girls then?' Billie asked.

'No.' The boys laughed and Billie waited patiently for them to explain.

'Arthur Toogood got a bit of a fright, that's all. He'd let our tyres down twice, so we offered him a ride, took him up there and threatened to chuck him down if he didn't promise to leave the bikes alone in future,' Pete laughed.

'Then someone told us it wasn't Arthur but Dawn Simmons who did it, so we gave him a bag of sweet and he's appointed himself guardian of the bikes.'

'Lots of good stuff in that old barn of a house,' Pete said as they roared off through the farm lane.

'Yes indeed. Makes our homes look a bit scruffy. Not fair is it, some having so much.'

'He works hard for it, mind. I don't think I'd like to start work at five and still be at it at ten o'clock at night like he often is.'

Billie watched them go and went inside to get ready to

303

take Amy to the pictures. He wished he had not telephoned her. He was stiffening already with the soaking and the effort of lifting the sheep up the slippery, steep bank. There was a sharp pain across his shoulder which he knew would take a few days to fade. 'Stupid animal!' he said aloud as he climbed the stairs stiffly to run a bath. He yawned as he undressed and threw his clothes into the washing basket. A day of inactivity then the sudden effort of dealing with the sheep had made him feel more ready for bed than going out gallivanting. Perhaps he was too old for this courting lark?

On that Tuesday, Fay did not go to the hotel where she had met Dexter. She did not even go into Llangwyn but had stopped for lunch in Swansea at a cafe overlooking a rocky beach. She sat eating her meal, watching children exploring the pools dressed in macs and wellingtons, ignoring the rain, determined to make the best of their holiday. The rain had eased only slightly and the day was gloomy, the only brightness the children's clothes moving like fantastic insects below her. The bright lights of the cafe emphasised the gloom of the day rather than improved it.

There were several families inside the cafe, the children restless with the inactivity the weather had caused, and Fay's meal was not a peaceful one. A coach arrived in the car-park and a pack of excited school-age children swarmed in and, as they fought to find places near their friends and argued about the positioning of chairs and tables, Fay picked up her handbag and umbrella and left, smiling at the people in charge of the unruly but happy group.

She ran to the shelter of the car and sat watching the determined explorers on the beach. She was undecided about the following day and it made her less able to concentrate on her business. She had to decide whether she would go to Pembrokeshire on the following day. The thought of seeing Dexter was a guilty excitement. In the few moments after Johnny had stormed out and she had followed, Dexter told her the name of a restaurant where she would find him on Wednesdays and Fridays. Sorely tempted, she opened her diary and considered the possibility of making the visit to Pembrokeshire a couple of weeks early.

It was innocent, she persuaded herself, and Johnny was being unreasonably jealous. She would go and meet Dexter for a brief hour and explain to her customers that the change of day was due to a forthcoming holiday. She thought Johnny would be content, knowing she had promised not to visit the hotel again on Tuesdays or any other day. She smiled at the small deceit.

She remembered how Johnny had looked when he had come upon her talking with Dexter, seeing her laughing with him and obviously enjoying his company. He had been hurt and almost frightened, but she still determined to go on the following day. Life was dull and there seemed to spread out in front of her a line of monotonous days with little to vary them apart from an occasional row with Johnny.

The rain continued to fall and she was soon chilled. Children skipped around the car, jumping into the dips in the macadam, splashing each other and laughing, determined to make some fun out of the dreary day. Everyone ran, scuttling to and from the cafe, where they steamed the windows with their damp clothes and filled the room with chatter.

Fay had eaten a salad and locally caught sewin for lunch but felt suddenly hungry again. She took out a packet of Penclawdd cockles she had bought for Johnny and which she did not usually enjoy, and ate them all. She was sure to be sick, shellfish did not always agree with her. She wanted something to take away the taste but could not face running across the car-park again. She started the car, feeling cold, damp and still hungry. She would call on two more customers then go home.

Johnny would be pleased to see her earlier than expected. Today was a day off and he would be finding it hard to fill in the time, with the rain pouring down. Wipers swishing, she drove carefully off.

The workmen in Nelly's house valiantly ignored the rain to finish the outside part of their work, huddled in what had been a porch room overlooking the back garden, filling up the huge hole they had made in the wall. The dogs lay close to the fire which burned sluggishly, their noses as close to the fender as possible.

When Nelly came home from work she had been horrified to see the mess of footprints both canine and human that carpeted the stone-flagged floor. While the men sat on the edge of the new bath to eat their sandwiches, she brought several buckets of water from the tap in the lane and sluiced the worst of it away through the door and down the garden in a brown river. When the worst of it had been brushed away she covered the floor with cardboard.

'All right, you lot. You can come out now!' she called and they trooped out like naughty children to find the kettle had finally boiled and the tea was made.

She flopped into a chair to recover, her legs aching painfully from her efforts. When the men had finished their work and turned off the blow-lamp that had been roaring for most of the afternoon, the place smelt of metholated spirits, the floors were again a mess of mud and pieces of litter but the bath, wash-basin and lavatory were all in place.

She heard footsteps but they weren't George's.

'Evie,' she groaned, looking round at the state of the room which Evie would be quick to complain about but not so willing to help clear.

'Mother, is Oliver here?'

' 'Course 'e ain't! I wouldn't invite 'im with all this mess about.' Nelly was ready to defend herself against Evie's criticism of the room but none came.

'I was late home, Mother, and I don't know where he is. I've phoned Amy but she wasn't there. I was supposed to be minding Margaret too. It's very worrying.

'I'll go an' see if 'e's at Amy's. If she ain't there they don't answer the phone. Amy tells them not to.' Wearily she heaved herself out of her chair and reached for her raincoat.

'Careless of yer, wasn't it, Evie?' she said. 'Leavin' two kids alone and wanderin'?'

'And what had you been doing with yourself all day?' Evie retorted, glancing around the filthy room. 'Sitting down listening to the wireless and waiting for George to come home to all this?' She was gone before Nelly could get breath for a reply.

When Amy stepped off the bus, trying to unfold the push-chair and keep Sian covered against the rain, she looked across at her house, hoping Margaret was there. How could Evie be so careless? She always felt guilty if Margaret was not in someone's care. Sheila's words about it being impossible to work and be a mother came back to her like a criticism. At this moment, as she hurried up her drive, she thought the girl was right. Opening the door she called and was surprised when both Margaret and Oliver came out to greet them. Behind them stood Victor.

'I came home early and saw these two trudging across the fields behind Oliver's house. They were going to spend the time until you came home in their tree house.'

'Sorry Margaret, love, but Oliver's mother promised that you could stay with her. She must have forgotten,' apologised Amy.

'It isn't the first time, is it?' Victor whispered when the

307

children had returned to playing records. 'How can you trust someone like that? It isn't like you to be so careless about Margaret's safety.'

Amy glared at him furiously. How could he think her less than a caring mother? 'Me, careless? How can you say that? I'm trying to do two jobs, shop and home, as well as look after Sian. I have to leave *her* with other people sometimes and I don't like doing that, but there's no alternative. Evie assured me she was not going out today, then I was told she was driving through Llangwyn! I've been frantic with worry!'

'Sorry, Amy, I didn't mean to criticise. You do a marvellous job, I know that. But it was such a shock, seeing them wandering out in the rain and heading for the wood. They're only ten years old and—' He stopped and took her in his arms.

Amy allowed herself the luxury of one kiss before pushing him away. She glanced at the door of the living room and he, seeing her concern, took her wet coat and hung it over a chair to dry.

'Can I feed Sian before I go?' he asked. 'My dinner will probably be in the dustbin so there's no rush. Imogine gives me half an hour and no more.'

'I'm cooking sausages and there's enough for an extra one if you'd like to stay,' Amy said, still with an edge of steel to her voice. 'But first I'm going to ring Evie and tell her what I think of her!'

While Victor sat and fed Sian, Amy tried to telephone Evie but there was no reply. Then there was a knock at the door and a voice called, 'Amy? Have you got Oliver in there? 'Is mother's gorn off an' fergot 'im!'

'Come in, Nelly.' Amy slammed down the receiver. 'He's here.'

'Evie failed 'er drivin' test an' today she was offered an extra lesson so she went, thinkin' she'd be back. But rain caused a flood the other side of Llangwyn an' when she got 'ome and found 'e wasn't there she ran up to me in a fine state. I said I'd come 'ere while she tried Netta and Ethel.'

'Road flooded, rubbish!' Amy said angrily. 'Sheila saw her driving through town just before our bus left! She forgot!'

Oliver insisted on eating the sausages Amy had cooked and Nelly sat waiting for him to finish. 'Let 'er sweat fer a bit,' she muttered. 'Call herself a mother!'

'The phone rang and Nelly stood to answer it. 'I'll see to this, Amy. You finish yer meal. I expect it's my Evie.' But it was Billie on the phone and Nelly smiled with a certain gloating satisfaction at Victor as she announced, 'It's Billie Brown and 'e wants to take you out. I'll stay with Margaret an' Sian if you wants me to.'

Amy thought of how chilled she still was after the afternoon out in the rain and of the ironing waiting to be done, but she was still smarting a little at Victor, so she nodded.

'Tell him yes, will you Nelly? And thanks for minding the kids.'

'I'm off then,' Victor said disconsolately. He kissed Sian and waved at the other two before leaving without a word for Amy.

Amy turned to hide the tears that had sprung to her eyes. She had to drive him out of her life, she *had* to.

Billie called for her at seven and they were in time for the main film. Half way through he fell asleep and Amy left him there and caught the bus home.

# Chapter Sixteen

The morning following the day of heavy rain broke calm and clear. The sun travelled across the walls of Fay and Johnny's bedroom and woke Fay, touching her face with the promise of warmth, disturbing her sleep long before the alarm began its strident demand. Johnny was still sleeping. He looked very young lying there completely relaxed, his moustache a dark shadow on his face, his black hair tumbled and long across his forehead. She must remind him to get it cut again, it grew so fast.

She stood at the window for a while, looking out across the newly washed fields, so rich a green they were dazzling. Sheep grazed contentedly as if the downpour had never happened. The sun touched her bare arms and she luxuriated in the glow. It was going to be an exciting day, she just knew it.

She closed the bathroom door quietly and began to run her bath. The water ran from the taps and caused a gushing, foamy swirly pool below and as she watched she gradually became aware of a slight churning in her stomach.

'Those cockles,' she whispered in dismay.

She climbed gingerly into the bath and lay back, hoping that the queasiness would go away, but it became worse and she had to leap out of the bath and lean over the toilet. Johnny heard her retching and came in, his sleep-dazed face a blur to her as she looked up.

'Fay, lovely, what is it?'

'Those cockles I ate yesterday,' she said ruefully.

'Cockles? I thought you weren't keen on seafood?' He put her dressing gown around her shoulders and led her back to the bed.

'I bought them for you and I ate them,' she explained. 'I can't understand why I was suddenly overcome with greed. I'd just eaten lunch.'

He propped her up on several pillows and went to make a cup of tea into which he put a slice of lemon, just as she liked it.

'Sip this slowly, lovely, and I think you should rest today, and not even think about work.'

'I'll stay here for a while and see how I feel,' she said. 'I doubt if it will last very long.'

An hour later, she got up, bathed and dressed and felt well enough to begin her day's visits. Johnny watched her go with consternation. She was still unwell, even though she had tried to hide her pallor under heavier makeup than usual.

'Call the depot if you don't feel well enough to drive home, wherever you are, and I'll come and fetch you,' he called as she went out of the door to the car.

'I won't go far,' she promised.

She was bitterly disappointed. Today, she had hoped to meet Dexter, spend an hour with him, enjoying the friendly conversation and the sensation of wickedness that added to the excitement. But how could she risk going now? The embarrassment of a further bout of sickness would ruin everything.

She drove slowly towards Swansea, having decided to make local calls only. She felt weak, standing was an effort and it was hard to be normally polite and interested in her customer's requirements. She wrote the small order in her notebook, then drove to her second call. From where she parked the car, she had to walk through the market, where busy stall-holders were selling

312

ing fruit, vegetables, fresh bread and meat, besides clothes, carpets and a dozen other requirements. At one end were the stalls selling the locally caught fish. She smelt the cockles straight away, and her stomach churned hungrily. Women gathered the cockles, going out with a horse and cart on to the sands of Penclawdd, then taking them home to clean and boil them. They then brought them to market in large baskets covered by spotlessly white cloth to sell them. One seller, seeing Fay's hesitation, held up the glass with which she measured the cockles and called, 'One bag or two, *cariad?*'

Fay shook her head and hurried out before greed could overcome common sense.

With schools closed for the summer holiday, buses were filled with families heading for the local beaches and trips into town and country. For those unable to go further afield, the streets were their playground. There were hoops, bowled along with short sticks, balls of every size, cricket stumps being drawn on the pine ends of houses and boys gathered into teams to compete. Whips and tops were in evidence on every corner, with applause rising for those able to keep the tops spinning longest. Skipping ropes both short and long were popular with the girls and several found ropes long enough to reach from pavement to pavement, allowing a dozen children to leap in and out of the turning rope, chanting rhymes.

Bicycles were in demand, boys and girls queueing for a turn, and bogies, made from the base of an old pram or a box on to which wheels had been added, a rope attached to the front to guide it, reappeared after the winter's hibernation. Up on the council houses a new craze had begun. Roller skates were placed on the ground with a large book on top of them and on this primitive transport, boys and girls would sit and whizz down Heol Caradoc or Hywel Rise, their feet up until they were needed for braking, then lowered so the back of the heel slowed their wild progress. The shoes worn by these book-riders were rapidly worn down to the linings, but the children were unaware of this as they screamed in fear-touched delight down the steep hill.

Evie had a nasty shock when she drove down from the top of the estate where she had been practising reversing and three-point turns with her driving instructor. She suddenly saw a swarm of children in front of her hurtling down the hill squatting on books and occasionally falling off into the road. She glared at her instructor.

'This is ridiculous. How some people can allow their children to be in such danger amazes me. It must be stopped, now.' She started the car cautiously driving past the halted, staring children and went to see Constable Harris.

So the game was stopped and before someone was seriously hurt, but the children were resentful and no one played with Oliver who, unknown to Evie, had been one of the instigators of the game. Disconsolately, he went from his new friends to tell Nelly, who for once supported his mother.

'Gawd 'elp us, Ollie. You might 'ave bin killed an' then where would George an' me be? Devastated, that's what.'

To compensate for the loss of his friends and fun, she suggested he and Margaret had a picnic in the den. As if on cue, Dawn arrived at the door and she was invited as well.

'Better hide them shoes of yours first, Ollie,' Nelly laughed, 'your mum'll guess quick as a wink what you've bin up to once she claps eyes on them!' She found the sandals she had bought for his day in Mumbles and threw the worn-down shoes in the ash bin. So the three children played in the wood, near enough for Nelly to hear if they needed anything, and Nelly sat in the garden, reading an article about the Duke and Duchess of Windsor, and listening to her wireless.

When Nelly's bathroom was finished, she hesitated for days before using it. She spent more time polishing the porcelain and cleaning the floor than actually making use of the facilities. With George's encouragement she began to find the toilet an advantage at night, then gradually accepted the value of it during the day and early morning. The floor of the bathroom was grey Welsh slate and this was scrubbed and buffed so the room shone and smelt pleasantly of soap and lavender polish.

George had taken the opportunity of a bath as soon as it had been available. The small back-sitting room which had never been used now had a fireplace which heated the water, and he lit it each Sunday and, on the third Sunday, Nelly decided she would bath too. It wasn't a new experience, she had bathed at Evie's once or twice, but having her own was different.

It was seven o'clock in the evening before she finally went into the small room that had been a porch room and turned on the taps. She poured in some pleasant-smelling powder that Amy had given her and, testing the water temperature nervously, stepped in. She lay in the deep warm foam and laughed aloud.

'Smashin' this is, George,' she shouted. 'Should 'ave 'ad one years ago. My Evie's done something right fer once.'

So the pattern of the summer days went on. When the weather was fine, the three children were either in Nelly's garden playing on the swing that Billie Brown had made for Oliver, or playing in the woods near by. Evie came occasionally to complain about the state of Oliver's clothes and to search for the pair of shoes that had gone missing, but seemed content to have her son out of the way, leaving her free to attend the coffee mornings and other social 'musts' for the wife of a man who planned to stand for the local council.

Life, for Nelly, with the children around her every day, was perfect. She went to and from work with the big dogs straining at their leads, and up and down to the shop to buy supplies for her temporary family, singing and declaring her contentment to the world.

When the days were wet or cold, Amy often gave Nelly the money to take the three children into town for a visit to the cinema, and they would frequently stand for an hour and a half to get in, and would sit enthralled, while Nelly produced sweets from her old leather-cloth shopping bag, and an occasional cake, ignoring the complaints about paper-rustling.

Dawn seemed content and no complaints had reached Nelly about her, but she gave Nelly a pound one day, saying it was from her father. At once Nelly thought she might be up to her usual tricks.

'What d'you think of that, George?' Nelly said, holding out the pound note Dawn had given her. 'Makes you wonder where Dawn got it. She *says* it's from 'er dad, but I 'ave me doubts.' Nelly suspected the girl of stealing, and had missed a few shillings from her own purse, but said nothing, hoping that as friendships grew and the girl felt less a stranger in the village, the thieving would stop.

'Besides,' she said to George, 'I don't fancing tellin' Tad what I suspect. It might be my turn for a black eye! Quieter 'e might be, but placid 'e ain't!'

For George too the end of the summer holiday was sad. He loved to see the children enjoying the freedom and took pleasure from hearing their shouts and laughter as he came across the fields after his day's work. Nelly and the children were often at the gate feeding the horses and making sure they had fresh water in the old bath they used as a trough. The three children would climb the gate

316

and run to meet him, arguing about whose turn it was to carry his food bag for him.

Nelly usually sent them home soon after George arrived, knowing he needed a rest after a hard day's work on the farm but not before he had heard all about their day and they had asked about his. Dawn had asked permission to visit Leighton's farm and take photographs and George had been impressed with the results.

'For a child she seems to have an unusual talent for seeing the picture in ordinary events,' George told Nelly. 'I wonder if she will continue with it and make it her career?'

'So long as she doesn't use 'em for blackmail, little devil,' Nelly said, reminding George of the exhibition at the school with a grim smile. 'I don't altogether trust 'er, an' she tells lies, George. She's bin saying things that ain't true about Delina fer a start. I 'ates lies, never could stand lies.' She did not add her fears about where Dawn was finding the money for her expensive hobby.

Tad left Dawn reading a library book and went down the hill and along the lane to Nelly's cottage. He was not going to find this easy, having punched George in the face once, but he had to thank them for the care and enjoyment they had given his daughter during the school holidays.

He found them both sitting outside their door, eating a meal. The wireless was playing softly from inside and the dogs, who had been sitting waiting hopefully for scraps jumped up at his approach. It was a such a contended scene that he felt a surge of anger that fate had deprived him of something similar. When he spoke, it was that anger that coloured his voice.

'Dawn has spent a lot of time with you,' he began and he made it sound like an accusation.

317

'What's wrong with that?' Nelly demanded, and her raised voice started the dogs barking. 'Fat lot of company she'd 'ave 'ad if she 'adn't!'

'I – I only wanted to say thank you,' Tad said, but his voice was still sharp. 'Dawn has enjoyed herself and it's thanks to you that she didn't—'

'Get into any mischief?' Nelly finished.

Anger flowed as always when Dawn was criticised. He felt that he was to blame for her wrong-doing.

'No. I didn't mean that. I was going to say that she might have become bored.'

'She ain't never bored, not that one,' Nelly said.

'What d'you mean by that?'

George stood up and raised a pacifying hand.

'I think you two are both defending Dawn and I don't think either of you have any need, do you?'

Tad did not answer. He lowered his head and studied the cinder path.

'I only came to thank you,' he muttered.

'There ain't no need,' Nelly said. 'Stay an 'ave a cuppa, why don't yer?' She went inside and returned with a cup and saucer which she proceeded to fill from the teapot near her chair. Tad came down the path and sat awkwardly on the edge of the lawn on an upturned bucket.

'I am too defensive,' he admitted. 'There have been so many problems that I can't stand the thought of anyone getting at Dawn. It isn't her fault her mother died and she has to make do with only me.'

'There's something you will 'ave to face,' Nelly said firmly, ignoring the warning look from George.

Tad looked at her, belligerence in the blue eyes and in the tightening of the thin jaw.

'And what's that?' he asked coldly.

'She tells lies. Real whoppers an' all. You should 'ave listened to Delina when she told you what really

318

'appened in town. She didn't refuse to 'elp Dawn and you know she wouldn't really—'

She did not say any more, as Tad rose to his feet, stormed off up the path and slammed the gate behind him.

'So much for my diplomacy,' Nelly groaned. 'Should 'ave kept me big mouth shut a bit longer, shouldn't I?'

'No, Nelly, love. Some time, somehow he has to accept the truth, and then perhaps he'll learn that we aren't his enemies.'

Tad walked home at a pace that had him breathless. He couldn't slow down, even when his lungs felt about to burst. He walked past his house and up to the top of the estate, out on the hill behind St Hilda's Crescent and only stopping where he could look down on the village nestling below him like a toy town. He felt ashamed of himself for allowing his stupid temper to force ill-considered words from him. If only he could calm down and allow time before he spoke.

He should have listened to Nelly. She was certain to have been trying to help Dawn. She would not have given the girl so much of her time if she were not interested in helping her. He wanted to go straight back down and tell Nelly and George how he really felt, listen to what they had to say about Delina. If he had been wrong about her—

He hugged himself in despair. Whatever he did seemed to make things worse and knowing he was his own worst enemy only added to his grief. He had arrived here with a small child and in need of friendship and help, but instead of accepting what had been generously offered, he had allowed pride and stupidity to ruin every chance of a good life here.

His breath was still ragged from the hurried walk up the steep hill as he slowly went back down. If only he could start again. Then his shoulders drooped. He would

319

only make the same mess of things as before. The past couldn't be changed. If anything altered it had to be himself. There was a smell of freshly cut grass on the air, a richness redolent of warm summer sun and happy days. He walked with his head low, avoiding the friendly stares of people working in their gardens.

When he got home, Dawn was not there. He did not worry, she was often missing when he expected her to be there. He sat and waited for her, the back door open and the kettle simmering on the cooker for her hot drink. After an hour had passed with miserable thoughts running through his mind, he went out to look for her. Anger again grew in him but this time not against himself but against Dawn. Why couldn't she stay put and do as he asked?

He found her sitting in the hedge not far from Nelly's cottage, staring through at where Nelly and George were talking together and laughing. His anger evaporated and he felt for her in her loneliness. He knelt down beside her and whispered softly, 'Come on, Dawn. Time for bed.'

She turned and hugged him with unaccustomed closeness, her head on his shoulder, her hands fastened tightly behind his neck. He stood up, lifting her in his arms and carried her home.

After weeks of waiting, and almost giving up hope of hearing from Maurice, Sheila received a letter from Australia. It was not very thick but she prayed silently that it would contain news of a passage for her to join Maurice. The paper was flimsy and crinkled and her fingers fumbled as she separated the leaves and began to read.

The tone at once shattered her hopes of a reunion with her husband and tears threatened. Curtly, he said he had nothing to say to her except to state his regret at the death of her child. *Her* child, she noted sadly, not theirs. He said he would be moving on and the address she had almost certainly stolen from Delina would no longer find him. It was signed just 'Maurice'.

She forced herself to continue to get ready for work and determined that no one would know of her bitter disappointment. She walked down the hill to the bus stop, eyes staring at the pavement, feeling exhausted and unwell. Why had he treated her so badly? Forcing her to make love and then abandoning her as soon as he met Delina? Unreasonably, she blamed Delina for everything, including the death of the baby. When she saw her setting off to Llangwyn on her bicycle, she wished fervently that the bicycle would swerve under a passing car.

She left the shop at five-thirty and wandered disconsolately towards the bus station. The day was warm but she shivered in her dress and short coat, hugging it around her and wishing she had somewhere to go other than home to Gran and the preparation of an evening meal. Then a voice called her and she looked across the road to see Nigel, and her face forced away its expression of misery. She was not in the mood for flirting with anyone, not even an accountant, but as soon as he crossed the road and smiled at her she shrugged off the unhappiness she had worn like a dark cloak all day and smiled back at him invitingly.

He persuaded her to wait for a later bus and go with him for tea and cakes.

'What's the excuse for spoiling me this time?' she asked. Widening her eyes at him. 'I'm not complaining, mind.'

'Something has upset you. *No*—' he stopped her denial with a wave of his hand. 'No, I can tell. I watched you walking along the road and I knew you were distressed about something.' He leaned on the table and touched her hands. 'I think I will always know, Sheila, when you are upset.'

Sheila warmed to his words and the admiration that glowed in his dark eyes. He was rather handsome in spite of his nose being over-long. She had liked dark-haired and brown-eyed men since seeing Cornel Wilde on the screen and using him as a dream-husband. His picture was still on her bedroom wall and she imagined taking it down and replacing it with one of Nigel.

'What are you thinking about?' he asked. 'You look as if you're in a daze? I hope I'm the cause?'

'I was thinking of having a picture of you on my bedroom wall,' she said slowly, 'instead of the one that's there at present.' She didn't tell him about the film-star. Add a bit more mystery, she thought as she sank her teeth into a cream cake with obvious enjoyment.

'Is it of your husband,' Nigel asked. 'The picture I mean.' Slowly she shook her head, still chewing the delicious cake.

'Perhaps one day you'll find out,' she teased, staring at him, wide-eyed and provocative. 'Perhaps.'

They arranged to meet the following evening and Sheila went home to re-read Maurice's letter again and again, determined to remove the pain it was causing, by constantly suffering the humiliation of her dislike and disregard until it faded and failed to hurt.

She finally tore it into shreds and went to bed to dream about Nigel and the escape he offered. If she could keep the secret of her marriage long enough for him to fall in love with her, then there was a chance. It would have to be kept a secret from her parents too, or they might consider it their duty to tell him. Oh, to get away from them all.

Secrets were never easy to keep in a small place like Hen Carw Parc. News of Sheila's new boyfriend travelled fast through the village, first on the tongue of the postman who reported in to Nelly as he brought her a letter one morning. He threw his sack down over the handlebars of his bicycles and settled in the chair near her door in the hope of a cup of tea.

'Heard the latest, then?' he asked, his finger rubbing the side of his nose in a conspiratorial gesture that presaged a confidence.

'Griff Evans 'as paid 'is debts!' she said sarcastically.

'No, no. Sheila, my poor little sister-in-law, has got herself a new boyfriend. Works as an accountant, so I'm told, daft about her too.'

' 'Ave to be daft to risk flirting with that one,' Nelly grumbled. 'What else is new?'

'Well, I shouldn't say this, but Archie says he's seen Griff coming out of the back door of the fish-an'-chip shop late at night.'

'So what?' Probably passin' on a message fer 'is wife. Hilda works there, doesn't she?'

'Yes, but this was when Hilda was away visiting her mother in Cardiff for the weekend.'

'Phil Davies, you're a wicked old gossip,' Nelly laughed. 'But tell me more!'

They sat drinking tea and eating some of the cakes Nelly had just taken out of the oven, while he reported all the current gossip about Griff and the daughter of Milly Toogood.

Ignoring the smattering of talk she had heard, Sheila began meeting Nigel regularly, and managed not to explain about her wedding ring and the lack of a husband. He seemed to presume she had been recently widowed and she allowed the untruth to become accepted simply by not denying it, and without ever have to state the lie herself.

She was pleased to see the admiration on the faces of the other girls in the salon when they saw him waiting outside the window for her. She delighted in appearing casual about his attentions. Twice he brought her

323

flowers and then she would sigh as she looked through the plate-glass window and tell them how very much in love with her he was and how hard it was for her to stay detached.

'I can't risk falling in love again so soon,' she said dramatically to the younger girls. 'Another disaster would make me run to the nearest convent. I've suffered so much at the hands of men, you know.'

Her late arrival at home was a constant source of annoyance to her parents, who still refused to treat her like the twenty-one-year-old who had been through the trauma of having and losing a child, as well as the embarrassment of the marriage that wasn't. They would watch from the window of the flat above the shop and study the passengers alighting from the buses from Llangwyn, anxious to see Sheila crossing the road and walk up Sheepy Lane. Often, when more than two buses had pulled away without her appearing, they would be at her grandmother's, both standing with disapproval on their faces and wanting an explanation and a minute-by-minute account of her lost hours.

'Treat me like a school-girl, you do! As if I can come to any harm in an hour or two in Llangwyn!' Sheila would complain with exasperation.

On the evening she and Nigel had gone to the pictures, she marched in, eyes glaring, daring them to say a word.

'I told you I'd be late and I told you where I was going. What more do you expect, for goodness sake?'

'Who's this young man?' her father said. 'I think it's time we met him.'

'What young man?'

'Don't take us for fools. Everybody in the village knows you've been going out with a man from Llangwyn,' Mavis snapped.

'What business is it of yours?'

'I want to be sure he knows the facts about you,' her father said.

'You want? You want to protect *him* from *me*?'

'No, of course not,' Mavis said quickly, glaring at Ralph. 'We just want everything to be straight and above-board.'

'Mam, if you don't keep out of my life I'll leave.'

'You can't, Sheila,' Ralph said mildly. 'You don't have a place to go and you don't earn enough to find anywhere. Be sensible.'

The complacency in his voice was the end. Sheila ran upstairs and began to throw some of her clothes into a suitcase. Mavis was beside her, begging her not to be foolish.

'Don't take any notice of your father, love. He talks before he thinks. We don't want to drive you away, really we don't. I can see how frustrating it must be with us constantly watching you but—'

'It's for my own good?' Sheila snapped. 'See where your concern got me before. You make me do things just to defy you. You make it clear you don't trust me. No wonder I rebelled and went out to find a bit of affection!'

'Sheila, we've always loved you. You've never lacked love, you can't say that!'

'But it's true, Mam, and in case you're worrying about what people will think, you can tell them I'm going to live in town, probably with a man called Nigel Knighton.'

It was midnight before Sheila went to bed: Gran had gone earlier, leaving Mavis and Ralph arguing with their daughter and trying to persuade her to stay. As she had no intention of going, Sheila enjoyed the battle of words and, when she went to bed, leaving her parents to walk home exhausted, she was smiling. Perhaps now they would leave her alone.

The following evening, she had made no arrangements

325

to meet Nigel but she did not catch the early bus. Instead, she went to a smart cafe and sat for an hour over a cup of tea and some sandwiches, then joined the queue for the pictures where she sat through the second film once and the first film twice before catching the late bus home.

Her parents had again been to the house; she knew that from the slightly disarranged plates. She wondered how long they had waited before giving up and going back to their flat to continue their vigil of watching each bus as it unloaded its passengers. She took a cup of cocoa to her grandmother and told her where she had been, inventing a companion for the evening. Describing him in detail to a worried Gran, Sheila hoped that every word would find its way into her mother's ear and cause her more concern. Serve her right, she whispered to the photograph on her wall, where one day she might hang a picture of Nigel Knighton.

She was unable to sleep, and the thought of the pieces of paper, torn up in a corner of her drawer, still waiting to be relegated to the ash bin, came to her mind. In the darkness, she felt her way to the drawer and took out Maurice's letters: the one to her and the one he had written to Delina. She knew his address off by heart, but she pieced the thin letter together and read it again, before writing it out, in the light of a torch so as not to disturb Gran, on a fresh piece of paper.

Tomorrow she would call and see Ethel Davies and give it to her. She would tell her Maurice had written but she had not opened it, but before tearing it up she had saved the address for her: a mother should always know where her son is. Yes, Ethel would be pleased with that story.

In the woods above Nelly's cottage a figure moved swiftly through the trees like a shadow driven by the wind. He did not carry a gun but he was intent on

326

poaching. He went to where a mound of earth revealed the ancient rabbit warren, and set up his nets. Taking a ferret from his pocket, he sent the supple creature down one of the holes and waited.

Soon the nets were twisting with the struggles of the rabbits trying in vain to escape. He went from one hole to another, attended to the terrified creatures and put the still-jerking bodies into a sack. When he had captured and killed them all, the ferret came back to his whistle and was replaced in his pocket. Taking the load to a motor-bike, he pushed the machine for some distance before mounting and riding off.

His keen ears and eyes were those of a man of the woods and fields, but he did not see the small figure who stood trembling, watching him as he worked, nor heard the click of the shutter as the camera was raised to frame him in the tiny lens.

Dawn followed the man for a while, her small feet making hardly a sound. When she heard the bike start up she was disappointed and held back, but the bike stopped again after a short distance. She edged carefully forward, her eyes and ears alert for the slightest danger. She saw the man hand over the bag of dead rabbits and receive money in exchange. Then the person he met disappeared and the man with the motor-bike stood for a long time, silent and perfectly still

Dawn's curiosity started to turn to discomfort. She wanted to go to the toilet, her feet were cold and she was becoming so edgy that she almost moved to end the terrifying stillness in which she imagined that the man knew she was there and was waiting for her to give herself away.

When he moved, it was towards her and she had to force herself to remain still. Then he went at an angle from her, towards the castle. She found that her leg muscles were knotted and stiff as she at last moved away.

Passing the uneven walls of the castle with the strange

327

shadows and eerie atmosphere she felt scared. Alone she was rarely frightened, but knowing the man was there she needed to keep him in her sight. She followed, staying within hearing of his footsteps as he waded through the long grass, and walked almost silently through the narrow animal paths.

Leaving the castle behind them, they walked across some open ground and Dawn knew she was now following the man because she was lost. She began to cry, silently, the tears welling up and coursing slowly down her cold cheeks. She wished she could see her house and be able to run through the back door which she had left open, and go in and warm herself in her bed in the room next to her father's. There was no moon, and the blackness of the night seemed to mass behind her and only allow her the slightest hint of the man in front. She was tiring now and wondered if she would be able to keep up with him for long enough to find a place she recognised. Stupid to take a photograph: it had been far too dark anyway, she thought. She should have gone home as soon as she had seen him instead of following him until darkness overcame her.

There was a risk that the man would hear her sobs if she could not hold them back. He would be angry at discovering her and she bit her lip until it bled. Then lights showed faintly in the sky and she knew they were near the council houses. Her cold hands covered her mouth to muffle sighs of relief and she found a new burst of speed and nearly caught up with the man striding ahead of her.

He stopped and looked around him and she crouched in panic, but he went on, apparently unaware of her, and she set off again in pursuit.

At the top of St Hilda's Crescent he slipped under a hedge and disappeared in the shadows. She knew the house. It was where two girls from school lived, Betty and Gillian Taylor. She did not wait for him to reappear, shivering with cold she ran around the Crescent and into her own garden. Her hot-water bottle was cold but she hugged it anyway and her father found her the next morning, dressed, dirty, her legs covered in scratches and he demanded to know where she had been.

'I don't know,' she lied. 'I must have been sleep-walking.'

'Dawn, don't be silly. Even I can't accept that!'

But she was asleep again, and he left her. He had better let her recover, then perhaps he would have some answers. And perhaps, he thought grimly, he would get the locks changed on the back and front door!

He was very worried when, on the news later that day, a robbery was reported in St Hilda's Crescent. He went up to look at Dawn, who had spent the day in bed after he had washed her torn legs, but had been given no satis-factory explanation for her dishevelled state.

'Dawn, you had better tell me what really happened last night. I think you might be in trouble and I have to know before I can defend you. Now, what happened after you left the house? Did you go into someone else's house? The truth, Dawn. I mean it this time, none of your lies, this definitely is not the time for them.'

'Dad, I don't remember. Honestly. I must have walked in my sleep. Remember you told me I did once or twice when I was a baby?'

'The truth, Dawn.' He stood beside her bed and glared down at her. Tempted by her smallness to abandon the questioning, he hardened his heart and waited. 'And while we're about it,' he added grimly, 'I'd like to know what really happened when you asked Miss Honeyman for help when you were in town a few weeks ago.'

Dawn rubbed her eyes and began to cry. 'Everyone hates me, and now they've got you hating me too. I haven't got anyone in the whole world to love me. I don't

329

remember, and what Miss Honeyman did was so mean, I can't think how you can pretend she's nice.'

Defeated, Tad comforted her and, tucking her under the covers, went down to make her a hot drink. Was she lying? If she were wandering around at night in semi-sleep, the dangers were enormous. Should he consult a doctor?

He dropped into a chair and held his head in his hands. He was so useless. Why had fate left someone as useless as him in charge of a small child? If only there was someone he could talk to.

Delina Honeyman came into his mind and he imagined her sitting opposite him and letting him talk about all that bothered him. But that was no way to think of her. Surely he should be thinking of the reverse, him caring for Delina? He would not want a woman just to lean on but someone he could protect and love and – he stopped, startled at where his weary mind was taking him. Delina could hardly bear to look at him, let alone be the recipient of either his complaining or his concern. But thoughts of her remained, refusing to leave him for an instant during the rest of the day, as he watched over the dozing child.

# Chapter Seventeen

It was raining and had been all night and Nelly decided that she would walk around the lane to go in through the back entrance of Amy's shop when she went to do some cleaning. There was always mud on her shoes from walking down the lane and since the new bathroom had been fitted, the mud was worse. Remnants of the trench-digging had spilled over on to the lane and the tractors and occasional cars, plus the lorries that had delivered the materials for the work, had spread the surface of the lane with a glutinous film.

Nelly skidded once when she reached the main road and her laughter rang out as she grasped at a branch for support. Walking slowly and giving the impression to the occasional passer-by that she was drunk, she went carefully across the main road and behind the row of cottages in which Amy's shop stood.

The rain was fine and misted her view of the fields behind the shop as she approached it, but, looking back, she saw a man she recognised coming out from the back of the fish-and-chip shop.

'Griff Evans,' she muttered, pulling the dogs to stop them barking. 'I wonder what 'e's doin' that I'm not supposed to know about?'

She opened the gate of Amy's yard and tied the dogs where they could sit just inside the shed that had once been Amy's storeroom and went to begin her work. As her hand touched the knob of the door, the gate opened and the constable stepped in.

'Nelly. Got a minute, have you?'

'O' course, so long as it won't take all mornin'.'

'I wondered if you've seen any strangers around the village lately? I know I've asked you before, but you might have remembered something or perhaps there's something you hadn't thought worth mentioning? You wander around more than most with those dogs of yours and you've a sharp eye.'

She leaned forward and grinned wickedly, 'I just seen that Griff comin' from where 'e ain't supposed to be,' she whispered hoarsely. 'Does Hilda know, I wonder?'

'I saw Griff too.' PC Harris showed slight disapproval at Nelly's innuendo. 'He told me he's called with a message from his wife. She won't be going in to work until later.'

Nelly grinned unrepentantly.

'Hilda's away fer the weekend, went last night. You don't think she'd 'ave fergotten to tell Bethan that, do yer?' He crooked teeth gave a cheekiness to her grin that made the policeman smile.

'Interesting,' he admitted.

'Yes, ain't it?'

'Well, if there's nothing more you can tell me—' He thanked her for her time and went back to the lane.

After a moment, Nelly went to the gate and pecred out. Harris was standing near the back entrance to Griff and Hilda's house, where the garage opened on to the lane. She crept along and stood peering through the weaker parts of the wooden doors into the dark interior. At first she could see nothing, but gradually she could make out the shapes of two motor-bikes and a bench on which there were several boxes, presumably of tools. There was the sound of voices and the further door, which opened on to the garden beyond, opened and Griff's son Pete, came in wearing large leather gloves and with a pair of goggles hanging loose around his neck.

332

The extra light revealed the floor covered with leaves and patches of mud from the boots that had walked across the garden. The boy called something, presumably to his father and closed the door. ' 'Ere,' Nelly said suddenly, 'come an' 'ide in Amy's yard, why don't yer?'

The suddenness of the voice behind him and close to his elbow, startled the policeman into a gasp of alarm. He had been so intent on studying the garage he had not heard her approach.

He allowed himself to be dragged by his sleeve back along the lane and in through Amy's gate. They heard the roar of the motor-bike as it turned down past the chip shop and out on to the main road.

Nelly continued to listen, her head on one side.

' 'E's gone up Sheepy Lane, to call for Gerry,' she decided as the whine of the engine faded.

'Thank you,' Harris said sarcastically. 'But there was no need for that, Nelly.' He pulled his sleeve straight fussily. 'I don't have to explain my presence.'

'But it's best not to let 'em know you're investigating 'em.'

'I'm not investigating them. Now you be careful what you say, Nelly.' He raised a warning finger. 'Say nothing about this, right?'

'Right.'

She added to his doubts about her keeping silent, by showing her teeth in another crooked grin, and saluting him. She laughed loudly then, and walked back to start Amy's cleaning. Harris adjusted his jacket and coughed, reorganising his dignity, before walking on.

When her work was finished and she and Amy sat on the bottom step of the stairs which led to the now-sealed door leading to the flat the shop suddenly filled up and Nelly watched while Amy served her customers quickly and efficiently. But after a while she could see there was little chance of a chat, so she stood up to leave. Phil, coming into the shop with his second delivery, stopped her.

'Heard about Sheila, then?' he asked the knot of people standing talking and blocking the doorway of the shop. 'And about Griff off work with a bad leg? Caused by Archie's carelessness *he* says.'

'What now with Sheila?' Milly Toogood asked. 'More trouble for her parents, is it?'

'Got herself a new boyfriend, that's what.' Phil said. 'A smart lad too by all accounts. Accounts, being his job,' he joked. 'An accountant in a building firm so I hear, don't know which one,' he added sadly. 'Posh that, isn't it?'

Nelly watched Amy's face on which surprise, relief and sudden doubt showed. She hoped Amy would not be the one to tell Freddie. He would hate whoever took it on themselves to do so.

'Blimey, 'ere's the farmer's union!' she shouted to take the talk away from Sheila and her new boyfriend. Everyone moved to make room for Billie and Mr Leighton and Sidney Davies, Phil's brother.

' 'Morning, Billie,' Amy said sweetly. 'Up early were you?' Even though Billie had repeatedly apologised for falling asleep in the cinema and had tried to explain his sudden tiredness because of the ewe that had fallen in the stream, Amy wouldn't let him forget it. Now, others heard of it too. Billie took the teasing in good part and joined in the laughter that followed.

The customers were still reluctant to disperse and Billie was obviously in a hurry. He came to lean closer to Amy and asked, 'Dare I invite you out again, Amy? I thought we could go to the pub for a drink or two then back to the farm for supper. Mary will leave everything ready for us. She's going out, see, to the evening class for lace-making.'

334

He groaned as his words were repeated with heavy emphasis and laughingly, Amy agreed. 'If I can find a baby-sitter,' she warned.

The shop finally emptied and Amy sat with Nelly for their belated cup of tea. As soon as they had poured their second cups, there were footsteps, and Victor came in.

'Y're late!' Nelly said. 'Missed Billie by ten minutes, yer did. You must be losin' yer second sense where 'e an' Amy's concerned.' She collected the dogs, damp and cold in their shed, and went home.

Evie had been made to feel guilty at the number of times Amy had looked after Oliver and had agreed to stay with Margaret and the baby until eleven o'clock.

'No later, mind,' she warned as Amy steped into the battered van in which Mary delivered her milk. 'I have to be up early in the morning.'

'Half-past-five, I'm up,' Amy replied. 'Can you beat that?'

Billie drove her to Llangwyn where they found a small public house a little way off the main road where they were not known and which Billie planned to make their own, special place. He told Amy as much and she smiled. He had some nice romantic ideas. Pity he was so slow telling them. He made everything mundane by his slowness, she sighed.

'We get along all right together, don't we, Amy?' he said after a lull in the conversation, which had been mainly about the troubles with sheep. 'I think your Margaret likes me, thinks of me as a favourite uncle. No trouble there. And as for little Sian, well, I'd love her like I love Margaret, and Freddie too. If we were to marry, I think you'd be very happy with how I treated them all.'

'Is this a proposal?' Amy stared at him. He'd made it sound like a contract with sheep-shearers.

'Well, you know how I feel about you—'

'No, I don't. Tell me!'

335

'I – I'm not very good at this sort of thing, Amy, but I – I'm fond of you, always have been, like—'

'Fond?' She was not going to help him at all. 'Is that all?'

'No, no. That's not all. I've always dreamed of us being married, you sharing my life and being there when I wake up every morning and there when I finish my work and never having to say goodbye ever again.'

'Billie, you need to feel more than fondness to take someone into your home and share your life.'

'Amy, you're teasing me.' He put a large hand over hers and smiled at her. 'Come on, let's go home, we can talk easier there.'

He helped her on with her coat and, with his hand resting on her shoulder, guided her out of the pub and across to the car park to the battered van, incongruous between smarter, newer cars. As if she had spoken of the comparison, Billie said, 'Sorry about this, the Landrover's in for a service. Anyway, first off, I'm going to buy us a really smart car, so when we take the children out they'll be really comfortable. Can't expect Margaret to sit in the back of a van much longer. Getting to be a real lady she is.'

Amy did not reply. There was no excitement in the prospect of marrying Billie, yet she did not discard the idea, afraid that there would never be another chance for her. Even Billie was better than a life spent alone, never experiencing the partnership of a man and woman living together, sharing everything and working in harness for the benefit of their family. 'Working in harness', she thought wryly, I'm even beginning to think like a farmer's wife!

She was silent as Billie drove her back to the farm. The countryside had changed colour with the approach of autumn, and the headlights caught patches of rich gold on the leaves of the hedges as they travelled along the twisting lanes, the tyres hissing on the road. As the farm house came into view at the end of the long drive between fields, they saw at once that the front door was open. Billie sighed with disappointment.

'Mary must be back,' he said.

'Night school finishes at nine,' Amy said, and felt relief flow through her. 'Can't expect her to stay away from her own home, now can you?' Dog in the manger I am, she thought guiltily. I don't want him, yet I hang on to him in case I change my mind.

Billie stepped out of the van and opened the door for her and she walked across the recently scrubbed yard to the house. In the living room door, Billie gasped in horror. The place had been ransacked.

'Stay there,' he warned Amy. 'I'll go and see if they're still here. Murder them, I will, if I catch them.'

'No, Billie, I'm coming with you!' Walking close behind him and looking nervously around her, she went from room to room along dark passages as they searched every corner of the rambling house.

It was empty but in several rooms drawers and wardrobes were open, their contents strewn across the floor. In the bedroom where Mary slept a small metal box was lying on the carpet, its lock obviously forced.

'Damn me, there's all her collection gone! I warned her. I told her this might happen. She used to take it straight to the bank regular, but lately she's been careless. I warned her!'

'Billie, don't you think we should ring the police?' Amy said.

She watched as, with hands trembling with rage, he dialled PC Harris's number, then they stood silently until he arrived together with two men from Llangwyn. They had waited in the doorway, Billie unable to go inside the ransacked house and face the chaos the intruders had left, and Amy needing to be close to him his warmth and his arms around her a protection from the fears the burglary had caused. She glanced around her, afraid that the events of the evening were not yet over, that someone would suddenly jump out at them. The mellow old building was no longer friendly, the evening already turning into an unpleasant memory with all the enjoyment fading from her mind.

Bert Roberts called a meeting in the church hall for the following Monday evening and the small building was crammed full. The Reverend Barclay Bevan was there to open the proceedings and the main speaker was Constable Harris, with one of his superiors to add information where necessary.

'Now, first of all, let me reassure you that this spate of burglaries is, so far as we know, *not* connected with the death of Harry Beynon. The methods used are so dissimilar as to make that very, very unlikely.' A murmur of conversation resulted from his words and he allowed it to continue for a few moments before continuing. 'I want you all to think about the past weeks and let me know of anything unusual, however insignificant, that might help identify the people responsible. Or anything that might be assisting them to get information. They are certainly aware of times when houses are empty and this suggests that information is being gathered.'

People looked at each other nervously.

'What are we doing here, then?' someone called. 'Best we were home, minding our property.'

'Yes, indeed,' another voice added, 'this meeting has been publicised, hasn't it?'

Harris raised his arms asking them to remain seated.

'Mr Chartridge will pass around some pieces of paper and I want you to write down anything you think might help.'

Timothy was standing near the constable and he

338

passed some scrap paper along the rows of people, and waited while pens and pencils were found and shared as the papers were filled.

'Ladies and gentlemen,' boomed Bert in his best sergeant's voice, 'we don't want to be here all night. Let's get them papers passed back so we can get home and see that our houses are safe.'

Too late he saw the constable trying to hush him. Several people stood and began pushing their way through the rows in panic at the thought of their endangered homes. Chairs scraped and fell in the sudden confusion and Archie, who was sitting in the middle of a row, crawled under some of the chairs, causing consternation to the ladies as he brushed their legs.

'Bleedin' chaos as usual, where Bert is concerned,' Nelly muttered to George. But she could not help laughing as the crush in the door became a tangle of arms, legs and umbrellas and no one could get in or out.

Order was somehow restored but not before over half the people had departed. PC Harris told Bert to sit down and he and the sergeant from Llangwyn began again. This time, there were several useful remarks, mainly regarding the various cafes and public houses frequented by villagers where tips about people's movements could be gathered.

Nelly wrote on her piece of paper:

1/ Gerry and Pete aren't the only ones with bikes.
2/ Ask at the garage where they work. They mend most of the bikes in the area.
3/ Have a look at Dawn's photographs.

George wrote:

Why motor-bikes? It's usually only money that's taken and that is easy to carry away.

339

They walked home in a night that was clear now the rain clouds had at last drifted on eastwards, both chuckling over the evening's events.

'You don't worry about being robbed, Nelly?' George asked.

'No, Gawd 'elp us. I ain't got enough to make it worth their while and we never has any money in the 'ouse, do we?'

'No, but d'you think we ought to start locking the door at night?'

Again Nelly shook her head. 'Doubt if it would lock anyway. It's dropped again after you tried to fix it.'

Down in the village, Ethel had managed to shut her front door firmly enough to turn the key but had been unable to open it the next morning. It was not until her son, Phil, called with the post that she had been able to go out, except by the back and through the field, so she abandoned the idea completely and decided to leave her door open in future.

Amy was uneasy about walking home with the day's takings as she occasionally had in the past, and Billie offered to come every evening and take it to the night safe at the bank for her. Victor added a bolt to each of her doors and checked her window fastenings. With the approach of the dark evenings, it seemed the risk of robberies would increase, but in fact there were no more. There was a spate of similar break-ins to some of the houses on the outskirts of Llangwyn, but these were far enough away not to cause much anxiety.

After the sickness following the bag of cockles, Fay avoided the markets and fish shops where the smell of them filled the air, mingling with the wonderful smell of freshly baked bread and boiled ham. Instead she ordered bread at Amy's shop and called each evening as she finished her day's work. Occasionally she would be too late, then Amy would send it over to Netta, and Netta would receive a rare visit from her daughter-in-law.

One evening in mid-September, Fay had not arrived to collect her bread at six-thirty and Netta walked to and from the front window looking for her. The television was on low so she half listened to it, and half listened for the sound of Fay's car. At a quarter to seven she decided that Fay had forgotten to call and she put on a coat and picked up a torch to walk up to St David's Close.

As she stepped out of her door, Fay's car stopped at the gate.

'Fay?' Netta called. 'Are you all right? Worried I've been, thinking of you trying to mend a puncture or something like that, all on your own in the dark.'

Fay didn't get out of the car, but just held out a hand to take the 'Swansea' loaf.

'I'm all right, Mother. I just got held up, that's all.'

Something in Fay's voice made Netta step closer and she bent down to enquire further, but Fay had moved back over to the driving seat and was revving the engine in a hurry to be off.

'Of course, I mustn't keep you chattering. Johnny will be worried too,' Netta said then added, 'Oh, of course, he's on the late shift and won't know, will he?' She had no time to say any more, the car moved on and she saw Fay's hand wave a brief farewell as she moved slowly past the school and on, to turn up Sheepy Lane to the council houses.

Fay drove up the lane, impatient to be home. The bread order was a nuisance. Tomorrow she would cancel it. It seemed to give Netta the right to check on her comings and goings, she thought unreasonably. There were plenty of shops where she could buy a loaf, for heaven's sake!

She was in a temper. The day had been a bad one from

the start. First of all, it being a Wednesday, she had promised herself she would avoid the place where she knew Dexter would be waiting for her. Then Johnny had asked her to go to some stupid skittles game at the Drovers. The landlord had decided to open a skittle alley that hadn't been used for years, hoping to make more money for the church-hall fund. Skittles! she thought with increased anger. She was sick of the village and the small, boring things they expected her to enjoy. Johnny knew how she felt about it, yet still insisted she joined in the silly nonsense.

The journey to her first call had been a nightmare of traffic holdups where mud from recent rains had blocked the drains. She had changed her route to get free of the area and the new one took her part of the way down to Pembrokeshire. On impulse, driven by the irritation brought on by the invitation to go and watch the stupid skittles match, she drove on.

She reached the place at twelve and decided to tempt fate and see if Dexter had arrived earlier than he had said. If he isn't there, she promised some imaginary overseer of morals, if he hasn't arrived, I'll go away and never come back here. Having passed responsibility for her behaviour into the hands of the fates, she walked into the restaurant.

He was there. Standing against the bar, tall, elegant, lean and very handsome and obviously delighted to see her. Her anger against the day faded in the warmth of his smile. She forgot her anger at Johnny, skittles, and the traffic that had brought her here and saw only him.

He kissed her lightly then found a table where he ordered wine and offered her the menu to choose her meal. He took her hand and pressed it against his heart. His obvious pleasure at her coming lit his hazel eyes so they glowed with those fascinating touches of gold. His reddish hair, so neat and well groomed tempted her to reach out and touch, his lips, full and generous, seemed close enough for her kiss them. She lowered her gaze, afraid he would see her thoughts in her eyes.

They both chose fish and as they ate their meal, slowly spending the time talking, getting to know one another Fay felt the tensions of the past days slip away from her. Dexter knew how to wine and dine a woman. He would never suggest taking her to watch a skittles match between the council houses and the village! She imagined being escorted to a London theatre, or to a grand ball, where she would wear a beautiful gown and Dexter would dazzle every woman in the room with his good looks and immaculate clothes.

Defiantly, she did not hurry to return to her calls. Johnny, having been disappointed at her reaction to the skittles invitation, had told her he would change his shift and work late to allow someone else to take part. Well, she was not going to hurry home and sit waiting for him. She hinted to Dexter that she was not rushing back and waited for him to suggest how they might spend their afternoon. He seemed delighted at first that she was free, but then told her he had to be back for a six o'clock appointment.

'But until then,' he whispered, gazing at her with adoring eyes, 'I want to spend every moment with you.'

They discussed places to go and finally admitted that for the limited time they had together, they could only walk and talk.

'I don't want to share you with anyone, I want you to myself. I want to know everything about you,' Dexter told her.

So they walked along the sea front of the small town, the wind making Fay wish she had worn something other than the thin costume and the lace-edged blouse she had chosen. But she hid the shivers she occasionally felt as they met a particularly windy corner and did not utter a

343

complaint. Dexter was wearing an overcoat and seemed unaware that she was less well clad. Holding his hand and feeling the chill wind on her face was heavenly compared with locals throwing balls down the stone floor of the skittle alley! What did a shiver or two matter compared with that?

At five-thirty he walked her back to the car and got in beside her. The comparative warmth of the car seemed to disturb her and she felt a twinge of discomfort as if she were about to be sick. Alarmed, she opened the window and took a few deep breaths.

'I love the smell of the sea,' she said as an excuse for her odd behaviour, but her voice was breathless when she spoke, as if her lungs could not contain enough air for her words. The wind was beginning to gust as the tide reached its height and the car rocked slightly. He turned towards her and she saw the desire in his eyes. His breathing became as shallow as hers.

Closing her eyes to receive his kisses, filled with longing, she suddenly felt its urgency leave her. Opening her eyes in alarm she saw his features swim before her and, pushing him aside, just managed to get out of the car before sickness overwhelmed her.

The moment was utterly and permanently ruined. She could not look at him, her eyes were filled with tears from the violence of the sickness.

'It must have been the fish,' she mumbled in a voice that did not sound like her own. She hid her face in a handkerchief. 'I'd better go home.'

He had left the car and had been standing well back from her. He stepped a fraction closer and asked solicitously, 'Will you be all right? I feel I should stay with you but—'

'I'll be all right. You go,' she whispered. 'I'll – we'll meet again, won't we?'

'Of course. Next week if you can manage it. Thank

344

you for coming, I'm so sorry the meal upset you.'

'It's so strange,' she said. 'I know fish upsets me. I can't think why I ordered it.'

She sat in the car for an age, with the windows down letting the now gusting wind cool her and clear the awful sensation the biliousness had left. Then she drove slowly home, wondering if she were ill. To have had two bouts of sickness was odd and she went over all she had eaten. It must have been the fish. Why did it attract her so when she knew it did not agree with her?

She was devastated by the unbelievably awful end of her few hours with Dexter and wondered sadly if he would ever want to see her again. Being sick, of all things, and timing it so that it was as if the thought of his kiss had revolted her. She was feeling humiliated and miserable by the time she stopped to collect the loaf of bread from Netta and could hardly bring herself to say 'hello'.

The house was empty and she thankfully stripped off and sank into a warm bath. She didn't dress again, but slipped on a nightdress and a silky dressing gown. When Johnny came home at eleven-thirty, she was asleep in the armchair they had recently bought and he carried her to bed without her waking.

The following morning she was sick before she had eaten, and knew with chilly certainty that she was pregnant.

Sheila continued to meet Nigel and, although she avoided discussing her recent past and avoided introducing him to others who might let things slip, they managed to develop a friendly relationship. She had not introduced Nigel to her parents, afraid that one of them would consider it their duty to tell the young man about the marriage and the baby, and Nigel had not, so far, suggested taking her home to meet his family, about whom he frequently talked with obvious affection.

One day they were meeting for a brief lunch-date in 'their' cafe, when a girl came in and hailed Nigel in surprise.

'Nigel, I've been looking for you. Fancy coming to the dance tonight? All the usual crowd will be there and we haven't seen you for ages.'

Sheila sat back in her chair as if stepping aside for Nigel to discuss things about which she knew nothing. Nigel was clearly embarrassed and showed it. Forgetting to introduce Sheila, he said he might come, and thanked the girl, who walked out with a final wave and a brief, curious glance at Sheila.

'Who was that?' she forced herself to ask lightly.

'One of the dancing crowd,' he said, taking refuge behind his cup of tea.

'The dance crowd? I never knew you liked dancing, Nigel?'

'We enter competitions, six of us. You must come and watch us one night. The new season's about to begin.'

'I'd love to,' Sheila smiled. 'Fancy you being a dancer. I never dreamed—'

'I haven't told you because, well, because I'd feel a bit silly with you watching me,' he admitted. 'Competitions are a bit tense and I'd be put off, knowing you were there. I can't concentrate on anything when I'm with you, Sheila.'

'Nigel,' she said softly.

'Perhaps later on when—'

'When you don't care as much?' This coyness was a surprising side to him. He had always seemed so confident. And the dancing suggested he was able spend a lot of money on his hobby: the dresses were costly and all the dancers must contribute to the cost of those yards of tulle and lace. She'd always known he was prosperous, but perhaps he was rich as well as attractive?

'When I'm used to being with you,' he corrected. 'You are so lovely, I can't believe my luck that you bother with dull old me.'

'Not so dull,' she said smiling up into his eyes. 'Full of surprises, that's what you are, Nigel Knighton. Full of surprises. I like that, mind, I like life to have a few mysteries, don't you?'

That evening, Sheila did not go straight home. Defying her parents, she wandered around the town and then went to a public house, ordered a drink boldly at the bar and sat with it, watching the faces of the men. They were put out with her being there and their eyes turned towards her as they whispered about the cheek of women entering a man's province. She sipped her drink and refused to be made to leave.

Although she appeared confident, she was relieved to see a familiar face. Victor Honeyman came in, went to order a pint then saw her.

'Sheila? Waiting for someone are you?'

'No, I just couldn't face the crowded bus, so I thought I'd wait and get a later one.'

'I see.' He didn't see why a young girl would want to wait in a public house instead of going home, but thought that she was in fact waiting for the boyfriend people had heard about. He did not approach her, and soon began a conversation with two men in the furthest corner.

'A gold watch, you say?' Victor said when the men offered him some jewellery. 'Yes, I might be interested in that.' They discussed prices for a while and Victor agreed to meet them there the following evening. When he went out, he was so excited at getting the watch he wanted for Amy, he forgot all about Sheila, walking past her without a word, his mind on the scene when he would give Amy the watch he had stopped smoking to save for.

\*　　\*　　\*

347

The number of televisions in the village had increased and this was having an effect on the activities. Neighbour invited neighbour in to watch favourite programmes so the conversation each morning in Amy's shop was often about the previous evening's offerings.

Netta, who was one of the first to have a television set, bemoaned the fact that the numbers joining the sewing circle to make things for the Autumn Fair were far too few.

'This sale of work we're planning won't be much of a success if we don't persuade our members to come back soon,' she confided in Amy one morning in September. 'There's a dozen of us where there used to be forty.'

'It's no use asking me, Netta,' Amy laughed. 'You'd spend all your time unravelling what I'd done and putting it right again!'

'Your Prue was good,' Netta sighed. 'I know she was a bit difficult, but she did work hard and she encouraged others so they did their best too.'

'Have you been to see her lately?' Amy asked.

'Yes, indeed. I see her regularly and, I must say Amy, she's improving. Getting back some of her spirit. I have to watch what I say now, whereas a few weeks ago she hardly seemed to know I was there.'

'She's coming home for the weekend on Friday,' Amy told her. 'The first time she's slept away from that place since she went in. I hope it goes well. It could be the beginning of her recovery.' She covered the cheese with vinegar-soaked muslin to keep it fresh and added anxiously, 'She seemed to want to come, but keeps asking if Freddie will be there. She says she won't come if he's home. Pretends she doesn't want to make things difficult for me but I know it's not that.' She laughed a bit harshly. 'Since when has Prue worried about making things difficult for me? No, she wants to avoid Freddie.'

'He was home a few weeks since. There isn't much

348

chance of him getting home again for a while, is there?'

'I told her that, but she still seems worried.'

'Perhaps it's her illness confusing her. Harry dying made Freddie leave the firm and join the army, didn't it? In her mind that must be what's worrying her.'

'Perhaps.'

'She'll soon be back to her normal self. Now she's started to get better things will improve faster, for sure.'

Constable Harris wandered down to the village and with apparent casualness went up the lane and behind the houses opposite the school and the church. When he reached the back of Griff's house he stopped and looked through the garage doors. He heard the gate open and started back, but Griff, who had come out of the back of the chip shop, saw him and asked, 'Anything wrong, Constable?'

'No, not really. I just wondered who those bikes belonged to, that's all. Being repaired on the side, like, are they?'

'One is my boy Pete's, and the other is Gerry's. Both in pieces again. Damn me, I've never seen a pair like them two for mucking about with bikes! All day in the garage then all evening here in *my* garage.'

'There's more than two bikes.'

'Oh, you mean, mine. Never touched it once the exhaust fell off. I haven't got the interest now Hilda won't go on it. Used to love the bike, she did, but now she won't bother, so I haven't got round to repairing it and I'm damned if I'm going to pay them boys to do it for me. Kids, they won't do anything without getting paid now, will they? Money-mad the lot of 'em.'

He led the constable through the gate and into the garage, where the floor was littered with fallen leaves and bundles of rags that had been used for wiping greasy hands and motor-bike parts. Harris lifted the old piece

349

of carpet that covered the bike belonging to Griff. It seemed the same as last time he had looked, and the exhaust was in the same sorry state. He knew very little about motor-bikes so there was little he could tell by standing looking at it. George told him once that he had owned a bike in his youth. Perhaps he might learn something talking to him.

'Thanks, Griff,' he said. 'If you hear anything about strangers on bikes, let me know, although I doubt if that will be the answer. George pointed out that these robberies don't need a vehicle to carry the stuff away, do they? Money fits easily into a pocket.'

'I wish some would fit easily into mine,' Griff laughed. 'Hilda spends it like there's no tomorrow!'

Harris walked back up the hill a niggle of unease in his mind. There must be something he was missing and not necessarily about Griff. He's a crook and that fact alone would account for *him* making me nervous, he thought. Poaching and carrying bets illegally were a regular and known part of Griff's life, *and* he was carrying on with Milly Toogood's daughter. All these facts were known to Harris, and almost a necessary evil in a place like Hen Carw Parc. The poaching and betting could hardly be considered real crimes, although he doubted if his superiors would agree. But somewhere in this village was someone who was not just cheating on the law, but bringing distress and fear to those who did not deserve it. If only there was something to give him a start on an investigation, but petty crime was all he had and there seemed nothing there likely to lead him to men who would break into houses and take all they could find. He went home and took out his notebooks to pore over them in the hope that a small, and unimportant detail would give him a lead. Hours later, he took out a fresh piece of paper and began all over again.

# Chapter Eighteen

When Prue arrived on the Friday morning, Amy was at the house to meet her. She had spent the previous evening cleaning and polishing the furniture ready for her critical sister's visit. The taxi pulled up at the end of the drive and she went out to greet Prue, who had brought surprisingly little luggage. She carried the one small bag up to the room that was Freddie's and then came down to make them some coffee.

'You're looking well, Prue,' she said as she set the kettle and milk to heat. 'Are you feeling better?'

'I want to forget how ill I've been,' Prue said rather gruffly. 'I'm determined to get well again and I'd rather not discuss how I'm feeling. All right?'

'Good idea,' Amy said brightly, thinking, it's going to be one of those visits! 'Shall we take the coffee out into the garden?' she suggested. 'I want you to see what we've done here. Only a patch of very untidy grass when we moved in. Not that I've done much, mind. I have to thank Victor and Billie for how it looks, and Freddie of course, for his planning. Coming home soon, he is. Got a few days' leave.'

Amy prattled on while Prue looked around her at the late summer flowers; michaelmas daisies and geraniums, fuchsias, gladioli and a riotous display of nasturtiums that made an attractive if untidy show in a rocky corner. Amy sensed that Prue was imagining the orderliness that would result if she were allowed an hour or two to tidy up.

'Not as neat as yours used to be, although that's a sorry sight now. Want to go and look?' Amy asked.

Prue was silent for a moment and Amy looked at her. Always thin, Prue's illness had reduced her weight further and now her eyes, deep in the lined face, were those of a stranger. Amy wondered how she was going to get through three days of entertaining her: the future hours stretched out long and exhausting.

An utter sense of loneliness overcame Amy and weariness pressed down on her shoulders. Why wasn't there someone in her life to help her? Someone to share the daily burdens and support her in things that worried her? She thought of Victor and how much easier life would be if he were always here, a part of her life. Then thoughts slipped to the offer of marriage from Billie.

That would be a different world but one in which she would have few worries. No shop accounts to bog down her weekends and no customers to press for payments. Margaret could have her piano and Freddie might leave the army instead of signing on for further years as he threatened. Billie was the answer to her troubles, perhaps the only one she would get, but definitely not, she sighed, the answer to her prayers!

She turned her head from where she was staring into the middle distance, unseeing and lost in her thoughts and brought herself back to the present.

'Yes,' Prue was saying. 'Yes, I would like to go and see my garden.'

'Great. I'll just take these cups inside and we'll go.'

Amy watched Prue carefully as they approached the village. Pushing Sian in her pram, she chattered about the people Prue remembered and gave her the latest news. She sensed Prue stiffen as they reached Gypsy Lane at the beginning of the group of houses in what had once been the grounds of Mrs French's house.

'All right?' she asked.

'I expect it will look a worse mess than yours,' Prue replied. 'Paying someone doesn't mean the work will be done satisfactorily.'

'No, but Victor has been a few times and Freddie did a bit of clearing up when he was last on leave,' Amy said. 'Don't expect too much, then you won't be disappointed.' She hoped that Prue would be pleased at how the garden had been kept, and surprised at how colourful it still was. Prue had paid someone to cut the lawns and Amy and her friends had done the rest.

Prue *was* surprised at how neat everything was but, being Prue, found it hard to admit it.

'The roses need dead-heading, the lawn edge is a bit uneven,' she said, but Amy saw from her face that the state of the garden had pleased her.

'It needs your expert and loving hand, Prue,' she said. 'But it has survived, hasn't it?'

'It will take ages for it to be put right.'

'We'll all help,' Amy offered. She was gratified to see a slight bloom of colour in her sister's cheeks and knew that in spite of the complaints Prue was pleased.

'I think your help would be more of a hazard,' Prue said, and there was a hint of a smile on the thin lips which made Amy laugh aloud.

'Best I stick to making the tea, is it?'

'I think so.'

They walked around the garden and Prue stopped occasionally to straighten a fallen stem, support a weak shrub or collect a few untidy leaves. Then, as they approached the back door, Prue stopped and, looking away from Amy, said, 'I want to go inside, on my own.'

'Are you sure, love?'

'Quite sure. You take Sian on home and I'll follow on.'

'No.' Amy spoke firmly. 'We'll wait. Take as long as you like but Sian and I will wait for you. Right?' The challenge in her blue eyes was not met and Prue agreed.

The house smelt surprisingly fresh as Prue unlocked the back door and stepped fearfully into the kitchen. It smelt of soap and disinfectant and not, as she had constantly believed, of death and stale flowers and blood. Nor did it have the atmosphere of horror that it had in her dreams and imaginings.

She closed the door and began to shake as she forced herself to look at the polished brass pokers that lay across the clean tiled hearth. She tried to imagine Harry lying there and courted his ghost to come and torment her. Instead the room remained friendly and calm. Slowly her heart settled to a steady rhythm and she began to breath evenly and easily.

She looked around the orderly kitchen with its scrubbed-top table and the bowl of flowers someone had placed there. Nelly had done well and for a brief moment she wanted to go and tell her so. She looked through the window to where Amy was playing with Sian, waving the branch of a fir tree and laughing at the child's reactions. Everything was so normal. She turned and faced the door leading to the hall.

A memory flitted across her mind. She had been back, she remembered coming here with, who was it, Netta? But when, and why? The brief memory faded and she stared at the door to Harry's office. Had she been back? Somewhere in her muddled mind there was a memory of a glance into that room, but the memory was faint and could be false. Her mind played such tricks on her.

The door to Harry's office was ajar and she stepped across and looked in. His books were still stacked on the shelves and his diary lay open on the desk. She looked at it and saw that the pages had been turned and the present week showed. Nelly again. She went out and closed the door.

It was difficult to go upstairs, although again she half

354

remembered being there since her illness. The stairs seemed steeper than she expected and the colour of the carpet deeper. It was red, blood-red, her mind quickly added, and for a moment she panicked and had to hold on to the banisters for support. She forced herself on although she imagined briefly that she was walking not on carpet but on blood. It's an illusion, she told herself firmly, and climbed upwards.

Her bedroom was cold and she shivered. It was here, if anywhere that Harry's ghost would wait. Here, where she had allowed her nephew, Freddie, to make love to her and give her the child that marriage to Harry had denied her. She faltered before making herself enter and touch the covers of the bed, trying to lay the ghost of her shame. She pulled back the covers and touched the pillows then re-made it, tucking the sheets in with fussy precision.

Out of the window she looked down on Amy and Sian. The child was not a part of her disgrace and deserved nothing but love. She had been selfish to make an innocent baby share her shame. The room began to feel warm and she went out, closing the door and walked with greater confidence than she had for weeks and she went down to rejoin her sister and her child.

The walk home convinced Amy that Prue was really on the mend. She talked mostly of the garden, and of her ideas for the following year's planting. She told Amy of the annuals she would grow to fill the beds with rich colour.

When they reached the house again, Prue went straight to her room and brought down her bag. From it she pulled out a child's dress. Beautifully made, its lacy pattern looked to Amy too perfect to have been created with only two needles and a ball of wool. They tried it on Sian and it fitted to perfection.

'Prue, it's wonderful. You really are clever!'

'Netta helped me to get started,' Prue said. 'For a while my mind wouldn't work properly. But now I can manage on my own. Shall we go on Sunday morning and show her that it's finished?'

'Lovely idea,' Amy smiled.

To Amy's delight, Prue wanted to see people she had not mentioned since her illness. Ordering a taxi, she called on several friends and seemed to grow in confidence as the hours passed. Her face was still thin, her eyes sunken and weary but there was animation in her that Amy had feared never to see again.

On the Sunday morning, she suggested the visit to Netta. For the first time, she pushed the pram in which Sian was propped up on a large pillow, wearing the new dress. After staying for tea, which Prue insisted was weak and only lukewarm, they waited outside the church for Margaret to come out after morning service.

Several people stopped to talk to Prue and admire the baby, and when they reached the house, the meat was overcooked and the roast potatoes shrivelled and hard. When Prue complained, Amy smiled in delight. She thought at that moment she would never again mind Prue's constant carping about how badly she did things. She was getting well and even the thought of losing the baby she had begun to think of as her own didn't spoil her joy.


Fay could not tell Johnny about the pregnancy. She tried not to think about it and hoped, childlike, that the problem would magically go away. People often had disappointments, didn't they? It was far too early to consider it a certain fact. She knew she ought to go to the doctor's and have the pregnancy confirmed but she could not. Once she heard the word 'pregnant' uttered aloud, it would be inescapable. Johnny would have to be told and there would be all the grinning faces of the women in the village and the usual crudities from the less pleasant inhabitants. She shuddered and wished she could suddenly move away to a place where no one knew her. She couldn't face it, she really couldn't.

Although she now felt the mild flirtation with Dexter had to be over, she still thought of him and in her dilemma began to imagine how it would have been with someone as suave and worldly as he, instead of the down-to-earth Johnny who, she was certain, would go into paroxysms of delight at the news. Dexter would have allowed her to discuss the full implications of it all. Foolishly and illogically, it was Dexter she wanted to tell first.

She knew so little about him. In their brief moments together they had discussed many things but had spoken little about their own lives. No, she decided, that was not really true, she had talked about herself and Johnny and Dexter had listened and sympathised with her on the differences between what she wanted from life and the little Johnny was prepared to settle for. She felt a flush of disloyalty, remembering, but knew it was still Dexter she needed to talk her through this difficulty.

He worked with his brother in an estate agency. She knew that much. But which one? She was not sure even which town the office was in and, although his name was Dexter Lloyd-Rees, there was no estate agency with that name that she'd come across so where could she begin?

Her customers, being business people, often knew others and she began asking about Dexter at every place she called. There was no joy in the area in which they had last met. In Llangwyn and Swansea no one had heard the name, and it was in a small town near Brecon that she eventually found him. The estate agency was not his, she was surprised to learn, but one of a chain. He was one of the salesman, his brother being the manager.

She was disappointed at the foolish deceit but still

357

wanted to see him. So what if he had told a few small untruths? People often did when they were with people they expected never to see again. And what was the harm in pretending you were better than you really were? Hadn't she done that herself?

She went to a cafe and after a light, cautious meal she applied fresh makeup with care and combed her long blonde hair until it hung in a neat, but loose under-roll, soft on her shoulders. She had on a new green costume with a pearl-grey blouse. Shoes and hat matched, in a darker green, and her handbag and umbrella were grey. Rain threatened and she hurried through the busy street hoping that the wind, now beginning to gust in the approaching squall, would not disturb her hair.

The office was open and as she stepped inside, a woman of about thirty-five looked up from her type-writer and smiled. 'May I help you?' she asked.

'I wondered if I could speak to Mr Lloyd-Rees for a moment, please?'

'About a property, was it?'

Fay nodded. 'Yes.'

'He'll be back in about five minutes, if you'd like to wait? He's gone for a sandwich for our lunch,' the woman explained. 'We haven't time to go out today.'

'That doesn't seem fair,' Fay smiled. 'I should complain.'

'I don't mind. We work together, Dexter and I. Having the children to see to, we work the hours that suits us best.'

'He's your husband?' Fay's throat was dry . . .

'Yes. People say husband and wife can't work together, but we manage very well in spite of all the awful warnings,' the woman laughed.

Before Fay could leave, the door opened and Dexter walked in, smiling at his wife. Then he turned and his face, prepared for conventional politenesses, was startled

358

into shock. His eyes widened as he recovered himself sufficiently to say, calmly, 'Ah, er, Mrs Evans, isn't it? About that property we discussed recently?'

'Yes,' Fay found herself saying, 'I've decided not to continue.'

'Thank you very much for letting us know. I'll find your file and make a note.'

He escaped by scrambling in a drawer on the pretext of finding some information and Fay rose, feeling sickness again overwhelming her. She had thought it was she who needed to be cautious. Discovering he was married had confused her. Why had she suddenly become the guilty one? She stumbled to the door and fled.

She was trembling when she reached the corner and was out of sight of the office. Then slowly, feeling the nausea that dogged her hours beginning to threaten, she walked to the car. The smell of leather increased the sensation of approaching sickness and as she opened the door, perspiration was running down her hot cheeks. People passed but fortunately none stopped to enquire if she were ill. Fay knew that if she tried to speak she would be sick at once.

Gradually the sensation eased and she drove back to the coast. She parked the car on a plateau overlooking the sea and watched the waves, their regular movements calming her. The spray dashing against the rocks of the shore rose, white and splendid, and she imagined them falling over her, cooling her. She felt better able to cope and after a while, drove home.

Johnny knew something had upset her almost before he opened the door. He sensed her moods as he approached the house these days. He saw the car parked outside the house and increased his pace to get home. As always the first sight of her thrilled him. Then his joy took a nose-dive as his fingers touched the door handle and found it locked. That usually meant she had come home early having had a bad day.

He took out his key and at once smelt the bath essence Fay used. That confirmed his guess. When things had gone badly she would come home, bath, then spend the evening searching through her notebooks and files, looking for additions to her round for the following days. Sales must always be up, never down on previous months. She took her work so seriously and was content only when things were going well.

She was sitting in the lounge with the curtains barely parted. She wore her dressing gown although it was only four o'clock. He slipped off his shoes, pushed his feet into slippers and went over to kiss her.

'Hello, my lovely, there's good to see you when I expected hours of my own company. I love you, Fay.' He kissed her unresponsive lips again. 'Would you like something to eat? Or what say we go out for a meal. Like that, would you?'

'I'm not hungry, Johnny. Get something for yourself, will you?'

'I'll leave it for a while. Too early for food. Perhaps later on you'll change your mind and eat with me.'

'No I won't.'

'You aren't ill are you, lovely? You look a bit green around the gills, like.'

'No, I'm not ill, I just don't want anything to eat.'

She spoke calmly, not as she would if she were trying to start an argument, and Johnny moved towards the kitchen door and studied her face. She was pale. No doubt she was unwell, but what could he do to help without making her angry? He sensed the tightness about her and decided to wait for a while in the hope she would tell him what was wrong.

Whistling cheerfully he put the kettle on to boil. He was cutting himself a piece of seedy cake, one of his

360

favourites that his mother still made for him, when she came out and leaned on the door-post.

She took a deep breath and for a moment he felt panic, afraid of what she was going to tell him. She was leaving him? She had become utterly bored with their marriage? When she did speak he did not believe what he had heard. He was hallucinating, imagining things. 'What did you say?' he breathed.

'I'm going to have a baby, Johnny, and I don't know what to do.' She moved towards him then, and at last he could take her in his arms and comfort her.

His head spun with wild thoughts. She was going to have his baby. She was not happy about it and she wanted him to sort things out. She was here in his arms and the sweet scent of her was driving him crazy with fear that he would lose her. He did not speak for a long time. He knew that what he said next was desperately important to them both.

'I love you, Fay, and I want only what you want,' he said at last. And he felt her arms tighten around him and knew the first hurdle was over.

She allowed herself to be led back to the lounge and together they sat on the armchair. Fay nestled against him and soon, to his surprise, she slept. He sat unmoving, facing the windows over which the curtains were still drawn. Outside, birds sang and the weak September sun shone but it was as if they were cut off from the rest of the world and Johnny was in a cocoon of happiness.

She woke after fifteen minutes and appeared rested and calm. He eased his stiffening arm from around her and kissed her gently. She smiled at him, her blue eyes drowsy with sleep and asked, 'Will you get me a drink, Johnny? Not tea. Anything but tea.'

'Troubled by sickness, are you, lovely?'

'Morning sickness but it lasts all day.'

'Now there's a funny thing. Mam said the same. Perhaps it will be a boy? Although I hope for a girl. Just like you, perfect.'

'Johnny, I don't want a baby. There are so many things I want to do first.'

During the brief time she had slept, Johnny had considered how he would treat the news. He decided that an acceptance of the situation without even discussing the alternatives was best. Give Fay no choice, not even hint at anything but the perfect solution, that she would give up work and care for their child.

'I know, it's a shock, and there's no doubt it will change our lives and our plans for the future. Not abandon our plans, mind, only shelve them for a while. Lovely mother you'll be, Fay. Show them all round here how it should be done.'

Fay was subdued for the rest of the evening and Johnny was careful not to say too much about the baby. They listened to the radio and it was not until they were going to bed that Fay broached the subject again.

'I don't want the baby, Johnny.'

He forced himself to sound calm as he replied, 'Of course you don't. Had great plans for us, you did. I know that. But your life doesn't have to be anything you don't want it to be. Once the baby arrives we can replan the next few years together, can't we? Nothing we can't achieve together, lovely.'

She slept in his arms and in the morning he had to wake her to ease himself out of bed to get to work. He watched anxiously as she opened her eyes, hoping to see contentment shine in them and was unable to hold back a wide grin as she smiled and said, 'Hello Dadda Johnny.'

They agreed not to tell anyone until they had savoured their secret for a while and it was more than a week later that they went to tell Netta that she was to be a grandmother.

'Oh!' she said, her round face beaming as she hugged Fay. 'Oh, how happy I am! But just think of all the knitting I've given to the sale of work! I'll have to get busy now, catching up, won't I?' She was busy sorting through patterns of baby clothes before they closed the gate.

On Sunday morning Nelly was cleaning the shop for Amy. As she gave the steps a final wipe with her cloth, she was surprised to see George walking towards her.

'George, what's wrong? I thought you was working?'

He showed her the hand he had been hiding behind his back. On two fingers were snowy-white bandages.

'Only cuts, nothing serious. But Mr Leighton insisted I went to the hospital and have it checked. He also insists I have the rest of the day off. Where shall we go?'

'Let me finish doing Amy's back room an' we'll go 'ome and decide,' she said after reassuring herself the injuries were slight. George agreed to wait while she finished her work.

The dogs, tied up in the yard, were barking frantically, aware that George was there and wondering why he hadn't come to release them. Nelly locked the doors and went through the yard and around to join George in the street.

He was looking at a motor-bike propped against the kerb and discussing the merits of that particular model with the constable.

'Do you know much about them, George?' Harris asked.

'Not really, I used to have one years ago and the only thing I remember was someone showing me how to disconnect the exhaust to give the impression that it was unusable, when my brother wanted to borrow it,' George laughed.

'Really? And how was that done?' The policeman looked interested.

'Oh, there's bolt, about here.' George bent down and pointed. 'If that's unscrewed and pulled out, the exhaust system comes away from the frame and falls down.'

'Fascinating, George. Thanks very much.'

'You haven't got a motor-bike and a brother wanting to borrow it, have you?' George laughed.

'Something much more intriguing than that, George,' Harris smiled as he walked away.

PC Harris went first to the owner of the garage where Pete and Gerry worked, then he spoke to his superiors.

'There might be nothing in it,' he explained. 'Perhaps the boys are avoiding repairing the bike for some completely innocent reason of their own but it's definitely something to check. And I have a feeling, only a feeling, mind, that it might be the father rather than those boys.'

'Oh, by the way,' the officer called as Harris was leaving. 'Those leaves you found on the site of the burglaries weren't privet, they were honeysuckle.'

Harris smiled his satisfaction.

Sheila had been meeting Nigel regularly for several weeks but had still not invited him to meet her parents. He had not invited her to the dance to meet his friends either and she wondered if their relationship would ever be close enough for her to tell him the truth about herself. She could not suggest going to meet his friends or family. That was up to him and he was probably waiting for her to invite him home first. It seemed a situation that could go on unresolved for ever.

She tried to imagine taking him home and shuddered at the prospect of her parents' inquisition. It would be worse than a police investigation! No, things would have to stay simmering for a while. Fate, she decided would eventually give things a push in the right direction. It seemed very romantic to await the kindly hand of fate.

They went to the cinema most weeks and he would

slide his arm around the back of her seat, squeeze her shoulder and nestle his face against hers, even stealing an occasional kiss when the film was particularly sentimental.

She would put her hand in his and feel his strong caressing fingers and desire for him would grow. But his show of affection and love never went further than the kisses he showered on her when they were alone on some dark corner of the street as they walked to the bus station and said goodnight.

She constantly thought of Maurice and, in rare instances, of Freddie, who at least made her feel desired and adored and very much a woman. Nigel was a gentleman and she loved to be seen with him, his smart clothes and fashionable trilby hat, his tall, lean figure making heads turn in admiration. He was like a knight-errant, guarding her from the passers-by who might, by the slightest touch, disturb her comfort. But he was not as exciting as Maurice, nor as infatuated as Freddie and she found that she looked forward to his company less and less.

One evening they were coming out of the cinema and hurrying to the bus station, when Sheila saw her parents who were obviously intent on catching the same bus as herself. She stopped, then, as Nigel looked at her for an explanation she pointed to them and said, 'Those two, they're my parents.'

'That's great,' he surprised her by saying. 'I'm longing to meet them.' He proceeded to hurry her along and be introduced.

He was his usual charming self and Sheila noted that her parents were impressed by his polite manner and his precise speech. They did not speak for long, but when Nigel's bus left before their own they waved Nigel off as enthusiastically as herself. The comments that followed made Sheila more dejected by the minute as the bus lumbered its way along the narrow roads and through the small villages on its way to Hen Carw Parc.

'Such a nice boy,' Mavis beamed. 'And you can see straight off he's a gentleman.'

This remark made him sound so dull and unadventurous that Sheila went home and cried herself to sleep thinking of Maurice Davies. If only there was some way to get to Australia and be sure of finding him. She went downstairs in the early morning and took out an atlas. Australia was enormous and such a long, long way. Six thousand miles. That evening she had arranged to meet Nigel and, remembering how delighted her parents had been when they had met him, she did not go.

He was waiting at the staff door of the shop the following evening and without asking for an explanation for the previous evening at once apologised for not inviting her to meet his parents sooner.

'I've told them all about you, Sheila and they're longing to see you, but I didn't want to rush you. The death of your husband must still be difficult to cope with. But, will you come for tea on Sunday?'

Sheila stared at him. For the moment she had forgotten what story she had told him to explain her wedding ring and no husband. Then she remembered. She had told him nothing, but had allowed him to presume she was a widow.

'You're so right, Nigel.' She smiled wanly and touched his hand. 'It comes over me some days as if it happened minutes ago. That was why I didn't come yesterday, as we'd arranged.' She pleaded a headache and went home on the early bus.

She thought about Nigel all the way home. Was he a better prospect for the future than hanging around Hen Carw Parc, or going to join Freddie Prichard in Devon? Coldly, she compared the three options. Financially, and so far as status was concerned, Nigel was the best. But

366

still the memory of Maurice intervened. Besides remembering Maurice as her lover, there was the inescapable fact that Maurice was her legal husband. It would be an age before she was free to marry anyone else, although Freddie seemed not to worry about this unalterable fact. She decided, as she walked up Sheepy Lane, that she would face Nigel with the truth and leave any decision until she knew what his reaction would be.

Instead of Sunday tea with his family he met her at the bus stop and took her to the park. It was drizzling and she complained that she had spent good money getting her hair set specially and didn't want to arrive at his house looking like a scarecrow.

'We aren't going,' Nigel said.

She looked at him and saw the tension on his face and guessed something was wrong. 'Has something happened, Nigel?' she asked, stopping, forcing him to look at her as she widened her eyes. 'I hope your mother isn't ill or anything like that.'

'Mam is fine. But I met a friend of yours yesterday, Pete Evans. He told me you aren't a widow but you have a husband in Australia who married you because you were going to have a baby, then ran out on you.' He gulped for breath after the long sentence and Sheila noticed with distaste that his adam's apple was quite large.

'Oh, he told you that, did he?' she said to give herself time to think. 'Fancy.'

'It isn't true, then?' He gave a weak smile. 'I thought it couldn't be.'

'Oh, it's true all right. In fact, I had decided to tell you today. Now you are becoming more and more important to me, Nigel, I wanted you to know everything about me. I didn't tell you at first because,' she thickened her voice and went on quietly, 'because it's hard to talk about what happened to me. Seduced the very first time I found

367

a boyfriend and then left alone to face having a baby and the sneers of everyone in the village. It's been hard for me, Nigel. I don't tell everyone I meet. How can I go through that with every new acquaintance? I try to forget it but now, now we are becoming so close, I'd decided to tell you exactly how it happened. Then you'll be able to judge how badly I was used and we can forget the whole sorry episode.'

She looked up at him through her lashes and saw that he was not softened by her words. They walked in silence across the soggy grass towards an area where swings and roundabouts stood silent and sad in the gloom of a wet Sunday afternoon.

'Do you want to know the truth, Nigel?'

'A divorce. It would take years,' he said blankly.

'Yes, that's what he did to me. Tied me to him for years and left me to face everything on my own. I don't know anyone else who could have brought me to the point where I can feel affection again, except you.' With a catch in her voice, she went on, 'Thank you for that. Thank you for making me feel human again.'

She walked away from him, convinced he would follow. She was devastated when he did not. Crossing to the far side of the park, where summer flowers lay beaten to the ground by rain and water ran down the path at her feet, she risked a glance back and saw that the park was empty. Away from the protection of his umbrella she could not be bothered to get out her hat, but allowed the rain to wash over her and soak her until she was shivering with the damp coldness.

Reaching the bus station, she climbed to the top deck, hoping to avoid seeing anyone she knew. Chosing the front seat she slid down low as she heard heavy ringing footsteps coming up the metal stairs. A voice she knew called her name and she turned to see Freddie standing beside her, big, powerful and so obviously concerned at her distressed state. He opened his arms and she clung to him sobbing.

He took her straight to his mother's, refusing even to allow her to go home and change while she was so obviously upset. On the bus journey where they were mercifully undisturbed, he had forced the story from her and sympathised, adding his conviction that she would be better to move right away from everyone who knew her. Then he began to describe the little market town in Devon where he would install her in a comfortable room and take care of her while she fully recovered and waited for her divorce papers to proceed through the early stages.

'Once things have started to move you'll feel different. At the moment there seems no end to it all,' he told her. 'Now you're tied to a man who doesn't love you and who treated you worse than Farmer Leighton treats his dogs. Once we start to untangle the mess, you'll start looking ahead again. Trust me, Sheila, you know I would never do anything to harm you, never.'

# Chapter Nineteen

Prue came home again that weekend and this time insisted on going to her house alone. At first Amy tried to dissuade her, but seeing the determined light in Prue's eyes and after a brief phone call to the hospital, she agreed. She accepted that her sister was recovering and able to deal with this next step. Prue tried to take baby Sian with her but bile rose in Amy's throat of the thought of her far-from-well sister taking the helpless child to the house that must still hold such fearful memories.

She held the baby in her arms as she watched Prue set off for her walk to the village. She wished she had taken a taxi or waited for the bus but Prue was determined to do this her own way. Uneasily, Amy began to prepare tea for when Margaret came out of church.

Prue felt tired as she reached the outskirts of the village and turned in past Mrs French's house to her own. The curtains were half drawn and the place seemed devoid of any life but she walked to the door and stepped inside without any hesitation. Today was the day she began to get on with the rest of her life. Of that she was determined. It was raining and a strong wind blew but she pulled back the curtains and opened all the windows and took pleasure in watching the curtains billow out in gusts of wind that threatened to soak the wallpaper from the walls. For once, orderliness was less important than the need to freshen the house and blow away all her bad memories.

She stood in the kitchen, wishing she had thought to bring some milk so she could make a cup of tea. She considered asking Mrs French, who she saw returning from church but abandoned the idea. Today she needed no one. Making tea, she drank it without milk, adding extra sugar instead.

A sound upstairs, a rumbling and crashing that startled her so she dropped her cup, paralysed her. She shook like a victim of the ague and wanted to run from the house, but if she did, she knew there would never be any coming back. Forcing herself to stay, she gripped the edge of the table and waited to gather her strength. Today was the day for facing things, wasn't it?

Slowly she went up the stairs and the wind was making low moaning sounds, sliding between the narrow gaps near the hinges of the window, singing a miserable dirge through the curtains. There was a slapping as another part of the wet curtain flapped against the panes. Three bedroom doors had slammed, and she had to push hard against the force of the wind to open them, one after the other and prop them open. A broken table lamp lay on the floor beside her bed. She went in and stood, looking down on the smooth counterpane.

She bent down and touched the cold bed, then pulled back the covers and plumped the pillow, denting it so it looked as if someone had just risen from its soft comfort. Another crash, this time from downstairs and she flew down, the phantoms of the bedroom chasing her.

The brass poker had slipped on the tiled surface of the fireplace and lay across it with the tongs she used to put coal on the fire. It had not been there when she went away. The police had taken it for examination. She went back up the stairs and gathered the pieces of the broken lamp in her skirt then, picking up the poker, which seemed to burn her hand as she touched it, she threw them all in the ash bin. Closing the windows, she collected

372

her umbrella from the porch and walked back to Amy's house.

There was only one thing left for her to face and that was Freddie. If she could sit in the same room as him, talk to him like an auntie, then the horrific events of Harry's death would be laid to rest. She saw the bus pass as she turned the final bend in the road and from the corner of her eyes, saw a soldier alight and help a young woman down, before shouldering his bag, as, with one hand on the girl's elbow, he guided her across the road.

She stopped as her mind registered the fact that it was Freddie. He seemed to have materialised out of her thoughts. She stood still, her feet wanting to retreat but after a moment, walked up the drive. At the door she glanced at Freddie and gave him a nod of recognition before going to look at Sian. Thank goodness that Sheila girl was with him, that would help to ease the conversation, she thought. But her heart raced with anxiety.

Amy was tired. Besides the strain of Prue's visit, the baby had been fractious with a tooth about to come through and she had been reduced to making food for tea time with the wriggling, protesting infant under her arm.

Margaret had tried several times to discuss the idea of the new school proposed by Mrs French, and had been hurt when Amy had asked her to leave the subject until later.

'Mam. You're always saying "later" or "now in a minute" or "after" or "tomorrow"!'

'I'm sorry, Margaret, love, but you can see how difficult it is for me just now.'

'Best if I do go away, then you'll have the peace you're always wanting!' Margaret grumbled.

Amy put the still-crying baby in her chair, held her daughter firmly by the shoulders, and stared into her dark brown eyes.

'Peace, I don't want. An hour or two until Auntie Prue goes I *do* need. Right? Then we'll talk. You and me.'

Prue returned as the last slice of bread was buttered and the salad washed. She came through the door in more than usual haste and announced, 'Freddie's come and he's got that Sheila girl with him.'

Margaret ran to greet her brother and Amy groaned and opened another tin of corned beef. Another precious leave ruined by having that girl here, she sighed.

The meal was not an easy one. Prue hardly spoke and Freddie never seemed to stop. Margaret refused to eat anything, still angry with her mother for refusing to discuss what was clearly an important subject. The baby cried throughout and only ceased when the dishes were washed and put away. Then, Margaret, despairing of ever having a moment of her mother's time, went to do her piano practice and woke the baby again.

To add to Amy's frustrations, Prue followed her into the kitchen when she went to fetch the coal scuttle and accused her of neglecting the baby who, she said, had been left to cry unattended. Amy bit her tongue. Prue was making good progress and she was afraid of causing a relapse into the unfeeling, uninterested woman of past weeks.

'Sorry, Prue, but it's been a busy day,' was all she said, and Prue seemed content to have made her point.

As they returned to the living room, Sheila held up a cup that had been forgotten, and Margaret took it from her and dropped it. Amy swore, Sheila laughed and it was Freddie who cleared up the mess.

It was not until the taxi came to take Prue away that Amy felt able to sit down. Then she smiled at Freddie and asked how he was, as if he had just arrived. She pulled a protesting Margaret on to her lap and invited her son to tell them all his news.

374

'Then,' she said, 'I want us to discuss something that concerns Margaret and me.'

To her dismay, instead of all the amusing anecdotes Freddie usually entertained them with, he began to talk about himself and Sheila.

'She's been let down badly, Mam, and went back to work before she had really recovered. I – well – I want to look after her, like. I want her to leave Hen Carw Parc and come to live near where I'm stationed.'

'But Freddie, what will you do for money?' You're only a boy soldier and your money won't keep Sheila! Four and sixpence a day for goodness sake! And besides—' she looked at Sheila defiantly, 'Sheila is married to Maurice Davies. Have you forgotten that? Married she'll be for a long time yet. It isn't something you can cancel like the milk, or pretend didn't happen.'

'Mam, we know all that. No point going over old arguments. I've thought this through and taken advice. There's a little town near the camp where several of the wives live. Sheila could get a job down there and I'll be on hand to see she's all right.'

'Sick of people looking at me as if I'm unclean,' Sheila said. 'And when I don't tell people about my situation, they find out anyway, thanks to the local gossips, and then I'm accused of being deceitful.'

Amy hardened her heart. She remembered the feeling all too well when she had returned to the village with Freddie a baby and no wedding ring.

'I understand that, Sheila, but it will pass. There's bound to be a more exciting bit of gossip soon to make your problems fade into memory. There are few people who can afford to criticise what you did anyway. Most have got a skeleton or two in their cupboards.' She turned to Margaret. 'Don't you worry about any of this, mind. I'll explain it all later. All right?'

\*   \*   \*

375

The discussion went on going round and round the same track no one changing their attitude and Amy felt she would soon fall asleep where she sat. She made the baby's final bottle and put her down in her cot. Freddie made cocoa for them all, and, when the baby woke again half an hour later, Freddie and Sheila stood up to leave.

'I'll be back after seeing Sheila home, Mam,' he said.

Once they had gone, Amy dragged herself up to change the bed in which Prue had been sleeping. She was undressed when she and Margaret finally began to discuss the proposition of the boarding school.

'To be honest, love, I don't want you to go. Growing up too fast you are and you'll be leaving me in a few years anyway. But it would be a marvellous opportunity for you. A chance to really do something with your music, and if you want to go, then I won't raise any objections. Now, what have you got to say?'

'I don't know, Mam. When I'm here with you I don't want to leave you, but when I'm with Mrs French she makes sharing with other girls and living away from home seem like a big adventure.'

'You don't have to decide yet. Take your time. Just remember that if you try it and you hate it, you can come back home again. No one would force you to stay.'

She kissed her daughter and went to bed after calming the baby once again. She tried to stay awake until Freddie came home but failed.

Freddie walked back to the shop with his mother the following day then returned home to cut lawns and plant more bulbs in the borders and under the trees. At four-thirty, when Amy was home and preparing the evening meal, he came in, bathed, and set out to meet Sheila.

They walked around the town for a while, Freddie enthusing to her about how contented she would be once they were together, Sheila half listening and planning how she would spend her next pay-packet. She looked into shop windows, studying the clothes on display while pretending to be absorbed in his words. Freddie took her silence for unhappiness and swore to himself to make up for every sad minute.

'If you want, later on, when I'm finished with the army we could share, like man and wife. Only if you want to, mind. There's another world outside Hen Carw Parc. We could live anywhere you like.'

'London?' she asked.

'If you want to, but I'd rather settle somewhere small, I want us to have a garden, see, where I can grow flowers and a few vegetables.'

'Sounds lovely,' she lied. 'So – caring.' She almost burst out laughing at the satisfied expression on his young, earnest face. Freddie was not her idea of the man to spend the rest of her life with, but she held on to him, knowing that for the moment he was all she had. She put her arm through his and pressed herself against him.

'Freddie, let's go to the pictures,' she said, and as he hesitated, mentally counting up his money to see if he had enough, she added in a whisper, 'Back row.'

Dawn had been missing from school quite a lot and Timothy noticed that when she did come, she was dressed in clothes that were often dirty and un-ironed. Her hands and face were in need of a wash too, and her legs were sometimes caked in mud and half-healed scratches that remained for several days without evidence of being attended to. He sent a note to her father but there was no response, and decided to discuss the situation with Evie.

She was out when he and Oliver got home from school that evening and there was a note telling them she had taken an extra driving lesson and would be back at six o'clock. So it was to his son that he spoke to about Dawn Simmons.

'Do you talk to Dawn much, Oliver?' he asked as Oliver spread treacle on to a thick slice of bread.

'Yes, *when* she's at school, and sometimes at Gran's.'

'Do you know why she is absent so much? I really ought to report her poor attendances.'

'She doesn't like school very much and she feels a bit cross when she's asked to take things that her father can't afford to buy for her, or that he forgets to do. So if it's a day for swimming lessons, she doesn't come because she hasn't got a swimming costume.' He said all this through a slippery and difficult sandwich and Timothy found himself watching the attempts of Oliver's teeth and tongue to prevent the shining golden river of treacle from sliding on to his plate.

'You had better hurry and clear that away before your mother sees you,' Timothy said, hiding a smile. 'That is not the way to eat a sandwich.'

'Dawn says she often has a treacle sandwich for her breakfast. I just wanted to try one, Father,' Oliver reported.

'I see, and your mother being out gave you the opportunity.'

Oliver was silent for a while, savouring the last crumbs.

Timothy watched him, then asked, 'Can you think of any way we can help Dawn? Would she accept some sports things outgrown by other pupils, do you think?'

'No. Her dad punches anyone who offers help. He even hit George. Granddad, I mean.'

When Evie returned, Timothy asked her for suggestions to help the little girl but Evie was unsympathetic.

'She and her father are unclean and common. Fisticuffs is his answer to everything. I don't even like her playing with Oliver. Of course, Mother encourages her in spite of my requests to send her packing! I don't

378

feel we have to do anything except report the situation to the relevant authorities.'

Going to school early the following morning, Timothy met Delina and asked her if, living on the council houses, she knew Dawn Simmons.

'Yes, I do, and I have also had the misfortune to meet her ill- mannered father.' Delina felt an unreasonable guilt as she said it, a disloyalty which she tried to ease by adding, 'He has many problems of course and that must account for his prickly manner, but he is not an easy man to deal with.'

'I'm aware that there's a problem but I don't know how best to handle it,' Timothy admitted. 'She's coming to school unkempt and I think the father is ill, or at least unable to look after her for some reason; she has never been as bad as these past few days. I telephoned a few people,' Timothy went on, 'and no one has seen him for several days. D'you think I should go there and offer help?'

On an impulse that she regretted for the rest of the day, Delina said, 'I'll go after school and try to see him, although I can't promise to be successful. I'll call and tell you what happens.'

With a relief he could not hide, Timothy thanked her and went into school feeling that a burden had been lifted from his shoulders. The last thing he wanted was a fight with a parent. He did not consider the risk to Delina, presuming that even someone with a reputation for outbursts, like Tad Simmons, wouldn't harm a woman.

All through lessons and the break periods Delina alternated between reaching for the phone to tell Timothy she had changed her mind, and wanting to see Tad again. This was at least a reasonable excuse to call and there might never be another. There was within her a genuine

379

concern for the girl too, and she knew that if, for some reason, she was not being properly cared for, then Tad would lose her. Holding the thought that it was because of Dawn she was facing that rude and aggressive man again, she walked slowly up the lane that evening, pushing her bicycle, and stopped outside his house.

She knocked the door and waited an age before knocking again. There was still no reply and she forced herself to go inside the kitchen and call. This time Tad's voice answered her and she went further into the house. Its bareness made her sad: no carpeting and no ornaments or extra touches that a woman would bring. A cupboard door hung ajar and she saw one solitary tin of baked beans and a packet of biscuits inside.

She called again and this time the voice asked who she was and what she wanted. Delina walked into the hall and called upstairs in the direction of Tad's voice.

'It's Delina Honeyman. I wanted to see Dawn. Can I talk to you for a moment, please?'

She heard the sound of someone walking across the floor above her and then Tad appeared at the top of the stairs. She was shocked by his appearance. The man was obviously ill. He came down, hanging on to the banisters and taking each step with obvious difficulty.

'You shouldn't have come down,' she gasped. 'Go back into bed and I'll go and phone for a doctor.'

'No, don't do that. I'll be all right in a day or so. But as you're here, you could get some food for Dawn. I haven't been able to get any money from the post office and we're short of a few things.'

He stopped half way down the stairs and as he swayed, Delina ran up to support him, guiding him back to his bedroom. She sat him on the edge of the bed and he explained that he hadn't felt well enough to go to work for a few days.

'I believed each day that I would be better the following

380

morning, but it's taken longer than I thought.'

'Look, I won't fetch the doctor if you really don't want me to, but I must do something. Where is Dawn? I can at least get her fed and bathed, and see to her clothes.'

He fell back on the bed and she hastily covered him up, left a note for Dawn and went to buy what she could carry, before Amy's shop closed.

For three days she called on the way to and from school and made sure Dawn was neatly dressed. After further discussions with Timothy, she bought the sports equipment Dawn needed to take part in the school activities as well. On the third day, when she went after school, Tad was up, shaved and dressed.

'Thank you for your generosity, Miss Honeyman. I don't know how we would have coped without your help.'

Delina smiled.

'It's what anyone would have done. There's plenty of people only too happy to help where it's needed, you know.' She stepped towards the door. 'Well, by the look of you, you won't be needing my help any more. So, well, I'm glad you're fully recovered.'

'Please stay a moment,' Tad said, 'Dawn will be here in a while and she wants to thank you too. She's promised me not to mitch from school any more and if she keeps that promise, then I owe you an even greater thanks.'

'It's been a pleasure.'

'It's been a rare pleasure for me too, anticipating your calls.' Tad said. 'I – I hope you won't forget us now there's no real need to visit us. I – we'll miss your visits.'

Dawn came in wearing one of the dresses that Delina had bought when she realised how few the girl had.

'Oh,' Tad added quickly, 'I will pay you for the clothes and food you bought.' Delina saw the firmness in his chin and decided not to argue.

'Thank you,' she said, 'but there's no hurry.' She stood to go and Tad walked as far as the front gate. She felt shy, like a schoolgirl instead of a teacher. Trying to find something brief and telling as a final remark, she found her brain refused to work. It was Tad who said, 'Please come again. I'd like to show you that I'm not really the ill-tempered lout I've appeared to be lately.'

'We all show our distress in different ways,' she said. 'I haven't been very good company these past months.'

'Since your wedding was cancelled?' he surprised her by saying. 'The man must have been an idiot to let you go. Think of him like that and you'll forget him easier. You wouldn't have been happy married to a fool.'

Delina felt a blush of embarrassment and anger flow through her veins. How dare he! Gossip about her and then offer his advice as if she were the one with problems! It was not her who hit out and alienated people offering nothing but friendship! She walked away without another word.

Freddie returned to his camp and Amy sadly washed his bedding knowing that the times he would come home to her were likely to be limited. He was determined to take Sheila into his life and soon would have a place, other than this, to call home.

Margaret was with Mrs French, having a piano lesson and the baby was sleeping, having produced her first tooth a few days before. Amy hung the washing on the clothesline and stood watching it blowing in the evening breeze. It was almost dark, but Mrs French always walked Margaret safely home after her lesson. She went back in the house which was already feeling hollow and empty, and turned on the wireless to fill the room with voices and music to push away the loneliness.

She almost shouted her relief when there was a knock at the door. She opened it and saw Victor standing there.

'Can I come in?' he asked.

Pleased as she was to see him, she did not show it, but

382

grudgingly offered him a cup of tea, hinting that Margaret would be home soon, and there were things she had to do. Then, as he sat and began to talk to her she relaxed and began to feel the warmth and love that was between them. If only life could be this simple, she thought. Just me and Victor like this every evening. He sensed her softening mood and gently kissed her.

'Victor, I can't go on like this,' she said when they sat, arms around each other on the couch. 'I'm going back to Nelly's idea of moving back to the flat. I have the strong feeling that I'm going to end up lonely here in this house. It was such a wonderful dream, me living here with Freddie and Margaret, but it's all gone wrong.'

'You can't move back to that poky flat. You'd be so cramped it would drive you mad.'

'In a while there'll be too much space. Freddie has gone and if Sheila has her way he won't be back. And Margaret, she's seriously considering taking Mrs French's offer to send her to a boarding school, and who's to blame her? Prue is improving and one day soon she'll take Sian back and I'll be here all on my own with all the space I want. I couldn't bear that, Victor.'

'I wish I could come here with you, love. It's my dream. The two of us and Margaret, and little Sian if possible, living here and being so content.'

'That's only a dream and it's no good tormenting me with it, is it?' Amy said, standing up and pushing his arms away. 'Forget about dreams and tell me what I should do!'

'I can't leave the boys, but if—'

'Stop using the word if and stop talking about dreams, will you? Go, Victor, it's best you go. I think I will marry Billie Brown. At least he's free and he loves me.'

'I love you, Amy. You must believe that?'

'Billie is free to love me. That you aren't, not ever will be. You won't leave your wife; the boys are just an

excuse. She doesn't need you and neither do they, but I
*do* need someone. If it can't be you then why shouldn't I
marry Billie? Victor, I'm sick of being alone!'

Victor said nothing for a while; the silence went on and
on as Amy glared at him, willing him to argue with her.
Finally he said, 'All right, marry the farmer, and pluck
chickens and see lambs going off to be slaughtered. I can
just see you enjoying that!'

'It won't be like that. I'll still have the shop.'

'Oh no you won't! Billie will expect you there, playing
second fiddle to that sister of his.'

Amy's shoulders drooped even more. 'What else can I
do?'

'I want you and I love you. Can't you wait, carry on as
we are, until the boys are old enough for me to leave
them?'

'Tell me why you stay with them? Can you honestly
believe that the picture of married bliss you and Imogine
display is better for them that a separation?'

'You'd hate me if I showed less concern for them.'

'Then I'll marry Billie.'

'You don't love him you love me!'

'Where has love ever got me? You haven't understood
what I've been saying. Yes, I love you, but I don't want
to spend the rest of my life waiting for something most
women have for fifty years! A man of my own, someone
sitting opposite me when I eat breakfast and supper.'

The baby woke at the same time as Margaret came
through the door. She kissed her mother and hugged
Victor then went to try out her new piano pieces. Amy
and Victor continued their discussion in whispers until
Victor burst out laughing.

'Talk about a farce,' he said. 'We can't even have a
good row. Standing here whispering insults at each
other, it's a waste of breath and kissing time.' He kissed
her again, leaning against the door so Margaret couldn't

interrupt them. They began dancing to a waltz coming from the piano, and laughing at the stupidity of it all.

'I have a present for you, Amy. Will you take it? It isn't a bribe to stop you marrying Billie.' He took a tissue-wrapped package from his pocket and handed it to her.

Amy stared at the gold watch in surprise.

'But how did you get it back?' she asked.

'What d'you mean "get it back"? I bought it for you.'

'But, Victor, it's mine. It was my mother's, the one stolen the night of the burglary.'

Victor sank into a chair in horror.

'But, I bought it,' he repeated. 'In a pub. I had the money from that win on the horses, weeks back and I've been adding to it and—' he took it from her and looked at it. 'Sure, are you, that it's the same one?'

'I'd hardly mistake it. Victor we'll have to tell Constable Harris, won't we?'

'Yes, but, will he believe me?'

'Of course he will. You're taking it back, aren't you?'

'I bought it from someone I don't know, in a pub I rarely visit. I got the money – thirty pound, I paid – from a win on the horses, but the bet was an illegal one with Griff Evans – and who will back me up on any of it? Certainly not Griff!' He looked at her, handing the watch back. 'Can't you say you found it, slipped down behind a cushion or something?'

'Who saw you at that pub?'

'No one I remember, so there wouldn't be anyone there who'd remember me. Oh,' he thought a moment, 'I think there was someone who would remember. That Sheila Davies was there, drinking on her own as bold as brass, she was. I spoke to her, only "hello", like but she'd remember, wouldn't she?'

'We'll go and see her now. Come on. Margaret won't mind a walk instead of bed.'

Sheila was surprised to see them, and showed them into the kitchen, explaining that her grandmother was in bed.

'Sheila, do you remember a few weeks ago, seeing me in a pub in town? Llangwyn, that is.'

'No? How could I? I don't go into pubs. My parents get upset if I do. Not worth the agony of their complaining. And Freddie wouldn't like it either. So, no, how could I have seen you in a pub in, where did you say?'

'Llangwyn. I spoke to a group of men who had some jewellery for sale. Surely you remember, Sheila?'

'Not me, you must have mistaken someone else for me; it's easily done, I should imagine.' She smiled and asked, 'Would you like a cup of cocoa? I'm just off to bed to read. I still need plenty of rest, Freddie says.'

Amy and Victor walked back along Nelly's lane, a torch touching the hedge with light.

'I don't need to tell you that I don't believe her, do I?' Amy said bitterly. 'I still think we should tell the constable. He'll know you're telling the truth.'

'I was convicted of stealing once before, remember? Why should they believe me?'

'I do, Uncle Victor,' Margaret said, putting her hand in his.

'Thank you, Margaret. You're my best friend,' Victor said.

They had just got back to Amy's house when there was a knock at the door. Victor opened it with a racing heart. If this were the police, he would regret not going to them straight away. But it was Nelly's face that greeted him. She held a torch below her chin that lit up her crooked grin.

' 'Ere, you 'eard the latest then?' she asked pushing her way in to Amy, the dogs searching the floor for

386

scraps. 'That Griff Evans 'as only got 'imself arrested fer burglaries. What d'you think of that, then?'

'Never!'

'Yes. 'E's bin 'oldin' on to bets and spendin' money on that daft Milly Toogood's daughter and got 'imself in a right mess borrowin'. He took to robberies to get 'imself sorted out an' made things worse.' She paused and beamed at them all, including Margaret who came down in her pyjamas to hear the news. 'An' what's more,' Nelly added, 'it was my George what set Constable 'Arris on the trail.'

'How was that, then?' Amy asked, looking at Victor in relief.

'He told 'Arris about knockin' the exhaust down so it looked as if it was broken or somethin'. George'll explain better 'n me. But it was enough to make the constable go and look proper at Griff's old bike and there you are!' She gasped for breath and said plaintively, 'Can I 'ave a cuppa? Rushin' 'ere to tell you 'as made me throat as rough as a coal-'ole.'

'For bringing us such good news I can do better than that.' Amy opened the sideboard and brought out a couple of bottles. 'It's a day for celebrations, Nelly. I found my watch today, under one of the cushions, would you believe?' She smiled at Victor, aware of how near they had been to making a lot of explanations that might or might not have been believed.

Victor poured drinks while Nelly filled in more details.

'Gawd 'elp, that Hilda was as mad as 'ell! Tried to thump Milly Toogood's daughter she did. Wish I'd bin there to see it,' she added sorrowfully. 'An' she said she'd murder Griff when the police 'ave finished with 'im.'

'Surely that was an act? A wife must know when her husband is out at night?' Victor said doubtfully.

'What an' 'im bein' a poacher? 'E's out more than 'e's

in! An' they say 'e's got a partner in crime! Someone workin' at the forestry an' livin' over near Llangwyn. I don't know who 'e is but Phil will be sure to find out by the mornin' post. Everyone is that relieved! In spite of what old 'Arris said, there's a good many convinced it was poor Harry Beynon's killer on the loose. Bad enough it being one of us but at least Griff ain't no murderer.'

Nelly sipped her drink, silent for a while, remembering the day of Harry's death, then she smiled at Margaret, sitting quietly enjoying the delay of her bed time.

'I heard you playin' when I came up the drive. Play somethin' fer me, will yer?'

As Margaret went back to the piano, Victor prepared to leave. Amy stopped him with a gesture.

'Wait a while, Victor, I want to talk to you,' she pleaded. Nelly lowered her head, warning Amy that she did not approve of Victor's presence.

'Walk back with me, why don't yer?' she said. 'I thought I'd go as far as Ethel's to tell 'er what's 'appened. That'll be a change fer me to tell 'er something before that son of 'ers!'

'No, Nelly,' Amy's voice was firm. 'I need Victor's help with the books.'

'Oh yeh?' Nelly whispered harshly, then settled down to listen to Margaret's playing.

They all listened silently, enjoying the romantic melody and the faultless playing, then Nelly noticed that Amy was upset.

'Lovely, that was,' she said when the music ended. 'As good as the wireless any day. That Mrs French is a good teacher, ain't she?'

'She wants Margaret to go away to a private school where she'll get regular tuition and encouragement,' Amy said softly. 'I know it's best for Margaret, but what about me?'

388

Nelly thought for a moment then said, 'Best fer 'er in some ways, Amy. But you'll lose your little girl if she goes. She won't be the same.'

'That's what frightens me,' Amy said. Then she forced a smile as Margaret returned and gave her daughter a hug. 'That was good, Margaret, love, although I think you lost the tempo a little towards the end. But I expect you're tired, it's very late.'

'It wasn't that, Mam. I found myself listening to you to see if you were talking about me and I forgot the music for a moment. You were talking about me, weren't you?'

'Only after you'd stopped playing, love.' Amy said. 'And everything we said was pride and pleasure.'

When Nelly had gone on her way to spread the news about Griff, Amy and Victor asked Margaret what she really felt about Mrs French's offer to pay for the private school.

'Mostly I don't want to go away, Mam. I wouldn't be happy, not seeing you for days at a time. But then it sounds so exciting and I think it's a wonderful idea. Oh, Mam I can't decide.' She turned to Victor. 'What should I do, Uncle Victor?'

'Only you can make up your mind, Margaret. I wish I could help, but the decision must be yours.'

'Would Mrs French be very upset if I said no?'

'You don't have to do anything you don't want to and I have to admit I would prefer you to stay with me,' Amy said. 'But I'm afraid my reasons are all selfish ones. You would benefit so much, love. It would widen your knowledge of music and many other things besides. So, think about it a bit longer, will you, then talk to me about it again. You don't have to rush and make a decision. Take all the time you want. All right?'

'Margaret.' Victor took the girl's hands in his. 'It's important you remember one thing. Whatever you decide you won't be letting anyone down.'

'Do you think we have time for a game of monopoly before I go to bed, Uncle Victor?' she asked.

Amy nodded at Victor, sensing that Margaret needed something trivial to take her mind off the decision she had to make. Amy regretted mentioning the subject of the school so near the end of the day when the idea might take hold and prevent Margaret from sleeping. While Margaret went to fetch the board she whispered to Victor, 'Let her play as long as needs, will you?'

'Until she falls asleep if necessary,' he agreed.

At ten-thirty, Amy carried Margaret upstairs and put the sleepy girl into her bed.

'Goodness, love, I won't be able to carry you upstairs much longer. You'll have to carry me soon!' Margaret smiled but was too tired to reply.

Victor was washing the cocoa cups when she went back down. She stood behind him, her arms around his waist and hugged him, her face pressed into his shoulder.

'Thank you, Victor, love.'

He turned, wiped his hands then took her into his arms.

'I love Margaret as I love you,' he murmured, his lips touching her sweet-smelling hair. 'For ever, for better or worse.' He paused and she felt him pull away from her before adding, 'As I once promised to love Imogine.'

'We all start out with ideas of perfection,' Amy said. 'For me it was Harry Beynon, who loved me yet married my sister, Prue.'

'With us it would be perfection. Wait for me, Amy. Please, wait.'

'If Margaret goes away to school we'd meet more often. We'd would have to be careful, of course. But there would be more time together.'

'Time. Now there's a luxury.'

Neither of them saw the small figure in the pink dressing gown stop half way down the stairs then return to her

390

room, sleep dispelled, to lie on her bed and stare at the ceiling. She saw in the cracked surface faces of disapproving people who didn't want her to come home ever again. Amy found her still awake when Victor had finally gone home.

'Do you want more time with Uncle Victor?' Margaret asked. 'If you like I won't ask him to play games with me again. That will give you more time.'

Amy guessed she had overheard some of the conversation and thanked heaven that she had been made aware of it.

'I shouldn't be seeing Victor, although we both like him very much and he loves you like his own daughter,' she said gently. 'He has a wife, and people talk, say unkind things. I don't want you to be upset by any talk. If you weren't here I would be so very unhappy. I'd want to see Victor more than ever; he's a very kind friend to us both. But if you decide not to go away, then I won't need him so much. But love, he enjoys playing games with you. You're much better at them than I am. Don't stop asking him to play.'

Amy turned out the light and tucked herself in beside her daughter and slept with her arms around her until morning.

# Chapter Twenty

The den in the woods near Nelly's cottage had not been a
success. Margaret had imagined it would be a place
where she and Oliver could meet, share books, enjoy an
occasional picnic and a place that was their own. Dawn
had spoilt it for her. She seemed to appear the moment
she and Oliver pulled down the rope-ladder Billie had
made for them. One evening, on their way out of school,
she asked Oliver if he would go there with her.

'But it's dark soon,' he said. 'Mother wouldn't let
me.'

'Tell her you're coming to my house. We won't stay
long. I'll tell Mam I'm coming to see you.'

Their plans made, they walked up the lane separately
and passed Nelly's cottage, where the door stood open as
always, her oil lamp already shedding a fan of light
across the path. They saw the vague shapes of the two
dogs at the door, staring into the evening gloom. The
dogs did not bark as the children passed the gate, the
only sign of their being aware of them the gentle thump
of their long tails on the cinders. The children ran on
undetected by Nelly or George.

In the tree house it was chilly and Margaret took off
her coat and wrapped it cloak-like around her to increase
its warmth. There was a blanket there but it was damp
and smelt of mildew, a symbol of the failure of the place.
Oliver looked in the tins they had brought earlier that
summer and found a few hard and inedible biscuits.

'Why don't you like coming here any more, Margaret?' Oliver asked.

'That Dawn! She always comes and spoils our games.'

As she spoke they heard rustling in the trees near by and they held their breath. Dawn was entering the clearing, the thin beam of a torch slanting ahead of her feet as she trod with care around the encroaching branches of bramble; painful prickly traps for the unwary.

Margaret gripped Oliver's hand, silently pleading to him not to call out. They sat, hardly daring to move as the girl walked to the foot of the tree on which they were perched, before departing the way she had come.

'We should have called to her,' Oliver whispered when the trees had swallowed up Dawn in their darkness. 'She is a friend and Gran says we should be nice to her.'

'She doesn't have to do everything we do!' Margaret grumbled. 'I don't want you to take her to meet the gypsies when they come back for the winter. And I don't want her to go to Uncle Billie's farm either.'

'Why?' Oliver asked in exasperation. 'You might be living there if your mam marries Uncle Billie and you'll be glad of friends calling. It's a long way from the village.'

'Mind your own business about my mam.'

'Well, she is going to marry him, isn't she?'

'Nothing to do with you. *Or* that Dawn!'

'Gran says we have to be kind to her because she hasn't got a mother.'

'Well, I haven't got a father, have I? So what?'

'It's worse without a mother. Everybody knows that.'

'You'd still have your Gran, and George.'

'You'd still have Mrs French!'

'She wants me to go away to a school where I'd live in and not come home every night. Just come back for holidays.'

'Your mam would never let her take you away!' Oliver

was so shocked his eyes were suddenly clear in the semi-darkness, the whites glistening like pale lanterns.

'Mam would be glad I think. There would be more time without me to look after.'

'More time for what?'

Margaret frowned, then answered irritably, 'Just more time, silly!'

Delina was leaving the bus at the bottom of Sheepy Lane on her way home from school when the books she held across her arm slipped and fell to the ground. Sheila, who had been on the same bus, stopped and looked around. There was a groan of sympathy but no offer of assistance came from her pursed lips.

'What a shame. You should have used a bag, much simpler,' she said as Delina picked up the last of the books and settled them once again on her arm.

'If I'd had a bag I'd have used it. If I had known I would have all this marking to do, I would have taken one.' Delina spoke quietly but with an edge of irritation. Really, it wouldn't have hurt the girl to offer some help.

'Yes, we don't always plan what happens, do we?' Sheila said, waiting for Delina to catch up with her. 'I wouldn't have expected the rain to stop or I wouldn't have brought my umbrella. Life is full of surprises, isn't it? And shocks!'

'Isn't it.' Delina wondered how Sheila could have had an affair with Maurice and not expect it to end in disaster.

'*I* didn't dream you'd steal Maurice from me,' Sheila went on. 'Now that was something unexpected.'

'Steal him?' Delina stopped and the books began to slide once again. 'How can you think I stole him? He wasn't yours, so how could I have stolen him?'

'I loved him and we had a baby on the way. What's that if it isn't belonging?'

'It wasn't as simple as that. He treated you badly, but I

don't think he loved you, Sheila. Even you must realise that.'

'You think he loved you?'

'Of course. We were going to be married.' Delina began to walk faster, wanting to get away from this stupid conversation.

'Don't talk daft! Love him? If you really loved him you wouldn't be here on your own, you'd be in Australia! You'd have fought to keep him. I would have. I'd have done anything to keep him. You only thought of yourself and what people would think! Come on, admit it. It was a fair-weather love that floundered as soon as there was a storm.' Sheila was pleased with that analogy. Quite poetic.

'You're very rude, Sheila. You ruined my wedding plans and now you accuse me of not loving the man I intended to marry!'

'Intended. Now there's a word. Intended to marry him as long as he was as perfect as you think you are! Why didn't you go on with the wedding? Why didn't you defy Ethel and all the old biddies of the village and tell Maurice that whatever happened he was your man? Tell me that, Miss Prim-and-Proper Honeyman. Tell me that!'

Sheila ran on, in a hurry now to get away from the woman who had ruined her life. She heard a squeal of rage and turned briefly to see the pile of books once more falling in an untidy heap on the lane.

Her eyes were full of unshed tears, her chest heaved with pent up unhappiness. She had not intended to speak to Delina in such a manner and had, in fact, been polite to her on the previous occasions when they had met. But today had been a bad day. She could see a future that held nothing but the ordinary and Sheila hated the ordinary.

She had failed to sell to the first customer and her

manageress was very superstitious about that, taking it as an augury for the day. Then Sheila had laddered her stockings and because of the manageress's insistence had to spend her last shillings on a new pair. But it was none of these things that had caused the outburst.

It had surprised her with its fury and she admitted that it had taught her the truth. Something she had tried not to admit to herself even in the darkest hour of the sleepless nights, when dreams of the future flitted through her mind in a stream of adventures and handsome men. The truth was, she still loved Maurice. Of all her dreams, the one in which he returned, or sent for her, was the one she spent the most time imagining. She felt a childish impulse to run back and kick Delina's books all over the lane.

Delina picked up the books and, shaking with anger at Sheila's outburst, did not hear the footsteps approaching. She had just succeeded in balancing the now disordered books on her arm when they slithered uncontrollably down. Tad knelt and gathered them into a neat pile and, placing them on his own arm, proceeded to take a bag containing the rest from her. 'Please, let me help you home with these.'

'Thank you, but I can manage.'

'You clearly can't, Miss Honeyman. I saw them fall twice and once you get angry with inanimate objects the chances of managing them decreases dramatically,' he smiled. 'I know all about anger and what it does to you.'

'There's no need—'

'No need, but I would be happy to help you.' He walked on, leaving her no alternative but to follow.

'The truth is,' he said, when she was close enough to talk, 'I envy you these books. Just carrying them gives me pleasure.'

'You envy me the hours of marking I have to do once I

have eaten? When most people will be sitting down enjoying the wireless or the television?'

'I would give a lot to be carrying books home, to study and do what I wanted to do before war interrupted everything. I – I suppose that's partly why I'm so ill-mannered at times, for which I am very sorry.'

'Oh, really, Mr Simmons. I can't accept that! Your behaviour can't be blamed on the fact you didn't recommence your studies once war finished. It's been over nine years, you know!'

'Dawn is ten. I had married in haste – a desire for the ordinary in a frightening world. I thought I would be happy in a completely different sort of life from the one I had planned as soon as I was relieved of my uniform, wanting nothing more than a peaceful and quiet life with my wife and little girl. I thought, during those dreadful days, that it would be enough. When my wife died it all seemed such a waste. Dawn was the only good thing to come out of it and even with her I have had more disasters than successes.'

'Do you resent Dawn for being the reason you didn't go back to your studies?'

'No!' For a moment the flare of anger threatened to stop the conversation. Then his blue eyes softened and the thin jaw relaxed. 'No, I have never, for a single moment regretted Dawn. I just wish there was some way I could look after her properly and go back to university.'

'There isn't, unless you find foster parents for her and I'm sure you've already considered that idea.'

'Yes. So I will continue working part time in a factory, brushing floors and clearing up mess made by other men. Men doing the sort of work I expected to be overseeing one day.'

'Bitterness is a disease and if you don't treat it, it will kill you,' Delina spoke firmly, and held out her arm for her books. 'Forget it, or do something about it.'

'What can I do?' He continued to walk beside her, still carrying the books, past his house and up the hill to the gate of Delina's house. There, he handed her the books and put the bag on her doorstep, before turning away, calling back,

'Thank you for listening, Miss Honeyman.'

Delina watched him go, a wave of sadness weighing on her shoulders more than the books had done. She wanted to help once her initial anger had gone. He really did need someone to talk to, someone sympathetic who would make him consider the options and come to some decision about his future before it was too late. For Dawn's sake, she told herself firmly, for Dawn's sake, she might start making enquiries and let him know if she discovered any way out of his situation.

Once Griff had been arrested for the burglaries, people in Hen Carw Parc relaxed. Archie no longer felt unease every time he returned home. Women began to be less fussy about locking doors when they went out for a few moments' gossip with a neighbour, and there was an air of relief that things could return to normal. Then food began to disappear.

Amy delivered orders from her shop by means of a boy on a carrier bike. Since Freddie had gone, the messenger boy had been Gerry Williams's younger brother, Merfyn. He came after school twice a week and took boxes packed with groceries, two at a time, on the carrier bike, walking up the hill and coasting back down. Amy had never missed a single biscuit since Merfyn started delivering for her and was surprised when a customer insisted that a full half pound had been missing from her order.

She replaced the biscuits and searched to see if the bag had been placed in another order by mistake, but they were never found. A few days later, apples were reported missing then a whole list of sweets from half a dozen orders. Amy told Victor, who promised to take an hour or two off and watch the boy on his rounds.

It was almost five-thirty one September evening when he saw a figure ease out of the shadows and run down the path of Nelly's house to take something Merfyn had just left at her door. He decided to watch the thief a while longer. There was always the chance that Nelly had told her to help yourself to something. It was Dawn Simmons, he had no doubt of that, although she wore an over-long grey plastic mac and ran at a crouch that succeeded in disguising her effectively from a casual glance. Victor had expected it to be her so he saw through the half-hearted disguise immediately.

He followed her to two more places where, as soon as Merfyn had deposited the box, rung the bell or knocked on the door, she would run to take something from it and disappear into the shadows once again. At the fourth place the order was a small one; only a few items in a small cardboard box. Dawn picked up the whole thing and ran with it, just as the door was opened, melting into the darkness as the woman came out of the lighted room, but clearly visible to Victor. He had seen enough.

Shouting for her to stop he headed after her, calling her name as he ran. She threw the box of groceries behind her as she turned a corner and, as Victor leapt aside to avoid it, off balance, he could not avoid running into the man coming towards him. It was Tad.

'Stop that daughter of yours!' Victor shouted as the girl darted away from them.

'What are you doing?' Tad demanded. 'Leave her alone!'

'Catch her, she's a thief!' Victor managed to avoid Tad's outstretched arm and grab Dawn. 'Come here you little pest!'

400

'Leave her alone.' Tad's fist shot out and caught the side of Victor's face. For a moment Tad's fist seemed to hover in the air, then suddenly Victor stood dazed by the blow, watching a stream of chocolate and biscuits fall from under Dawn's mac. Then he pointed and in a nasal voice distorted by the pain in his face, he said, 'See, man? Bloody little thief, she is, and all you can do is pretend it isn't true!'

'Dawn?' Tad questioned, and as the girl began to sob, he asked, 'Dawn, why have you done this?'

'I didn't do anything, Dad. Nelly gave me the sweets and he frightened me, chasing me in the dark and—' she dissolved into a tearful, shaking child.

Tad's impulse was to hug her, tell her it didn't matter, that he would sort it all out. But he knew that this time he couldn't presume she was telling the truth. This time he had to find out exactly what had happened. If Dawn was not lying, then he would make sure Victor Honeyman remembered this night for a long time. His fist pulled back ready for another fierce jabbing blow. But the thought that this was Delina's father made him hold back.

Nelly had heard the knock on the door which, having given up the effort of trying to close it over the uneven stone-flagged floor, she'd left ajar. She put down the fish she was preparing to bake for the following day in time to see Dawn push through the gateway. She glanced down at the order at her feet and checked the most likely items and saw at once that the chocolate she had ordered was missing. She called the dogs and gave chase. Dawn had obviously knocked to check if the house was empty and, receiving no response, presumed it was and helped herself to the chocolate.

Fear for the girl was uppermost in her mind as she lifted the long apron she wore over her dress and ran up the path and out into the lane. The dogs, thinking it was a game, raced round and round her, threatening to trip her up and she stopped and pretended to throw a stick to send them chasing back the way they had come. She puffed up through the council houses, heading for Dawn's house, and was in time to see Tad hit Victor.

' 'Ere, you! Less of that!' she shouted and the dogs, who had been searching for some invisible stick, swooped, barking on the trio.

'What you 'itting *'im* for?' Nelly demanded between gulping breaths. 'It's 'er what wants a smacked arse if you ask me!' Still panting, she held her hand out to Dawn. 'Come on, 'and it over. Me an' George an' Oliver was goin' to enjoy that chocolate while we listened to the wireless tonight.'

In the light of the street lamp she saw the pile of chocolate, sweets and biscuits on the ground at Dawn's feet. She pointed to it and glared at Tad.

'Well? What you goin' ter do about it then? First off you ought to apologise to Victor.'

'He can keep his apology, Nelly. All I want is for him to stop his daughter being a bloody nuisance before she gets into real trouble.' He turned away and Nelly stared at Dawn, her face threatening with the lamplight twisting her features into mask-like shadows.

'Dawn?' she asked, in a growling voice. 'What 'ave you got to say?'

'Nothing,' the girl muttered, her head bent low.

'I think you 'ave. And fer a start off, I think you 'ave to tell your dad a few truths. Like what really 'appened when you asked Delina for a lift 'ome from town.'

'I have only raised a hand to you once in all your life, Dawn,' Tad said quietly, 'but I swear that if you don't start telling the truth now, I'll make you so sore you won't sit down for a week. Now, as Nelly suggests, we'll start with when you say Delina refused to lend you money to get the bus home from town, shall we?'

'I don't want you to marry Delina and have me sent away to school like Mrs Prichard is sending Margaret!' Dawn sobbed.

Nelly pricked up her ears. 'What's this about Margaret goin' away to school? What's that got to do with pinchin' things?'

'Let me, please, Nelly,' Tad asked.

'Margaret's mother is sending her away so she can marry Billie Brown the farmer. She told me.'

'I see, so you think that by stealing, you will stand a better chance of not being sent away? This is ridiculous, Dawn.'

'Not the stealing. That was a dare. I make myself do three dares every day. Sometimes I spit on the floor in front of Mr Chartridge's house, sometimes I spread mud on someone's car and once I let down the tyres of Pete Evans's motor bike. I – I take things – for a dare,' she finished lamely.

They all stood huddled around the lamp-post, the stolen items still at Dawn's feet, no one making the decision to move somewhere more private.

'Stealing could get you sent away from me. I've already told you that, Dawn. They'll say I'm not bringing you up properly and take you away to someone who will keep a sharper eye on you.'

Tad turned to Nelly and Victor. 'Will you please leave this to me? I'll try to get the sweets back to where they belong. I'm sure Mrs Prichard will help. I know the police should be involved, but if you will let me try to deal with it, I promise you that if I fail I'll go to the authorities myself.'

'I don't want the kid to grow up with a police record,' Victor said gruffly. 'I blame *you*, not her!' he added angrily.

'I agree,' Tad replied. 'Thank you, both of you.' He

403

picked up the collection of sweets, biscuits and chocolate and hesitantly handed them to Nelly. 'Do you think you could— Perhaps if Amy got them all back she wouldn't—'

Nelly lifted the edges of her apron and Tad dropped the items in.

'She's an understanding sort, Amy. I reckon she'll give you a bit of time to sort things out. Only a little while though, she ain't soft!' said Nelly grimly. She walked away and Victor followed her, the dogs dancing around them; they could smell the chocolate and were hoping for a share. They strolled past the trees and when they reached Nelly's cottage, she asked, 'Come in fer a cuppa why don't yer?'

'Thanks, I'd enjoy that. Then I'll go and tell Amy that her thief is caught.'

'I'll come with yer. I think she'd like to know about Margaret's worries, don't you?'

'The thought of Amy marrying Billie Brown is worrying me too, Nelly,' Victor admitted quietly. 'She'd be marrying for all the wrong reasons.'

Billie had been a regular suitor since the embarrassment of falling asleep in the cinema. He had avoided such places since, prefering to invite her and Margaret to the farm or for rides out in the Landrover to places of interest and beauty. Mary would occasionally go with them and she would always pack a fine luncheon basket so all Amy had to do was dress herself and the two children and go.

Amy found she looked forward to the outings more and more. The freedom of not having to plan for the whole of Sunday from the moment that Margaret came home from church was a joy, the baby seemed to like the movement of the car and the fresh air made them all sleep contentedly. Only Margaret seemed less than content.

Even when Oliver came to keep her company, the day

404

seemed long for her. She would sit quietly and look at the waterfalls or the mountains or wander along the beaches, deserted now the summer visitors had left, and pick desultorily at the food Mary had supplied and was obviously relieved when it became time to return home.

As soon as they were inside and the roar of the Landrover had faded away, she would go in to her piano and play for as long as it took Amy to get the baby settled and put Margaret's night-clothes to warm by the fire. Then she would climb on her mother's lap while Amy tried to discuss the day before seeing her tucked into bed.

When Nelly and Victor came that evening to tell her that Dawn had been caught and her father informed, Nelly stayed on after Victor had left. She told Amy about Dawn's fears, fears that had come from Margaret. For Amy it explained much.

'I knew there was something, Nelly. I've tried to persuade her to talk but she insisted nothing was wrong. I really thought we had settled the worries about school. All the time she's been thinking I wanted to send her away!' She looked towards the stairs, wanting to run up and reassure the child straight away. 'Thank you, Nelly. Now I know what's troubling her I'll make sure she understands how I feel about losing her.'

'You going to marry Billie, then?' Nelly asked in her forthright way. 'Think that's fer the best, do yer?'

'I'd be cheating on him if I did, Nelly,' Amy admitted. 'He knows this and still wants to marry me. I've been completely honest with him about how I feel about Victor.'

'So?'

'So, I still don't know. It would be goodbye, Victor. I wouldn't cheat on him that way. But I don't know if I could accept not seeing him again.' She sighed and her long diamante earrings sparkled as she shook her blonde head. 'Why do I always fall for the wrong one, Nelly? Can you tell me that?'

405

'P'r'aps it's the right one but only the wrong time. Could you wait? You're 'eading fer forty. It's sometimes 'ard fer people to deliberately change their lives and take another into it when you're gettin' on an' stuck in yer ways.'

'You managed!' Amy laughed. 'And you said goodbye to forty a long time ago!'

'Ah, but me an' George is different. Like a pair of kids we are, Amy, and none of that sex nonsense to upset things. No, like an egg without salt I am, when George ain't there an' that's a fact.'

Nelly left soon after that and Amy crept upstairs to see if Margaret was sleeping. She found her daughter propped up in bed with an Enid Blyton adventure story against her raised knees.

'Can't you sleep, love?' Amy asked. 'Something bothering you?'

'No, Mam. I just want to finish this story.'

'Have you thought any more about the school idea?' Again Amy knew she was chosing the wrong time, just before Margaret slept, but urgency made her refuse to wait.

'I'll go if you want me to.'

'Oh.'

'Aren't you pleased?'

'Well, no, I'm not. Margaret, love, I think it's time for honesty. I hoped you would say you prefer to stay here with me. I won't stand in your way if you are really keen to go, but I'd be devastated to lose you. There would be holidays, I know that, and the terms aren't very long.'

'You mean you don't want me to go? I thought you wanted more time, like with Uncle Victor, or if you married Uncle Billie.'

'No love. I don't want you to go away. And as for Billie, there's nothing decided about that. He wants us to be his family and go and live with him at the farm. Would you like that?'

406

'Yes, I think so, but we'd still have this house, wouldn't we? And we could come back sometimes. Freddie would like the farm I think, as long as you let him plan a garden for you. There's no flowers there at the moment and he'd want us to have flowers.'

'Let's say that if, and only if, mind, *if* I should consider marrying Uncle Billie and taking us to live at the farm, we'd all discuss it, you and Freddie and me, before anything was decided. It's like everything, Margaret, love. We are a family and we do what's best for us all, not just me, or even you, much as I love you. Right?'

She bent to kiss Margaret and tuck her in. The book lay forgotten on the counterpane and as the beautiful brown eyes closed, Amy placed it on the bedside table and snapped off the light. She looked back at the dark shadow of her daughter's long red hair spread across the pillow and hoped her words had helped and not muddled her more than ever.

It was ten o'clock when there was a knock at the door. She opened it to Tad, and a neatly dressed Dawn, standing hand in hand at the door. Tad carried a torch with which he had been lighting their way. He flicked it off and asked politely if they might come in.

'Dawn has something to say to you, Mrs Prichard.' He turned to Dawn, who stared boldly at Amy and said briefly, 'Sorry.'

'That, Dawn,' Amy said firmly, 'is not enough!' The girl looked surprised and looked at her father.

'I think you should explain to Mrs Prichard what you did and promise never to touch anything that doesn't belong to you again,' Tad coaxed.

Amy led them from the hall into the living room where the fire was dying and the lights were low.

'I'm tired, it's late. If you haven't thought about what you did sufficiently to be able to tell me you really regret what you did, Dawn Simmons, then I would rather wait until you have.' She glared at the little girl. 'You have caused me a lot of trouble beside making my delivery boy believe he was suspected of dishonesty. Now, what have you to say to that?'

'I'm sorry.'

This time the girl's lips quivered slightly and Amy went on,

'Sorry isn't enough, Dawn. Do you know how badly you have let your father down?'

'Yes, and I won't do it again, I promise.' Dawn's face began to crumple and Amy forced herself to ignore the tears brimming and beginning to course down the thin cheeks.

'I think you should do something to make up to me for all the inconvenience, don't you? I've lost customers over this.'

The tears stopped, the eyes became bright with curiosity. This was something unexpected.

'I want you to come tomorrow after school and sweep my yard for me. You'll have to do it properly, mind, and move all the boxes that get thrown out during the day. I want to see it cleaner than it's ever been before. Right?'

Tad began to protest but Amy silenced him with a glare.

'All right, Dawn? Tomorrow, or I'll inform the police.'

'Can I go home first to change my clothes?'

'Yes, but I'll be timing you so don't go wandering off. I mean what I say.'

Tad hesitated as if wanting to protest but afraid of something worse than the punishment Amy had chosen. Amy saw them out and, in a better mood, prepared herself for bed.


Margaret seemed more relaxed the following morning and talked happily of staying put and only visiting the farm for occasional treats. Amy was relieved that she was free from the fear of being 'sent away' but felt that life was closing in on her again. The option of marrying Billie seemed to be fading. There were her own doubts and now the relief clearly felt by Margaret at not having to leave their home.

Philosophically, she decided to let life continue for a few weeks and see if something happened to alter things without her assistance. Life was never static, and perhaps Margaret would come to think of living on a farm an exciting idea. She would discuss it all with Freddie on his next leave, *if* she could get him away from Sheila for long enough!

Children weren't your own for long, she thought sadly. When they were babies the future seemed to stretch endlessly ahead with teething, and napkins, then going to school, joining the Brownies or the Cubs, plus the thousand and one everyday things to deal with besides. Before you realised it they were young adults making their own decisions and leaving you behind like a discarded fashion. She dressed the baby and, tucking her cosily into her pram, set off for the shop, with Margaret skipping happily beside her.

It was pleasant walking in the crisp, clean early morning air. Around them the distant hills were still green and with the sheep dotted on the sides of them a pleasing sight. Margaret trod on the crisp brown leaves and laughed at the crackling they made. Amy looked at the rather bedraggled remnants of the summer flowers in the gardens they passed and made a mental note of some she would like Freddie to add to hers.

Margaret stopped skipping and jumping about and came to walk by her side. 'Mam, if we did go to live with Uncle Billie, we wouldn't see Uncle Victor, would we? I like him better than Uncle Billie really.'

So do I love, Amy wanted to say, so do I! She busied herself tucking in Sian's blankets and did not trust herself to reply.

*     *     *

Phil-the-Post called cheerfully from the shop door.
'Letter here from your Freddie. Shall I leave it or deliver
it at the house?'

'Give it to me and quick about it!' Amy laughed. She
stuffed it into her apron pocket and continued serving.
'And if you're hoping for a cup of tea you're unlucky
this morning,' she added.

'Right then. Two next time, is it?'

Amy laughingly agreed.

'*She*'s got one as well, mind,' Phil added, poking a
thumb in the direction of the council houses. Then, seeing Mavis behind the counter, he added, 'Your daughter,
Mrs Powell, she's got a letter from him as well.' He
shuffled out past the waiting customers.

It spoilt the pleasure of the letter slightly but when she
found a moment free and opened it, she forgot about
being one of two and read it aloud.

'Freddie's coming for the weekend.' That at least
meant he was staying with her and not Sheila, she
thought with relief. 'He's got leave before he goes to
Devon, and asks me to invite Sheila to tea on Sunday.'

'If she's free, that is,' Mavis said, a hint of satisfaction
on her face. 'Found herself a nice boyfriend, she has.
Knows all about what happened too, so there's nothing
underhand.'

'Good. I'm glad she's getting out and about.' She had
heard that the romance with the young man from town
was off, but declined to mention it.

'He's an accountant,' Mavis went on. This was news
to Amy but she was lost in Freddie's letter and hardly
acknowledged the remark.

When Victor came to the house a few days later he
found her polishing and arranging the few late flowers
she had found in the garden and rearranging the furniture.
Her face was flushed and glowing with her efforts and,

410

as she opened the door to him, her fair hair slightly fuller than usual, the earrings she wore sparkling like her smile of welcome. Victor could not hold back words of admiration.

'Amy, love, you are lovely.' He stepped inside and took her into his arms and held her close. She was warm and smelt of perfume and polish. He trembled with longing as she reached up and kissed him lightly on the cheek.

'Freddie's coming home,' she said. 'I've been cleaning and I must look a mess.'

'If this is a mess,' he laughed, holding her away from him and gazing at her, 'I'd love to see you when you're dressed up smart!'

He went into the living room and sat on a chair, pulling her to sit on his lap.

'Prue is coming too,' Amy said. 'And I suppose I'll have Sheila for most of the time. I'd better start some cooking.'

'I'll help.'

Together they made a pile of bake stones and a Teisen Lap, a delicious fruit cake that was just out of the oven when Margaret came home. Victor brushed the flour from his clothes and smiled at Margaret.

'And there's no starting them till tomorrow,' he threatened. 'For your brother, they are.'

'Just one, Mam?' Margaret pleaded. 'And Uncle Victor, can you stay and talk for a moment? I want to tell you about the quiz show.'

'I've seen notices about it. But what's it in aid of, do you know?' He knew but didn't want to spoil the telling for her.

'Well,' Margaret began in her precise way, 'they're having a Quiz Show in the Drovers, which means I can't go, of course. And it will be two teams, the Farmers and the Village.'

'Who's running it?' Amy asked. 'If it's Bert Roberts,

411

I'm going somewhere else that night!' Her groan was echoed by Victor when Margaret said, 'Mr Roberts.' She laughed at the faces they pulled. 'He's in one of the teams too. There's Mr Roberts, our headmaster and Uncle Johnny Cartwright. Then on the other side there's Mr Sidney Davies, Nelly's husband, George, and – guess who?'

'Not Uncle Billie?' Amy said.

'Yes, Uncle Billie too. I wish I could go. Will you go, Mam?'

Amy looked at Victor. 'I might, love, if I can find someone who isn't going to mind you and Sian.'

Victor had intended to do some painting for Amy on Sunday morning, but now he thought it best he did not. With Freddie there, Amy would prefer he stayed away. He explained this as she saw him out.

'But I'll call in,' he said. 'It won't seem odd to call and say hello to Freddie, will it?'

'Of course, come,' Amy said. 'He'd like to see you, I'm sure. And so would I, love.' she whispered.

Victor called goodbye to Margaret then went slowly home to a wife who never spoke to him and sons who seemed indifferent to his unhappiness. There was only Delina who, while not supporting him, at least showed some understanding of his miserable situation.

Remembering how uneasy Prue felt in Freddie's presence, although not understanding why, Amy telephoned to the hospital and asked that Prue be informed that Freddie would be there at the weekend. Half an hour later, she was told that her sister would not be coming home as planned. She felt a bit mean, spoiling Prue's break from the hospital, but could not deny a sense of relief that there would be one fewer to worry about. It was Freddie she wanted to spend the time with, not her sister, who was becoming increasingly difficult as she regained her health.

412

# Chapter Twenty-One

On Saturday, Sheila woke with a headache and felt the beginnings of a cold. She hated having a cold, which frequently ended with her having an ugly cold-sore on her lip. The day did not improve.

As first sales, she always dealt with the first customer of the day, and the superstition that if she failed on that the day would be an unsuccessful one always made her nervous.

She knew she pressed too hard, aware of the tension of the manageress in her little cash desk near the door. When their first customer walked in her she insisted on her looking at just one more dress and then another until she was practically following the poor woman out through the door and almost certainly ensuring that she would never step foot inside the shop again! She glared back at the manageress who was showing her disapproval in a stare that made her wriggle in her chair.

'What has got into you this morning, Mrs Davies?' she asked. 'I think the third sales would have done better.'

'I have a cold,' Sheila excused, 'my head is pounding.'

'Really.' There was disbelief on the woman's face as she stepped forward to open the door for another interested customer.

'Madam,' she smiled encouragingly. 'May we help you?'

She looked at the second sales girl and, when the woman explained her wants, beckoned the girl forward.

Irritably, Sheila stepped back and began to straighten already straight sleeves on a row of coats. It was the third time that week she had been reprimanded, and in front of the other girls too. It was inconsiderate of the manageress to make her look foolish in front of girls she had to instruct and correct. Even the alterations girl was chuckling behind her sewing machine. If only she could leave, get away from these people with their small-minded spite.

Sheila's day was further spoilt by seeing her parents outside the shop at lunchtime. She could hardly ignore them but at once made it clear that she had very little time to talk.

Ralph led them to a cafe, where the lunchtime trade made finding a table difficult. He eventually found seats for them in a corner, squashed between a group of noisy school-children on a visit to the shops and some work-men from a nearby building site. Sheila pulled her coat around her as if fearing contamination from the dusty clothes of the workmen or the sticky fingers of the children. This was definitely not her kind of place and her face clearly showed it.

'What is it?' she asked with a sigh. 'I have shopping to do for Gran and I've only an hour.'

'It's about Freddie,' Mavis said and Sheila sighed again, only louder. 'He's coming home this weekend but we won't be staying at your Gran's, understand that. It isn't right, you being a married woman, and going out with that Nigel too.'

Sheila took a bite from the sandwich her father had bought and stared insolently into space.

'Sheila, answer your mother,' Ralph hissed.

'What's there to answer?'

'Why don't you settle down and wait for your divorce to come through? It's not right to get yourself a name for – carrying on.' Mavis whispered the last words,

414

which, to Sheila seemed to carry more easily than her normal speech.

'What has it got to do with you, Mam? Or you, Dad? I'm twenty-one and I was abandoned by my husband. It's for me to sort out. And if you think I'm waiting years for a divorce then you've another think coming!' Her high-pitched voice made several people near them stop eating to listen. Throwing the half-eaten sandwich onto the table cloth she pushed her way to the door.

She made her way to the bench where she had once or twice met Freddie, but her thoughts were on Maurice. Whenever she was feeling particularly low, as today, she thought of Maurice. He filled her thoughts more and more and even when the way he had messed up her life became more apparent, she still felt a longing for him, a desire to see his face, feel his arms enfold her, to hear him telling her he loved her. She was late back after her lunch-hour but fortunately the manageress was out so there was no further trouble.

Foolishly, Sheila felt disappointed not to have another complaint levelled at her. Her parents had upset her with their concern for what people thought of them, with no offer of help to her, their only daughter. She would have welcomed a row with someone today, even if it cost her the job she was beginning to hate.

When the stop closed she did not go for the early bus but wandered around the shops, looking at nothing in particular, trying to decide how she would spend the next few years of her life. Perhaps Freddie was the best offer she would get? After all, he knew everything about her and there would be no need to pretend about anything. That in itself would be a relief. She had told so many different stories, she was half afraid to open her mouth for fear of changing what she had previously said.

She was confident also, that with Freddie, she would be able to avoid a sexual relationship. He wanted her, she

415

knew that. Her eyes sparkled at the prospect of a little teasing. But it was impossible to take any chances now. If she succumbed to her need for a man's loving and became pregnant, there would be no possibility of marrying the father, not while she was still tied to Maurice. But then again Freddie had offered to live with her, as man and wife, and who would know the difference outside Hen Carw Parc? But it was with a picture of Maurice in her mind she wandered back and caught the next bus home.

Freddie didn't reach Hen Carw Parc until early on Saturday evening. He spent the previous night with a friend and on Saturday had been shopping. When he jumped off the bus near his home he ran in and put his kit-bag in his room. He had a brief look at the garden, ate a few welsh-cakes and cycled up to see Sheila.

It was a disappointment to learn she was still on her way home from work. He wondered if perhaps she had not received his letter. If she had gone to the pictures there wouldn't be much left of his leave. Disconsolately, he rode back down Hywel Rise and Sheepy Lane and stopped outside his mother's shop. He saw Amy taking in the vegetables in from outside the shop and went to help her.

'Freddie! Where did you spring from? We'd given you up!'

'I've been home to drop my bag, then I went to see Sheila but she isn't home from work yet.'

'There's a shame, and she knew you were coming, too.'

'You're late leaving, Mam.'

'Yes, Mavis wanted the day off and I couldn't refuse. I think she and Ralph were going into town to meet Sheila. Perhaps they're all up in the flat?' Amy knocked on the side door while Freddie carried in the last of the boxes.

416

'No reply,' she reported, 'so they aren't back either. Gone to the pictures, perhaps?'

'I wrote to tell Sheila I was coming. She wouldn't have forgotten.'

'Go and fetch Margaret, will you, love? Over with Oliver she is. I'll just gather my own shopping and I'm ready to go.'

They walked back to the house, where the smell of spices and fresh cake-baking still lingered.

'There's bake-stones if you want something while I get dinner,' Amy said.

'Mam!' Margaret exclaimed, opening the tin. 'He's already found them, and you wouldn't let me start them last night while they were still warm and tasty!'

'And you aren't to eat any now young lady,' Amy scolded lightly. 'You'll spoil your dinner.'

Brother and sister muttered their opinion of the nonsensical rule, and taking a handful of the fruit-filled flat cakes that had been cooked on a griddle-stone, they disappeared into the front room and exchanged news.

It was Freddie's intention to go back to Sheila's as soon as he had finished his meal but a knock at the door while they were still eating changed that. Sheila stood there, carrying a basket of shopping and looking, to Freddie, quite beautiful.

She had found a seat upstairs on the bus home and, unseen by the rest of the passengers, had repaired her makeup and carefully combed her hair. She had not gone straight home but had continued on the bus to alight near Amy's house to see Freddie and make her apologies for not being home earlier.

'So excited I was, coming to see you, but there was a hold-up at work,' she lied. 'Some rearranging to do. You know what a fusspot the manageress is. Then I missed the bus, and had to wait for the next one. Frozen I was, standing in the bus station for ages.'

417

Freddie ushered her in and sat her near the fire and Amy handed her a cup of tea and offered food, which Sheila declined.

'Too upset to eat, I am,' she said in her high voice. 'I was so looking forward to seeing you and there I was, stuck in Llangwyn. What must you think of me for not being home early when there's so little time?'

'Glad you're here now.'

Sheila looked at him, and was surprised to realise that she too was glad. Excitement glowed in him and was reflected in her own sensations of joy.

Freddie smiled a wide smile, so like his father's, his glasses glinting in the light, the eyes so blue that for a moment, Amy felt a choking sensation of love for the man whom she had once hoped to marry all those years ago, her brother-in-law, Harry Beynon. With his happy attitude to life and carefree ways, he was brought to life again through Freddie and sometimes it hurt to realise that she would never see Freddie's father smiling at her as Freddie was smiling at Sheila, ever again. When Harry had been killed she had not even been able to show grief over the loss of her love. She was thankful to at least have Harry's son. No one could take that joy away. Not even Sheila.

They walked back to Sheila's house, Freddie carrying her shopping and pushing his bike. Sheila leaned against him, gazing up so the occasional street light gave him an adoring view of her. Sheila was beginning to think of him not as a boy, but as the man with whom she might be content.

It was completely black when they left the main road and turned into Sheepy Lane. The lights behind them making the lane into a dark tunnel with no break in the darkness until they passed Ethel Davies's cottage, where a fan of light spilt, golden, out of her open door.

'Can't feel the cold, that one,' Sheila shivered,

snuggling close to Freddie. 'Never has the door shut. I need warmth, I do.' He looked down at her and, dropping the bike and the shopping took her into his arms. The kiss was so sweet he gave a sob of disbelief that he was here in the secret dark with Sheila, tasting her lovely, promising, lips. He was shaking when they finally separated.

'Sheila, I love you. I want to look after you,' he whispered against her hair. 'Will you let me? I'll never do a thing to harm you, I promise.'

'Oh, Freddie, if only it were that simple. I'm not free, you know that.' She turned slightly to glance towards Ethel's cottage. 'Him over by there spoilt everything for me. Years it'll be before I'm free to even think of sharing your life. Go and find someone else, someone who deserves your love.' She drooped her head and he lifted her chin with a finger and gazed down at her, so small and defenceless.

'Sheila, you're my love. I don't want anyone else, now or in the future. You must know that.'

'But it isn't fair.'

'Come to Devon and find a job there. It will be a wonderful new start. No one need know that we're anything but a happily married couple. There won't be much money for a while. I can't claim for a wife I haven't got. But we'll manage and we'll be happy. Think about it. A small town and a lot of new friends. Lovely it will be.'

Sheila's mind was made up and, swept away by the romance of the moment, she agreed. 'All right, Freddie, if you're sure, but no pretend marriage, at least for a while, right?'

'You'll come? Oh, damn, this is great! You'll never regret it, not for a minute.' He kissed her again, but this time the excitement of her agreement made it less emotional as plans and ideas teemed through his brain.

Picking up the bicycle and the shopping, he managed to put an arm around her until they reached the first of

419

the council houses, then they walked with the bicycle between them in case anyone saw them and caused a fuss.

'Can't be too careful with parents like mine,' Sheila said. 'But I feel lonely with this old bike between us. I want you close where I can feel your warmth, Freddie Prichard.'

The house was silent when Freddie went home, the lateness giving the place an air of disapproval. There was a small light in the living room and a plate of sandwiches left for him. He ate them before going to bed to lie awake, imagining life with Sheila.

The following morning he rose early and, after having breakfast with his mother and Margaret, he walked with his sister through the village, leaving her at the church and going on up the hill to see Sheila, half dreading that she would have changed her mind.

They came to tea with Amy as planned and Amy was worried to see how close they looked, the exchanged glances and intimate touches, the way each helped the other when no help was necessary. Amy was unhappy at the prospect of her son waiting for years for a girl who was already married and who, she strongly suspected, did not really love him.

When she went outside to put the empty milk-bottles out for Mary-dairy, she saw Fay and Johnny walking past the end of the drive and called to them. If another couple came in the conversation would be easier. Freddie and Sheila were saying very little, their attention taken up with each other.

'Fay? Johnny? There's a cup of tea just made if you're interested,' she called and Johnny at once guided Fay along the drive to the front door.

'We've been for a walk,' Fay said. 'Johnny insists that expectant mothers need a lot of exercise.' She covered

420

her mouth with embarrassment when she realised that Margaret and Freddie were there. 'Sorry,' she mouthed to Amy.

'Johnny's quite right,' Amy laughed. She helped them off with their coats and Margaret came to take them from her.

'I'll put them upstairs, shall I, Mam? Glad to get away from those two,' she whispered, her dark eyes frowning in disapproval in the direction of the living room. 'Freddie's very boring when she's here!'

Sheila stood as the newcomers walked in.

'Want any help, Mrs Prichard?'

'No thanks, there's only a bit of extra bread to slice,' Amy called. It was Fay who followed her into the kitchen and rolled up her sleeves, accepted an apron and sliced the loaf.

'We just saw Evie and Timothy, with poor little Oliver, in their car. Evie's driving and, in my opinion, a long way from being ready for her test even though she's had two tries already!'

'I often think it would be handy to drive,' Amy said.

'Plenty of vehicles on Billie's farm,' Fay reminded her. 'I'm sure he's teach you to drive the tractor so you can help with bringing the harvest home, or whatever farmers do with tractors.'

'I don't think I'll ever enjoy anything as mucky as helping on a farm,' Amy admitted.

'Oh, I thought you and Billie were—'

'Well, we're not!'

'Nice to have Freddie home for a while, isn't it?' Fay tried to change what was obviously a tender subject.

'It would have been nice of he *had* been home! Spent all his time with her in by there.'

'I suppose he'll always be fond of Sheila. She was his first love. Special that is.'

'She's using him again, I'm sure of it,' Amy whispered.

'Well then, how about you? Are you getting excited at the prospect of being a mother?'

'I find myself getting caught up in Johnny's excitement,' Fay laughed. 'He's like a child on Christmas Eve. I was upset at first, but I'm coming around to the idea.' Fay stopped and Amy guessed she had something more to say. She waited while Fay cut the last of the sandwiches into neat quarters.

'But you have moments of doubt? Of panic even?' Amy asked gently.

'Oh, why do I feel trapped?' Fay said at last.

'I know a lot of married women who experienced that. Happily married, wanting a baby desperately, and then feeling as if life had locked them into an irrevocable situation. Felt it myself of course, but it was different for me. I *was* trapped. And afraid. I wasn't in a marriage, happy or not. I was alone.'

'Like Sheila,' added Fay, reflecting that other people had been in far worse positions than herself.

'Like Sheila.' Amy paused, then added, 'She is coping with it all, isn't she? Starting back to work, facing all the tittering that goes on behind her in that shop where all the girls know what happened. She's trying to make a new life for herself, like I had to.'

'You just wish it wasn't Freddie.'

'I wish she was a thousand miles away from Freddie. He's so young. She's twenty-one and he's barely sixteen.'

'He's mature though, and so sensible. I hope I make as good a job as you have when I bring up my baby, Amy.'

Amy smiled her thanks and laughed.

'Don't use me as an example of how to live!'

Amy finished putting the sandwiches on a plate, then suddenly relenting in her attitude towards Sheila, took them off and called for Sheila to help.

'Sheila, I would be glad of your help. Come and

arrange these sandwiches, will you, there's a love.'

It was an uneasy evening for Amy. Seeing Fay and Johnny so happy and excited about their baby, and Freddie with his arm possessively around Sheila made her feel old, as if life had already discarded her in favour of the young. She was so relieved when Victor came that she had to remind herself of Margaret's presence and force herself to act as casually as she would if it had been Nelly who had walked in. And it was such an effort she found herself overacting.

Victor was puzzled by her apparent indifference. Even with Margaret there she did not usually treat him so coolly. He beckoned to Margaret and invited her to play for them to calm the atmosphere.

Freddie had to leave at eight and it was Sheila who walked him to the bus stop. Fay and Johnny left at the same time and soon after Margaret went to bed.

'Do you want me to go?' Victor asked.

'I don't want you to, that's the trouble, but I think you must.'

She sat alone in the living room, watching the fire slip lower and lower until it was just a grey bed of ash with the faintest lining of red satin hiding in its depths. The shapes of the dead coal did not make any pictures for her. There were no pretended dreams of a church and a steeple, with herself a bride, coming out of the ancient doorway amid flowers and confetti, to be greeted by her friends. She could not imagine Billie at her side, and there was no possibility of Victor ever being free. The red faded and there was only greyness.

It was dark when Delina walked up Hywel Rise one evening after school and knocked on the door of Tad's house, waiting for him to answer, with little hope of him doing so. The house appeared to be empty. The curtains were open and the fire glowed and sent a rosy pattern

423

over the walls, yet it was still apparent that the place was deserted. There was a hush, like that of a long-neglected ruin, that made Delina shiver.

She waited a moment, fingering the pile of papers on her arm before walking round to the back door. She was still half afraid of starting off on the wrong foot with Tad who, when angered, rarely gave anyone a chance for explanations, and this time, it was important he listened.

The back door was propped open and inside there were the makings of a meal, half prepared: a loaf of bread, a packet containing margarine and an opened tin of meat. A few tomatoes were beside the meat and it looked as if someone had been hurriedly called away. She stepped closer to the door and called but again there was no reply. She still had the impression that the house was empty.

She scribbled a note and placed it near the loaf to say she had called and would like to speak to them both. She stayed a few more minutes, first at the door, then at the gate and finally at the top of Hywel Rise, but neither Dawn or Tad appeared.

When she had almost reached home she saw them, and even from a distance it was plain to see that Tad was angry with his daughter. She walked a short distance behind him, her head bent low, kicking at things in the gutter as Tad urged her on, his arm waving at her, his voice, as they drew near, sharp.

'I was hoping to see you,' Delina said hesitantly as they approached. 'When you have a moment, will you come to the house?'

She knew instantly that she would have been better to have walked past with only a brief nod and left her news for a later date, but Tad stopped, grabbing Dawn as she tried to dart past, and with her squealing and protesting, asked, 'What do you want this time?'

'I can't explain when you're in this mood!' Delina was immediately on the defence.

424

'I'm sorry—' He sounded anything but sorry '—but now is not a convenient time.'

'Come and see me as soon as you can, will you? It is important.' She tried to explain, but he and the still-firmly-held Dawn walked on and he did not reply.

'Oh, the rudeness of the man! I don't know why I bothered!' she muttered and, screwing up the papers she intended showing him, hurried home. She did not throw them away though. Some faint hope that he would stay civil long enough for her to explain made her take them home and throw them on her bed.

After she had eaten, there was a knock at the door. She opened it, expecting to see her father, but it was Tad and a subdued Dawn.

'Once again I come to apologise, Miss Honeyman,' he said but his voice did not sound apologetic and she told him so.

'From the tone of your voice it appears that the fault was mine,' she said quietly.

'Can we come in for a moment, please?'

Delina stood aside and allowed them to enter, then gestured them towards the front room. Tad and Dawn went in and at another gesture from her sat down.

The room was over-filled with dark, heavy furniture that would have been better suited to an hotel or some grand mansion. Dawn was dwarfed in the wide, deep armchair, and Tad, who was a small man, sat on the edge of the sofa as if afraid of being swallowed completely.

'Well?' Delina asked coolly.

'Dawn has been in trouble again and I was so angry with her that I allowed my fury to spill over on to you, and you did not deserve it. I am most sorry,' Tad said. He stared at her all the time he spoke and there was something in his eyes that disturbed her greatly. A need for understanding and something more.

Delina nodded and relaxed her stern expression into a

425

smile. She shook her almost white-blonde hair and the sight of her fair beauty in the sober room made Tad catch his breath in wonder. He felt his attraction for her glue his tongue to his mouth and with difficulty he whispered to his daughter, 'Have you something to say?'

'No,' Dawn said defiantly. 'I want to go home and go to bed.'

'I don't think it's unreasonable for you to give me an explanation of why you go out of your way to make people angry with you, Dawn,' Delina said. 'I don't want to know what you did to make your father cross, but why are you misbehaving now? If it's something I have done, then tell me what it is and we'll talk it out.'

Dawn remained silent, her head lowered and, Delina suspected, tears imminent.

'Dawn, would you like a drink of lemonade while I talk to your father?' Delina saw the girl shake her head, but went to the door and called to her brother. 'Daniel, will you take Dawn, please, and give her a drink. Then perhaps she would like to see your rabbits and guinea pigs.' She gave the girl no chance to argue but led her towards the door.

Daniel, who was almost eighteen and fair, like Delina, came in and took the girl's hand to lead her out.

'Now,' Delina said, 'I will tell you what I wanted to talk to you about, then I needn't interfere in your life any further.' She left him sitting there and went to her room to fetch the papers she had brought home. Handing them to him, she said, 'I made enquiries about studying for your exams at night-school. All the details are there and I think, after a short refresher course you will find it possible to get back to university and complete your degree.'

He looked briefly at the papers then up at her. She was standing, a little apart from him and, feeling himself at a disadvantage, he stood also. He stared at her for a moment and asked, 'Why do you bother? I've

426

done nothing to deserve your time or interest.'

'I don't know,' she said with honesty. 'Unless it's because I hate to see anyone as unhappy as you are. If you really want to become an engineer, then you must. There's always a way, if you really want it. All the details are there. Now, if you'll excuse me, I have a lot of marking to do.'

He hesitated for a moment, then thrust the papers back at her. 'It's no use me looking at these. It would only make me more frustrated than I already am. There isn't always a way, Miss Honeyman. I have Dawn and no money. She is more important to me than a career, even if I do seem to be making a right mess of bringing her up.'

Delina deliberately let the papers fall and as he bent to recover them, said, 'I was going to suggest that I took responsibility for Dawn while you went to the evening classes, but I realise you don't think enough of anyone, certainly not me, to trust them to help, so there's no point discussing it. Good evening, Mr Simmons.' She called her brother and Dawn and held the door for him to leave.

'You'd be willing to look after Dawn – I don't know what to say.'

'Please don't apologise again, Mr Simmons, it's getting quite tedious.'

He looked down at the untidy pile of papers and then looked at Delina and this time his blue eyes were not cold, but showed a spark of excitement.

'Let me take you out one evening, will you? So we can discuss it? That is, unless you have changed your mind about helping?'

His invitation startled her. Her heart beat faster as she realised how much she wanted him to notice her; think of her as a young woman as well as a teacher who might be willing to help him with his daughter. However quick-

427

tempered he might be, the man behind the façade of an irritable, suspicious, over-protective parent, attracted her greatly.

He was very different from her previous love, Maurice, who had been as easy to read as a 'Trespassers Keep Off' notice on a farm. She quirked her lips in a secret smile at the thought that in fact those very words seemed to be written in the frown lines on Tad's face!

'Well, have you?' he asked again and she saw the expression in his blue eyes begin to close him in again, as if preparing for her refusal, hardening himself against being hurt. She answered in a firm voice, hiding her desire to make things easier for him, her sympathy for his brittle arrogance put resolutely aside.

'No, I haven't changed my mind. But if I agree, you can be sure that Dawn won't find me a soft option.'

Dawn rejoined them and Tad held out his hand to Delina.

'Thank you, Miss Honeyman.'

Dawn, looking far happier than earlier, said goodnight and added, 'The rabbits are lovely. Can I come and take some photographs, please Miss?' She was already planning how she would arrange the rabbits for the photographs she wanted to take.

Delina was reminded that Dawn, like most children, needed very little to make her happy apart from someone to show love and interest.

Tad and his daughter walked away and, after thanking her brother for amusing the little girl, Delina went to try and put her mind to marking the essays of her eight-year-old pupils. Her thoughts constantly wandered and she began to wonder if Tad would repeat his invitation and whether, if he did, she would accept.

Delina got up the following morning and, as usual, took her mother a cup of tea before helping her to dress. Since a fall, her mother's arm had been stiff and occasionally painful. Physiotherapy seemed to help for a while but there was little overall improvement. Once she was helped into her clothes, she managed well enough. Her father had already left for work, his job at the wholesalers beginning at seven o'clock when he loaded the van ready for his deliveries. He caught the bus into Llangwyn at six-thirty.

As she reached the school gates, the caretaker handed her a letter. It had been given in by a man, at seven o'clock when he had opened up and was stacking up the crates of milk bottles ready for the deliveries.

It was from Tad, and he asked if she would meet him at the Drovers that evening to discuss the return to study. She was smiling as she went to greet her class.

He had added a phone number where a message could be left for him. She phoned at lunchtime and was able to speak to him.

'The Drovers is not a convenient place to meet and discuss this,' she said briskly. 'And besides, if I went there, I would expect to be escorted, not hang around waiting for you.' She saw no advantage in walking on eggshells where he was concerned; there had been too much of that already.

'What do you suggest, Miss Honeyman?'

Did she detect a hint of a laugh in his voice? 'This concerns Dawn as well as you, so I suggest we meet at my house. All right?'

'Thank you. We'll be there at six-thirty, if that suits?' Delina rejoined her class with a smile lighting her lovely features.

They arrived at six-thirty as arranged and Dawn was wearing a neat skirt and jumper, with long socks that, on her thin legs, reached well past her knees and kept slipping down. Her skin was mottled with the cold and she was grateful to sit on one of the huge armchairs which Delina turned closer to the fire.

'Now, Dawn,' Delina began in what her brothers called her 'teacher's' voice. 'This concerns you and your father and I am only an outsider offering to help. Your father would like to study for a big exam and to do so he will have to go several times a week to a school that opens in the evenings. I have offered to look after you while he is out. Now what do you think of the idea?'

'No. I don't want you to look after me. I want to go to Nelly and George.'

'I doubt they would think that a pleasure, considering how you let their chickens out and stole from them.'

Tad was about to protest but hurriedly subsided in his chair as Delina glared at him. Dawn looked at her father for support but for once did not get it. Silently, Delina sighed her relief. So far so good.

'If you wish, I'll ask Nelly and George, but Dawn, because of your past stupidity, I doubt they will help, and who's to blame them?' She knew she was risking Tad taking Dawn and walking out in a temper but she had to start as firmly as she needed to be, to handle this wild-mannered child and her equally wild-tempered father. She glanced at Tad. He was balling a fist, but his gaze, when he looked up and caught her watching him, showed no anger against her. She guessed his anger went inward.

'I want to go to Nelly.' Dawn began to cry and Tad stood and said, 'It's no use. Forget it. It isn't going to work.'

'Dawn!' Delina spoke sharply and the girl stopped crying and again looked at Tad.

'Go and fetch your coat from the hall, will you? We'll go now to see Nelly. And, on the way, I think you should consider how your behaviour has caused her, and many others, so much trouble.' She fastened the girl's coat and they went out.

The evening was cold and a keen wind swooped on them as they reached the top of Heol Caradoc and began to walk down to the top of Sheepy Lane. Dawn shivered loudly and Delina felt pity for the little girl make her waver in her intentions. But she only told Dawn to walk faster when she complained of the cold.

It was dark when they walked past the woods and the first light they saw was from Nelly's doorway. The dogs pushed their way out through the half-open door and ran, barking, up the path. Delina hesitated, but Dawn called to them and they began fussing around her in welcome, their bodies, in the faint glimmer of light, twisting into circles, long tails swishing madly.

'They are pleased to see you, Dawn,' Delina said.

'So will Nelly be. She doesn't make a fuss about things like some people,' Dawn said belligerently.

'Dawn—' Tad warned.

There was a delicious smell as they walked down the path, with the dogs leaping about them like ecstatic idiots. George appeared in the door and they heard him call to Nelly.

'Kettle, Nelly love, we have visitors.'

One of Nelly's chickens had learnt to knack of pushing against the door of the run and, when it swung slightly back, push her way out. As the run had not yet been locked for the night, the procession, which had begun with three people, grew to include the two dogs, and a scattering of hens, who chortled and clucked as they headed for the living room and began to peck oddments of food from the stone floor. Laughing, George went to shut them in, taking some bread to coax them back to their run.

Nelly found them seats, pushing magazines she had been reading on to the floor and throwing some cushions beside them for Dawn to sit on. Dawn settled at once in her favourite place and the dogs rested their large heads on her lap.

When George returned, Tad and Delina explained the problem and Nelly turned to George who gave only the slightest shake of his bearded head.

431

'George an' I agree that we couldn't look after yer, Dawn. It would be too much of a responsibility. Sorry.'

'It's unfortunate she isn't better behaved, isn't it, Nelly,' Delina said, giving Nelly the lead she needed to know how to handle the conversation.

'Yes, that's the trouble, Dawn. We're fond of yer, me an' George, but you're not the best be'aved and we've got busy lives, what with one thing and another. We wouldn't 'ave time to go chasin' to see what mischief you were findin'. Come an' see us though. We'd like that, wouldn't we George?'

'Any time, but we couldn't look after you, not like Miss Honeyman could. It's her job, knowing about children, just like it's mine to help Mr Leighton on the farm.'

The girl started to protest, but her arguments were slowly being worn down. She began to be afraid that if she did not agree, the only possible step her father could take was to send her into care, and although she was unclear what it entailed, she did not think she would enjoy it.

'Just think 'ow lucky you'd be to 'ave someone like Miss Honeyman to talk to. Blimey, Dawn, you'd be top of yer class in no time! Just by bein' with 'er, you bein' as bright as a newly opened buttercup! Make yer dad proud, that would. Dawn, dads want to be proud of their kids, even if they are daft and stick up for 'em when they've been idiots, like you've been more times than them dogs 'ave 'ad a slice of cake. Try it, why don't yer?'

'Can I still come and play on the swing?'

'More than that,' George interrupted. 'I've got a job for you.' He smiled and said, 'Come and see the garden.'

'The garden? But it's pitch-black out there!'

George picked up a lantern, lit it and guided her through the house to the back, where the door now opened freely on to the recently cleared back garden. In

432

the distance, they could see the lights of the village nestling below them, the church spire faintly lit by the street lamps and its silhouette showing touches of gold.

'I've cleared it you see,' he explained, 'and we thought of planting a lot of spring bulbs. Would you like to help?'

As their voices faded, Tad looked at Nelly. 'I'm sorry to burden you with my problems.'

'In this village, everyone shares, good things and bad. Sorry we can't 'elp, but kids is 'ard work.'

'We didn't come to persuade you to mind Dawn,' Delina smiled. 'We were showing her she has no choice. I should have spoken to you first, but there wasn't time. I just knew you'd say the right things.'

'Me say the right things? Blimey, I bet my Evie wouldn't agree with you!'

George returned with a shivering but happier-looking Dawn.

'George wants me to help plant dozens and dozens of bulbs, Dad. Can I?'

'If Delina is going to look after you, you must ask her.'

'Yes, young lady,' George warned. 'You never go anywhere without telling your father and Miss Honeyman first. Is that understood, first mate?'

'Understood captain,' Dawn laughed.

'Stay an' 'ave a bit of supper, why don't yer?' Nelly offered, wondering how she could make the meal spread to five plates. Tad and Delina stood to leave, shaking their heads, regretfully.

'We've taken enough of your time. I hope we haven't spoilt your meal. It smells delicious.'

'Only a bit of stuffed bream. Can't beat this old oven fer cookin', can you George?' She turned to where Dawn and George were still deep in conversation. 'What you two talkin' about that we should know?'

'Dawn thinks the garden lacks something,' George explained.

'Yes, why don't you dig a pond?' Dawn asked. 'It would be perfect then. Frogs are nice and I could take photographs of them. And there would be tad – er – frog-spawn in the spring,' she amended. She blushed as she realised how easily she might have reminded her father that he had been nicknamed Tadpole by her school friends as he was so small.

She saw her father's face tighten. Nerves made giggling a certainty. She ran from the house to hide her unreasonable merriment and in the blackness of the garden ran unerringly to the swing.

She pushed herself higher and higher, above the hedge to where she could imagine seeing the tree in which the den stood. Her laughter rang out unrestricted, like the calling of some strange bird of the night and making the people inside the house smile with her. For some reason she could not understand, Dawn felt light-hearted and ridiculously happy.

# Chapter Twenty-Two

The morning started with a mist that filled the valley, and traffic crawled along the road outside Amy's house, making its way to Swansea. She came downstairs much later than usual but it felt like the middle of the night, the day refusing to make its presence felt in the gloom.

Her first job was to clean the grate of the remnants of the previous day's fire. Putting on the thick gloves she used for the messy work, she re-laid the fire, washed her hands and made herself a cup of tea. Going to the fridge, she found there was no milk.

'Damn,' she said aloud. 'That's having all those extra people to tea.' She tried to drink it without milk but curled up her face and threw it away in disgust.

Still in her dressing gown, she considered her life and how she could change it. The way she lived was not satisfactory and surely she was intelligent enough to improve things? For one thing, the flat above the shop would make better sense than living here.

If only they could go back without such unheaval. She sighed at the thought of it all. Renting this house wouldn't be difficult but all the new furniture, and especially Margaret's piano, would not fit into the tiny rooms above the shop, no matter how she tried. She looked at the clock and tried to motivate herself to move. It was late and she should be dressed, getting the breakfast cooked and rousing Margaret by now. The baby would be waking soon and would want bathing and feeding.

None of the automatic tasks seemed important this morning. How nice it would be just to sit and spend the day reading a book that wasn't an order or an accounts book, and be utterly lazy.

A sound outside made her rise. It was the clink of the milk being left on the doorstep and she opened the door to take it and saw Billie walking down the drive.

'Where's Mary, Billie?' she called. 'Not ill, is she?'

'No, gone to Cardiff on a bit of business, so I offered to do the round for her.' He hesitated. 'Any chance of a cup of tea?'

'Come on then.' She picked up the bottles and went inside.

He followed her into the kitchen, filling it with his size. He seemed larger than ever, wearing overalls on top of the coat he had put on for extra warmth.

'Amy,' he reached out and put his cold cheek against hers so she gasped at the shock of it. 'I want us to get married.'

'Billie, love, this is hardly the time. I have to call Margaret and see to—' He silenced her with a kiss that again shocked her, this time with its suddenness and intensity. 'Billie,' she gasped when he released her.

'Mary won't interfere, if that's what's worrying you.'

'I never thought she would. Mary isn't the reason I'm saying no.'

'I think I've always loved you, Amy, although it took me a long time to realise it. You're the reason I haven't married before this.'

'No I'm not, love. Tell the truth and shame the devil, you've been too comfortable, you and Mary. You've never had need for a woman.'

'That isn't the truth. I've wanted a wife and a family like most men.'

'Not badly enough.'

'I love children.'

'I know you do, but as for loving me, well, I don't want to hurt you, Billie, but I think what I represent isn't love. It's a need to have that family other men have. Now you've realised it's getting towards the time when it will be too late.'

'Isn't it the same with you? Haven't you thought how late it's getting? I know you aren't forty yet but in a few years – and time passes so fast. Can't we spend what's left of our lives together? All right, you don't love me with a great passion, but we get on so well and the children would be happy on the farm. It's the perfect place for children. And you'd have the life you wanted, any kind of life. Just tell me what you want and I'll arrange it.'

'You tempt me, you really do. But there are so many difficulties, even if Margaret and Freddie were happy about it. How would I get to the shop from the farm? There's no bus that crosses the fields and goes through the wood!'

'Amy, you wouldn't have to work!' Billie looked outraged at the suggestion.

'And what would I do?' she laughed. 'I've got too much to do now, but I'd soon be fed up with nothing at all!'

'Keep turkeys for pin-money. Mary would help start you off, and you could join women's groups, things you don't have time for now.'

'I'd be completely off my rocker in a month!'

'What would you want to do then?' he asked, pouring himself a cup of tea.

His action was so at odds with the important discussion Amy wanted to scream. 'I want to run my shop of course! It will be for Freddie or Margaret one day, if they want it. I own it you know, it isn't rented.'

'We could sort that out. But won't people think it strange, me sending you out to work and not keeping you as a husband should?'

'Billie, love, I'll think about it, I promise. And I'll write to Freddie and talk to Margaret – it's their future we're talking about as well as ours.'

'At least you've said "ours". That's progress of a sort.'

He smiled at her and in sudden affection for the big, gentle, sincere man, Amy hugged him and he kissed her in a way that gave him hope, and her a glimpse of a life infinitely more exciting than her present existence.

He looked away from her almost shyly and stammered, 'Got to go. The milk will be late and there's a row I'll have from Mary.' He opened the door but stopped and asked, 'Will I see you tonight, at the quiz?'

'It depends if I can find someone to mind Margaret and Sian.'

'That might be difficult,' he admitted. 'Everybody's going to the Drovers for the quiz!'

'Margaret says you're in the Farmer's team?'

'Yes, and I hope we don't win. I gave part of the prize! There's four chicken dinners, a fowl, vegetables and some fruit for a pudding.'

'I'll be there to cheer you if I can,' she promised.


Amy was late. She hurriedly called Margaret and prepared a hasty breakfast before setting off for the shop with the baby in the pram. Margaret urged her on, anxious not to miss Oliver, who waited for her at the corner, and when Amy reached the shop she was breathless, Margaret's impatience having made her almost run the last few minutes.

The shop was already full but Mavis ran out to meet her as she opened the back-lane gate. 'Thank goodness you're here. My Sheila is threatening to go off and live with your Freddie,' she spluttered as Amy lifted Sian out of the pram.

'What are you talking about? She's married, and Freddie wouldn't—' As she spoke the words she knew

438

with certainty that Freddie would. 'What's happened?' she demanded.

'Going to live in Devon, they are. Him in the army with not enough to keep a pet mouse, and her finding work in some shop.' She began to sob. 'Why is she like this, Amy? Where did we go wrong?' From inside the shop, voices began to call, insisting on being served.

'Come on, Mavis,' Nelly's voice yelled. 'Let's 'ave some bacon before World War Three starts and they ration it again!'

'We're coming,' Amy called back. 'Hang on a minute, will you?'

'We'll have to go back to my mother's,' Mavis said, her voice muffled by the handkerchief she hid her face in. 'First time we've been on our own since we were married, and now we'll have to go back to look after Mam.'

'You'll be leaving the flat?' Amy tried to ignore the chanting from the shop. 'Well I never! And there's me thinking I might prefer to live there instead of trekking to and from the house like this.'

'How can you think of the flat after news like this?' Mavis wailed.

'You did! And besides, there's customers waiting and we have to deal with them first. Now we'll get a cup of tea made then I'll see to that lot in by there.' She put Sian into the play-pen Victor had made for her, looked into the shop and smiled brightly at her customers.

'Now then, let me see to the kettle then I'll see to you all in a flash.'

'Let me do that for yer, Amy.' Nelly pushed her way unceremoniously though the short-tempered people into the small kitchen behind the shop. Amy was standing staring into space as if mesmerised.

'What's up, Amy?' Nelly asked.

'Do you believe in auguries?'

439

'I might be able to tell you if I knew what they were!'

'Signs to head you in the right direction.'

'Yes, I do.'

'Mavis is thinking of leaving the flat and I have been undecided about whether to come back. D'you think that's a sign?'

'I think if you don't get servin' you won't 'ave no business to live over the top of!'

Amy laughed and went into the shop to be greeted by a storm of teasing about being unable to get up in the mornings. Good naturedly she quickly served the men who had called for the morning paper and some cigarettes on their way to work and then dealt with the rest.

She looked at the clock. Still not quite nine o'clock. What a lot had happened in a short time! She glanced across the road to the school from where the roar of children at play met her ears. She had to tell Margaret and find out what she thought of the idea. As always, she made sure her children were involved in any decision that would affect them. Some might think that foolish but being without a husband, she had determined that Freddie and Margaret would always know they were a family.

'Mind the shop for a minute, Nelly. Mavis is outside. I won't be long.' She ran across the road.

She reached the railings – wooden replacements for the old iron ones taken down during the war – and asked one of the children to find Margaret. Looking anxious, Margaret ran to her, glancing back to where the children were already beginning to form lines ready to go into their classrooms.

'Margaret, love. Would you prefer to live above the shop again, or with Uncle Billie on the farm? Mr and Mrs Powell might be leaving and we now have a choice.'

Still looking anxiously at the children trooping into the building behind her, Margaret said seriously, 'It would be nearer to Oliver if we were in the flat, but where would I put the piano?'

'If that could be arranged, love?'

'Well, there's more room and lots to do on the farm, but d'you think Uncle Victor would still be able to come and see us? He's very good at Monopoly.'

'That is expecting a lot, love. Uncle Billie might be jealous.'

'Wants us all to himself, does he?' She looked at the disappearing tail of the line of children. 'Mam, I'll have to go or I'll get a late mark.'

'Bye, love, we'll talk about it later, right?'

At lunchtime Margaret wanted to go and live at the farm, but by the time school finished for the afternoon she had changed her mind and thought she would prefer the flat.

'Margaret, you're more mixed up than I am!' Amy laughed. 'I've written to Freddie and asked him to phone and tell us what he thinks.' She did not tell Margaret about Sheila's intention to live with Freddie; she did not trust Sheila not to be inventing the whole thing. Besides, there were some things even *she* thought too complicated to discuss with a ten-year-old.

There was no time to talk further about the move as it was the night of the long-waited quiz show, which Bert had decided to call 'Chuck It In Charlie's Churn'. Charlie was Mr Leighton, the quiet farmer who was supplying the fifteen-gallon milk churn to receive the money exacted as penalties for wrong answers.

Evie had agreed to mind Margaret and baby Sian, although Amy had needed to put pressure on Nelly's socially minded daughter by reminding her of how often Oliver spent time with Margaret, while she and Timothy went 'gallivanting.'

The baby was put to bed in Evie's and Margaret and Oliver were given some colouring books so they could

441

play quietly and not disturb Evie, who was studying the meanings of road signs ready for her third attempt on the driving test. Amy set off for the Drovers in Timothy's car, as he was one of the village team-members.

The bar was already crowded, with the other five team-members looking very respectable in smart suits which rarely saw the light of day. Billie wore a brown tweed suit that he occasionally wore on market day; Sidney, Phil's brother, who, like George, worked for Mr Leighton, was in a newly knitted pullover and grey trousers, and George, who to Nelly looked the smartest of them all, wore a neat grey pin-striped suit which they had bought from Mrs Greener, the second-hand clothes dealer in town.

The village team consisted of Bert, in a formal navy suit and a dashing heather buttonhole, Johnny, in sports jacket and grey trousers, and Timothy, who, as always, looked held together in a dark grey suit that fitted him so precisely Nelly whispered to George, 'That explains why he can never get 'is 'and in 'is pocket to pay 'is round!'

A low rostrum had been placed in a corner of the room and in front of it stood a polished milk churn with, standing beside it, Farmer Leighton. It was Timothy who explained the rules and Bert who insisted that the audience, on cue from him, should all shout out 'Chuck it in Charlie's Churn' every time someone had to pay a forfeit.

'So, it's one point for every correct answer, and two pennies in the churn for every wrong answer,' Timothy summed up. 'So let us begin.'

Nelly sat beside Netta Cartwright and they laughed and they called encouragement for opposing teams. Nelly looked around the room, which was already filled with smoke, and saw Mrs French sitting with Fay and Delina. Standing near the bar was Victor. When Amy arrived she had found a place near the churn facing

Billie's team, but close to Victor. Nelly thought the time must soon come when Amy would have to make up her mind about the two men in her life.

'Thank gawd I've got George and no complications,' she said with a loud sigh. Netta agreed, although not understanding what her friend referred to.

'You've got to admire 'er nerve,' Nelly went on. 'There's Billie wanting to marry 'er and there she sits, smilin' at 'im and playin' footsey with Victor under the bench!'

'Hush, Nelly, they'll hear you,' Netta chuckled.

The greatest laughter and applause of the evening was when Timothy became over-confident and rattled off the spelling of 'parsimoniously' at great speed and got it wrong! He joined good-naturedly in the laughter and added extra coins to Charlie's Churn, as the crowd chanted in delight. 'Just to show that meanness simply isn't in my vocabulary,' he joked.

' 'Ow do yer spell that then?' Nelly shouted.

Later, Timothy was asked what number came next to twelve on a dart board and he was wrong again.

'Blimey! My Ollie would've got that one right, and 'e's only nine!' Nelly shouted in delight.

Billie surprised them all by being able to name the seven dwarfs and Sidney by spelling 'autocratically', but it was Timothy's team who eventually won the chicken-dinners supplied by Billie and Farmer Leighton.

It was almost impossible for Mrs French to push her way through to present the prizes, but, amid much good-natured teasing,she reached a place near the bar where the prizes were displayed. There was one each for Bert, Johnny and Timothy and everyone waited to see who was to be given the fourth.

Mrs French looked around in the expectant hush. 'We decided on an extra prize to add to the fun,' she said. The hat which had been so neat when she arrived, was now tilted at a saucy angle across one eye and her face was rosy and shiny with the heat of the room and the generous offers of drinks she had received throughout the evening.

'We have decided to give it to the person with the loudest and happiest laugh.' All eyes turned to Nelly.

'To Nelly Masters, whom we all love.'

Nelly hugged George and laughed, her excited, gap-toothed smile distorted by the uneven light into a grimace.

'Smashin'. Thanks very much. Me an' George will feel like king and queen eatin' this!' She sat down quickly as her head began to spin. 'George,' she said, urgently, 'take me 'ome!'

But the evening was far from over. Leighton shook the churn and there was a call for more contributions. The landlord threw in a handful of coins and people began to throw money across the heads of others while Leighton struggled to retrieve the coins. Several customers were unseated in the scramble and the landlord called for order as the door opened and Mr and Mrs Norwood Bennet-Hughes came in.

'Anyone willing to make an offer for the contents of Charlie's Churn?' the barman shouted, after nodding a greeting to the newcomers.

Offers began to come in and there was the murmur of voices as people tried to guess how much the churn contained. Eventually the impromptu auction reached thirty pounds, offered by Mr Norwood Bennet-Hughes.

Constable Harris, squashed in a corner, tried to stand up and protest that the proceedings were not legal. But Phil put another drink in front of him and threatened to sit on him if he didn't pipe down, so he closed his eyes and pretended not to know what was happening.

The contents of the churn were counted and the amount announced, as Mr Norwood Bennet-Hughes handed over the thirty pounds. 'Thirty-three pounds, seven shillings and threepence. 'Timothy announced and Mr Norwood Bennet-Hughes stood with difficulty, to say he was handing it back to the fund.

More money was thrown and the amount reached seventy pounds. With the tickets sold for the evening's entertainment the final amount was almost eighty.

The Reverend Barclay Bevan, who had arrived late and stood near the door where he could gasp an occasional breath of fresh air, tried to give a speech of thanks, but no one was listening. In fact several, including Nelly and Archie Pearce, were fast asleep.

In the council house she shared with her grandmother, Sheila was busily making preparations to leave Hen Carw Parc. She had joyfully given her notice at the gown-shop and, after working her week's notice, had begun to sort through her clothes before packing her suitcase ready for the journey to Devon.

She had spent the morning washing and, having dried her clothes around the fire, was selecting which were worth ironing and which could be discarded. On a chair were a pile of nylon stockings awaiting repair. She hoped to persuade her grandmother to deal with that tedious task.

The jobs had become boring and although the excitement of the approaching adventure boosted her spirits for most of the morning, by two o'clock she was throwing more on to the pile destined for the ash bin than on the pile to be ironed.

Her grandmother's irons were solid metal and had to be heated alternatively over the fire. While she waited for one to reach the heat necessary for pressing a skirt, she sat down and counted her money and made a shopping list for the following day.

She felt a little sorry for her grandmother, who prefered

her granddaughter's company to having Mavis and Ralph looking after her, as had become apparent when Sheila had taken Gran her early-morning tea.

'They mean well, but they do fuss so,' Gran had complained.

'Don't I know it! Why d'you think I'm leaving?' Sheila had confided.

'You don't love this boy, then?' Her gran's watchful eyes followed Sheila as she struggled to find an answer approaching honesty but that would also satisfy the old lady.

'You aren't leaving because you can't bear to be parted from him?' Gran pressed.

'I do feel something for Freddie, of course I do. But it isn't love,' Sheila admitted. 'Anyway, we can't get married or anything for ages, so we'll have time to think about how we feel about each other, won't we?'

'I suppose so. But Sheila, be careful. It's all very well to defy convention but something else to pretend that other people's good opinion of you doesn't matter. It does.'

Sheila had tried to block her grandmother's advice from her mind, as she started her ironing. Now, as she waited for the iron to heat on a fire that had burnt low, she saw Ethel Davies passing the kitchen window.

She stepped back and hoped, with Gran dosing in the living room, she might get away with not answering her mother-in-law's knock. She felt guilty when she thought of Ethel's painful struggle up the hill and, after hearing the door knocked three times, she relented and opened it. At least Ethel could have a rest before walking all the way back down, even if she had no wish to hear what the woman had to say to her.

Ethel went in and had a brief word with Gran while Sheila discarded her attempt to finish her ironing. She offered tea and Ethel followed Sheila back into the kitchen to make it.

446

'I've had a reply to my letter to Maurice,' Ethel said, sinking with relief into a chair. 'There was a note for you included with it.'

Sheila's heart leapt. She had difficult holding her voice calm as she said, 'Oh, I don't think I want to read it, but thank you for bringing it all the way up here. I suppose he's furious with me for telling you where he was? I had a stinking rude letter I did! I don't want to read another one. Let your son keep his whereabouts a secret if he wants to, Mrs Davies. He's hurt me quite enough.' All the time, Sheila stared at the letter, pushed temptingly close across the table.

'He wants to thank you for your generosity,' Ethel said, her deep, dark eyes watching Sheila's agitation.

'He what?'

'He says he was touched by your generosity in passing on his address to me. You have no cause to thank him for what he did, or be kind to me. We've treated you badly, far worse than you deserve. Yet you knew how I was worrying and took the trouble to pass on his address. Maurice says you have a generous and forgiving spirit and are a lesson to us all.'

Sheila sat down and stared at the notepaper.

'There's poetic. Well, I don't know what's happened to change his mind, but I still remember how he answered *my* letter, telling him about the baby. If I were stupid enough to open this one, I'm sure I'd find more of the same. He might tell you that he's grateful and appreciative, Mrs Davies, but I'm a lot wiser than you, when it comes to Maurice.'

'He's ill.'

'Oh, so now we're getting it. He can afford to be forgiving can he, now he's ill and wanting someone to write and tell him how sorry they are?'

'Please, Sheila, open it.'

Sheila rattled the lip of the jug against the rim of the

447

cup as she poured the tea she had made and only after the tea was half drunk did she reluctantly pick up the sealed letter.

'Read it,' Ethel pleaded as Sheila held it and looked at it contemptuously. With a thumb, the seal was broken and the paper, blue and crinkled, was spread flat.

The first thing Sheila noted was an address at the top of the page.

'My Dear Sheila', she read. 'I have no right to expect you to even read this, but please let me tell you how I feel. Remorse for the way I treated you is uppermost in my heart. I used you, then discarded you for someone I thought I loved more. I was wrong. I know that now. I want to come home and repay you for my cruelty. I want to be a real husband to you, Sheila. Can you forgive me, or at least allow me the chance to try and make amends? I'll have to try, somehow, to raise the money to refund my passage before I can come home, but believe me, home is where I want to be. Will you let me come home to you, my wife?' It was signed, 'Your foolish, your loving, Maurice'

Sheila felt tears burning her eyes and she wished she had had the sense to wait until she was alone before reading it. She had expected to throw it down and tell Ethel she was a fool to think it would contain anything other than more insults. Now her heart was in turmoil and she knew that if she spoke she would cry. She threw the flimsy notepaper in front of Ethel and whispered, 'Go on, read it,' before sobs began to shake her shoulders and wails of pent up despair filled the room.

Ethel's brown eyes were as tear-filled as Sheila's when she read the letter. She reached out her arms and tried to comfort the girl.

'Please go, Mrs Davies, I'll come down and see you later. But, please, I want to be alone now.'

Ethel made her slow way back down the hill. She too

wanted solitude to fathom out whether her son's words were honest or the result of his being ill and far away from anyone who cared. She crossed her fingers as she pushed the door open, and prayed fervently that if he did return, it would be to make a real effort to settle into marriage with Sheila, and not start something up again with Delina Honeyman.

Sheila did not go to Ethel's to discuss the letter. She needed someone independent of both herself and Maurice and there was no one. She threw her things, so carefully pressed, back into cupboards and drawers and tried to write to Freddie. She wrote three letters, the first asking for more time to decide, the second telling him she was no longer sure what she wanted and the third being brutally frank, and explaining that a letter from Maurice had turned her decision to live near him on its head. She posted the third and immediately felt better.

She bathed and put on the suit in which she had planned to travel to Devon and went out. Her hair shone and for once hung exactly as she wanted it to. Her shoes were fairly new and had been polished to a mirror finish. Wearing a few pieces of jewellery and with carefully applied makeup, including her favourite Max Factor creme-puff, 'Tempting Touch', she set off to see Delina.

Within her she felt a need to hit back and punish the girl who, in her mind had stolen Maurice from her. The prospect of distressing the young woman sent the last hint of unhappiness speeding off into the night. Maurice had come to his senses. He loved her.

'I thought you'd like to be the first to know,' Sheila said when Delina opened the door. 'My husband is coming home. To me, of course, to his wife, Miss Honeyman. Goodnight.'

She was disconcerted to hear the door close without Delina uttering a word. She would have been even more

449

surprised if she could have seen through the door. Delina was smiling. A ghost had been well and truly put to rest. She had heard the news without feeling anything except relief that for her the love affair was over.

Sheila returned home, took down the picture of Cornel Wilde and from a drawer pulled out a small photograph of Maurice. She stared at it and wondered anxiously if she would still feel the same about him. She also wondered if he genuinely wanted her or knew that coming back to his wife would ensure his family's compassion and their financial help.

She regretted going to gloat over Delina. If it were Delina he really wanted then, legal wife or not, she would lose him again. Had she set herself up for another disaster? Reading and re-reading the letter, she took comfort from it, interpreting from its few lines much more than Maurice, poetic or not, could possibly have intended.

A few days later, Amy, who knew nothing of Freddie's disappointment, received a phone call from him, begging her to go and see Sheila and persuade her to change her mind about taking Maurice back.

'Freddie, I can't do that! It isn't up to you or me to tell her to ignore the chance of a reunion with her legal husband!'

'She's sueing him for divorce, Mam. He's never been her husband and how can you support him after the way he treated her, him and that family of his!'

In Amy's mind was the retort that Sheila had not treated Freddie as anything more than a dupe, but she held the comment back. Freddie would not thank her for the reminder.

'I won't go to see Sheila but I will talk to Ethel and see what Maurice really said. If there's anything Sheila hasn't fully explained, Ethel will know. Ring me tomorrow and I'll tell you all I've found out.'

Amy replaced the receiver and stood trembling with indecision. She knew that if Sheila wanted to mess Freddie about, maybe for years, there was nothing she could do to prevent her. She could only be constant in her support of him, always be there and willing to do what she could to help. This was no exception. After the shop closed she went, with Margaret and Sian, to see Ethel.

'So what Sheila told Freddie was true then?' Amy said when Ethel had repeated what had been in both letters. 'What shall I tell Freddie then? That once more Sheila is playing silly-buggers with his affection? Nice girl that is! Honestly, Ethel, she's nothing but trouble, and your Maurice is no better!'

'Look, Amy, I can't help you. I only know how glad I am that Maurice is coming back. I'm prepared to let everything else wait till then. Things will settle one way or another and what *we* think doesn't really come into it. Go now, and we'll talk again. Tomorrow perhaps.'

'You're right and I'm sorry. It isn't for me to burst in here and blame you or your son.' She lowered her voice and added sadly, 'I have to keep reminding myself of *my* past. It's so easy to forget and accuse others of misbehaving.'

'Easy too to forget that if Sheila had been brought up with less anxious parents she might have been different. She's never been allowed to have a thought of her own, poor dab.'

Amy called Margaret who was out in the garden, staring up at an old birds' nest in a hawthorn tree with the aid of a torch. 'Come on, Margaret, love, we'll come and see Auntie Ethel another time. We'll have to get this baby home or she'll soon let us know she's unhappy.' She apologised again to Ethel and they set off home through the dark lane.

451

When Nelly was cleaning the shop later that week, news of Maurice's intended return had leaked out and most people were of the opinion that when he did, it would be to Delina he went and not his wife.

'I'm selfish enough to wonder how it will concern Freddie, and how it will affect me,' Amy admitted.

'Another of them auguries, you mean?' Nelly said.

'Yes, I suppose so. I'm wondering whether this will alter what I decide to do about marrying Billie and going to the farm, if Freddie's still a part of the family.'

'Ask 'im, did yer? Ask Freddie 'ow 'e felt?' Nelly rested on her bucket to enquire.

'Well, no. I think we've hardly mentioned it since Sheila's latest change of heart.'

'When in doubt do nowt!' Nelly said, puffing as she lifted the bucket of dirty water to empty outside. 'Wait an' see'.

'For how long? I can't expect Billie to wait much longer. Had him on a string long enough, I have.'

' 'E ain't goin' nowhere.'

'Neither am I, Nelly, neither am I. Unless it's round and round in circles!'

452

# Chapter Twenty-Three

Prue came home for a week and the extra work made Amy very tired and irritable. Prue had regained her sharp, accusatory manner together with her health and seemed to criticise everything her sister did. She took over most of the responsibility for Sian and seemed at last to delight in her little daughter. Amy knew that soon the baby would no longer be hers to care for and love. Life was so hectic she knew handing the baby back to her real mother would ease the burden but she dreaded the moment when Sian would no longer be her responsibility. It would be a long time too before she felt happy about Prue looking after Sian, she knew that already.

She was loath to allow Prue to take the baby out on her own and was alarmed one day to find the pram and Sian missing from the garden, where she had put her as she hung out some washing. Prue was not in her room and Amy paused only long enough to grab a coat before running from the house to search for her. Not knowing which way she had gone, she settled for the most likely and, taking her bicycle for speed, peddled past Mrs French's house to where her sister had lived before her illness.

The windows were all open and she could hear Prue singing as she approached. Looking through the kitchen window she saw Prue rocking the little girl and singing to her while Sian crowed her delight. Amy crept away, wondering what to do. She did not think Prue well enough to be left alone with the baby, but feared to do or say something to upset Prue and set back her progress towards full health.

Fortunately the decision was taken for her as Prue opened the door and called to her. 'I thought I would show Sian the house so it won't be a complete surprise to her when she comes home,' Prue said, smiling. 'Shall we walk back now?'

'Yes. There's pleased I am that you're making plans for the future.'

The following morning Amy went to see Prue's doctor and between them they decided that the safest plan was for Amy to appoint a housekeeper for Prue. That way the baby could visit in safety until Prue was well enough to care for her. Several people were asked to keep their ears open for someone suitable but it was several days before Amy interviewed Florrie Gwyn.

It was Billie who found her. He was in almost daily contact with Amy either at the shop or the house, still hoping to persuade her that her future lay at the farm.

'She's a Mrs Florrie Gwyn,' he announced one Monday morning as he helped Amy put the vegetables out on to the pavement. 'A customer of Mary's she is, and an ex-nurse. Widowed a couple of years ago and she'd be glad of a place. Shares now with her daughter and they both find it a bit of a strain, like.'

Florrie Gwyn was a tall red-haired woman with angular features who, to Amy, looked cold and rather hard. When she spoke though, the lines on her face softened and her surprisingly soft voice reassured Amy.

'It's with children I've worked mostly,' Florrie explained. 'Sick children for the most part of course, but children need the same things wherever you find them, don't they? Warmth, food and the knowledge that they are needed and loved.'

'You'll have to get on with my sister as well, mind,'

Amy said, after Florrie had looked at the child and cuddled her in her capable arms. 'She might be a bit more difficult to get on with than our lovely Sian, but you'll soon know when you meet her whether you can cope.'

They arranged to meet at Amy's house the following Sunday morning and Prue made an extra effort to look smart. Florrie arrived on her bicycle and, although Prue was very formal and almost suspicious at first, the two women soon found shared interests and began talking like friends. Amy breathed a huge sigh of relief. At least that was one hurdle overcome.

Florrie started living at the house straight away so that Prue could go home whenever she wanted to. It was strange to see the curtains billowing out each morning and lights showing at night after the months of dark, still silence.

Billie went several times to see if Florrie needed anything and provoked in Amy a jealousy that surprised her, making her show more affection towards Billie than she truly felt.

At weekends, Prue began to examine the books left by Morgan and surprised Amy by her swift understanding of them.

'Satisfactory, are they?' she asked one day as Prue put the books back into the briefcase Morgan used to carry them to and from the office.

'Well, to be honest, I'm very impressed with the way that young man is managing the place. He's thorough and honest and very keen to increase the business.'

'Good. I'm glad you don't have to worry about that.'

'In fact I think I'll continue to let him manage, even when I'm well enough to take back the reins. There'll still be plenty for me to do and, with Sian to look after – yes, I think I'll leave things just as they are, and give Morgan a good increase in wages. I'll keep an eye on things of course, but yes, I'll leave things stay as they are.'

Mavis was busily polishing the table, trying to remove a stain left from placing a hot teapot on the polished surface when Sheila had called to see her.

'You get me all agitated you do, Sheila.'

'What are you bothering with that, for? It's Amy's and you'll be leaving it behind soon.'

'When I leave here and go back to Gran's, you mean? Well I don't want Amy telling people I didn't look after the place,' Mavis retorted, rubbing more furiously than before.

'Amy won't make a fuss. Why get so bothered?'

'That's the way I am. I care about people's opinion of me, I do. Pity you don't!'

'Oh, Mam, don't start. I've come to tell you I won't be going to Devon, after all.'

Sheila was surprised at the look of relief on her mother's flushed face. She had not realised how much her mother had hated the gossip her intention to join Freddie had caused.

'Best for you, too!' Mavis said, returning to her polishing. She sat on the floor and pulled the duster around the table legs, back and forth, back and forth, making the dark wood gleam. 'Glad you've come to your senses about that, my girl.'

'Maurice is coming home,' Sheila said and once more succeeded in stopping her mother from her work.

'Maurice? He can't! Having you on, he is. He has to stay in Australia for at least two years.'

'His family are paying his fare and refunding the passage money so he can come back. I had a letter a few days ago but I haven't said anything until the money was all fixed, in case there was a disappointment. Mam, he's hoping we can get together again.'

'You'd better move right away from that Delina Honeyman then!'

'It's me he's coming back to, Mam. He's had time to think and he's coming back to me.'

'Don't rely on him, Sheila. He's let you down badly once and there's always a chance he'll do it again.'

'Mam, can't you be happy for me?'

Mavis sank into a chair and nodded. 'I'm sorry, Sheila, I know I always expect the worst, but, fair play, when has it ever been anything else with you?' She went to put the kettle on. 'Have another cup of tea and we'll talk about what to do when Maurice comes home.'

'Can't you wish me luck?'

'I do, but I'm afraid you'll—' Mavis stopped, smiled and said hurriedly, 'I do wish you luck, Sheila. I really do.'

'I'm still moving out of Gran's. I'm going to live with Ethel, get to know my mother-in-law. I'll find a job and stay with her. Best I get to know my new family at last, isn't it?'

'Why bother? Your own was never very important,' Mavis sighed.

They drank their tea in silence then Sheila stood to leave. 'I'll come and see you soon. Say hello to Dad for me.' She felt the weight of her mother's presence slide from her like an unwanted coat as soon as she was outside and she ran, joyfully, as excited as a child. She saw herself in the romantic role of wronged wife, loyal and loving, waiting for her husband's change of heart and winning through by patient devotion. Her footsteps slowed as she walked up Sheepy Lane. She hoped Maurice wouldn't hear about Nigel and of her plans to go and live near Freddie.

The last main item the village had organised in aid of the church-hall fund was the sale of work. It was to be held on the following Saturday in the school, where there was more room for the stalls to set up their assorted wares.

Lights shone from the building from early in the

457

morning as Mr Evans the caretaker made sure everything was clean for the invasion of enthusiastic ladies who would arrive in cars and on foot with heavy boxes and baskets of things to sell.

Mr Evans fixed ribbons across the front entrance which Mrs Norwood Bennet-Hughes had been invited to cut as she declared the sale of work open. All the helpers went in through the back entrance, leaving their rain-coats on the pegs used during the week by the children.

The rain, which had begun the previous day and showed no sign of stopping, disappointed the organisers. Glum-faced, they gathered in groups, discussing the like-lihood that numbers would be down because of it. Many would chose to stay home rather than face dressing up in raincoats and hats and carry umbrellas to push their way through similarly dressed women, all hoping for a bargain.

Bert was there early, and he helped Mr Evans set up the tables which the ladies would decorate and fill with their handiwork, which represented many hours of patient labour.

Prue came home for the weekend and, instead of handing in her usual pile of knitted and crocheted gar-ments for the handicraft stall, said it was her intention to buy.

'Bound to see some home-knitted dresses and cardi-gans to fit Sian,' she told Amy. 'I hate to see a child of mine in shop-bought clothes.'

'Baby-minding I can manage standing on my head, running a shop, and organising a home, fine, but knit-ting and I don't get on at all!' Amy laughed.

'I wasn't criticising—' Prue began, then changed back to her usual ways and added, 'But as you mention it, I will be glad when I'm dressing her myself. You haven't the flair, Amy.'

\*      \*      \*

As Amy and Mavis both wanted to go to the sale of work, they had agreed to share the hours at the shop, which would probably be very quiet, anyway. As Amy slipped on her coat and went through the shop she saw a bus load of people from Llangwyn alight and enter the school, to wait outside for the arrival of Mrs Norwood Bennet-Hughes. The crowd at the entrance swelled minute by minute and Amy recognised Delina and Dorothy Williams, for whom Nelly worked, walking past with Fay, all huddled inside their coats and umbrellas against the weather.

Margaret had gone to help set out the stalls and Amy wondered where Oliver was. Her question was answered a while later when the Chartridges' car hissed past. Evie was driving and she recognised the small face of Oliver looking out of the back window.

'Who was that with Evie?' she asked Mavis. 'It can't be Timothy, he'll be over there waiting for Mrs Norwood Bennet-Hughes.'

'I think it was Johnny,' Mavis said. 'I know she's asked him to help with her driving. Determined to pass her test, she is. She seems to get plenty of practice, what with Timothy and your Victor.'

'He isn't *my* Victor. Married he is, remember?'

'Poor little Oliver, stuck there with nothing to do for ages while she practises her three-point turns or whatever.'

'Yes, he doesn't get much consideration, does he?'

An ambulance drove past a few moments after Evie turned up Sheepy Lane.

'Going to collect Ethel for her treatment,' Mavis said. 'Victor's wife goes too, something about a painful shoulder.'

Amy did not reply. Why was Mavis talking about Victor with every breath? She knew that was an exaggeration but Victor was on her mind and each time

459

his name was spoken her heart gave a leap. She imagined guilt showed clearly on her face.

That evening, she and Victor were going on a rare evening out. First to town, where they planned to have a meal together, then, after a drink in some out-of-town pub, they would travel home on separate buses.

'Evie should have left Oliver with me,' Amy said, to take the conversation away from Victor's wife. 'He'd have been better off here than driving around the council houses on a morning like this.'

The rain had not eased and a chill wind blew through the shop each time a customer entered. Mavis looked out and the streets seemed empty of people, apart from the growing crowd at the school. Only the cars parked on the green verge showed the presence of extra people.

'I think everyone is staying indoors by their fires, or are already at the school,' Mavis said.

Just then a large Vauxhall car drove up and the crowd cheered a welcome to the large, fur-coated figure of Mrs Norwood Bennet-Hughes.

'You'd better go and get in quick or there'll be nothing of the best things left.' Mavis said.

'Yes,' Amy agreed, pulling the hood of her coat higher. 'I want to buy a couple of embroidered tray-cloths, mine are in ribbons!'

Inside, on the stage, Mrs Norwood Bennet-Hughes was aware that the Reverend Barclay Bevan was avoiding standing near her. She wondered at first if it was because of the perfume with which she had covered herself before setting out, but later decided that he was shy of her. The thought amused and flattered her. Whenever they were together he shuffled about nervously and always managed to arrange that someone stood between them. She would have been more amused if she had known the real reason. Barclay Bevan was short, plump, balding and vague. From past, well-remembered experience he

460

knew that as she spoke, Mrs Norwood Bennet-Hughes
had a habit of turning her body rather than just her head,
as she addressed an audience. He lived in constant fear of
being buried in her fur-covered bosom.

During her speech, Phil sneaked in and helped himself
to a cup of tea from the large urn and a welsh-cake which
Brenda Roberts had been about to offer to her husband
Bert. Brenda slapped his hand and the sound of it travelled through the crowd but it was Brenda's face that
blushed and debates began about the possible cause,
making her blush deepen. Phil chuckled and went on
with his deliveries.

When Amy had finally paid her entrance fee and
walked into the school hall she saw it was packed with
women, each trying to push their way through to the
front of the stalls and find what they needed from the
wide selection. The cakes were almost sold out and the
handiwork stalls, always so important a feature of these
affairs, were spreading their remaining pieces to fill gaps
in the displays where items had been sold. She found
three tray-cloths and stayed a while, looking to see if any
of her friends were present.

Nelly was easily found. Amy only had to follow the
sound of her laughter to see her talking to Netta and Fay,
in the corner where Brenda Roberts was selling tea.

'Bought anything, Nelly?' she asked.

'No, just lookin' Amy. Always good fer a laugh, this
is. Blimey, you should 'ave seen Tedious Timothy trying
to get things started! Waited fer Evie fer ten minutes!
She still 'asn't arrived. Gorn with young Johnny, Gawd
'elp 'im, fer a drivin' lesson.'

'Yes, Mavis and I saw them going up Sheepy Lane.
Poor little Oliver was stuck in the back. I bet he'll be glad
to get here!'

Amy left them and began looking for Prue. She was
glad she had left the baby with Mavis; it would have been

461

frightening for the little girl amid all these shouting people, and the smell of plastic macs and ancient rubber-backed coats was overpowering. She thought she would find Prue and then leave.

Trade was so brisk that several of the stalls were already clearing away the last of their goods but there was no sign of people leaving. In the corner near the door of school kitchen Brenda's tea-and-cake stall continued to do business and it was there that Amy found Prue.

Florrie was with her and it was clear the two women were becoming good friends. Prue had an armful of baby clothes and she was extolling the quality of the dresses and the embroidered cot-covers she had bought to anyone who would listen. Amy smiled. Her sister's health was improving by the minute and her joy in her baby daughter a joy to see.

When Amy tapped her on the arm, Prue turned and a blush suffused her thin cheeks. Amy guessed that her name had been spoken and probably in criticism of the way she had dressed Sian.

'Got some nice dresses and coats, I see,' Amy said. 'Have you bought anything for yourself?'

'No,' her sister replied, 'but I bought you a present for Christmas so you mustn't look.'

'There's lovely! The excitement's starting already and it's only October!'

Timothy was clapping his hands and asking for silence. It was time for a few closing remarks for Mrs Norwood Bennet-Hughes.

'Oh my goodness!' Amy gasped, 'and I promised not to stay a minute. Mavis will be too late for anything!'

Timothy stood on a chair and looked over the heads of the people gathered. He was obviously looking for some-one.

'Has anyone seen Mrs Norwood Bennet-Hughes?' He

462

asked. 'I would like to prevail upon that lady to give us a few closing words.'

'She's 'ere, talkin' to me.' Nelly stood up, spilling the sweets she had just bought and she scrambled down to gather them up from the parquet floor as Mrs Norwood Bennet-Hughes stood and began to walk towards Timothy.

'Goodbye, Nelly. Thanks for talking to me,' she smiled. 'I'll come as soon as I can to see the improvements in your lovely home.'

'Come any time yer like,' Nelly shouted back, the look of pleasure on her face diminished only by her daughter's absence: it wouldn't be the same just telling her what her grand friend had just said. 'Cor,' she whispered to Netta, 'if my Evie 'ad only 'eard that!'

Evie was driving in ferocious slanting rain through the council houses. Up Hywel Rise, she went, along St Illtyd's and around St Hilda's Crescent, stopping to reverse into the small streets and closes. She grew more and more agitated as her driving became worse and not better as time went on. She was determined to master this reversing and turning the car before she went back down to the village, although she sensed that Johnny had had enough.

Oliver began to complain. He wanted to see if there were any second-hand toys at the sale of work as there sometimes were, and he had promised to meet Margaret there. That increased Evie's tension and the fact that Johnny had his hand hovering over the hand-brake did not help either.

'Do you have to look as if you are about to jump out?' she said irritably. 'I've been driving for weeks and weeks, you know. I'm not likely to do anything stupid!'

'Look out! *Duw annwyl*!' Johnny shouted as Mary-dairy's van moved slowly out of St Non's Road.

'It's all right, I did see it!' Evie said, although she was shaken. Putting the car into fourth gear instead of first, she struggled to move off up the hill. Patiently, Johnny suggested she went into neutral and tried again.

'Don't you think we should call it a day, Evie? *Jesu Mawr*, poor Oliver must be fed up sitting there all this time.'

'Just a couple more hill-starts, Johnny, then we'll go back. I promised to show myself at the sale of work before Mrs Norwood Bennet-Hughes leaves.'

'Cutting it a bit fine, then.' Johnny glanced at his watch. 'Once more up Heol Caradoc and we'll call it a day. Right?'

'Very well.'

In the back seat, Oliver shared a look with Johnny and gave a sigh of relief.

Johnny relaxed slightly as they climbed the hill and, as they approached St David's Drive, he suggested they reversed in. They had not seen the ambulance cross over from collecting someone in St Illtyd's Road and when Evie suddenly put on her brake she missed her footing, panicked and touched the clutch and accelerator and the car went backwards down the hill. With a crash, they hit the ambulance which went skidding on the brown decaying leaves as the driver tried to avoid her.

Johnny pulled hard on the brake and clutched the wheel, swinging the car deftly into its skid and straightening it up in seconds. When they were still, he checked Oliver, who had fallen to the floor, and found him frightened, crying but apparently unharmed.

He ran then, swearing at the sobbing Evie, to where the ambulance was slewed across the pavement, its side against a bent lamp-post. He helped the driver to open the door, asking as he did so.

'Ethel Davies, is she in there?'

'No, no,' the driver said as he struggled to open the

damaged back doors. 'Dropped her on the way up.'

The doors gave under their combined efforts and they went in to find Victor's wife on the floor between the two bench seats. She was lifted back on to the seat and, with her assurance that she was all right, they ran back to see Evie and Oliver.

Oliver was still crying in the back seat and Johnny swore at Evie, who was sobbing and trembling, oblivious to her son's distress. He hauled the little boy out and told Evie to get him home.

'*Uffern dan*, Evie. Can't you see the boy is frightened?'

He stood the boy down and saw that his thin legs were trembling too much for him to walk. 'Go you,' he said irritably to Evie. 'Sit in the car. We'll have to wait for the police.'

'I think I'd better get Mrs Honeyman home,' the driver said. 'I can't leave her sitting there while we find the constable, can I?'

He walked back to the ambulance and opened the doors again then he gave a horrified shout. 'Here, come quick, I think the woman's dead!'

Mrs Norwood Bennet-Hughes was announcing that they had raised enough to make a start on the new building, when the news reached them. PC Harris came in and asked for attention. Voices rose then fell silent as he asked, 'Is Mr Honeyman here?'

It was Delina who pushed her way through to the constable. 'Why do you want my father, what has happened?' she asked anxiously.

'I'd like to talk to your father first, Miss Honeyman. There's a bit of bad news I'm afraid.'

'You'd better tell me,' she insisted.

He led her out into the empty school kitchen and told her about the accident.

465

'Can't say for certain, like, but they think it was a heart attack. Rushed to hospital she was, but there was nothing they could do for the poor lady. I'm sorry, very sorry. Is there someone who could stay with you for a while? At least until we find your father.'

Tad appeared at her elbow and asked if he could help.

'I heard the crash and went out to see what I could do,' he explained. 'I'm so very sorry. Can I go with you to tell your brothers, or help find your father?'

'Dad is meeting Daniel in town after he finishes work, Daniel needs new shoes.' Delina spoke as if in a daze.

PC Harris explained the situation in a few whispered words to Tad.

'Can Dawn stay with you, Nelly?' Tad asked, before leading Delina out to walk with her, silently, to wait until her brothers and her father could be found.

'I'll wait for the next few buses and try to catch them before they get home,' Harris told Tad.

Bert pontificated to anyone too polite not to move away about women drivers.

'Best not let Johnny hear you talking like that, mind,' Archie warned. 'His Fay's been driving safely for years.'

In the school hall people seemed unwilling to leave. They stood around in groups, talking in hushed voices, waiting for further news, sharing the little that was known. Few of them knew Mrs Honeyman as, apart from exchanging her books at the mobile library, she rarely joined in the life of the village. But Delina and Victor were liked and, for them and the boys, they all felt sympathy.

Prue was upset when the news of the sudden death reached her. It revived for her the shock of Harry's death. Florrie Gwyn, seeing the distress on her face, insisted they went straight home. Others slowly began to leave, some leisurely, hoping for more details, others, like Nelly and Dawn pushing their way through the doors in haste. Amy followed her sister, but seeing that Florrie was taking care of her, went back to the shop with Margaret. She was numb and it was Margaret who told Mavis what had happened.

'Go home, Mavis,' Amy said when she had recovered sufficiently to speak. 'I'm closing the shop.'

When Mavis had returned to her flat, Amy sat close to Margaret after lifting Sian out of her playpen. She was glad of the little hands grabbing her and the warm dependent body against her own. Sian and Margaret were all she had, and soon there would be only Margaret.

She walked home with mixed feelings. Suddenly Victor was free but in such a wretched way it was like a punishment to them all for having wished it. Achieving their right to be together in such a manner – depriving Delina, David and Daniel of their mother – how could they ever rejoice in it?

Nelly took Dawn's hand and ran to Evie's house, where she found her daughter crouched in an armchair, head buried in her hands.

'Where's young Ollie?' was Nelly's first question.

'He's gone to lie down,' Evie sobbed. 'Oh, I feel terrible. Causing a death! I'll never sit in a driving seat again!'

'Wasn't your fault, Evie. No one could 'ave known she'd 'ave an 'eart attack, could they? I'll just go up an' see if Ollie's all right. I don't think 'e should be on 'is own and worryin'. Come on, Dawn.' She clumped up the stairs, followed by a hesitant Dawn, and for once Evie did not complain about the mud they had brought in.

Oliver was sitting on his bed reading a Rupert Annual.

'All right, young Ollie?' Nelly asked brightly. She carried with her the shopping bag she had brought from the sale of work, and from it she produced a bag of home-made toffee. ' 'Ere, stuff one of them inside yer. Good they are, sugar's good fer shock. You too, Dawn.'

'Did Mother make that lady die, Gran?'

'O' course not! What an idea! Feelin' a bit upset by what 'appened she is, but she didn't do nothin' except bash yer dad's car.' She sat reading to him for a long time, then, realising he had fallen asleep, crept downstairs and rejoined Evie.

Mrs Norwood Bennet-Hughes had arrived with Timothy and they were sitting, talking quietly.

'I give 'im a couple of toffees, Evie,' she reported.

'Oh, Mother, he'll be sick.'

'Good fer 'im, a bit of sugar. 'E's 'ad a shock too, for Gawd's sake! Tell you something else. My mother told me the best thing fer shock is to 'ave a pee straight away and that takes the shock from yer.'

Timothy winced and glanced at their visitor, who only nodded and smiled.

'That might 'ave been a worse shock fer Evie if she 'ad, though,' Nelly went on. ' 'Er being so fussed about what people thinks of 'er!'

'Mother, please!'

George came to Evie's as soon as he heard and he and Nelly walked back home with Dawn.

'Your Dad will know where to find you, Dawn,' George assured her, 'and in this rain I think you're better with us than in your house on your own. It can make you lonely, looking out on rain.'

'The dogs'll be that pleased to see yer,' Nelly added.

As they passed they saw PC Harris sheltering in the doorway of Amy's shop. They heard a bus approaching and paused to see him go and greet Victor and his youngest son. The group huddled together for a moment, a sombre sight in dark raincoats and a large black umbrella. Then they turned, and walking slowly, disregarding the pouring rain, they disappeared up Sheepy Lane.

'The bleedin' weather suits the occasion fer once,' Nelly groaned. She put an arm around Dawn. 'They'll cope though, won't they, Dawn? Just like you did when you lost your mum, eh?'

Amy did not see Victor immediately after the accident. She felt unable to go to the house and offer sympathy so, apart from a brief note addressed to the family, there was no contact at all. It seemed that in death, Imogine had come between them as she had not managed to in life.

A week after the funeral Victor finally called to see Amy, who was packing her things, preparing to go back to the flat. She opened the door and he walked in, ill at ease and not, for once, going straight to the kitchen to make himself a cup of tea. He spoke to Margaret, asked about her new piano pieces, and seemed unable to meet Amy's eye.

For her too the encounter was a difficult one. She was uptight, embarrassed, stiff. She could not imagine leaning towards him and greeting him with a kiss, even if Margaret had not been there as chaperone. He was a stranger. She stood near Margaret as if using her as a shield, and invited him to stay for tea and, when he refused, she felt only relief.

'Come again soon,' she said as he left a few minutes later, explaining that he had only called to see if they were both all right.

What had happened to them? The dream had come true but the process had distorted what they thought they had, making their love for each other unimportant, almost childish in its romantic furtiveness.

Victor returned to work the following week and, when he called with a delivery, Amy tried to act as if nothing had happened to change things.

469

'Go on in, Victor, love, and make us a cup of tea, will you?' He did so and, between serving customers, they talked.

'There's so much to sort out,' he said, and the remark was so ambiguous that Amy did not reply. Did he mean between them or with his family?

'Delina will run the house, for a while at least,' he went on. 'Hardly seems fair, does it, for her to be lumbered with looking after us when only months ago she was planning to start a home of her own?'

'It's odd how things work out sometimes,' Amy said. 'If Delina *had* married Maurice, things would have been very different.'

'If she had, would you have offered to take us all on, Amy? Me and David and Daniel?'

Amy thought carefully before she spoke.

'My first instinct was to do just that, Victor, even with Delina to help you. But now I think we both need time to adjust to the death of Imogine, don't you?' She watched him and felt a blow to her heart as a look of relief flickered across his face. She forced herself to go on. 'Delina and the boys will need time too. If there's anything I can do—'

'Thanks, but I think they only need each other.'

'And you, love.'

'And me, for what use I am.'

'Does Delina know that Maurice is coming home?'

'Yes, Sheila took great delight in telling her.'

'It's been a stormy year, hasn't it? Glad I'll be when it's over and the new year gives us all a fresh start.'

'What about our fresh start?'

'That's up to you.'

'What about you and that farmer?'

'I won't marry Billie. I told him that and apologised for keeping him on a string. Nice man, but I couldn't marry someone I don't love. I couldn't see me wading through cow-pats to gather eggs for breakfast, either, can you?'

She was rewarded with a smile and for a moment the old Victor was back, but the smile faded and when she returned to him after serving Netta with some liquid shampoo and a box of Bel cheeses, he was preparing to leave.

'Thanks for being so understanding, Amy.' He lowered his head, unable to look at her.

'Goodbye, Victor.'

'Goodbye?' He lifted his head then and stared at her, his pale-blue eyes full of alarm. 'Not goodbye, for God's sake! How can I get through these next weeks without knowing you'll be there at the end of them? Amy, don't let me down now.'

'But I thought – I – this isn't goodbye, then?'

'No. Just a few weeks' pause before we go forward again, together.'

He strode past her through the empty shop and slammed the door. He locked it and pulled down the blind then took her into his arms.

Nelly and George had been to the pictures in Llangwyn, and had continued on the bus as far as the Drovers for a drink. It was raining but the rain was soft, purring down rather than hissing, on the hedges and the grass verge. They walked along, arm in arm, both wearing navy, rubber-backed coats. Nelly held up an umbrella, the cover of which had become detached from the frame, so it was half-moon shaped instead of round.

She found them a seat near the Drovers' fire by the simple expedient of shaking her outsized coat. She pushed nearer to the blazing logs and looked hopefully at Phil, who was standing near the bar. Phil tilted his head questioningly.

'What are you having, George?' Nelly asked.

471

'Don't know that I need a drink. I'm that wet outside I might dissolve away,' he laughed, his white beard revealing a clean pink mouth. 'But I'll force one to be sociable, Phil.' He joined Phil at the bar.

There weren't as many as usual in the pub. Gradually, people were buying television sets and staying at home to watch them.

'Things is changin' George, even 'ere in Hen Carw Parc,' Nelly remarked sadly.

They did not stay long and, gathering their coats and umbrella to the discomfort of all, went out again into the night. They walked slowly, ignoring the steady rain, discussing the more interesting parts of the film they had seen. When they reached the bottom of Gypsy Lane, Nelly stopped.

'George, I can smell smoke.'

'Nelly, you can't be surprised at that! Every house in the village will have a fire on a night like this!'

'Bonfire smoke. Up there.' She pointed into the blackness of the lane leading to Leighton's farm. 'I reckon the gypsies are back fer winter. Fancy that, winter 'as really arrived and we can stop worryin' about anything except keepin' warm and eatin' plenty of suety puddin's. And just think! We've got an indoor lav! No need to go into the woods through the ice an' snow in the dark of night and the early mornin's. We 'ave Mrs Norwood Bennet-'Ughes to thank fer that. We can sort of hibernate, can't we? Stay 'ome, warm and comfortable, till the spring. Nice thought, ain't it, George?'

'Yes, Nelly, love. It's a very nice thought.'

He put an arm across her shoulders and, singing 'Show me the Way To Go Home', they wandered on towards the cottage.